A CHRISTMAS WISH

"This can't happen," she muttered into his chest, "we can't happen."

"It can, and we can." He tipped her chin upward to meet his eyes. Midnight black, framed in gently brushed lashes, they promised her the world and more. "If we want it to."

She licked her lips, still damp with the taste of his mouth and the feel of his tongue. Yes, she wanted him. But she knew she needed more than one night of passion with this man. She needed a lifetime plus a day.

"You'd better go now," she said, defying the words even as they left her mouth.

"Patricia," Pierce said as he stood reluctantly. Leaving her at this moment was the most difficult thing he'd ever had to do. He nodded, then moved to the door and placed his hand on the brass knob, but refused turn it.

She knew she should have turned away, but she didn't, couldn't. She watched as he walked across the bare wooden floors. When he stopped and turned to her, her heart leaped.

DEDICATION

To Fate & Fortune

A CHRISTMAS WISH

Celeste O. Norfleet

BET Publications, LLC
http://www.bet.com
http://www.arabesquebooks.com

ARABESQUE BOOKS are published by

BET Publications, LLC
c/o BET BOOKS
One BET Plaza
1900 W Place NE
Washington, DC 20018-1211

All Kensington Titles, Imprints, and Distributed Lines are available at special quantity discounts for bulk purchases for sales promotion, premiums, fund-raising, and educational or institutional use. Special book excerpts or customized printings can also be created to fit specific needs. For details, write or phone the office of the Kensington special sales manager: Kensington Publishing Corp., 850 Third Avenue, New York, NY 10022, attn: Special Sales Department, Phone: 1-800-221-2647.

First Printing: October 2002
10 9 8 7 6 5 4 3 2 1

Printed in the United States of America

ACKNOWLEDGMENTS

Much thanks to my critique group. As always, your input was invaluable. Also to my family and friends for their constant motivation and endless support.

Special thanks to the incredible men in my life who bring truth to my writing.

Charles, Christopher, Otis, Anthony, China, Steve, Butch, Garry, Jenkins, Michael, Adrian, Timothy, Michael Jr., Christian, Joshua, Charles, Prince, Kyle, Guy, Doug, and Mr. Monroe.

You, Reese, are my strength.

Prologue

It was two weeks before Christmas.

Patricia peeked into the gift box, her eyes wide in wonder and delight. At twelve years old, she still believed in the magic of Christmas. All around her, colorful tiny lights sparkled and twinkled in the windows and on the mantels and trees. Silver- and gold-tinted glass balls hung from the hooks surrounded by shredded icicles of silver lace.

This was her favorite time of year.

Enraptured by the glorious decorations, she reached in and pulled out a carefully wrapped box. Gently she placed it on the table and lifted the lid slowly. Sparks of delight brought a twinkle of joy to her face as she peered inside. Carefully, she unwrapped the Christmas star and handed it to her mother.

As was tradition every year, when the star was placed atop its lofty post, her mother would utter the same phrase: "Falling stars and rising stars, it's time to make your Christmas wish." And she would.

Sometimes she wished for new clothes, other times she'd wished for a new bike. But this time, she wished for something very special. She wished that Pierce Franklin would ask her to the Christmas Ball. She smiled, secure in the knowledge that her wish would come true, as it always had in the past.

After all, this was Christmas, the time of year when

wishes came true and dreams were realized. She didn't need Aladdin's magic lamp and enchanted genie. All she needed was the simple hope of the holidays and a whispered Christmas wish on a star.

"Star light, star bright,
First star I see tonight,
I wish I may, I wish I might,
have the wish I wish tonight."

One

This was not going to be pleasant. There was no way she could talk her way out this time. Kimberly Franklin was used to getting into trouble, she just wasn't used to getting caught. So, to purposely get into trouble and purposely get caught went against all the rules of the universe as far as she was concerned. But now, she had no choice; he had left her no alternative.

At first, she'd done everything conceivably possible not to get her uncle's attention. Dutifully, she'd rerouted any and all communications attempted from her school to her home. Because, of course, who would believe that the perfect Kimberly Franklin could possibly get into trouble?

In trouble. The words vibrated in her head like a snare drum. She was in major trouble, and they didn't even know the half of it. For the first time in her young life, she was in over her head. Suddenly, the thought panicked her as tears welled in her eyes. She admonished herself. Crying was not going to help her now.

The problem was, she'd always been the perfect student with perfect grades, leading the perfect life as the perfect niece with the perfect uncle. But all of that had changed and was about to change even more. And now, even worse, she'd broken her first and only rule. Never, never let them see you cry.

No one could fathom why her behavior had suddenly taken a 180-degree turn. For the past three weeks, her teachers and instructors had admonished, warned, and cautioned her about her recent behavioral change. But she refused to comply.

She had a plan, and she needed to jump-start it in a hurry. Even if it meant sacrificing her dean's list grades and her honor roll standing and everything she'd ever wanted and worked so hard to attain. It would be worth it. After all, when you make a Christmas wish as difficult as hers, there were bound to be sacrifices. Besides, she could always catch up on her falling grades later on.

This was far more important.

She'd done her part weeks ago. She had studied, planned, and investigated, until everything was in place for the first meeting. Then, nothing. The meeting never happened. Her uncle had canceled out on the scheduled parent-teacher conference—first, because of an unexpected business trip, then an unscheduled meeting, and finally, some dire emergency at the office.

Kimberly was perplexed. Unfortunately, she hadn't considered being faced with the complete lack of cooperation. So, now it was up to her again. Desperate matters called for desperate measures, and she was as desperate as it got. So, tonight her uncle had no choice but to show up; this time she'd made sure of that.

She roughly wiped the falling tears from her damp face and stiffened her lower lip. She refused to go out like this. After all, she wasn't a baby. She was almost thirteen years old—a teenager, almost an adult. In many cultures, she was already considered fully grown and of marriageable age.

A final sniff of composure ended her teardrops as she regained control. She needed to assess the damage and reevaluate her exposure. If she was going down, she had to come up with another plan quickly. Her mind whirled at all of the possibilities. Then, one came to mind.

This unexpected meeting would definitely put a snag

in her self-imposed timetable. But, with her new idea, she was sure she could handle it. The hard part was handling her uncle and her counselor.

Granted, this wasn't exactly how she'd planned the first meeting to go, but she supposed that it had to happen sometime. This was as good a time as any. And, since everything depended on this first meeting, the next hour or so would be crucial to her plans.

She looked up at the poster-size school calendar displayed on the near wall. December 25th immediately caught her eye. That was her target date. So she had until the winter break, or just eleven weeks, to make her Christmas wish come true.

Unconsciously, nervously, she bit at her lower lip, sending a myriad of ideas and scenarios racing through her mind. If she could get into the school's computer system a few more times, she was sure she could crack the mainframe and get even more information.

What she'd gotten so far had been useful, but she needed more. Kimberly frowned thoughtfully. She had a lot of work to do and very little time to do it. Then, moments later, a slow satisfied smile appeared. She was proud of her accomplishments so far. For once in her life, she was going to have a very merry Christmas and get exactly what she wished for.

Suddenly, she startled with a jump. The sound of a door closing and the jingle of keys in the far distance caught her attention. He was here, and Mr. Wilson, the school's janitor, was escorting him to the office. This was the moment Kimberly had anticipated for weeks.

Pierce Franklin, her uncle and sole guardian, had arrived, and he most assuredly wouldn't be happy. He didn't like having his time wasted, so he most certainly didn't have time for this. Pierce was owner and CEO of PEF Software, Inc., a rising star in the computer software industry. He was a very important man, with very important clients, and he valued his time above everything else. Work was his sole focus, leaving very little time for what he often referred to as nonsense. Translated, anything not related to business, software, or computers was deemed trivial. This meeting, she presumed, he'd surely consider was just that: trivial nonsense.

Kimberly looked up at the calendar again. This, in particular, was the wrong time of year to upset her uncle. In another few days it would be Halloween and the unofficial beginning of the dreaded holiday season. Somewhere between October and January, Pierce Franklin turned into a cross between the Grinch and Ebenezer Scrooge. Not that he was stingy—he was anything but. His problem was that he despised any- and everything pertaining to the holiday season—in particular, Christmas.

He'd always done the expected, the required, and the obligatory, but his heart wasn't in it. He dutifully sponsored the office parties but never attended, and he sent huge baskets as gifts to their family but never visited. He tolerated the occasional holiday cheer, but everyone knew that he was just going through the motions.

At first Kimberly thought that he'd always been like this, but later, she found that wasn't true. So, Kimberly reasoned—rightfully or not—that her uncle's sour mood, which had become increasingly prolonged over the years, had something to do with her.

As far back as she could remember, she and her uncle had lived a very separate, very controlled, and very orderly existence. She lived in his house, ate his food, and spent his money, but very seldom found it necessary actually to interact with him. Simply put, he lived in his world and she lived in hers. They were always just an e-mail apart. It was the perfect solution and the perfect life until that unexpected e-mail message slipped through.

For weeks Kimberly had intercepted, delayed and

blocked any and all communications attempted from her school to her uncle. She needed time for everything to be perfect before the first meeting. Unfortunately, Ms. Burke had found out about her behavior problems and sent a message to her uncle.

Butterflies began to flutter in Kimberly's stomach. This was it, the meeting she'd been excitedly dreaming of for weeks. She took a deep breath to calm her frayed nerves. She only hoped that she could pull this off.

Then, like any typical sullen teenager, she crossed her arms, pouted, and rolled her eyes. Regretfully, after this meeting she knew that there'd surely be a confrontation with her uncle. That was the last thing she needed.

Still, if he knew what she'd really been up to, he'd have her hide, take away her credit cards, and ground her for life. But, as any good computer hacker would tell you, interpretation was in the mind of the beholder. It wasn't her fault that the school's computer system was so easy to get into and manipulate.

Pierce followed the older man through the labyrinth of first-floor offices. A flood of memories surrounded him as walked through the empty corridors. He hadn't set foot in this school in five years, and before then it had been almost twenty. If memory served correctly, it hadn't changed drastically since he had attended years ago.

The library was still on the left, the auditorium on the right, and directions confirmed that the music conservatory, cafeteria, and study halls were still in the same locations. There were numerous renovations and additions, including another connected building, an upgraded gymnasium, and fully operational computer and science labs. But overall, it was the same Ida B. Wells Academy.

The solitary sound of determined footsteps echoed through the deserted halls and drowned out squeaking sounds of the janitor's well-worn soft-soled sneakers. It had been too long since he'd been here. Maybe he should have come sooner, been more attentive and hands on with Kimberly's education. Maybe he shouldn't have left it up to someone else. After all, she was his responsibility. *No,* he chastised and corrected himself mentally, *she isn't a responsibility. She is my niece, my heart and my joy.*

As Pierce proceeded down the main hall, he eyed the poster-covered walls with indifference. Numerous notices announced upcoming school events: a book reading, a mentoring program, Career Day, a harvest dance, the Thanksgiving Dinner Volunteer Program at a D.C. shelter, and the Annual Christmas Ball in late December. Pierce, unimpressed, nodded his approval, then curiously wondered why he'd never heard anything about any of these events from Kimberly.

Thinking back, he hadn't received anything—a flyer, a letter, an E-mail, or a phone call—since the start of the school year in late August. Surely something must have been sent home in the ten weeks since Kimberly had begun attending classes. The one and only communication he'd received was an E-mail that insisted he be here tonight. The exact words practically ordered him to appear. He didn't take orders well.

He mentally replayed the sharp tone of the woman's e-mail message on his computer screen. She was crisp and sharp and lacked the warmth he would have expected from an educator of the young. The woman was obviously either unprofessional or unsuited for the job of school counselor.

A few seconds later, the office door opened and an older gray-haired gentleman with skin wrinkled with time and age entered. He gave Kimberly a sympathetic smile, then winked at her. Against her will, she smiled just as her uncle Pierce walked in. Pierce frowned, curtly nodded to thank the janitor, and crossed the small reception area to his niece.

"Hello, Kimberly," he said as he walked over and sat down beside her.

"Hi, Uncle Pierce." She mumbled what might be considered a greeting and half smiled. The sparkly clear glitter of eye shadow glimmered as she looked down nervously at her silver painted nails.

Meticulously, Pierce looked around the small area. It was the typical school office: sturdy, functional, inexpensive furniture piled high with personal mementos frozen in time to forget the reality of work. A mass chaotic clutter of papers, folders, and desk gadgets, interrupted by a telephone and computer, lay accessible on the desks. It was all far from the sterile environment in which he immersed himself daily. He grimaced and turned back to his niece.

"So, what's going on, Kimberly? I'm told that there's a problem." She shrugged evasively. "Are you okay?" She shrugged again. "Kimberly, we've spoken about this before. Shrugging isn't an acceptable answer. Talk to me."

"I'm fine," she grumbled into her newly blooming chest.

"Then why does the school's principal want to speak with me?"

"She's not the school's principal. Mrs. Simmons is our principal," she specified loud and clear. "Ms. Burke is my counselor, and she's just an acting assistant principal until Mrs. Rodger comes back in January from maternity leave."

Impatiently, he corrected himself using her exact words. "Fine. Why does the school's counselor and acting assistant principal until Mrs. Roger comes back in January from maternity leave want to speak with me?"

She shrugged, then remembered his admonishment.

"I don't know. She's just mean like that. She calls parents in for no good reason. I think she's a lonely old woman who calls people in just to keep her company at night."

Pierce frowned. "I don't think that's very likely, Kimberly."

"For real, Uncle Pierce, she called my girlfriend Jasmine's stepmother in just last week and Jasmine didn't do anything, either. Ms. Burke is just a mean old lady who likes to torture kids." At this point Pierce wasn't sure what to believe. He knew Kimberly's friend Jasmine and was always impressed by her good manners and equally good sense. Sure, she was immature, talked nonstop, and shopped endlessly, but didn't all teenage girls her age? That hardly made her a problem child.

Then, the vision of an old crotchety, toothpick-thin, Coke-bottle-eyeglasses-wearing schoolmarm with squeaky orthopedic shoes and bad breath entered his mind. He cringed mentally.

Kimberly saw the wavering thoughts in her uncle's eyes and continued boldly. She leaned in closer and whispered, "I'm not supposed to tell you this, but they say she's even got some kind of torture device sitting right there on her desk, and if you don't do what she says she uses it on you."

"Now, Kimberly, I think you're being rude and more than a little melodramatic."

"No, Uncle Pierce, for real, she's really whacked."

"Kimberly, if there's a problem, I'm always available. You know you can come to me."

She huffed deeply, anchored her arms across her chest, and slid away from him. "You never listen to me."

"I'm listening now, Kimberly. Tell me what's going on."

She sucked her teeth miserably. "Nothing."

"Kimberly," Pierce began again just as the counselor's door opened. Two sets of identical midnight black eyes framed by long curly lashes turned to the woman standing in the doorway.

Pierce's jaw dropped as his breath caught in his chest. Counselors never looked like that when he was a young boy in school. He wasn't sure exactly what he expected, but he was sure it wasn't this long-legged goddess with shimmering curls and skin the shade of dark rich cocoa. It wasn't until after a few seconds that he realized he was just staring at her.

This wasn't an altogether unique reaction, but coming from Pierce Franklin, Patricia was more than flattered. Men had been staring at her since puberty. And since puberty, she'd ignored their generous attention for the most part. Still, with Pierce Franklin, there had always been something, a feeling as quick and fleeting as the twinkle of a shooting star. There was an instant pull of attraction, an instant something that she was certain made them both notice.

She smiled generously, betraying the thunderous beating of her heart as she stood in the doorway. Nervously, anxiously, Patricia rearranged the single strand of white pearls around her neck and smoothed the deep emerald sleeveless cashmere knit sweater.

"Mr. Franklin?" she questioned needlessly as Pierce came to his feet and approached her with his hand readily extended. They shook with professional courtesy.

Pierce cleared his suddenly dry throat. "Yes, I am Mr. Franklin, Pierce Franklin." Patricia caught a twinge of something sparkling in his eye. Her heart sailed, dreaming as her hopes raced. *He remembered.*

He didn't remember. Her hopes dashed as she chastised herself. How could he possibly remember someone he never knew? *Get ahold of yourself, girl,* she warned mentally. She immediately suppressed her disappointment. After all, this was one of her student's parents. Nothing would or could ever come of it.

"Hello. I'm Kimberly's counselor and the school's assistant principal, Patricia Burke." A low rumble of "acting principal" traveled through the outer office. Pierce ignored Kimberly's hushed remark and nodded as Patricia tilted her head to acknowledge his niece. "Hello, Kimberly."

"Hi, Ms. Burke," Kimberly muttered under her breath.

Patricia smiled, knowing the growing pains of a brand-new teenager. Speaking and greeting adults wasn't high up on their things-to-do list. Actually, very few social graces were. But that was fine with Patricia, as long as her students showed some form of respect for themselves and others.

Kimberly rolled her eyes in complete embarrassment. She moaned inwardly. Since when did her uncle get tongue-tied around women? If anything, he had the reputation of sending *them* into tailspins. She was just glad that it was after school and no one was around to witness this horrifically embarrassing nightmare.

"Mr. Franklin, please come in." Kimberly stood reluctantly and approached as Pierce walked into the inner office. Patricia turned as Kimberly approached. "Kimberly, would you please give me a moment or two alone with your uncle? I'll call you when or if I'd like to speak with you."

"Whatever," she muttered, then immediately went back and plopped back down in her seat. She'd began sulking, her second favorite thing to do right after shopping. Patricia began to close the door, then paused and opened it again. "Kimberly, you might want to take this opportunity to start working on your history paper. I believe it's due in two days, and I'm sure you don't want it to be tardy." Patricia smiled and closed the door quietly.

Kimberly instantly mimicked Patricia's words while making a funny crinkled face. She tossed her book bag on the seat next to her, unzipped it roughly, and pulled out her history textbook, a spiral notebook, and her favorite purple gel pen, then grumbled, "Tardy? Who uses that word anymore?" Exasperated, she sucked her teeth and began to write.

Inside, Pierce crossed to the large neat desk sitting in front of the window, in the far corner of the small office. He remained standing, waiting for Patricia to be seated. As soon as she sat down, the telephone rang. "Please excuse me, Mr. Franklin. I've been expecting a call." She motioned for him to sit in one of the two large standard-issue chairs facing her desk. Pierce nodded curtly, but instead chose to remain standing and look around the small office.

Patricia picked up the phone. Unfortunately, it was the call she had expected. With lackluster enthusiasm she listened patiently to the irate ramblings of a parent on the other end of the receiver complaining about another parent who was also on the Christmas Ball committee. Squarely placed in the position of referee between the two overzealous parents, it afforded Patricia little time to get her own committee work done.

She offered little in the way of commiseration, but instead suggested that the parent focus on the larger picture, which was the success of the Christmas Ball and the funds raised for the much-needed scholarships. Momentarily placated, the parent went on to elaborate about several new ideas she recently had.

Pierce walked around the tiny cramped space, which gave him an uneasy sense of claustrophobia. It could easily fit into his enormous office six times over. Yet the one thing that came to mind as he looked around was order. It was obvious that she was a neat freak. He imagined she was one of those type A workaholics who needed to control everything in her immediate surroundings.

Patricia watched as Pierce casually moved around her

office. *Umm, he still looks good,* she thought as she eyed the
fit of his suit jacket across his broad shoulders and the
smooth creased length of lightweight wool down his long
legs. He turned, his perfect profile showing the small dark
mole on his lower jaw. She fell in love all over again.

*Mindless psychobabble bookworm with delusional visions of
Freudian grandeur,* Pierce surmised as he casually eyed the
various psychology and child psychology textbooks lining her bookcase shelves.

*He still has the trim, firm athlete's physique, the same hand-
some features and superb taste in clothes,* Patricia continued
thinking. *Very impressive, Mr. Franklin. You've done very well
for yourself.*

Pierce continued to mentally mull over her obvious
outdated puritan attributes. *Authoritative, glacial, humor-
less*—no surprise here, he knew the type. Satisfied that
he'd summed her up nicely, he turned to the far wall.

Attractive, intelligent, caring, Patricia blushed in spite of
herself. Theoretically speaking, he was just her type. He
was everything the many newspaper and magazine articles had said. He was handsome, rich, and handsome
some more.

With as much decorum as she could muster under the
circumstances, Patricia ended her telephone conversation, then stood and pulled her jacket from the back of
her chair and slipped it on. Pierce turned as she approached, now more professionally attired.

She began as she always did when in conference, with
polite conversation to put the parent at ease in a tense
situation. Unfortunately, it was quite obvious that Pierce
Franklin did not want to be at ease.

So, at precisely the right moment, she ended their
brief social conversation on the unusually nice weather
for the end of October. "We'd better get started. Please
have a seat." She again motioned for him to sit in one of
the chairs opposite the desk.

"First of all, thank you for taking time from your busy schedule to meet with me, Mr. Franklin. I'm just sorry it had to be under these circumstances." Pierce frowned instantly. He had no idea what she was talking about.

"These circumstances?" he repeated, the perpetual frown on his brow deepening to a scowl.

"Yes." She pulled out and opened a folder on her desk. "We've been having a few problems lately with Kimberly's behavior and scholastic achievement. She's usually an excellent student with extraordinary talents, which is why we're so concerned."

"Ms. Burke, what exactly are you implying Kimberly has done?" he asked defensively.

"Mr. Franklin, Wells Academy has experienced a rash of thefts and vandalism recently. We have reason to believe—"

Outraged at the pending implication, he cut her off. "Are you accusing my niece of vandalism and theft, Ms. Burke? Because I assure you, Kimberly wants for nothing, therefore she has no reason to steal."

Patricia took a deep breath and proceeded cautiously. "Of course not, but I'm sure you're aware that oftentimes teenage stealing has very little to do with need and more with desire for parental attention."

He quickly interrupted again. "You're implying that I don't pay enough attention to my niece?"

"The fact remains that Kimberly was spotted in the vicinity of the school on two separate occasions."

"As were several hundred other students, I'm sure."

"No, not at 8:30 at night."

"Are you saying Kimberly was in the school at 8:30 one evening?"

"Yes, and that would be on two separate evenings."

"I assume you have verifiable proof, or at the least a viable witness?"

Patricia smiled, warming. "Mr. Franklin, I would not

have called you in this evening if I didn't have irrefutable proof. The fact is, Kimberly was in the school at the time of the recent offenses." Her voice hushed to almost a whisper.

"Who is your witness?" he sternly insisted.

Patricia smiled. "Mr. Franklin, I've not brought the matter of Kimberly's presence each time of the offenses to the attention of Mrs. Simmons, our principal. But, if her behavior continues, I'll have no choice but to take action."

She was ready to continue when the phone on her desk rang a second time. She excused herself again and picked up the phone. He nodded curtly, looked at his Rolex, then looked away impatiently. His mind whirled with questions, all ending with the same certain answer: There must be some kind of mistake, because Kimberly would never do anything like this.

This time the telephone conversation was short. When she hung up, she continued. "Mr. Franklin, please understand, Kimberly is a very sweet child. We all adore her here at Wells Academy. She's just going through some growing pains and she needs a bit more guidance right now."

Pierce stopped and stared, unbelieving. "Now you're implying that my niece lacks parental guidance or that I have not been diligent in raising her?"

"Not at all."

"Ms. Burke, I want to know who this witness is and what proof you have that my niece is involved."

"Please understand, Mr. Franklin, we're not formally accusing Kimberly of anything. We're speaking to a number of our parents to merely inform them of the situation."

Pierce was hardly satisfied as he stood to leave. "Thank you for your unwarranted concern, Ms. Burke. I'm sure it will be proved that Kimberly had nothing to do with the school's security problems. Is there anything else?"

"Yes, there is," she said, not at all alarmed by his obvious impatience. He paused and stood behind the chair. "We're also concerned about Kimberly's recent academic behavior." Patricia looked down at the scribbled notes in the folder and began to read from the page. "She's been absent from school six times since August. She's been late to classes eight times, missed quite a few homework and class assignments. At this point, a tutor might be a consideration." Patricia looked up into the coldness of Pierce's jet-black eyes. A rush of sadness hugged her before she continued. "And, most alarming, she's been belligerent to some of her instructors. This behavior is unacceptable."

Pierce frowned, causing a series of tiny creases at his brow to furrow. "There must be some mistake. Kimberly goes to school and she does her homework."

"I don't doubt that's what she tells you."

Pierce went silent, realizing that he'd never actually seen her go to school, do her homework, or even read a book, for that matter. "I'm rarely home until late," he admitted reluctantly. "My neighbor, Kimberly's companion, is there with her most of the time. She tells me that Kimberly is always in her room doing her homework. I believe her."

"Of course." Patricia sat back in her chair and templed her fingers under her chin. It was obvious to her that Pierce was angry and defensive. They had reached an impasse, and he was too protective of Kimberly to continue the conversation rationally. She closed the folder.

Pierce had been staring at the mock miniature guillotine on Patricia's desk. His thoughts were clouded. He smiled, remembering Kimberly's remark about the eighteenth-century torture and execution device. Kimberly had never lied to him before.

Patricia stood and walked around to stand next to Pierce, who was still standing behind the chair. She touched his arm gently, and he looked down at her thin fingers attached to his suit jacket. "I realize that this is a lot to contemplate, Mr. Franklin. But if we work together, Kimberly will do just fine."

He didn't answer. He was too troubled by Patricia's pronouncement. Maybe she didn't have an actual guillotine, but the blade of her words had cut just as deep. "Is there anything else?" he asked calmly.

She removed her hand from his arm and stood back. "Yes." He looked at her, dreading what else she might disclose. Patricia smiled hopefully. "Thank you for coming in, Mr. Franklin." He nodded, then turned to the door.

As soon as he stepped into the outer office, he noticed that Kimberly was not where she'd been earlier. Pierce looked around. She'd changed seats. She was now seated at the secretary's computer terminal, staring at computer solitaire. "Kimberly," Patricia began, "I've talked to your uncle about some concerns that were brought to my attention recently."

"But, Ms. Burke, it wasn't me, I didn't do anything," she immediately pleaded.

"No one said you did, dear." Patricia smiled and moved a long tendril of hair from Kimberly's face. "We're just a little concerned about your grades. They've been slipping recently and your homework and class assignments have been tardy. You're going to have to be more diligent in the future."

Kimberly gave a deep sigh of relief. She was safe. All Ms. Burke wanted to talk about were her falling grades—big deal.

Patricia turned back to Pierce. "Mr. Franklin, it was a pleasure meeting you, and thank you again for coming out this evening. I'm sure Kimberly will be more attentive to her studies in the future." She looked pointedly at Kimberly, then to Pierce. "My door is always open. Please feel free to call or come by at any time."

For a few seconds, the two stood staring at each other wordlessly. She'd never felt such intensity. The old feelings of attraction were back and just as strong, much to her dismay. She'd hoped that they were long gone, but here they were, just as strong as ever.

Pierce continued to stare at Patricia without responding. When he finally spoke, he directed his statement to his niece. "Let's go, Kimberly," he said, finally pulling his eyes from Patricia.

Kimberly picked up on the intense interaction between her uncle and her counselor. She smiled to herself victoriously. She looked at both adults as they stared at each other silently. She shrugged her narrow shoulders in satisfaction, then picked up her backpack and heaved it over one arm. She began walking to the office door, followed by her uncle.

"By the way, Kimberly," Patricia began slyly, "our school has been experiencing a rash of thefts and vandalism lately. Have you heard anything or do you know anything about them?"

Kimberly's eyes burst from her tiny face. She didn't know what to say. She decided quickly to go with the easy answer. "No, Ms. Burke," she singsonged innocently.

"Thank you, dear, that's all I needed to know."

Kimberly stared at Ms. Burke a second. Their eyes glistened intentionally. A split second of complete knowledge passed between them. Kimberly knew more than she was saying, and Patricia knew it.

Pierce, on the other hand, didn't notice Kimberly's guarded reaction. His eyes were hooded and riveted to Patricia's face. When Patricia finally looked at Pierce, a twinge of hammered lightning shot through her. There were definitely sparks between them; she just wasn't sure what kind, or what she going to do about them.

TWO

Patricia shook her head and went back into her office, realizing that her investigation was far from over. As the faint sound of Mr. Wilson's floor-polishing machine hummed in the background, she walked over to her desk. She removed her jacket as a familiar blast of heat that had nothing to do with the seventy-degree temperature tore through her. She stood at the window and watched as Pierce and Kimberly climbed into the shiny black Jaguar parked in front of the school building.

She glanced down just as Pierce took a last look up at the one light still on—her office. Even in the dusk of evening, she could plainly see the classic features of his chiseled face. He was even more attractive than she remembered.

No, *attractive* was definitely an understatement. The man was drop-dead gorgeous. With eyes as black as night and skin of singed almonds, he was sinfully perfect. The deep melodious rhythm of his voice seeped through her each time he spoke, and the broad width of his chest begged to be explored. She smiled, letting her mind savor the possibilities as her thoughts drifted back to their very first meeting. . . .

A hush fell as she quickly walked into the room and took her seat in the front of the class. All eyes were on her, again. Tech-

nically, she was an anomaly, a twelve-year-old sixth-grader in an eighth-grade class, a freshman in a senior world, never really belonging in either. So, as usual, she lowered her head, made herself as little as possible, and hurried to her desk.

She sat quickly and quietly, then pulled out her notebook in preparation for the morning's lesson. She looked up at the board and watched as Mrs. Simmons, her English literature teacher, scripted an assignment on the board. It was the typical busywork used to challenge the stagnated intellectual minds of the school football team.

Patricia frowned, thankful the assignments came in two phases, one for the serious students and one for the team. She was one of the few serious students in this class. With a grade point average leveled at four-point-seven, she had quickly advanced beyond her sixth-grade curriculum and been placed in eighth-grade classes. The assignments were still tediously boring, but she handled them in stride.

The flying airplane caught her eye as it whizzed past her on the right. It was instantly followed by another one on the left, then another and another. Then, the final blow hit its target. Slowly she reached up and pulled the paper airplane from her small Afro and placed it on her desk.

Being scholastically advanced was one thing; being constantly harassed with juvenile antics was another. It was the same old thing, the Richies versus the Poories. She closed her eyes in tolerance, stiffened her lip, and tried her best to ignore them. But the childish laughter of Aidan Franklin and Lewis Carter, the two ringleaders, could not be ignored.

"Miss Burke." Patricia opened her eyes with a start, surprised to see Mrs. Simmons standing in front of her holding the airplane in her hand while slapping it against the other hand. She'd let her half-frame reading glasses dangle from a beaded chain around her neck. "I'm not sure what you're accustomed to in your previous school, but we do not fly paper airplanes in this school. I will not tolerate anymore of your mischief. If you cannot handle yourself as a mature young lady in this school,

*then perhaps you should return to wherever you came from. Do
I make myself crystal clear?"*

Patricia, too scared to utter a word, simply stared wide-eyed
as laughter crackled all around her and chanted whispers of
"Ratsy Patsy" made tears spill.

*"Either you behave yourself and pick up this trash, or leave
this class immediately—your choice,"* Mrs. Simmons said.

Patricia opened her mouth to rebut, but closed it almost immediately. There was no way Mrs. Simmons would believe that
she was innocent. In her eyes, Patricia not only didn't belong in
her class, but she didn't even belong in the prestigious Ida B.
Wells Academy.

Mrs. Simmons was one of the most vocal disputants of the
new Wells Academy ruling that opened the gold-tinted doors of
the academy to deserving but underprivileged scholarship students. Patricia was one of the first to be accepted. From that day
on, her life had changed forever, and Mrs. Simmons made sure
of that.

It didn't matter that she was smarter than anyone in her class
or that she was already taking preparatory college classes. The
only thing she saw was that Patricia was poor.

Slowly Patricia stood, bent down, and began picking up the
discarded paper airplanes around her seat. A slow tormented
tear fell onto the polished wooden floor as the laughter continued around her. Suddenly, a hand reached down and picked up
a piece of trash next to her.

"Why don't you leave her alone?" he said to the jeers and
sneers of his friends and peers. *"Don't pay any attention to
them,"* he whispered to her as he handed an airplane over. *"My
brother and his friends are just kidding around."*

She stood and walked toward the trash can by the front door.
She smiled. Suddenly the childish teasing didn't matter anymore. It was the first time that Pierce Franklin had actually
spoken to her. . . .

* * *

Patricia jumped as the ringing telephone drew her attention back to her desk. Feeling slightly ridiculous about revisiting her schoolgirl fantasies, she quickly picked up the ringing telephone. "Patricia Burke."

"Girl, don't you ever go home?"

"Hey, Juliet, what's up, girl?" Patricia sat down at her desk and began clearing and neatening the litter of files piled in the bins.

"Nothing. I left a couple of messages on your machine at home, but I should have known you'd still be at work."

"Where else would I be?" Patricia admitted truthfully.

"How about at home chilling?"

"Are you kidding? With budget meetings, restructuring curriculums, planning placement assessment strategies, child development programs, and site-based management evaluations, not to mention the staff development exchange program in a few months, who has time to chill?" Patricia said, then blew out a sigh of exhaustion.

"I can't believe you," Juliet said.

"I haven't told you the worst yet. I have a couple of spoiled rich moms on the Christmas Ball committee who are constantly complaining about each other. Every day I get to hear some whining complaint about what the other has done. The whole thing is so childish. They forget the whole meaning behind the Christmas Ball in the first place."

"Which was it tonight?"

"All of the above, but I also had a parent conference with one of my students."

"Patricia, it's well after seven o'clock at night. Enough is enough. Go home, girl. Couldn't your parent conference wait until tomorrow morning?"

"Sometimes you have to yield to the schedules of the parents. And unfortunately, I've found that most of the parents here are borderline workaholics. I've been try-

ing to get this particular parent in my office since the beginning of this semester. So, I have to meet them when
they're available and when it's convenient for them,
even if it means waiting until seven o'clock at night."

"Screw that," Juliet said with her typical trash-talking
cool. "Patricia, you have a life, too. No one is that important that you have to plan your schedule around
them. You shouldn't have to wait for anyone. You need
to learn that work shouldn't consume your entire life."

"Look who's talking. You need to stop frontin'. I bet
you're standing at a bar in front of a wall of mirrors in
the middle of an empty dance studio right now. Am I
right?"

"Rehearsals are different. If I wanted to stay in the
back chorus waving a plastic rose, I could have. But I
didn't. Being principal takes more work, more time, and
more dedication," Juliet weakly defended her late-night
solo dance. "Besides, I don't have to wait around for anyone else. Nobody's worth that."

Patricia thought about Pierce Franklin, then smiled
openly. "I don't know about that. Some things are definitely worth waiting for."

"That sounds too cryptic. What's it supposed to mean,
and what are you up to?" Juliet lowered her leg from the
bar and relaxed from the extended toe point then she
rose up onto her toes again.

Patricia fibbed, "Nothing, I'm just tired and babbling."
She'd cleared her desk and pulled her purse from the
bottom drawer of her file cabinet, then inserted a key
and locked it. "If it makes you feel any better, I'm on my
way out the door right now. Believe it or not, I still have
a lot of packing to do."

"How's that going?"

"I never knew I had so much stuff. I finished my closets
last night, so I just have my Christmas stuff left to pack."

"Oh, man, your Christmas stuff alone could take a few

months to pack. Honestly, Patricia, I've never met anyone else who starts decorating for Christmas in April."

"Don't start on me about my holiday spirit. And I don't start decorating in April."

"Oh, girl, please, the average person has holiday spirit in December, maybe November. You, dear lunatic friend, have Christmas spirit all year round."

"There's nothing wrong with keeping the joy of the season with you year round."

"Playing Christmas music, singing carols, and keeping a lit and decorated tree in the house year round is just plain nuts."

"Are you calling me nuts?" Patricia asked defensively.

"Yes, you are a nut," Juliet confirmed without a second's thought or consideration. The two laughed on the phone like a couple of schoolkids at recess.

"Thanks, I appreciate that," Patricia finally said. "Are you still coming next weekend?"

"I'll be there and I'm bringing a friend. I think we might need another pair of hands."

"Oh," Patricia drew out with lengthy sarcasm. "A friend. What kind of *friend?*" she asked teasingly.

"A buddy kind of friend."

"Just a buddy?"

"Girl, please, this particular buddy happens to do a pirouette better than I can. You know what the men in my world are like. They're either gay with a capital *G* or paranoid assholes afraid of being labeled as gay, so they act like sex-hungry jerks with egos the size of their codpieces."

Patricia shook her head, chuckling at her friend's dramatic play on words. "Don't pull any punches, Juliet, by all means, speak your mind."

"I just call it as I see it. So, believe me, I'm definitely not his type, but he's cool." She waited until Patricia's laughter faded. "Girl, you know D.C. is drying up. I haven't had a real date in weeks. I can't wait to move on to another town when my contract's over."

"The odds of finding someone are no better anywhere else."

"True love," Juliet said with an extended dreamy sigh, "is that too much to ask for?"

"Are you still looking for that old thing?" Patricia asked, then thought for a moment as she dug in her purse searching for her car keys. "You're such a romantic, but sorry, you're asking the wrong person. I've given up on looking for and finding true love. As a matter of fact, I've decided not to wait for anything anymore."

"Liar." Juliet laughed as Patricia spattered an appalled reaction. "You've been waiting for a certain Mr. Right since the first day I met you."

"Am not. School and work, work and school, that's all I'm concentrating on these days. I just need a few more credits for my doctorate, then I hang out my own shingle. Dr. Patricia Burke, child psychologist."

"You can have the shingle and true love, too."

"Ha. You know good and darn well it doesn't work like that. The last thing most men want is an intelligent, professional, established woman with her own mind."

"You have to have more faith, girl. Since when did you become such a cynic? What happened to the Christmas fanatic we all know and love?"

"She woke up," Patricia spouted uncharacteristically.

"I doubt that. Where's your faith?"

"Oh, yeah, I got your faith," she said as they both laughed, knowing that faith was the last thing in the world she lacked. "We'll have to continue this conversation later. I'm on my way out the door." They hung up promising to call and continue the conversation later.

Patricia smiled as she hung up the phone. Juliet was the best thing to happen to her. From the very first time they met they had been best friends. Her wit and fast talking had saved Patricia on more than on one occasion. Patricia continued locking and clearing up her desk as she thought about their first eventful meeting. . . .

"Oh, grow up," Juliet yelled out after the boys while she helped Patricia pick up the books they'd purposely knocked to the hallway floor. Aidan, Lewis, and their friends laughed with roaring humor as they continued down the emptying hall. "They're such bullies," Juliet, a fourteen-year-old senior, added to a frenzied and nervous twelve-year-old Patricia.

All Patricia could think was that she was going to be late for class. She hurried and grabbed all the books, then ran down the hall to her next class, world history.

It wasn't until the next day that she realized she was missing her math notebook. Then, while she sat in her class panicking, Juliet Bridges came up to her and placed the notebook on her desk. She pointed to a large heart beautifully sketched with a red marker on the last page with the words PATRICIA LOVES PIERCE written inside of it. Patricia was mortified.

"I'd leave that page at home next time if I were you," Juliet said with a polite smile. Patricia quickly tore the page out and ripped it into tiny pieces. They'd been best friends ever since. . . .

Even now, years later, Patricia couldn't imagine why she'd drawn that heart and written the names. All she could fathom was that at twelve years old she'd been too infatuated by her first love to even think straight.

Patricia shook her head as the memory faded. She closed and locked her office door as a sense of sadness washed over her. The reality of seeing Pierce Franklin again was more pungent than she'd anticipated. There hadn't been a shred of recognition or familiarity in his dark hooded eyes. The truth was hurtful, as reality often is. He didn't even slightly recognize or remember her.

* * *

The ride from Wells Academy to the Regency Towers where they lived was a relatively short one. Kimberly had ridden it several times on her bicycle, making the trip in less than twenty-five minutes flat. But now, listening to her uncle drone on about honor, success, and pride made it unbearably long. It was the same speech he'd used before, one she'd heard all her life. Absently she rolled her eyes and stared out of the window into the settled dusk of sunset, watching as children still played outside in shorts and T-shirts.

It was still Indian summer, and the unseasonably warm weather had spoiled everybody. She lowered the car window to let some of the warm October air blow in. She closed her eyes, tilted and leaned her head farther out of the window. The warm breeze felt wonderful as it rushed through her soft curly hair.

"Kimberly?"

"Yes, I'm listening, Uncle Pierce," she responded automatically, knowing that was sufficient to keep him talking.

The bright glittering headlights of oncoming traffic held more interest for her at this point. The residential streets of McLean, Virginia, were always busy this time of night, but the warm weather only added to the evening's activities. With restaurants lining the main streets like Monopoly boxes and the Tyson's Corner shopping center just two minutes away, Leesburg Pike was the place to be, and they lived in the center of it all.

The Regency Towers, also known as "Money Towers," was a high-rise condominium built at the onset of the major influx of computer companies into the area. When the computer companies arrived, they brought with them money and expensive tastes. The luxury units were high-priced, rich and classy. Every executive in the area wanted a home in the Regency Towers.

Pierce had moved into one of the four two-story penthouse units soon after it was built. The spectacular view of the Washington, D.C., beltway and stellar monuments was incredible from the top floors. It was often said that on a clear day you could see right into the West Wing.

Kimberly had lived in the Regency Towers since she was eight years old. Before that, she couldn't really remember. She had photos of her mother and father in a beautiful house in a suburb of Boston. But that was all she had—not a single memory, just photos.

"Are you listening to me?" Pierce repeated a second time as he steered the Jaguar sports car through the security gate. He nodded and waved to the posted guard, then continued to the parking garage.

"Yes," she grumbled roughly, "I'm listening." Satisfied with the answer, Pierce continued. Kimberly knew this game well. She'd played it as far back as she could remember. Her uncle Pierce was sweet, but his parental graces were sorely lacking. The harshest punishment he'd ever doled out to her had been after she accidentally crashed his computer system at home, and even then, the best he could muster was a day without television. It had been a Friday night, and nobody watched television on Friday night anyway. She'd eventually gone to the mall with her friends.

"You have to think about your future, Kimberly. Life is not just going to hand you a career. You have to work for it, and that starts right here, right now," he droned on.

"I know that, Uncle Pierce," she admitted truthfully. Her future happiness was exactly what she was thinking about.

"Making and having money is fine, but doing something you love for the rest of your life, that's the real challenge." He looked over to her and smiled. "You can do anything you want, Kimberly, *be* anything you want. But it takes work, hard work. Wells Academy is only the beginning. But it's an excellent beginning. Your dad and I worked very hard there, and you will, too."

"I know, Uncle Pierce," she repeated soberly, as if set on automatic by response remote control.

"Wells Academy is one of the foremost private schools in the country. Just getting in there is an honor. I realize that this is your last year, but you have to keep up the same steadfast and dedicated work habits as the previous five years. This summer you'll be in the Banneker summer program, and next year you'll begin high school at Benjamin Banneker School of Computers, Mathematics, and Science. After that you're off to college. These years are the ones that matter most and will mold you for the rest of your life." Pierce looked over to the somber Kimberly. "You're an excellent student with a promising future. But I realize that some classes at the academy can be overly challenging, so maybe you want to consider a tutor to help bring your grades back up." Kimberly nodded, still on mental automatic.

The lecture lasted right up to the front door of their penthouse condo. Kimberly was sure she'd burned out a million or two brain cells by the time the door opened.

Mrs. Hopkins, their neighbor, opened the door with her usual cheerful demeanor. "Hello, Kimmy. How did the meeting with Ms. Burke go?"

"Great," Kimberly muttered sarcastically, then breezed past her and hurried up the stairs to her bedroom sanctuary.

Mrs. Hopkins, a round woman with plump features, shook her head, not at all surprised by Kimberly's quick remark and abrupt departure. She was used to Kimberly's moodiness. As far as she was concerned, it was all part of being a teen and growing up.

Mrs. Hopkins, whose other half ran the Regency Towers' management team, had been a true lifesaver in the years since Kimberly had first arrived to stay with Pierce. She had immediately assumed the grandmotherly position in their lives and was well on her way to permanent sainthood. Pierce had no idea what he'd have done without her. As a cook and companion to Kimberly, she was irreplaceable.

In the early years of PEF Software, Pierce's late hours at the office weren't exactly conducive to raising a young child. That's when Mrs. Hopkins had stepped in. Knowing that she was always there was an assurance and made his long hours at the office less damnable.

Now, as a teen, Kimberly had a companion and friend in Helen Hopkins. But still, she was his niece. That twinge of guilt had again escaped from the little place just inside his heart. Had he truly given up too much for success? Had he given the important years of Kimberly's young life to a computer company?

"Good evening, Pierce," Mrs. Hopkins greeted him as he walked in following Kimberly.

"Good evening, Mrs. Hopkins." He dropped his briefcase on a chair by the front door, then picked up the mail and casually flipped through it, a nightly ritual.

"How was your day?" she asked him.

"Busy as usual." Pierce really wanted to say that it was one of the worst days he'd had in a long time. But he didn't.

"You've got to find some time to relax," she scolded mildly, "or you're going to be burned out before Christmas day."

Pierce had heard this gentle warning numerous times from Mrs. Hopkins. It was her favorite forewarning: "before Christmas." To her everything had to be measured by, defined by, and compared to the Christmas holiday. Pierce smiled at her steadiness, "I'll be fine, Mrs. Hopkins," he assured her.

"Yep, that's what they all say just before they keel over. Same thing happened to Dr. Wright. He just passed out right in the middle of his wife's heart transplant. Poor woman, her ten-year-old son had to finish the operation." Mrs. Hopkins shook her head woefully. "It's a good thing that boy remembered what his mother told him about sewing and knitting, or she'd be in a world of trouble."

Pierce laughed at the absurd tragedy of the soap opera story lines as he flipped through and studied each envelope. "Anything new and interesting happen today?"

She threw her hands up in the air in mock surrender. "Same old same old, so don't go getting me started."

Pierce smirked again and did just that. "Did amnesiac Melissa Crane finally catch Jeffery with her sister in the hospital linen closet?"

"Lord, no, not yet, that poor dear child. She'll be making the biggest mistake of her life if she marries that low-down two-timing devil. And her mother, she's just plain slow-witted. She thinks the sun rises and sets on the boy. Lord, I don't see why Melissa don't see through him. He's just plain evil. But I guess being run over by that train and having amnesia can do that to a person."

Pierce smiled as usual. "Maybe things will change tomorrow. They always do somehow." He always made time to patiently listen to Mrs. Hopkins commiserate over her soap operas. She watched a bevy of them beginning at eleven o'clock and ending at four. Recently, she'd even found herself addicted to the Spanish-language soaps.

It didn't matter that she didn't speak or understand a single word of the language; she insisted that misery was misery, no matter how they spoke it.

"I sure hope you're right. The wedding's in only two days' time. It'll take a miracle for Melissa to see the error of her ways by then." Mrs. Hopkins knew, of course, that the people in the soaps weren't real, but still, she enjoyed their tragedies, trials, and struggles nevertheless.

Pierce placed the opened mail back down on the foyer table and picked up his briefcase.

"You had three or four telephone calls on your private line earlier this evening. I didn't answer them, so you might want to see what was so important. I'll go get dinner warmed up for you." Mrs. Hopkins turned and started down the hall leading to the kitchen. "How'd it go at school this evening with Ms. Burke?"

"Fine," he answered absently, "Kimberly's just got to buckle down more on her homework and adjust her attitude."

Mrs. Hopkins shook her head as she walked. "She's a piece of work, that niece of yours," she called out as she entered the kitchen.

Pierce went straight to the library, then to his desk. Slowly, thoughtfully, he looked around his domain. The dark rich burgundy textured walls lined with massive bookcases gave him the sense of total seclusion. When he entered here, everything else was left outside. This was his sanctuary. It was the one place he could go to shut the world out completely as he so often did.

The caller ID displayed a well-worn number on the key pad: Lewis Carter, the company's new department manager and his brother's close friend since grade school. The number indicated that he'd called five times from his home, so Pierce assured himself that Lewis had taken his advice and gone home to his wife after their talk.

Lewis, although a close family friend, had turned out to be more trouble than he was worth. Having been hired less than ten months ago, he was already up to his nose in crap.

Insulting one of PEF's oldest and most respected

clients in order to bilk him for a larger order was one thing, but now he was in hot water for sexual harassment of a staff secretary. That was both incorrigible and unforgivable.

Pierce prided himself on PEF's strict ethics and skilled professionalism. Every employee worked to the best of his or her ability and was paid accordingly with the top salaries and stock options. Each employee deserved and received optimal security with a comfortable, safe, assured environment. Lewis had threatened that environment.

The secretary wasn't going to press charges; she just wanted Lewis to leave her alone and to be placed as far away from him as possible. Pierce had immediately accommodated her by giving her a position in his office, which he knew was far enough away from Lewis.

He'd also had a long serious talk with his old friend about this latest indiscretion. But Lewis, playing his usual charming self, blamed the whole thing on the secretary and a grave misunderstanding on her part. Listening to his obvious lies had been truly frustrating.

"Pierce, man, if I'd known for one minute that she wasn't interested, I would have just backed off and dissed her. But man, she was, like, all over me. I was just going with the flow, you know what I mean," Lewis had offered up as some kind of an excuse.

Pierce had known the particular young woman of Lewis's desire. She'd been employed at PEF for more than two years. She was kind, efficient, and trustworthy. She'd been married since forever to a man she adored and was blessed with three overzealous boys who regularly came to the company picnics and drove her crazy.

Pierce smiled at the memory of the boys running around and her trying to catch up with them. He knew that there was no way she would have come on to Lewis, as he had adamantly claimed. Pierce shook his head. Regrettably, he'd have to handle Lewis eventually, but not now. He had other things on his mind.

Suddenly feeling anxious, Pierce stood and walked over to the small bar set up near the terrace's sliding glass doors. He poured a drink of amber liquid, then moved to his reflection in the glass doors. Looking past his despondent expression, Pierce stared out into the darkened night sky. It had become an increasingly familiar posture when his old demons reared their heads, as they did so often lately.

Recently, Pierce had become increasingly introspective about his life. By all accounts he should be ecstatic. Ideally, he had the best of all worlds. He had a thriving business, a fabulous apartment, his health, and Kimberly. What could possibly be missing?

Everything had been perfect until just a few months ago. He was certain that it wasn't the usual Christmas holiday blues that usually gripped him. It was something else. There was something missing, something just beyond the horizon that he just couldn't seem to grasp.

Questions tangled in his mind as he reviewed his day. Each time he focused, his mind's eye took him back to Patricia Burke's warm patient smile. It was too mesmerizing and couldn't be as genuine as it appeared. She definitely couldn't be as she appeared. Her fiery, ill-mannered e-mail proved that.

Ultimately, he wondered what her chink was. Armor that bright and shiny had to come with some deep-set cuts or nicks. Nobody could be that dedicated and giving. He continued to stare out into the night as thoughts of Patricia danced around his head like fallen leaves on a windy day. She was just too perfect.

Upstairs, Kimberly was once again safely locked behind the confines of her closed doors. She wasted no time. In a single sure-fingered swoop, she'd managed to turn on her television, her CD player, and her computer and speed-dialed her best friend in less than three seconds flat, a personal record. The phone on the other end was picked up on the first ring.

"Kimmy?"

"Yeah," Kimberly responded while kicking off her shoes and loosening her school uniform's striped tie.

"What took you so long? I thought you'd never call. I've been calling you for the last hour. The phone kept ringing and ringing and ringing. I thought it was broken or something, so I must have sent you two dozen E-mails. I couldn't figure out what was taking you so long. I was starting to get worried. I thought Ms. Burke had had you arrested or something."

Since third grade, Jasmine had successfully acquired the knack of giving an entire monologue without bothering to take a single breath. It was a unique talent that required Kimberly to either listen very carefully to gather each thought as quickly as possible or to tune out entirely. Tonight she chose a combination of both. "Nah, my uncle was running late as usual. So it took longer than I thought."

"How did it go? What did Ms. Burke tell him? Oh, my God, I know she must have spilled her guts. Your uncle Pierce hasn't been to the academy in, like, forever or something, like since you first got there, right? I can just see Ms. Burke telling him everything about your last five years. She probably brought up every single incident since third grade."

"I don't know. I had to wait outside. They were in the office together. I heard them arguing mostly." She pulled the school sweater over her head and pulled the white shirt out of her plaid pleated skirt. She tossed the school uniform on the chair and belly flopped across the bed. Her head landed on a pile of decorative pillows and plush stuffed animals.

"Arguing?" Jasmine balked in stunned surprise.

"Yeah," Kimberly said, encouraged as she flicked the remote control and a blur of channels whizzed by.

"Oh, no, that means we're screwed."

"No, it doesn't. It's a good sign, it means that it's working."

"How is arguing a good sign? They weren't supposed to be arguing. They were supposed to be attracted to each other. Not trying to kill each other."

"They were communicating," Kimberly said while peeling down her socks and sliding her purple polished toes into her slippers.

"Nobody communicates like that."

"Sure they do. My family does it all the time. Uncle Pierce and Grandpop and Grandmom go at it loud enough to wake the dead."

"Kimberly, this is serious. This whole Christmas wish rides on them at least getting along."

Kimberly smiled. "That's just it, *they were* getting along. I told Uncle Pierce that Ms. Burke was old and ugly and mean."

"Why did you do that?"

"Reverse psychology."

"Are you kidding? You chose this moment to try out your Introduction to Psychology notes. Are you nuts? We're in enough trouble already."

"But it worked, just like the textbook said it would. Implant a dramatic negative idea and the reverse opinion will be that much stronger. And it worked, Jasmine." She paused to think. "I'm sure of it."

"Kimmy."

"No, listen, the first meeting wasn't so good, but you should have seem Uncle Pierce's reaction when he first saw Ms. Burke. He was floored. He practically fell out of his chair."

"Hello, earth to Kimmy, I repeat, they were still arguing."

"And I repeat, they were communicating."

"You're impossible. I'm beginning to think that this whole thing was a big mistake."

"Jasmine, listen, if Uncle Pierce and Ms. Burke were arguing, that's just because he didn't agree with what she was saying about me. You know how overprotective Uncle Pierce can be. Don't you get it?"

"Get what?"

"Sparks."

"What?"

"Sparks," Kimberly repeated in the sweet dreamy way she did after reading a teen romance novel. "Adults are like computer programs—" she began.

Jasmine interrupted, "Oh, not that again."

Kimberly cleared her throat loudly. "As I was saying, adults are like computer programs: Sometimes you have to reboot or even do a quick restart after you add a new program."

"That makes absolutely no sense at all."

"Okay, think of it this way. Not everybody experiences love at first sight, so the fact that they were arguing means that emotions were high, and when emotions are high, then you know what happens next?" she ended.

"No, what?"

"Then adrenaline starts to pump. The fact that they were arguing means that emotions were high, and when emotions are high, then you're bound to get excitement. Don't think of them as arguing, think of it more as pregame warm-up or an overture to the main event." Kimberly smiled, remembering the look on her uncle's and counselor's faces outside the office. She was sure that there was something more than just anger raging in their eyes.

"This was a lousy idea. You never should have made that stupid wish. Now look at us. I can't believe we actually broke into the school, hacked the computer system, and lied just for a stupid Christmas wish. We should have just stuck with the safari in Africa idea."

Kimberly picked up a catalog from the stack she kept by her bed and began flipping through it. "Remember, it's not just a Christmas wish, it's *the* Christmas wish, the perfect Christmas wish."

Those exact words had stayed with Kimberly since that late-night meteor shower and that lazy afternoon in August when the idea first hit her and it had all started. . . .

Jasmine had spent the night at Kimberly's house. The two sneaked outside onto the roof to watch the late-night meteor shower, which had now become an annual ritual. It was almost three o'clock in the morning, and still no sign of a single falling star.

"They're late," Jasmine complained as she finished off her second Popsicle.

"You can't predict the exact time of these things," Kimberly said, chewing on the wooden Popsicle stick.

"Are you sure it's tonight?" Jasmine asked.

"Positive, you just have to be patient, that's all."

"We've been out here for over an hour and not one meteor," Jasmine said as she adjusted the zoom lens on the telescope while Kimberly searched the northeast corridor.

"Look, there!" Kimberly shrieked excitedly. "Did you see them?"

"See what?" Jasmine hurried by Kimberly's side. Both girls stared up at the sky in silence. Then, in the twinkling of an eye, two flashes of light streaked across the night sky. "There's one! And another one!"

For the next ten minutes they sat watching meteors streak down in a shower like rain from the heavens.

"There's another one," Jasmine said, eagerly pointing skyward.

Kimberly watched the tiny flash of light streak across the sky and disappear in an instant. "Last year I wished on a falling star that I would be accepted to the Banneker summer program, and I was."

Jasmine nodded. Her eyes were glued to the heavens.

"So," Kimberly wondered aloud, "if you get to make a single wish on a shooting star, making a wish on a meteor shower ought to really make it come true, right?"

"Sounds about right. You should try it and see if it works," Jasmine said with enthusiastic encouragement.

"I'll make a wish on the next one," Kimberly said.

Seconds later, a myriad of shooting stars streaked through the sky in simultaneous abandonment. As they watched them streaking, one right after the other, both girls held their mouths open in awestruck wonder. Jasmine grabbed Kimberly's arm tightly and jumped excitedly. "Come on, do it now, make your wish!"

She took it as a sign and whispered the familiar child's poem:

Star light, star bright,
First star I see tonight,
I wish I may, I wish I might,
Have the wish I wish tonight.

Kimberly closed her eyes real tight and made the most ardent, fervent, heartfelt wish she could think of. "I wish I could give Uncle Pierce the perfect Christmas gift this year, please."

Jasmine looked over to her friend. "Oh, you are seriously tripping. What kind of wish was that? It's impossible, totally hopeless. What do you get the man that has everything?"

Kimberly shrugged and looked out at the vastness of space. "That's the wish, to find something that would be perfect for him. Something that he doesn't already have and something that he doesn't even know he needs yet. The perfect gift to make him love Christmas again."

Both girls sat quietly for a few moments, thinking about the vastness of their surroundings and the vast hopelessness of Kimberly's wish.

"It's hopeless," Jasmine commiserated.

"Not if you wish on a falling star or a lot of falling stars," Kimberly said with a surge of eager optimism. "Come on, let's get to bed. We have to get up early. We've got a lot of work to do tomorrow."

The following morning, back in Kimberly's bedroom, Jasmine and Kimberly decided to help her wish along. Together they flipped through tons of magazines and catalogs and searched the Internet for the perfect Christmas gift for the man who has everything.

"It's not just a Christmas wish. It's the *Christmas wish*," Kimberly said as she tossed the catalog she'd been scanning on the floor and picked up another one.

"It's the beginning of August, Kimberly. Nobody except you is even thinking about Christmas presents this time of year. It's like a million zillion degrees outside," Jasmine said, still scrolling through the myriad of Internet screens she had opened.

"It was my wish, and I'm sure that whoever it is who grants wishes could use all the help they can get on this particular one. So I need as much time as possible for this particular present."

"So, what's the present anyway? Another certificate for a galaxy named after your uncle, like last year?"

"No," she said absently, still searching through catalogs, "and that was a star named after him, not a galaxy."

"Whatever. So, what's the big gift idea this year?"

"I wish I knew. I have no idea," Kimberly said, tossing then picking up another catalog.

"You don't know?"

"I have no idea, that's what we're looking for now. I've been collecting these magazines and catalogs for months. There's got to be something in here somewhere that'll be the perfect gift."

Jasmine continued to scroll through the dozens of Web sites that Kimberly had saved earlier. "I never knew that there were so many specialty gift sites for executives. Look at these. How did you find them all?"

"I hacked into my uncle's computer a few weeks ago. All these companies sent sales announcements to him about their products. I simply forwarded them to me. I'm hoping that one of them has something special."

"Wait a minute, you hacked your uncle?"

Kimberly nodded nonchalantly.

"You are so dead meat."

"It's okay. He's so busy he never checks all his mail. You know he doesn't have time for anything except the office. I hacked in months ago and he hasn't even noticed it. Besides, it's an address he rarely looks at anymore."

"Whatever," Jasmine said skeptically, then continued looking. "These things are serious. You're gonna have to drop some mad cash this year if you want something from this place."

"That's another thing, the numbers are practically worn off my credit cards. I have to find something reasonable or Uncle Pierce is gonna be suspicious when the bill comes in."

"Why are you trippin'? You know he's gonna roll with you. You can spend whatever you want and he'll just sign over a check. You are so lucky. My evil stepmom watches my credit cards like a hawk," Jasmine complained as she scanned another Web site. "Hey, check this out. How about a ride on the space shuttle with Russian cosmonauts?"

"Let's try something a bit more local," Kimberly said with a frown.

"What about a six-week safari in Africa?"

"Uncle Pierce would never leave his office that long. It has to be something spectacular but personal."

"An English manservant?"

"That's too personal." Kimberly laughed at the idea of her uncle having his own servant to wait on him hand and foot

and follow him everywhere he went. "Find something more im-pressive."

"How about a full-length mink coat, with matching hat and boots?" Jasmine said, barely able to contain her laughter.

"I don't think so. Let's go with personal, but less spectacular and more fun. I definitely want something that's fun."

"A fire-engine red James Bond prototype Ferrari of the future with solar panels, electric power, and aquatic ability," Jasmine read from the screen, giggling with each word.

"Aquatic ability?"

"That's what the ad says. Not only does it drive on highways, but it also has some kind of hovercraft thing underneath that enables it to float on water."

"Nah, I don't think so, too dangerous. I want something more exciting and provocative."

"Oh, here, wait, I got it, check this out. A weeklong stay at the Playboy Mansion. It says here that you get to party with all twelve Playmates and a private party with the man himself."

"Nah, too crowded, I need something more exclusive."

"How about . . . oh, never mind," Jasmine began, then paused. "What do you get the man that has everything?" she wondered aloud.

"I've got it!" Kimberly tossed her catalog aside and nearly jumped off the bed with excitement. "I've got it! It's perfect, I've got it. What do you get the man that has everything?" she asked rhetorically, then smiled brightly.

"What?" Jasmine hurried to Kimberly, still sitting on the bed surrounded by magazines and catalogs. "What?" Jasmine scanned the catalog Kimberly had been looking through. She flipped through the pages quickly. "What did you find?"

"Love, and the perfect woman."

Jasmine thought for a second. It was perfect. "He's got tons of bimbos hanging around, so this woman had better be really spe-cial," she warned.

"I know," Kimberly said, still smiling at the unbelievable idea. "She will be." Kimberly stood and began pacing the floor.

"Who is she?" The charged excitement in Jasmine's eyes was evident as she sat expectantly.

"I have no idea." Jasmine looked crestfallen until Kimberly added, "Not yet, anyway."

"Do you already have someone in mind?"

"No, but it can't be that difficult to find someone, can it?"

Jasmine shrugged her shoulders. "You're right about one thing: It can't be just any woman, it has to be the perfect woman."

Kimberly nodded. "The perfect woman for the perfect gift." She plopped down across her bed and rolled over with a broad smile. "She has to be patient and strong."

Jasmine laid back on the bed next to her friend. Their heads met at an angle. "Yeah, she has to be beautiful and smart, too."

"Really smart with a good sense of humor."

"Yeah, and single, she has to be single," Jasmine added.

"Definitely, and she's got to like Christmas."

"No, she's got to love Christmas. Remember, we're talking about your uncle Bah-humbug Scrooge."

"You're right, since Uncle Pierce is so totally the Grinch, we'll need someone who really loves Christmas to balance him out," Kimberly said as she sat up.

"Okay, what do we have?" Jasmine asked, sitting up also.

"Patient, strong, loves Christmas, single, and smart."

"Don't forget a good sense of humor."

"Right, she's got to have a great sense of humor."

Kimberly and Jasmine smiled.

Kimberly turned to Jasmine. "Are you thinking what I'm thinking?" she asked. Kimberly nodded eagerly. Jasmine nodded along until they both were nodding and squealing gleefully.

"She's a Christmas fanatic, he's Uncle Bah-humbug Scrooge. Together they'll be perfect," Kimberly said. Jasmine nodded again, totally agreeing as Kimberly continued, "If they don't kill each other in the process, that is." Together they giggled uncontrollably. "Ms. Burke is perfect," Kimberly stated to a very agreeable Jasmine. . . .

* * *

"Kimberly, Kimberly, are you still there?"

"Yeah, I'm here. I was just thinking about my uncle and Ms. Burke. They'll make a great couple."

"Okay, but we still have to make sure that nobody knows what we're doing. This whole thing could blow up in our faces. Breaking and entering plus hacking computers aren't exactly college prep courses, and I have no intention of taking up residence in juvenile hall."

"We'll be fine, trust me," Kimberly assured her friend. "Ms. Burke asked a lot of questions, but I don't think Uncle Pierce believed her."

"That's such a relief," Jasmine said. "You're so lucky that your uncle Pierce didn't believe Ms. Burke. My evil stepmom came right home and told my dad everything."

"What exactly did your stepmom tell your dad?"

"That I'd been cutting class and that my grades were falling. Dad had a major fit and grounded me for life.

"Is that what Ms. Burke told your uncle?"

"I guess so. That's probably what they were arguing about."

"Probably."

Kimberly wondered aloud. "But you know what was too perfect? Right before we left, Ms. Burke and Uncle Pierce looked at each other like they were either going to kill each other or kiss." She smiled happily and made a wistful face. "Can you believe it? They were, like, making eyes at each other. It was so perfect."

"That's exactly what I was saying." Jasmine sighed dreamily. "Ms. Burke and Uncle Pierce, they are so perfect together. I can't believe we didn't see it years before."

"You think?"

"Totally."

"I hope so," Kimberly said, "'cause if this doesn't work, I'm in a load of trouble."

"They are so totally perfect together, it has to work," Jasmine said. "Besides, you wished on a falling star, right? Your wish has got to come true. Wait, actually, you wished on a lot of stars. This whole thing is like fate or something." She grinned. "What better way to get rid of a Scrooge than to hook him up with Ms. Burke? They're the perfect gift for each other."

"I can't believe we're actually doing this. I can't believe we're actually hooking up Ms. Burke with my uncle."

"Why not? You know how Ms. Burke gets around the holidays. She's like Ms. Super-Christmas-fanatic. So, if she and Uncle Pierce hook up, then it's bound to rub off and you'll have your wish. Besides, Ms. Burke is a babe and Uncle Pierce is the biggest and only catch. She could be like your aunt or something. That would be, like, so cool. We wouldn't have to do homework anymore, we could get to school late, we could get away with, like, just about anything."

Kimberly mulled over Jasmine's suggestion. It was true, she had always wished that her uncle would stop being such a Scrooge around the holidays, and Ms. Burke *was* the personification of Christmas. A slow easy smile crossed her lips. If her wish came true, this would be the perfect solution. While Uncle Pierce was wooing Ms. Burke, she could continue to hack into the system for more information on her.

"So, what did Ms. Burke say to you?" Jasmine asked.

"Nothing really. She asked me about the school thefts and the vandalism, then told me to do my homework. I got the ten-hour lecture from Uncle Pierce all the way home. I was so not listening." Kimberly decided to omit the part about her uneasiness when Ms. Burke looked at her just before they left. "Oh, I almost forgot, while I was at school I got a chance to check out the computer system again while Ms. Burke and my uncle were in her office."

"Did you have any luck getting in?"

"No, but I did find a letter Ms. Burke was writing. I can't believe she forgot and just left it on the screen like that."

"What did it say?"

"She's leaving at the end of the semester."

"To do what?"

"I don't know. It mentioned some new program." Kimberly was silent. She felt odd. She didn't tell her friend that Ms. Burke had also turned down a permanent position as assistant principal. "I also found out that Ms. Burke was definitely a student at Wells."

"That had to be a million zillion years ago, like just before the dinosaurs roamed the earth." Jasmine laughed.

"She's not that old. She's about as ancient as my uncle."

"Did you get that application approved?"

"Yeah, Mrs. Hopkins mentioned that we'd be getting a new neighbor real soon. I'm sure she was talking about Ms. Burke."

"Perfect." A second later, Jasmine shrieked into the receiver. "Oh, my God, turn on BET quick. It's Usher's, it's his new video," she squealed. "He is so delicious and I heard that his girlfriend is so rank. He and I would be so perfect together."

Jasmine had the tendency to live in a dream world at times. She would make up detailed scenarios complete with Shakespearean tragedies or multilayer dramatic intrigues. But the one common thread was her romantic happily-ever-after endings. No matter the quandary, in her dreams everything always worked out perfectly in the end.

By this time, Kimberly had completely tuned Jasmine out, a trick she'd perfected years ago. Her mind whirled, warping to the speed of light. Ideas blinked before her like twinkling lights on a Christmas tree. Every conceivable scenario zipped through her mind. They all ended with the same thing: her wish coming true and her smiling.

But it wasn't going to be easy. Her uncle was a very sought-after bachelor who usually dated what she classified as brainless wonders or arm candy, whose singular thought was the dollar sign and prestige that came with marrying him. They were all the same, all wanting one thing: money.

Kimberly knew that all of her research had shown that Ms. Burke was nothing like that. She just hoped that her uncle could see that. After all, she spoke aloud, "Ms. Burke is totally not Uncle Pierce's usual type."

"True that, she's like a superbrain," Jasmine chimed in, thinking that Kimberly was talking to her. "And we all know the brainless types he dates," she said sarcastically.

"Brainless is a compliment," Kimberly added.

"But remember, Uncle Pierce is very smart, too. That's why he never married any of the others."

Jasmine, totally unaware of her innocently blurted remark, suddenly whispered into the receiver, "I gotta go, I'm still on restriction and my paternal carbon unit and his wife just got home. Don't forget we're going shopping tomorrow night. See ya at school," she said in her usual single breath of excitement.

Kimberly held the receiver for a moment before hanging up. She barely heard her friend's final good-bye. She was still strategizing her reverse psychology scenario. It could work, she fathomed with a sneaky smile. Satisfied with her brilliance, she dumped the insides of her book bag on the bed and scrabbled through its contents. Tossing books and notes aside, she grabbed a single printed sheet of paper and reread the contents. This was perfect.

* * *

Pierce set the untouched drink on his desk and turned on his computer. It felt odd to be home at this hour. He sat down in the large executive chair and smiled, also an oddity. But since leaving Patricia Burke's office, he'd found himself smiling for no apparent reason. There was something about the knowing smile in her eyes that intrigued him.

"Pierce," Mrs. Hopkins repeated a second time. Pierce finally looked up. "Sorry to disturb you, but I'm on my way out. Kimberly says she's got homework and wants to eat later. So I left both meals in the oven warmer."

"Thank you, Mrs. Hopkins. Have a good night."

Mrs. Hopkins walked over to the desk and saw the untouched drink. She shook her head and frowned. She reached over and took the drink while placing a plate of chocolate chip cookies in its place. Pierce smiled knowingly. "I'll just take care of this," she said as she disappeared into the bathroom at the far side of the room and dumped the drink into the sink.

When she came back, Pierce was munching happily on the large homemade cookies. He exhaled lovingly. "This really hits the spot," he admitted with much zeal and appreciation.

"I was sure that it would," Mrs. Hopkins said with smiling eyes. Her chocolate chip, macadamia, and raisin cookies could brighten the worst day. They were the cure for anything that ailed you, as far as she was concerned.

Pierce finished the cookie in three consecutive bites. "Mrs. Hopkins, you're the best bartender in the world. You should send a box of those cookies to Melissa Crane from that soap opera of yours. After a few of these, she'll come to her senses and dump that bum."

"From your mouth to the screenwriters' notes," she said as she voiced her agreement, turned to leave, then paused. "Did everything go all right with Ms. Burke this evening?" He smiled, which prompted her to do the same. "My, my, from that bright smile I'd have to say everything went extremely well with Ms. Burke. Good night."

"Mrs. Hopkins," Pierce called out, "after Kimberly does her homework, does she ever show it to you?"

"Me? Nah, I wouldn't know what I was looking at with all the newfangled learning the kids do these days. Computers, slide rules, little tiny calculators." She threw her hands up in the air. "Bah, I wouldn't know what I was looking at, nor where to begin." She chuckled. "Been a long time since I was at school, and even then, we didn't have any of those newfangled gadgets." She chuckled again.

Pierce smiled at her honesty. "Thank you, Mrs. Hopkins, have a good evening. I'll see you tomorrow." She turned to leave a second time. "Mrs. Hopkins," Pierce began, then paused a second and decided to forge ahead, "do you think I've been a good parent to Kimberly?" The question, spoken aloud, surprised him even as he asked it.

Mrs. Hopkins smiled the big round smile that always exaggerated the crow's-feet around her eyes and laugh lines beside her dimples. She pondered a moment or two, then nodded the way the old folks did when they sensed a need for reassurance. "You are a wonderful parent to Kimberly, and make no mistake about it, she knows it," she stated emphatically.

He nodded his appreciation and barely whispered the words, "Thank you, Mrs. Hopkins, good night."

"Good night, Pierce." He heard her contented sigh as she walked to the foyer. He listened as the soft pad of her comfortable heels ended when the front door closed soundly behind her.

Momentarily content, Pierce found himself walking to

the kitchen as troubled thoughts of Patricia Burke sparked in his consciousness. He was a good parent, he affirmed to himself adamantly, and it would take more than a few words from a psychobabbling shrink to shake his self-confidence.

As soon as he pushed through the swinging doors and entered the kitchen, the heavenly aroma of cinnamon and candied sweet potatoes with toasted marshmallows sent his mouth watering. He smiled and looked to the ceiling, giving his usual thanks to God for sending an angel in the form of Mrs. Hopkins. He would have been lost without her, and she was a godsend in both of their lives.

When Kimberly arrived on his doorstep years ago, he'd had no idea what to do or where to start when it came to raising a small child. After all, she'd just lost both parents and hadn't quite understood what was going on and why her life had changed so drastically.

Both of his parents had insisted on raising Kimberly, but as godfather and legal guardian, he'd adamantly refused. The arguments had raged on for months and still, to this day, his parents insisted that Kimberly would be better off with them than with a confirmed bachelor. Pierce always stayed firm and Kimberly remained with him. He had never regretted his decision.

Unfortunately, with PEF Software just turning a major corner, Pierce needed to focus, which left little time for parenting. That was when Mrs. Hopkins had instantly stepped in to take care of both of them. She'd become the answer to his prayers. She basically ran the house much like her husband ran the building: with care and loving attention.

Mrs. Hopkins, after retiring from her lifelong government position a few years earlier, needed a distraction, so Pierce and Kimberly became the perfect outlet. Since her children were all grown and scattered around the globe, she needed to be needed, and Pierce and Kimberly needed to be cared for. The fit was perfect. Contented, theirs was the best of all worlds.

Aside from overseeing the cleaning crew twice a week, one of Mrs. Hopkins's main joys was cooking. Coming from a very large family, she loved to cook large meals in large quantities. Unfortunately, only cooking for her husband and herself wasn't much of a challenge. So she'd begun preparing home-cooked meals for Pierce and Kimberly.

Mrs. Hopkins, as usual, had set up a tray of napkins and silverware. Pierce reached in the warming oven below the microwave and pulled out two covered dishes. He placed the warmed meals on the tray and walked up the stairs to the second level.

His feet on the thick plush pile of the carpet made hushed sounds as he passed the first open door, his bedroom, the master suite. He continued on past two guest bedrooms, a hall table with chair, lamp, and mirror, then came to the last door at the end of the hall. It was closed, as usual.

Kimberly's door was always closed lately. She'd changed so much in the five years he'd been her legal guardian. As a child, she'd been a delight filled with inquisitive questions and joyful exuberance. She'd spent most of her time in his library right beside him at the computer.

The sparks of light had shone brightly in her eyes from the day her father had proudly introduced him to her through the plate-glass window of the maternity ward.

His brother, Aidan, had been so proud of his precious Christmas present. He had always wished for a little girl. And on Christmas day, he'd gotten his wish. He'd beamed each time he held her in his mighty arms. Pierce was equally proud of Kimberly. She was to be the daughter he'd never had. In so many ways, she was the spitting image of her mother, with just enough of his brother to make her a handful.

Pierce balanced the tray on his arm and knocked gently. The sound of thumping bass slammed against her door. He knocked again, louder and harder. Hearing no movement, Pierce frowned. Then he heard the rustling of paper and the scamper of bare feet on the mahogany floor.

Kimberly jerked open the door, expecting to see and hear Mrs. Hopkins repeating her lecture of last-minute dos and don'ts before she left each evening. She was surprised to see her uncle standing with a tray of food in his arms. She stood unblinking for a second, then remembered he'd left work early to meet with Ms. Burke.

Pierce smiled. "May I come in?"

Kimberly stepped aside and headed back to the bed covered with books, paper, pens, and pillows and stuffed animals. She picked up the remote control and increased the volume.

"I thought we could eat dinner together." He set the tray down on the desk.

"I'm not hungry," Kimberly said, and turned back to the television screen.

"Kimberly," Pierce began, more sternly this time, "we need to talk."

"We already did," she whined, referring to the long conversation they'd had in the car after leaving the school.

"Not about school or homework. I want to talk about us, about you and me, our relationship." He removed the warming covers and brought over two plates of roast beef, candied sweet potatoes with biscuits, and green beans, her favorite meal. He sat down on the bed next to her and gave Kimberly a plate with silverware and a napkin. She took the plate and inhaled the delectable aroma. She dug right in, eating with gusto. Pierce smiled at her zeal.

"I guess I haven't been very attentive the past few months." He corrected himself. "Better make that the past few years. I want to apologize about that. The company has taken more and more of my time. I realize now that wasn't fair to you." He brushed the strand of hair from her face as he'd seen Patricia do earlier. "Look at you, you're almost all grown up and I'm missing it all. It was only yesterday that I was waving at you for the first time in the hospital nursery."

"Uncle Pierce," she moaned and rolled her eyes, then slipped a tender slice of roast beef into her mouth. It melted instantly. Mrs. Hopkins was the best cook in the world as far as she was concerned.

"I know, I know, I'm embarrassing you. I just wanted to say I'm sorry and that things are going to be different around here."

"How different?" she asked skeptically with a mouthful of food.

"I intend to be more involved in your life from now on."

She groaned miserably. This wasn't supposed to happen. "Ahh, Uncle Pierce."

"This'll be a good thing, Kimberly," he assured her. Kimberly groaned again. This was definitely not part of the plan. Pierce smiled. They ate in silence for a few moments until he picked up the handset controller and switched on the game system. By the time they'd finished eating, they were in hot pursuit of enemy aircraft, evading relentless air-to-ground missiles and saving the universe from intergalactic alien invaders.

"That's it." Pierce tossed the controller on the bed, "I surrender."

"Wimp," she teased jokingly.

Together they wrapped the cording and placed the plates back onto the tray.

"So," Pierce began, "tell me about the history paper that's due in a few days."

Kimberly stood with her hands on her hips. "I thought that you said we weren't gonna talk about homework."

"I lied." Pierce smiled and chuckled. Kimberly cracked just enough to let a small smile escape. "So, what do you have to do?"

A half hour later, the two were listening to her music and talking about her history instructor. They'd narrowed down a subject for her paper and begun surfing the Internet for information. An hour later, the paper had taken shape with an outline, notes, and bibliography.

"Tell me about Ms. Burke," Pierce queried as nonchalantly as possible. Kimberly smiled and deliberately ignored his question. "How long has she been at the academy?"

"All her life."

Pierce frowned. "What do you mean, all her life?"

"They're always talking about how she's some kind of success story. She had a scholarship to go there when she was a kid. Then after college she came back to teach English literature, then she became a counselor."

"I see, so she has been there all her life," Pierce said, now understanding the literal nature of her remark. "What did she mean when she asked you about the thefts and vandalism at school?"

Kimberly shrugged. "I don't know. She's asking all the kids about it."

Pierce nodded slowly. "It's funny, some things never change." Kimberly looked at her uncle questioningly. "I remember the same thing happening when I was at Wells. The administration even kicked out one of the kids. Turned out it was just a simple kid's prank and the kid they kicked out didn't even do it."

"Then why did they kick him out?"

Pierce looked away in thought. His memories clouded over. "I don't remember."

"What happened to the kid?"

"I don't really know. I seem to remember that he refused to come back to Wells. But it was just one of the poor scholarship kids, no big deal."

"It was a big deal to him. Just because he was on scholarship didn't mean he had no feelings."

Pierce looked down at his niece's clear dark eyes. The impact of her innocent remark was sudden and staggering. Without realizing it, he still carried the same prideful and prejudiced feelings after all these years. He reached out to Kimberly and brought her into a welcoming embrace. "I'm proud of you, Kimberly. You're a very thoughtful young lady. You respect the feelings of others. You should be very proud of that."

"Don't you?"

"I didn't always."

"Why not?"

"Good question."

"I'm glad you're not like that anymore," Kimberly said.

"Me, too," Pierce said and hugged her again. "It's getting late, you'd better get ready for bed."

Kimberly looked over to the clock. "Uncle Pierce, it's like Friday and only 10:45. I go to bed later than this on school nights."

Pierce, completely astonished, realized that he had absolutely no idea of her schedule. "So, what do you usually do on a Friday night at 10:45?"

Kimberly smiled. "I usually invite friends over and have a wild party." Pierce gasped in horror until she began laughing. "I'm joking, Uncle Pierce, I'm joking.

I usually just watch some television, talk on the phone, or surf the Web."

Pierce nodded vaguely, not completely assured of her humor, but troubled that it added more fuel to the fire. It was true, he really didn't know Kimberly at all. Troubled by the realization, he thought of the instigator, Patricia Burke. How could she have possibly known?

Together they began gathering the many notebooks and printed-out papers from her desk and bed. Pierce slipped the assignments into her backpack while Kimberly emptied her bed of the dozens of pillows and dolls. He picked up the tray and walked to the door, then turned. "Kimberly."

"Huh?"

"I saw a poster in the school corridor about the Annual Christmas Ball. When is it exactly?"

"You should call Ms. Burke, she's in charge of stuff like that."

Pierce nodded and shrugged. "I might just do that." He continued nodding. "I might just do that." He turned and paused a second time. "Is she married or does she have children?"

"I don't think so. Why do you want to know?"

"Just curious," he said casually, not completely sure himself of the reason for the question. He closed the door as he left.

Kimberly shook her head, not believing his wet tissue-paper excuse. She turned back to the computer screen and grinned to herself. This was going to be easier than she'd thought. She flipped the Awake switch on the system and immediately received an instant message. It was Jasmine. They talked and planned until the early hours of Saturday morning.

Three

A heavy fog drifted across the academy campus, then decided to stay as a typical miserable rainy day greeted Kimberly when she arrived at school on Monday morning a little more than two weeks later. She zombied through her morning classes, only slightly paying attention to her instructors and their neverending chatter about mind-numbing subjects she knew she'd never use again as long as she lived on this planet. Thankfully, her one saving grace was lunch.

The cafeteria was packed as usual. Kimberly got in line and grabbed a slice of pizza, a diet soda, and an apple. After paying, she stood and looked out over the sea of students until she spotted Jasmine waving across the room. She smiled and waved back, then began the arduous trek in her direction. A few moments later, the two girls sat talking about their mornings.

Having different class programs—Kimberly with computer-advanced and Jasmine with performance—they met only at lunchtime. Jasmine was right in the middle of complaining about her drama instructor when she stopped and smiled at a new student as he approached their table.

"Girl, did you peep him? He's got mad props. He's in my second-period math analysis class. His name is Jamal Scott, and the dude is for real smart. It's a shame he's a Poorie, 'cause he is too cute."

Kimberly looked at Jasmine and frowned. She despised the distinctions of the Poories and the Richies. She hated it even more when she found out that her father was that one who'd come up with the whole idea years ago.

"If Jason hadn't already asked me," Jasmine continued with a giggle, "I'd seriously think about letting him take me to the Christmas Ball." Jasmine watched as Jamal walked by with his eyes glued to Kimberly. "Ooh, check him out, trying to roll up on somebody." She nudged closer to her friend. "Kimmy, you should hook up with Jamal and get him to take you to the Christmas Ball." Kimberly frowned and shook her head without even looking. "What's wrong with you?"

"Nothing, I'm just thinking." Kimberly looked down at the huge pile of food on her friend's tray. Jasmine, a strawberry blonde with a mass of thick curls atop a face loaded with tiny brown freckles, was the size of a twig but ate like an NFL linebacker marooned on a desert island for a month. Today was no exception.

"Thinking about what?" Jasmine lowered her voice and looked around, then back to Kimberly. "Hacking into the system again?" she asked. Kimberly shook her head. "What then?" Jasmine asked between mouthfuls of carrot dipped in dill dressing. She swallowed hard. "Oh, wait a minute, I know that face. You have an idea. You're up to something. What?" She nudged Kimberly and grinned endlessly. Just as their two heads connected, they were interrupted.

"Good afternoon, ladies." Both heads bobbed up when Patricia Burke spoke to them as she walked by the table.

"Hello, Ms. Burke," they responded in sweet innocent unison. Jasmine immediately went back to eating, but Kimberly merely picked at the pepperoni loaded on her pizza. She was confounded.

It had been two weeks and her uncle still hadn't called Ms. Burke. Kimberly was completely frustrated. What was wrong with her uncle? What was he waiting for? Last week he'd even gone out with Caroline Carter, the queen of brainless twits.

"So, what are you up to?" Jasmine, her brow raised in interest, asked as soon as Patricia moved to the next table. "Oh, wait, don't look, here comes Jason." At that moment several eighth-grade boys walked past their table carrying lunch trays. They laughed loudly while pushing and shoving jokingly. Kimberly rolled her eyes to the ceiling. She couldn't concentrate on anything until she figured out a new strategy, since it was obvious that the reverse psychology didn't work.

Jasmine grabbed her hand and squeezed. "He is so in love with me," she confirmed, whispering confidentially. She went on to elaborate about her wedding gown, the house they'd live in after they were married, how many kids they'd have, and where they'd take summer vacations. Kimberly only half listened as Jasmine continued in her fantasy world.

Instead, she looked around the cafeteria. The ever predictable scenario was in place. Richies on one side and Poories on the other. Since her attendance at the academy was paid in full, she was considered a Richie and sat in the appropriate location. The Poories sat in the back of the cafeteria.

There had to be something that she was missing. She was sure that her uncle was interested. That meant that maybe the problem wasn't with her uncle but with Ms. Burke. Maybe she was already seeing someone. Kimberly frowned miserably and looked across the cafeteria.

Ms. Burke had stopped by several tables, but chose to stop and sit with a few of the kids in the back of the cafeteria. Specifically, she sat with Jamal Scott, who usually sat alone.

Kimberly watched as she casually sipped from her cup while listening with great interest to whatever Jamal was saying. She nodded agreeably, smiled, then stood and moved to another table and eventually back out into the hall.

Patricia looked up at hearing the timid knock on her door. She closed the file she'd been looking through and motioned to enter. "Hi, Kimberly, how are you today?"

"I'm fine, Ms. Burke."

Patricia looked over to the crystal clock on her desk. "Aren't you supposed to be in class now?"

"I'm in study hall for another five minutes."

Patricia nodded her understanding. "Come on in, have a seat." Kimberly eased into the office and took a seat across from Patricia's desk. "What can I do for you today, Kimberly?"

"It's about my uncle Pierce."

Patricia's stomach flipped at the mention of Pierce's name. She flushed red and experienced her first hot flash in over two weeks. "Your uncle, is he all right?"

"Oh, yes, he's fine. It's just that he wanted to help with this year's Christmas Ball. But"—she looked down at her hands in her lap and squirmed uneasily in her seat—"uh, he needs, I mean, he wanted more information. He asked me, but I didn't know what was involved, so I told him he should call you since you were in charge this year."

"I see."

"But he's been really busy at work so I was thinking that maybe you could call him instead of him calling you." Kimberly looked hopefully across the desk at Patricia.

Patricia templed her fingers under her chin and smiled at the obvious fabrication. She knew Kimberly was lying, but couldn't figure out her reasoning. What would be gained by a phone call to Pierce Franklin? Patricia wondered. "Was there anything else you wanted to talk about, Kimberly?" She asked of the now smugly smiling preteen.

"No," Kimberly responded much too quickly to sound calm and composed. She frowned at the slip.

"I haven't heard from your uncle since our meeting a couple of weeks ago." Kimberly frowned at the confirmation that she'd been right: Her uncle hadn't called. "If he's still interested in volunteering, I'd be happy to talk to him about the Christmas Ball."

Kimberly nearly jumped out of her seat. "That would be great," she exclaimed. "I have his work number, his pager, and his cell phone number right here."

"Kimberly, I'm sure calling him this evening at home will be soon enough."

"But, Ms. Burke, he's expecting you to call him this afternoon."

"I'll contact him," Patricia promised. Kimberly stood still, then balanced from one foot to the other nervously. "Is there something else?"

"Yes, kind of."

"Yes," Patricia prompted.

"My uncle and I talked about a tutor."

"That's a great idea, Kimberly. You've missed quite a few assignments and a tutor might be just the thing to get your grades back up. If you don't have anyone in mind, I can make arrangements to have someone give either you or your uncle a call."

"Well, actually, Ms. Burke"—she shifted to the other foot, then back to the first again—"I was kind of hoping you'd be able to tutor me. I know that you taught English literature, and I just have a few problems with this book we're studying, and since you're my academic mentor, I was hoping that maybe you could do it." Before

Patricia could answer, Kimberly began pleading her case. "I promise to pay attention and do my best. I won't be any trouble and I'm usually always on time."

"Kimberly, I don't tutor students."

"I know, but I was thinking that just this one time you could help me, 'cause it's just this one book and the exam's in a few weeks and it's really not that much. I think just one or two sessions will do it. Please help me, Ms. Burke, pretty please."

Patricia shook her head regretfully. Kimberly had said the two words she never could resist, *help* and *me*. Although she didn't usually tutor her students, she decided to make an exception, just this one time. "All right, Kimberly, I'll be happy to tutor you. But I expect you to work hard. Don't think just because I'm your counselor that you'll get an easy ride."

"No, I wouldn't think that. Thank you, Ms. Burke." The school's bell rang, signaling the change of classes.

"You'd better get to your next class now or you'll be tardy."

Kimberly reluctantly turned and moved toward the office door. She turned back quickly. "Don't forget to call my uncle Pierce, okay?"

"I promise I'll contact your uncle later this evening. Now go to class, Kimberly." Patricia made a shooing action with her hands.

As soon as the door closed, Patricia stood and walked to her single window. Overcast clouds, thickened and darkened by droplets of water hung heavy in the late noon sky. The rain had slackened, but there was still the unseasonable warmth in the air. It was a warm November. Pierce Franklin had entered her thoughts again. Lately she'd been distracted too often by thoughts of a man she didn't even know and could never have.

* * *

It could easily be said that Pierce Franklin was a tyrant. He worked long hard hours and expected each and every employee to do the same.

After a four-hour bull session, Pierce Franklin dispersed his staff to their respective offices with new data and detailed instructions. His mandates were simple: Utilize the existing matrix to increase and update software productivity.

The office emptied; production managers, product engineers, system analysts, and system programmers all filed out of his office recharged and excited to get started on the next phase of development. Lewis Carter stayed behind.

"All right, what's going on?" Lewis asked as he took a seat opposite Pierce's desk.

Pierce sat down. "What are you talking about?"

"I'm talking about you. You aren't your usual charming self." Pierce raised a warning brow. "Seriously," Lewis joked, treading lightly, "you were distracted the entire meeting, not to mention the last two weeks. Something's up. What is it? Is there something wrong with the company?"

"No. Business is fine, better than ever, as a matter of fact. We're forty-two percent above last quarter's projected annual forecast."

"That's great," Lewis stated exuberantly. "Of course, it'll be even better when I can actually take advantage of the stock options."

Pierce raised his brow again, this time choosing to ignore Lewis's continued reference to the company policy of waiting a full year before offering new employees stock in the company.

"Then what's up?"

"There's nothing up. I'm just dealing with some personal issues."

"Caroline?" he asked hopefully of his younger sister, who'd been after Pierce since grade school.

Pierce grimaced. "No, Kimberly."

"Is she okay?"

"She's thirteen and a teenager. She wears makeup, talks on the phone twenty-four hours a day, seven days a week, and has suddenly noticed that boys exist."

"I see." He chuckled.

"Not just that, she's skipping school, not doing homework, lying, breaking into the school after hours, and heaven knows what else."

"Kimberly, lying and breaking into the school? Are you sure?" Lewis asked, unbelieving.

"That's what her counselor says."

"Breaking into the school, that doesn't sound like Kimberly." Lewis chuckled to himself again. "It sounds more like something Aidan would do. I remember this one time. . ." Lewis began, then changed his mind when Pierce frowned at him. "There must be some mistake. That definitely doesn't sound like something our sweet little Kimberly would do."

"No, it doesn't. But the counselor said that someone actually saw her in the school after hours."

"Maybe she was there for a good reason." He paused to consider. "You know, if this got on her permanent record, she might not get into Banneker this summer as planned."

"Yes, I know." Pierce ran an angry hand roughly over his head in frustration. He'd thought of that. Kimberly had her heart set on getting into the Banneker School's summer program.

It was the most comprehensive, advanced computer specialty program in the area. It offered admission to a very select few. Kimberly getting accepted was a tremendous honor and something for which she had worked very hard.

Pierce frowned. He had to find out who accused her of breaking into the school. "I've got some serious damage control to do."

"Ah, yes, this is where the real parenting gig begins," Lewis confirmed.

"That's just it. For the past few years I've been so consumed with making the company number one that I've let Kimberly do most of the parenting alone. She practically raised herself for the most part."

"Come on, I know for a fact you've been in there all along."

"Don't get me wrong, she's a terrific kid but, but all of the sudden she's not a kid anymore, she's a young woman. In a few years she's going to be off to college, then married, then having children of her own." Pierce practically cringed.

Lewis began laughing. "I get it. You just realized that life moved faster than the speed of a microchip."

"How did it happen, when did it happen?"

"Man, little girls have been turning into young women since time began and their fathers have done the same thing—dealt with it. But it hits home when it's your little girl, doesn't it?"

"I had a meeting with her counselor last week," Pierce admitted. He shook his head, still not believing Patricia's audacity. "Kimberly's into things I had no idea about. When did it all happen? Where was I?"

"Man, you can't be there every second of the day. Don't beat yourself up about it. It's impossible to know everything she's doing. Just be thankful she's a good girl with a clear head on her shoulders."

"I can't help but wonder what happened to our relationship. Lately with me she's withdrawn, indifferent, and distant. How do I get my little girl back?"

"You don't," Lewis stated plainly. Pierce looked at him, troubled. "Kimberly, the little girl you knew, is gone.

What you have to do is learn to develop a relationship with Kimberly, the young woman."

"When did life get to be so difficult?"

"When you became a father and Kimberly became a teenager."

"True that." A moment of silence passed between them as each man was lost in thought.

Lewis stood and walked to the door. "What did Kimberly's counselor have to say? I'm sure he had a few creative ideas on communication."

Pierce smiled devilishly as his thoughts went straight to his first sighting of Patricia.

Lewis turned and came back into the room. "Whoa, whoa, whoa, what was that?"

"What was what?" Pierce looked at him innocently.

"I mention talking to the counselor and you start leering like the big bad wolf at a Little Red Riding Hood convention. Give."

"There's nothing to give. Kimberly's counselor, Patricia Burke, is another whole story."

"A real dawg?"

"On the contrary, she's tight. She's built like a brick house with legs that go on forever. And"—he paused to wonder—"and I can't put my finger on it, but there's something familiar about her."

"I was just about to say the same thing. Doesn't that name sound familiar to you?"

Pierce shrugged and shook his head.

Lewis thought for another few seconds, then shrugged it off. "You gonna hit it?"

"Nah, man. She's got serious issues. The last thing I need right now is a woman with attitude."

"Attitude?" Lewis questioned. "What kind of attitude?"

"First of all, she practically orders me to attend a meeting with her, then she spends the whole time chastising me and accusing Kimberly of God knows what. I have half a mind to go back there and step to her but she's the only one who knows who this person is who saw Kimberly break into the school." Anger began to well up in him as he spoke, remembering the particular details of their meeting.

"So, do it."

"Do what?"

Lewis shook his head and headed for the door. "Do it. Step to her if it'll make you feel better. Look, we both know that Kimberly's a great kid. So she's a little rambunctious lately in school. What kid isn't?"

Pierce was silent for a few moments as he pondered his options. "Go, you've got a lot of work to do. I'll check you later."

"Yeah, I'm leaving. But I want to hear more about Little Red Riding Hood later." He turned to leave. "Oh, before I forget, I spoke to Caroline, and she wanted you to know that she's available next Friday if you're still interested." Pierce nodded his understanding as Lewis left, soundly closing the door behind him. He was alone.

Pierce looked around the enormous expanse of his office. It was as his life had been expensive, excessive, and empty. The once-full conference table, moments ago crowded with the top software and programming developers in the country, was now littered with writing pads, pens, and papers filled with calculations.

His office, like his apartment, had been professionally decorated. The sectional sofa, wing chairs, and Italian marble coffee table sat poised and ready in a desolate corner of the room. The traditional office furniture, credenza, and floor-to-ceiling bookcases stood before a massive window that overlooked the front of the building, which in turn overlooked the Washington, D.C., Beltway. The perfect emptiness of his life was reflected in his office and apartment. He realized now that there was something missing.

Reflectively, Pierce looked out of the window and scanned the view until his eyes fell upon the multilaned interstate beyond the treetops. He continued to be amazed even now, after all this time. Within seven years' time, a mere eighty-four months, PEF Software had grown into a multimillion dollar conglomerate right before his eyes.

Pierce turned back to his desk and sat down. He chose a shiny CD from a container of dozens and unconsciously spun it on his finger several times before placing it in the drive opening. He pushed a single key on the keyboard and was instantly connected to his files.

Lost in his empty thoughts, he barely paid attention to the numerical calculations that appeared on the screen.

Instead, he chose to browse the Internet.

Pierce typed in *Ida B. Wells Academy,* then impatiently waited a split second for the Web site to connect and appear. A photo of the school's buildings surrounded by the floral greens of late spring greeted him. He sequenced through each screen until he came to the one screen for which he was looking.

He clicked on *faculty,* then *support services,* then *administrative services,* until finally, pleased, he had the screen he was seeking. Patricia Burke smiled back at him from across her desk. She was absolutely lovely, sitting at her desk dressed in a navy blue blouse and suit jacket with a double strand of white pearls.

Pierce's thoughts went back to the brief time they'd spent together in her tiny office. Patricia Burke was everything in a woman he'd abhorred. She was self-righteous, self-centered, and arrogant—traits usually associated with himself. Still, there was something about her that piqued his interest.

Absently, he touched his screen, lightly stroking the soft-edged pixels of Patricia's computer-generated image. He had to admit, he was still impressed by her

professionalism and poise. She had a unique and com-
forting quality of putting order and balance in her
surrounding. He was certain that the calmness of her
voice could soothe away the most horrendous day. He realized he wanted to see and hear her again. He picked
up the receiver and dialed the main office number displayed on the screen.

A few moments later, he found himself pulling away
from his parking space and pointing his car toward Wells
Academy.

Patricia was on the phone when Pierce peered into
her open door. She looked up at him behind small wire-
framed glasses and smiled openly while beckoning him
inside. She held up a single finger, indicating that she'd
just be a minute or two. He stepped inside and closed
the door behind him.

The call lasted longer than she expected and gave him
ample time to thoroughly examine her wall hangings.
A brow lifted in interest at a watercolor drawing from a
young child, a poster announcing the school's annual
Christmas Ball on December twentieth, and several small
Leroy Campbell prints. *Good taste,* he decided reluctantly
as he moved to the next wall of diplomas. *Impressive.*

He moved to the side wall and scanned the narrow
credenza. Four neatly trimmed bonsai trees and several
framed candid photos paraded along the top. He picked
up a frame and looked deeply into Patricia's smoky
brown eyes. They twinkled with laughter as she sat beside
a man, his long muscular arm draped lovingly around
her shoulders.

Pierce frowned, bothered by a distant twinge of emotional attraction. The photo seemed to make her more
human and less like the stamped-out administrator he
imagined her to be. The genuine smile of happier times

drew him closer. She was dressed in blue jeans and a T-shirt with bold red writing across the front: SEAMAN'S SLUGGERS. Her hair was divided into two long pigtails that draped over her shoulders and was topped with a backward baseball cap stitched with the same logo. The man beside her, holding a baseball bat and glove, was identically dressed, as were the three other people in the photo. The man's arm around her, as if he had every right to have it there, drew Pierce's attention again. Bothered by the strange sensation, he set the frame back in its place.

He took a step and picked up the next item, an illegibly signed baseball, and tossed it in the air. He caught it and smiled for the first time since he'd arrived. Suddenly Patricia Burke had become more human, more approachable. He placed the baseball back on its pedestal and turned to the room with new eyes. The first thing he noticed was its quiet serenity.

After a few moments, Pierce decided he liked the office. It was warm, cozy, and unpretentious. It seemed more like a comfortable living room than a counselor's or principal's office.

Its overstuffed sofa on the side was balanced by a fringed shaded floor lamp. A wooden rocking chair sat in the corner surrounded by a basket of children's books on one side and a basket of puzzles and games on the other. A tiny table of coloring books and crayons with matching chairs sat near the rocker and was covered by a hand-knitted throw.

He smiled, remembering his niece's warnings of torture chambers and medieval devices. This hardly looked like the dark sinister picture of a medieval chamber of horrors that Kimberly had painted.

Patricia finally ended the telephone conversation. "Good afternoon, Mr. Franklin." She stood and came around to stand next to him. "This is a pleasant coincidence."

"Really? Why is that, Ms. Burke?"

"I was going to contact you this evening if I didn't hear from you by this afternoon." She stood and held her hand out to shake.

"Hear from me? Why is that?" he questioned, puzzled by her comment.

"Kimberly told me that you might be contacting me this afternoon, and if not that I should call you."

"Is that so?"

"Yes. When can we get together? I have a few ideas already and I've recruited several other parents who I'm sure will be delighted to get the extra help."

Pierce frowned with confusion. There was definitely a miscommunication. "Help with what exactly?"

She paused cautiously, then stated the obvious. "This year's Annual Christmas Ball."

"Of course, yes, the Christmas Ball." He remembered seeing the help wanted posters hanging around the school.

"I beg your pardon. I presumed that's why you came by. Kimberly told me that you were interested in helping out this year. Was there something else you'd like to talk about?"

"Yes, as a matter of fact there is. I'm troubled by our conversation a few weeks ago."

"I see." She moved back to her desk and sat, then motioned for him to sit in the seat across from her.

"Mind you, I'm still not satisfied with this vandalism witness incident. Also, I find it hard to believe that Kimberly is missing school and not completing assignments, but I'm willing to get to the bottom of this."

"I'm glad to hear that." She noticed that his anger and defensiveness from his last visit had greatly subsided. He seemed reasonable and more willing to discuss solutions.

They spent the next twenty minutes discussing Kimberly's falling grades and missing assignments. Then, together they blocked out a strategy to help motivate her and stimulate her desire to learn.

"So, what do you suggest I do first?"

Patricia smiled, stood, and came around to lean against the front of her desk. "That's the easy part. Just talk to her. Explain to her how important school is at this point in her life. She already has a good foundation, we just need to keep it strong and build on it. She's in the eighth grade, and by the end of this school year, she'll be on her way to an excellent high school, then she'll have the college of her choice."

Pierce waved his hand toward the degrees and diplomas hanging on the side wall. "I see you attended Howard University for undergraduate studies."

She nodded. "Yes, I did my graduate studies at Georgetown and now I'm back at Howard for my doctrine in child psychology."

"Good schools."

"Yes, they are. Where did you study, Mr. Franklin?" She asked.

"MIT."

"Also a very good school." He nodded his agreement. "Is that where you developed your software program?"

"That's where the idea started," Pierce began, surprised by her knowledge of his work. The conversation lasted for close to half an hour. Patricia asked question after question about his infamous computer software, and Pierce was all too delighted to answer. When he talked about computers, he was in his element. He lived, slept, ate, and drank computers and software. His latest software was destined to revolutionize the work-based computer industry.

Patricia listened intently. It was impossible not to. When Pierce spoke, it was as if every other sound in the world silenced just to hear his words. His voice commanded strength and demanded attention. And she gave willingly.

Unexpected laughter rang throughout the office as Pierce relayed details of his early trials, attempts, and failures. Patricia's eyes were moist with tears of laughter when he spoke of the ten computers he'd burned and blown up with his revolutionized new software.

Pierce was surprised how easy she was to talk to. She asked pertinent knowledgeable questions that kept him talking while she seemed to understand his technical responses.

"I think Kimberly has a lot of your qualities in her."

"You think so?"

"Yes. She's inquisitive, curious, and extremely proficient in her computer lab classes. I understand she's been approved to attend Banneker's early admission program next year."

"Yes, she's already taken and passed the early admission exam. I understand that you had a lot to do with that."

"It's all part of my job. Kimberly's a very determined young lady. She'll do very well at Banneker."

Pierce looked into Patricia's clear brown eyes. They sparkled with understanding and intelligence. "You make it sound so easy."

Patricia laughed. "On the contrary, it's anything but. Teenagers these days have it a lot harder then we did when we were growing up. There are so many distractions. I don't envy them. But given the right instruction, the sky's the limit."

"Sounds like you've been through this before."

She smiled wide. "Yeah, well, I was a thirteen-year-old teenager a while back. I remember getting into a bit of trouble with some of my antics." She winked. "I wasn't always a counselor. I bent and twisted a few rules in my day."

The earlier tension in the room had completely dissipated, lightened by Patricia's warmth and honesty.

"You don't look like the type that would get into trouble."

She laughed warmly. "We never do look the type, but, oh, the stories I could tell."

"I'd like to hear a few of those stories sometime." Pierce looked at Patricia. Their eyes held a moment. The conversation had slipped into more social banter. There was a curious personal quality that had quickly entered.

"You're a busy man, Mr. Franklin. I'm sure you don't have time to listen to my youthful indiscretions."

"On the contrary. I'd like to know more about you at age thirteen. I think it'll give me an interesting insight to my niece's recent behavior problems." He'd realized that he was actually seriously interested in seeing her again. The dreaded Ms. Burke had a remarkable gift for defusing tense situations with her calmness. He liked that and he liked her.

Patricia laughed and shook her head. "Be that as it may, I'm confident your talking with Kimberly will help guide her back in the right direction." She held out her hand to shake. Pierce held on to her hand longer than needed.

"I bet you were a prankster."

She paused long enough for a flood of humorous memories to affirm his prediction. She bit at her lower lip anxiously, shyly, like a child having been caught in the cookie jar. He nodded knowingly as they laughed together.

"Thank you again for coming by, Mr. Franklin. I hope our talk helped clear up any confusion and more thoroughly explain my intentions."

"Yes, you were very helpful. And I will consider what

we talked about." She nodded as he left and closed the door.

Patricia went back to her desk with a joyful spirit. She sat down, played with her glasses a second, hummed a pleasant Christmas tune, then went back to work.

Moments later, a heavy knock on her door drew her attention away from the student file she'd been studying. The door opened without warning. She removed her reading glasses and looked up, seeing a small slight man standing in the door frame. "Good afternoon. May I help you?" Patricia asked pleasantly.

The man stood authoritatively, legs apart, arms firmly secured in the "at ease" military position behind his back, and head erect. He looked down at the school ID hanging from around Patricia's neck. His eyes lingered beyond the tag for a moment longer than necessary. She didn't seem to notice. "You Patsy Burke?" he questioned gruffly with an attitude giving him half ownership of the universe.

She stood and came around to the front of her desk, having always detested the shortening of her name to Patsy. "Patricia Burke," she corrected and forced an agreeable smile. "How may I help you?"

The man stepped into the office and closed the door behind him. "The name's Shields, Vincent Shields. I believe you were expecting me." His head dipped slightly as he eyed her full frame from top to bottom.

Patricia looked puzzled. "I'm sorry, Mr. Shields." She moved back to her desk, leaned over, and ran a clear polished fingernail down the current day of her appointment book. Her only appointments that afternoon were with a student, then later with prospective parents. "But I don't seem to have you on my schedule for today. Perhaps you're scheduled to meet with someone else at the academy."

Vincent, still donning his mirrored sunglasses,

watched her long legs as they leaned across the desk. "Only if there's another Patsy Burke in the school," he quipped humorlessly as he quickly diverted his eyes when she turned back to him. He quickly scanned the general office, then concentrated on the tree just out-side her window.

"I'm the only Patricia Burke here. Perhaps if you tell me what you've come to discuss, I can be of more assis-tance, or possibly direct you to the appropriate office."

"Shields ProTech Security, Incorporated," he in-structed. He handed her a card he'd drawn from his jacket pocket. As he pulled the card out, she noticed a filled arm holster tucked against his chest. Patricia took the card and read the wording, *Vincent Shields, Supervis-ing Consultant, Shields ProTech Security*. Above, the company logo filled the card with patriotic red, white, and blue.

Patricia nodded her understanding. "The security of-fice is down the opposite hall, fourth door on the left. I'll be happy to escort you there."

He smirked. "I've been deployed to take care of your security problems." He pulled a small notepad and pen from his jacket pocket and efficiently flipped through several pages. "A mutual associate, Matt Grover, re-quested that my company personally look into this matter. We intend to apprehend the culprit or culprits responsible for your recent crime wave."

"I would hardly consider a few stolen items a crime wave, Mr. Shields."

"That's why I'm the professional and you're not," he quipped rudely, revealing his diluted personality and less-than-adequate charm.

"I see. Well, Mr. Shields, why don't I take you down to the principal's office? I'm sure she'll be able to help you more than I can."

"I was informed by my men that you were my primary

contact." He looked down at the open pad again. "Says here you've already begun an investigation into the matter, and already have suspects. I'd like to have all your notes and I'll need the names, addresses, and phone numbers of all your students and faculty."

"Mr. Shields, I'm afraid you've been misinformed. There are no 'suspects,' I merely made a few inquires of some of the students. And we are not in the habit of divulging our faculty and student information to outsiders."

"I'm a security professional, not an outsider. Names?"

"I will not tell you names of innocent students."

"Then you'll be guilty of obstructing the investigation. That's a serious charge," he warned.

The size of the office, cramped as it was, made it almost impossible for Patricia to ease around the small man's enormous ego, but she managed. "Please come with me, Mr. Shields."

Patricia escorted him through the back office of the administrative area of Wells Academy. As they walked the narrow corridor and approached the last door, she paused and turned to him. "Mr. Shields, I would appreciate it if you'd remove your sunglasses while you're inside the building. And the next time you come, if there is a next time, please be sure to leave your weapon in your car," she chastised him, then emphasized pointedly, "inside your locked car." Vincent cocked his head and glared at her behind his mirrored sunglasses. "In this school, we instruct our students to respect themselves and one another. Hence, weapons of any kind are not permitted on this campus."

Begrudgingly, he removed his sunglasses. "According to the number of thefts in recent years, I'd say you need to do more punishment and less instructing."

"I beg your pardon." She was just about to ream him when the door to the principal's office opened. Audrey Simmons appeared with her usual pinched, pruned expression. She stared at the two with an expression that bore an uncanny resemblance to the Wicked Witch of the West.

The older woman standing at the door gave a forced smile to Patricia and the man standing by her side. Then she directed her attention to Patricia. "Ms. Burke, I could hear you all the way in my office. This is not how we maintain order in this school, and certainly not in front of our guests." She attempted to smile again at Vincent, and he smugly responded with a curt nod.

Patricia chose to ignore the obvious slam to her character. "Of course, Mrs. Simmons," she gritted out with great difficulty. "This is Vincent Shields of Shields Pro-Tech Security. He's been asked by Matt Grover and the board to assist with our security needs. He would like a copy of our student and faculty listing."

Audrey Simmons nodded evasively, then directed her attention to the man standing beside Patricia. She smiled and extended her hand to shake. "Mr. Shields, please come in and have a seat." She stepped out of the way. "I will be with you momentarily."

Vincent followed her instructions and walked into the office, chose a seat across from the desk, and sat down. Mrs. Simmons softly closed the door and leaned in closer to Patricia. "Patricia," she spoke quietly, "have Matt Grover send me the information on Mr. Shields and ProTech."

Patricia nodded her understanding. "Of course." She walked down the hall and returned to her office. *This is strange,* she wondered aloud. *Why would Matt Grover have Vincent Shields look into the thefts when they already had Pro-Tech as their main security team?*

It made no sense. Matt Grover was on the board of Wells Academy and a respected member of the business and scholastic community. How could he have known about the thefts and vandalism in the school? Patricia picked up the phone, dialed, and waited for the line to connect. "Matt Grover," he answered.

"Matt, this is Patricia Burke at Wells Academy."

"Patricia, how are you?"

"Fine. How are you and how's the family?"

"The kids are good, Marla's got a head cold, but other than that we're all good. What can I do for you?"

"We need you to forward the bio on a Vincent Shields."

"Vincent Shields?" He paused to ponder the name. "Oh, you mean Henry Shields, of Shields ProTech Security, big fellow, military type, real mean-looking, thick mane of salt-and-pepper hair."

"No, the exact opposite," she said.

Matt paused for a moment. "Oh, small fellow, kind of mousy with a big mean attitude."

"One and the same."

"Yes, of course, Vincent. He's your district supervising security specialist. His father, Henry, has impeachable credentials, ex-CIA specializing in kidnapping and terrorism operations. His company is also proficient in theft, security disturbance prevention. He has a lot of experience in school security."

"What about his son, Vincent?"

"I'm sure he's every bit as thorough as Henry. I understand that he specializes in school theft and vandalism. He and his team have a success rate of one hundred percent. They go from school to school, whenever there's a need. And, to tell you the truth, with all these school shootings these days, it might be a good idea to have someone look into and beef up the school's security measures, just in case."

"We already have three new security staff from Shields ProTech."

"Yes, and they do a fine job. But I feel it's time we need to get in tune with the times. This is a troubled world,

Patricia. The recent rash of thefts and vandalism prove that."

"So, you asked Henry to look into this personally, or rather his son?"

"Yes. This is only tentative, Patricia. He still has to go before the board and be approved."

"He's meeting with Audrey Simmons right now. She asked me to request his bio for our files."

"I didn't know he was going into the academy so soon."

"He was a big surprise."

"I'm sure he was. I intended to forward a memo in a few days, but there's no need to now. Henry's doing me a big favor on this one, Patricia. He's got his son looking into this one personally. He only uses his most discreet associates, that includes his son. Henry is good at what he does, that I can assure you. I'll pull the company's information packet and forward a copy to you."

"Matt, I have a question. How did ProTech Security even know about the theft problem? Nothing was ever reported officially."

"I believe Vincent brought it to his father's attention like all the others."

"Others?"

"Yes, there's been a rash of thefts in the vicinity. Not even my office was immune. Vincent and his team came in and cleared the whole thing up in no time."

"I see, but how did Vincent know about our problem?"

"His security team at the school probably told him."

Patricia frowned. That made no sense. It was like ProTech knew about the thefts before they even occurred. "Thanks, Matt. I'll let Audrey know that the information is on its way."

"No problem, I'll send it out this evening."

Patricia hung up the phone, still wondering about Vincent Shields. There was something about his demeanor that didn't sit well with her. The fact that he requested access to the academy's student roster was highly unusual, not to mention unethical. As a security specialist, he should have known that no academic administration would ever comply with such a request.

She stood and moved to the window. There was something about Mr. Shields that she didn't trust. His stern menacing expression and straight back posture bespoke of military exposure. Patricia shook her head. The last thing this school needed was a goose-stepping trigger-happy almost cop with which to contend.

She turned when her phone rang. "Patricia Burke."

"Patricia, when you have a moment, would you come into my office?"

"I have a student appointment in half an hour. I'll postpone it and be right there."

Patricia knocked and cracked open the principal's office door. Vincent sat across from the desk, his stubby muscular legs crossed as he sat relaxed in the chair.

"Patricia, come in," Audrey said as she looked up to see the cracked door open wider. Patricia came in and sat down in the seat next to Vincent. "Patricia, Mr. Shields will be monitoring and reviewing our school's security procedures and policies for the next few months. I'd like you to give him a basic tour of our facility and your full cooperation. He'll be reviewing whatever notes you have on the vandalism and thefts and anything else that might be pertinent."

Reluctantly, Patricia nodded her understanding. Vincent sat smugly smiling to himself. Audrey continued recapping their discussion. She ended with a request that Patricia work closely with Vincent to end the theft problem as soon as possible. Patricia stood and turned to Vincent. "Mr. Shields, if you'll follow me, I'll show you the grounds."

Once outside the administrative offices, Patricia began her memorized lecture on Wells Academy. "This is the main hall, as you can see." She pointed to the tiled floors inlayed with quotes from famous people. "We are extremely proud of our vision and mission statements and go to great lengths to keep our exceptional scholastic standards. The Wells Academy is comprised of three separate buildings connected by two two-story bridges. The campus sits on thirty-five acres of land and is the largest private specialized facility in the county. The main facility is over seventy-seven thousand square feet with an average student-teacher ratio of ten to one."

She paused to speak with a few students as Vincent looked on. She continued with a polite nod to Vincent. "One hundred percent of our tuition stays right here at the facility. As you can see, our students are required to wear uniforms at all times when they are on campus. Our grade levels begin at kindergarten and run through eighth grade. At the eighth-grade level, we assist our students with placement in specialized senior-level institutions. The main facility houses the administrative offices, auditorium, study hall, and cafeteria. The other two buildings, located on either side, house the classrooms and labs."

Vincent walked behind Patricia. When she paused to step into the elevator and push the button for the second floor, he asked, "You don't agree with me being here, do you?"

"Whether you're here or not is beyond my control, Mr. Shields." She continued relaying the Wells Academy history until he interrupted a second time.

"You didn't answer the question."

"This conversation is pointless, Mr. Shields. Shall we continue the tour?" She stepped out of the elevator and walked down the hall to the connecting bridge. Continuing the tour, she spoke of the innovative art and sports afterschool programs, the vast number of students in attendance, and their overall achievement percentage.

The brilliant openness of the glass-covered space gave the overcast day a bright cheerful feel.

"Are you going to answer the question?"

"Mr. Shields, I have a meeting in less than half an hour." Patricia looked at her watch to confirm the time. "My personal feelings regarding your security company are irrelevant. Shall we proceed with the math and science wing?"

"No." He stopped. "I'd like to hear what you have to say."

"My opinion is my own and of no consequence."

"Then you should have no problem stating it."

Patricia took a deep cleansing breath. "No, I don't think your presence is necessary in this school, not in this case."

"Security is and always will be a top priority in this country and rightfully so. Highjackings, hostage crises, kidnappings, and school shootings are unfortunate realities of our present culture. When security fails, I'm the one you call. My company is merely an answer to the world's plea for peace of mind. We are the solution."

"Security is an illusion. You're a Band-Aid at most, and for this school, an extreme Band-Aid."

He smiled with all the cockiness and confidence of a lion poised for the kill. "A Band-Aid with a semiautomatic weapon armed and loaded for your protection."

She stopped walking and looked at him with a you-asked-for-it expression. "You're Big Brother with your monitoring security cameras, intrusive surveillance, and all the other false protective devices used to pacify a paranoid public."

Vincent bit right back. "Industry analyses prove that

we are effective. Hundreds of schools, government agencies, and companies both private and public scramble for our services. Prevention is the key. We protect."

"You profit off the fear of others and incite an already festering paranoia."

Vincent smiled. "Complacency is the reason my company exists. I have over two thousand employees worldwide who put their lives on the line every day for people like you, cynics. But we're the first you scream for when your life is in danger."

"You're missing the point, Mr. Shields. This is a school, not a prison. We already have an excellent security team. We don't need you."

"But for the time being, Patsy, you have me. I'd take full advantage of that if I were you."

"Shall we continue the tour?" she asked, seeing the futility of the discussion. He nodded curtly.

Patricia smiled hopelessly. She knew her point had fallen on deaf ears. He was never going to gain understanding from her perspective. She continued the tour, verbalizing only the necessities and answering only his related questions. It saddened her to think that the school had come to this.

Thankfully the abridged tour lasted less than twenty minutes. Vincent, seeing Patricia's obvious resentment, requested that his lead security guard continue at another time.

Patricia, delighted to comply, bid him good day and went back to the main building and her office.

The remainder of the day was troubling and long. The excitement and joy of seeing Pierce again was quickly overshadowed by the sudden appearance of Vincent Shields. By six o'clock that evening, Patricia was ready to leave for home.

Four

Patricia had been awake since before dawn. She'd tossed and turned for hours but to no avail; sleep eluded her. She was much too excited just to lie there staring at the ceiling, so she got up. With the rooms still shrouded in darkness, she stumbled through the apartment to the kitchen. She placed the water-filled tea kettle on the stove and pulled a single cup from the cabinet.

She showered, dressed, and then stepped out onto the balcony of her apartment with a steaming hot cup of Earl Grey and watched as the rising sun slowly peered from behind the condemned building across the street.

She smiled happily. Thankfully, this was the last time she would see this sight. Empty crack vials strewn on the streets, loud obnoxious music blasting from passing cars, and an occasional armed robbery were all things she would never miss.

She'd grown up in this neighborhood and spent most of her adult life in the immediate area. She'd seen childhood friends married, with kids, jailed, and killed. She'd watched as her beloved childhood home slowly sank lower and lower into the bottomless pit of despair and desperation. This wasn't the life she wanted for herself anymore. She needed freedom. She needed to breathe.

Patricia smiled, reminiscing. This neighborhood would always be in her heart, but it was time to move on. Time to fill her heart and fulfill her dreams. Never again would she have to put up with the monthly drug raids next door, the passionate fistfights of the couple above her, and the obnoxious catcalls from the shiftless jobless men hanging on the street corner all day and all night.

Regency Towers was now her future. After months and months of waiting, she finally, suddenly, without warning, had received a call notifying her that there was an available apartment in the building she'd coveted for years. The Regency was the epitome of distinction. Its gated security, private parking, and exquisite surroundings made it the most desired real estate in Northern Virginia.

Regency Towers was a twenty-story building shaped like a gigantic U with hundreds of condominium apartments. The smaller studio and one-bedroom apartments were scattered on the first through fifteen floors, leaving the top floors for the two-, three- and four-bedroom apartments. The very top floor housed four two-story penthouses, four-bedroom suites which Patricia presumed were stunning and included an equally stunning monthly mortgage.

She'd already seen her new home. It was a one-bedroom rental apartment on the seventh floor on the left side of the U shape. The living room–dining room combination was smaller than she'd like, but the bedroom was huge and she was thrilled.

Patricia stepped back into her dismal apartment and looked around the crowded room wearily. Boxes surrounded her at every turn. She didn't know where to start. Then, without thinking, she grabbed an empty box and some packing paper and dived in.

After an hour and a half of steady packing, she picked up paper and began wrapping the last few items remaining in her kitchen. Once she'd filled the box, she scribbled its destination on top with a black marker and stacked it on top of the others.

She looked over her handiwork proudly. In ninety minutes, she'd managed to box her entire kitchen. She searched the emptying apartment for her next assignment. It stood patiently waiting for her in the corner of the living room. She moved to her desk.

Pulling memory after memory from the drawers was more difficult that she imagined. Years of savings had found their way into every crevice of the antique secretary desk. She'd saved student letters, photos, and small gifts given from the heart. Useless trinkets to anyone else, these precious valuables would be with her a lifetime plus a day.

Leaving Wells Academy and the worries of her job behind at the end of each day was always difficult for Patricia. She was simply too dedicated. She loved what she did and she loved the kids who made her job a pleasure. As a single woman, it was the best of all possible worlds. She helped raise her young charges for up to ten hours each day, then sent them home to their parents.

Unfortunately, most of the time, she had a hard time divorcing herself from the academy that easily. She brought her students' troubles, problems, and concerns home with her more times than she cared to remember. But today was different; today was all about her. So, with trudging determination, she continued to pack the treasures of a lifetime.

At 7:30, the doorbell rang with alarming persistence. With several rolls of masking-tape bracelets up her arm and wrapping paper tucked under her arm, she opened the door wide.

A grungy, grumpy, half-asleep woman cracked an eyelid behind her sunglasses and peered over the rim of her grande coffee cup. "You own me big-time." She yawned.

Patricia smiled joyfully, then looked at her watch. "You're late. You were supposed to be here a half hour ago. "And"—she peeked behind her friend—"I thought you were going to bring your buddy."

"Don't start with me. You're lucky I'm here at all, and my buddy Richie twisted his ankle at rehearsal. He's down for six weeks."

Patricia opened her arms and welcomed her best friend. "I'm sorry to hear about Richie. Please give him my well wishes. Come on in," she offered. "I've got plenty of Earl Grey tea and donuts."

"Tea! My God, woman, are you delirious?" Juliet nearly shouted. Patricia laughed at the astonished expression on Juliet's face. She was one of those people who required at least three cups of coffee to put a single foot on the floor. "Coffee, coffee, coffee," she repeated louder and louder, emphatically holding up her cup of café latte with four shots of espresso. "Coffee in the morning, not tea."

Juliet Bridges was like a sister to Patricia, who had only an older brother. They'd met in grade school and quickly become best friends for life. Their lifestyles and backgrounds were as different as where they grew up. A world apart, Patricia grew up in the inner city of Washington, D.C., and Juliet in the pristine suburbs of Northern Virginia.

While Patricia was the soft-spoken, shy intellect, Juliet was the popular, hip talking, graceful dancer with the honesty and chutzpah of a street thug. And, in direct contrast to Patricia, being all neck and legs, Juliet was perfectly suited as the principal prima ballerina for the prestigious Washington Dance Company.

"I'm sorry, my mistake. Coffee next time, I promise." Patricia apologized profusely while following Juliet through the maze of boxes into the kitchen. "I might have some instant decaffeinated coffee in one of these boxes," Patricia added, and immediately began poking around in the top boxes until she ran into Juliet's back.

Juliet stopped as if struck by lightning. "Instant and decaffeinated," she repeated in disgust, then dumped herself onto the nearest kitchen stool. She shook her head. "Never, ever say those words when discussing coffee. You owe me big-time."

Juliet looked around the apartment filled with sealed boxes of all shapes and sizes. "I'm sure glad you're getting out of this dump."

"Hey, watch it, this was my home for a long time."

"Still a dump," she muttered loudly enough for Patricia to hear.

Patricia stood next to Juliet and looked around. "You're right." She finally chuckled. "It is a dump." They both laughed. "But it's almost impossible for a single woman to find an affordable apartment in a safe neighborhood without spending an arm and a leg or ransoming her firstborn."

"You're so dramatic. You know that you could have always moved in with me."

"You have no furniture."

"I do so," Juliet said, defending her spacious three-bedroom town house in Alexandria.

"You have wall-to-wall mirrors and a bed. That's not exactly what I'd call a fully furnished home. Besides, you know I can't tolerate roommates, and you know that you and I would probably kill each other after the first two days."

"True that." They looked at each other and laughed again. "I have to admit, you really hit the jackpot getting into the Regency Towers. That place is the bomb."

"I know, the whole thing was too weird. I only just filled out the application a few months ago, so I know they have a waiting list a block long. I didn't expect to hear anything from them for a least another two or three years."

Juliet chuckled. "Maybe there was a murder in that apartment or a poltergeist ripping the place apart."

Patricia looked at her friend menacingly. "You see, if you were my roommate I would have just choked you."

After another bout of laughter, Juliet said seriously, "Don't look a gift horse in the mouth. Take and enjoy."

"Most definitely," Patricia agreed wholeheartedly.

An hour and a half later, and after a quick trip to the local minimart for more coffee, Juliet and Patricia opened the door to three brawny men in well-worn back braces, work jumpsuits, and steel-toed boots.

The moment Patricia had been waiting for for so long had finally arrived. It was time to move. The movers took a quick inventory of the boxes and furniture, then began the arduous task of loading the truck.

While the men worked busily with the furniture and large boxes, Patricia and Juliet talked and laughed endlessly as they pulled out memories to pack into the backseats and trunks of their two cars.

Soon it was time to bid her farewell to the only home she'd ever known. With no regrets and a host of fond memories, she closed the door of the apartment and drove away, followed by her best friend and all of her worldly belongings.

Kimberly and Jasmine had just made another pass around the massive parking lot when the moving truck turned into the loading bay and nearly ran them over. Giggling at the near miss, the girls curiously inline-skated over to meet the new tenant.

"Ms. Burke? What are you doing here?" Jasmine exclaimed in astonishment as Patricia pulled a muslin bag from the passenger seat of her car and placed it into a terrarium.

"Moving in, Jasmine, duh, remember?" Kimberly teased.

Jasmine looked confused for a second, then brightened up. "Oh, yeah, that's right. You're moving in."

Patricia, not sure how either one would know in advance that she was moving in, decided to ignore the statement. "Hello, Kimberly, Jasmine."

"Hi, Ms. Burke," they responded in unison. Kimberly welcomed her to the building, then Jasmine spoke up. Her conversation, as usual, was unending. Luckily one of the movers came over to get information on Patricia's new apartment and interrupted what would have surely been a half hour monologue. Satisfied with the answer to his question, the mover went back to the truck and conversed with his coworkers. "Juliet, I'd like you to meet two of my students, Kimberly Franklin and Jasmine Penbrook. Ladies, this is a good friend of mine, Juliet Bridges."

"Juliet Bridges the dancer," Jasmine exclaimed ecstatically. "I adore you," she screeched. "You are, like, the best prima ballerina in the whole world. I saw you dance *Gizell* last spring. I couldn't believe my eyes, you are so graceful. I take lessons at the Sparks Studio, but I'll never in my life be as good as you. I know you're dancing principal in *The Nutcracker* this December. I can't wait to see you. My father has season tickets, you know."

Juliet smiled and leaned over into Patricia's ear. "Does she ever shut up?" Patricia shook her head sadly.

"You are so beautiful. Although my older sister, Cynthia, says you're too thin, but I don't think so. I think Cynthia is just jealous because our dance teacher said that I have the same graceful qualities that you have." Jasmine continued for another few minutes until Kimberly finally spoke up.

"It's nice to meet you, Ms. Bridges. I remember my

uncle told me that he and my dad went to school with you at Wells Academy. I even saw you in their yearbook."

"See, told ya I was famous," Juliet said, nudging Patricia teasingly. "Well, thank you both very much, ladies, you are too kind. But it might be a good idea to continue this another time. Those guys are being paid by the hour." Four heads turned in the direction of the moving van. The men had stopped unloading the truck and were now standing around smoking cigarettes, laughing, and joking with one another.

Patricia immediately sprang into action. In no time flat the moving crew had returned to work loading her furniture and boxes onto the freight elevator. Juliet and Patricia picked up a large terrarium from the backseat of her car. Patricia reached in and gently soothed the anxiously jumping bag.

"Oh God, look at that!" Jasmine exclaimed to Kimberly in astonishment. "Look, the bag's moving. What's in there?"

Patricia and Juliet shifted the glass-covered cube in their arms. "He's my roommate, Rupert," Patricia said. They carried the large square terrarium from the backseat of the car to the bank of freight elevators. The girls rolled closer and peered curiously through the glass. Their eyes brightened with wonder as they asked question after question in rapid-fire sequence.

Once inside Patricia's new apartment, the girls removed their skates and walked around the empty space. "It's kind of small," Jasmine said, frowning as she looked around.

"It's supposed to be, it's a one-bedroom," Kimberly defended. After a quick tour, the girls went back to the living room to make friends with Rupert.

It took them half an hour to muster enough nerve to touch Rupert. Then fifteen minutes later, and given exact instructions, they argued whose turn it was to hold

him as the questions continued. "How old is he? Is he a
he or a she? How can you tell it's a he? Why don't you
bring him to school? What do iguanas eat? How big will
he get? Where did you get him? Why'd you name him
Rupert?"

Happily, Kimberly and Jasmine kept busy and out of
the way with Rupert the entire time.

Slowly, boxes began crowding the rooms of her brand-
new one-bedroom apartment. Soon there were more
boxes in the apartment than on the truck. Then, eventually, the truck was empty and the move was complete.

Patricia and Juliet collapsed on the sofa after their unexpected helpers, Kimberly and Jasmine, left under
protest, closing the door behind them.

Exhausted silence drifted between the two women as
they sat looking around the box-filled living room. "Are
you ready to start unpacking?" Juliet asked wearily.

Patricia just looked at her friend. She didn't have the
strength to answer. She awkwardly rolled her head from
side to side against the back of the sofa, indicating that
her answer was no.

Juliet understood the silent response. "So," she began
again after another momentary silent pause, "tell me
about Uncle Pierce."

Patricia suddenly gained a burst of energy as evi-
denced by her abruptly sitting straight up. "What?" she
gasped out barely containing her stunned surprise.

Juliet smiled at seeing her friend's unbalanced behav-
ior. Apparently, what she'd heard about her and Pierce
Franklin was at least in some part true. "You heard me.
Tell me about you and Uncle Pierce Franklin."

"There's nothing to tell," Patricia began guardedly,
then added, "Pierce is simply the uncle of a student at
the academy."

"Pierce Franklin, *the* Pierce Franklin, *your* Pierce
Franklin."

"He's not *my* Pierce Franklin," Patricia said defensively. Juliet looked at her unbelievingly until she continued, "That was more than twenty years ago. I was a kid. It was a silly schoolgirl crush. I'm an adult now. I do not have any feelings for him."

Juliet began laughing at Patricia's comical denials. "You're pathetic. I've seen better acting in B movies. Try it again, this time with feeling."

"I refuse to participate in this inane conversation. You're way off base."

Juliet bent over in hysterical laughter. "Somehow I doubt that."

"I have no idea what you're talking about," Patricia vowed, then sat back and shifted her shoulder indignantly away from Juliet.

"Sure you don't."

They sat quietly for a few moments until Patricia, unable to stand it any longer, blurted out, "Where did you hear about Pierce?"

Juliet smiled slyly, knowing her friend too well. "Your little friend told me."

"Kimberly?"

"No, the other one, the one that talks continuously, Jasmine."

Patricia smiled at Juliet's quick assessment of Jasmine's nervous habit. "There's nothing to tell."

Juliet eyed Patricia suspiciously, then chuckled menacingly. "That's not what I heard."

"What exactly did you hear?"

"You know what." Juliet slapped her thigh and stood. "I'm hungry." She sashayed into the kitchen and opened the refrigerator door. Patricia hurriedly followed her. "What did you hear?" She repeated. Juliet frowned finding the refrigerator empty. Patricia reached over and opened a box on the counter marked 'kitchen refrigerator.' Juliet smiled and pulled out a still chilled bottle of spring water, twisting the cap, and taking a long swig. "Juliet." Patricia raised her voice slightly. "Tell me."

Juliet burst with laughter and leaned back against the closed refrigerator door. "Little Miss Jasmine told me that you and Uncle Pierce were making googoo eyes at each other in your office the other day." Patricia's mouth dropped open. "Ah, ah, close your mouth," she instructed her friend, "no need to deny it, not after that reaction."

Patricia sucked her teeth and looked away. "You know better than to believe everything you hear." She nudged her friend with the refrigerator door to move her.

"So, you're telling me that there's nothing between you and Pierce Franklin?"

Patricia quickly emptied the box and filled the refrigerator. "That's exactly what I'm telling you." She pulled out a bottle of water then looked back at Juliet indignantly as she slammed the door.

"Look at your face. You are so full of it," Juliet accused, with her hand planted firmly on her hip. "I can't believe you're standing there lying to me."

Patricia's mouth gaped open in shock at her friend's allegation. "I am not lying," she said innocently.

"Girl, please, I've known you too long and we've played poker too many times for me to believe that face. How many times do I have to tell you? You don't bluff well."

"I'm not bluffing and I'm not lying. Pierce Franklin is Kimberly's guardian. She's one of my students. End of story."

"What do you mean, end of story? Is he all of a sudden gay, married, or crazy?"

"No, no, and no. As a matter of fact"—Patricia paused and smiled shamelessly—"he's more along the line of tall, dark, and to-die-for."

"So?" Juliet questioned.

"So, it's my job and possibly my career. I can't get involved in a relationship with a student's parent. It's unethical."

"Says who?"

"The board of directors of Wells Academy, for one."

"That's ridiculous."

Patricia thought for a while. It was ridiculous. Although there was no actual verbiage in the bylaws of the school charter that expressly forbade a relationship between a parent or guardian and faculty, the hint of impropriety would be scandalous.

Patricia looked over to Juliet and smiled with naughty delight. "He's still as delectable as ever," she admitted. The smile that played on her lips spoke volumes. She shook her head, then unconsciously bit at her lower lip, allowing an impish grin to spread wider. Juliet watched the battle of conscience displayed on her friend's face.

"Mouthwatering?" Juliet asked, already knowing the answer to her question by Patricia's expression.

Patricia slowly nodded in complete agreement. "To the very last drop," she said, obviously tempted by the possibility of Pierce. "He hasn't changed a bit. He's still way too serious for his own good and way too tempting for mine." She smiled inwardly, wickedly, and continued. "Tall, lean, with just the right amount of muscle in the right places." Juliet smiled at Patricia's dreamy description. "His eyes are still the blackest I've ever seen. They sparkle beneath his long curly lashes like spikes of coal turning into diamonds. Oh, and his lips—full, sensuous, kissable." She was about to continue when she noticed Juliet's expression.

"So go for it," Juliet nudged her on.

Patricia smiled in naughty abandonment. "I wish I could."

"You can, just do it. You've been giving into loneliness all your life. It's about time you find a little happiness.

Besides, you've been dancing around this thing for, what, almost twenty years?" She draped her arm around Patricia's shoulder and whispered in her ear. "'Patricia loves Pierce,' I remember you writing that all over your math notes."

Patricia blushed, much the same as she had when she and Juliet first had met.

"All right, yes, I know, enough of your flashbulb memory." Patricia smiled with childlike embarrassment.

Juliet looked down at her watch. It was getting late. "Listen, girl, you do whatever it takes to make you happy, okay?" Patricia nodded. "Good, now I've gotta go. I have to soak in a hot tub and get some sleep. I have an early rehearsal tomorrow morning and my new *pas de deux* partner is about as strong and limber as a wet noodle."

"Thanks again, Juliet," Patricia said as she and Juliet linked arms and walked to the door. They hugged. "I really appreciate all your help and support."

"You know I got your back."

"I know." Patricia opened the door. "Drive carefully."

After Juliet left, Patricia went back into the living room and gazed around her new apartment. A giddy surge of laughter bubbled within her. She smiled with satisfied delight. She had finally attained a long-awaited dream. She had moved into the prestigious Regency Towers. After a moment of gleeful reflection, she sat in the silence of her solitude until the loud rumbling noise broke the quiet.

She smiled and rubbed at her stomach. She realized that she hadn't eaten all day. She remembered driving by a small family restaurant a few blocks away and decided to get some take-out food, then dive right back into unpacking. She quickly grabbed a light jacket for the cool November evening and trudged on foot to the restaurant.

Patricia walked up the two marble steps leading to the

huge wooden doors and thick brass handles. She looked up. The sign read Elwood's Grill.

The heavy door opened easily, letting an array of delectable aromas escape. Patricia inhaled deeply and her stomach growled again. She smiled, certain that Elwood's Grill would be her new favorite eatery.

Patricia quickly glanced around the open foyer. This was obviously a very popular restaurant. Several couples and families were standing and sitting around, patiently waiting their turn to be served. Beautifully gilded stained-glass windows adorned the partition that divided the quaint eatery from the take-out section.

Patricia peered into the dining area before getting into the take-out line. The atmosphere was festive and lively. Every available table was taken as aproned waiters and waitresses darted around, in, and out, attending their assigned tables.

Patricia patiently stood in line for fifteen minutes, then finally stepped up to the counter. She placed her order, paid, grabbed a take-out menu for future trips, then moved to the side and prepared for a lengthy wait.

It was obvious by the crowded dining room and lengthy take-out line that no one within a three-block radius cooked on Saturday night. Laughter and joyful applause rang out as a group of waiters and waitresses gathered to serenade a happy couple with a special anniversary song. The manager brought out a small layer cake with a single candle burning bright.

The very appreciative couple and their guests laughed and applauded before the couple blew out the candle.

Then, instantly, the restaurant returned to the same hustle and bustle as before. Patricia smiled and watched the loving couple. Someday . . .

Five

Kimberly sat across the dining table from Pierce. She smiled like a Cheshire cat. Pierce noticed her changed mood immediately. For the past few weeks, she'd been almost impossible to live with. Now, this evening, she giggled wildly and sparkled like a shiny new penny. Pierce put his fork of pasta and sauce back down on the plate. "All right, that's it. What's going on with you? What are you up to?"

"Nothing, Uncle Pierce," Kimberly said innocently.

Pierce shook his head and grinned. Whatever had caused the change in his usually sulky, moody teenage niece was a godsend, and he was grateful for it. Kimberly looked around the crowded restaurant. This was one of her favorite places because most of her friends met and ate here. She scanned the dining area to no avail. So far, no one was there but her. She looked over to the take-out section and gasped in surprise. "Oh, look, there's Ms. Burke," she nearly shrieked in glee.

Pierce turned in time to catch a glimpse of Patricia before a family of four stepped up to be seated. Kimberly instantly sprang from her seat and raced to the take-out counter.

"Hi, Ms. Burke," she exclaimed eagerly.

"Hello, Kimberly." Patricia looked around the restaurant expecting to see Pierce, which she did. He smiled and waved from the far booth on the opposite side of the large open dining room.

"Where's Ms. Bridges?" Kimberly said, still too excited and encouraged by her counselor's presence.

"Home. She has an early rehearsal tomorrow morning."

"Are you getting takeout?" Patricia nodded and wiggled the receipt in her hand. "Why don't you come eat with us? Uncle Pierce is right over there." She pointed to a booth table near the window. Pierce was still looking in her direction.

"Thank you, Kimberly, but I'm just going to grab takeout, go home, and get started unpacking." She looked down at the extensive take-out menu still in her hand. She needed a distraction quickly. Piece looked too good, and even from across the room, his eyes were too intense.

"Aren't you gonna at least come to say hello to Uncle Pierce?"

"Yes, of course." After all, what harm could that do? This was a public place and she was merely saying hello to a student's guardian. She was only being sociable. It was only good manners to greet someone you knew. Right? she questioned. Then she listened to that little voice in her head whisper *trouble* as she walked over to Pierce's booth. "Hello, Mr. Franklin, how are you this evening?"

Pierce stood as they came to the table. "Good evening, Patricia. I'm doing well, and you?"

First-name basis? Patricia sparked. When did they start using first names? she wondered. "Tired," she admitted truthfully, then wondered why she'd said that, knowing of course that it would inevitably open a line of dialogue about her move. It did.

"Uncle Pierce, Ms. Burke and Rupert just moved into the building this afternoon."

"Is that right?" Pierce said as his brow rose with interest at the mention of the man's name Rupert. "Welcome to the neighborhood."

"Thank you," she responded, mentally noting his raised brow of interest.

"Yeah, and I met one of Ms. Burke's girlfriends." Pierce was slightly disappointed, expecting to hear about Rupert instead of a female friend. "Her friend is Juliet Bridges. *The* Juliet Bridges, the dancer with the Washington Dance Company. She is so cool. She told Jasmine and me all about being a dancer and invited us to see the company's next production, *The Nutcracker.* Isn't that too exciting? She even invited us to her rehearsals."

Pierce looked at Kimberly as if she'd turned into someone else. He couldn't get over her newly acquired spirit. She was gay instead of miserable, happy instead of sulky, and joyful instead of surly. It was as if she'd changed into a whole new person.

"You went to Wells Academy, right, Uncle Pierce, with Juliet Bridges?" Kimberly said.

"Yes, I did."

"Do you think she'd remember you?" she asked.

"It was a long time ago, Kimberly, I doubt it. We didn't travel in the same circles."

Patricia looked away as the shadow of pain crossed over her. He didn't remember her, either. They also hadn't traveled in the same circles.

Just then, Kimberly looked up and saw her friend Jasmine walk into the restaurant with her older sister. "There's Jasmine and Cynthia. I'll be right back." Without waiting for a response, Kimberly dashed through the thickening crowd and disappeared.

Pierce looked over to Patricia with a brilliant hopeful smile that was totally infectious. He shook his head in dismay. "Is raising a teenage girl ever going to be easier and less confusing?"

Patricia returned his smile and shook her head. "I'm afraid not."

"Any words of advice?"

"You're doing a great job. She obviously loves and adores you." Patricia watched as Kimberly and Jasmine peered through the crowd and waved. She smiled, nodded, and waved back. They giggled and were again swallowed up by the mass of waiting customers.

Patricia had always relied on her instincts. And lately, her gut instincts told her that those two were up to something. The appearance of innocent youth was often deceiving; with Kimberly and Jasmine, it was downright cunning. Patricia made a mental note to keep a keen eye on them in the future, just in case.

The exchange of pleasantries and the trite dance of polite small talk ended almost as soon as Kimberly left the table. But, to Patricia, conversation with Pierce Franklin was as easy and comfortable as talking with an old friend on a rainy afternoon in April. He was funny, attentive, and smart. He seemed so different from his public persona, which more closely resembled the impatient beast from the first time they'd met in her office.

Of course she'd seen him interviewed on television about his company. Who hadn't? PEF Software, Incorporated, was a fast-rising product with unending possibilities and venture capital worldwide. He'd been courted by governments from all over the globe, all clambering to get what he had.

Patricia would be the first to admit that she wasn't the greatest or most knowledgeable when it came to megabytes and gigabits. She'd even go so far as to say most of the students at Wells Academy were more proficient than she on the computer. So imagine her surprise at relating to Pierce without a computer keyboard and zero-one code.

She'd read articles and seen advertisements, but nothing compared to sitting down and just talking with Pierce. He was a remarkable man, to say the least. His humorous anecdotes on raising Kimberly were witty gems of absurdity.

By the time her take-out order was ready, the disappointment of ending their conversation was obvious to both of them. She really enjoyed herself in those few short moments. Reluctantly, she said her good-byes, picked up her food order at the counter, and went back to her new home.

Half an hour later, Pierce walked into the darkness of his empty apartment. The sound of silence all around him was deafening. His pensive mood had returned. He found it odd that the absence of human contact never before bothered him until recently. All of his life, he'd focused solely on his computer software. The solitary position of sitting alone at a computer terminal was all he knew and all he cared to know, until now. He didn't want to be solitary any longer.

He walked into his library, turned on the bright desk lamp, and pushed the key to bring his computer back to life. Instantly the screen brightened, it chimed its readiness, and programs blinked to attention, ready for his instruction. Pierce turned and walked away, another first for him.

The sound of a system booting up was usually music to his ears. But now, all he could hear was the joyous laughter and sweet lilting voice of Patricia Burke. Patricia Burke filled his thoughts more often than he wanted to admit, even to himself. Never had he allowed a woman to get under his skin as she had. Forcefully dismissing her from his thoughts, he inserted a black disk into the drive and began to work.

* * *

Frustrated and discouraged, Pierce looked up at the reflection of himself in the darkened sliding-glass door across the large room. Two hours of wasted work was dumped into cybertrash. How had he lost control? he pondered. Slowly he stood, walked over to the door, and stared out into the abyss of darkness. He unlatched the pin and stepped out onto the library's balcony. The late autumn evening breeze blew stronger on the top floor as a swirl of summer battled to the end.

An icy chill of almost winter hadn't yet begun to fill the night air. Pierce looked down at the center patch of land brightly lit from the numerous security spotlights. The landscaped grounds, green with summer's grass, were still accented with vibrant blooms of floral color. It was a pleasant evening, the kind you'd share with someone you cared about, someone you loved.

The luxury of relaxation had become foreign to him; he was so used to the strenuous pace of PEF Software. Restless and impatient, Pierce looked down and across the courtyard to the apartments below, a sight he'd seen for numerous years. Each balcony aligned perfectly, one atop the other, in military precision. The Regency was home to hundreds of families; some he knew, some he didn't. There, on the seventh or eighth floor, he caught his first glimpse of his new neighbor.

Still smiling madly, Patricia arrived back to her box-filled apartment. Traversing the maze through the living room was a lot easier than maneuvering the chaos in her kitchen. She opened and scanned several boxes in search of basic eating essentials, only to realize that the restaurant had included plastic utensils and a napkin in the bag.

Patricia stood in the kitchen and looked around at the mass of boxes surrounding her. Her brilliant plan of eating and unpacking in the kitchen was not going to happen. There was way too much to be done, and she was way too exhausted to do it tonight. So she chalked the kitchen up to tomorrow's task. She grabbed a cup of peppermint tea, took her meal into the living room, and collapsed on the sofa with her feet up on the coffee table.

Patricia opened the first food container and sighed in serene delight. The smallest whisper of anchovy paste was added to the perfection of the Caesar salad dressing. She devoured it within minutes. Pure ecstasy. She opened the second container. Huge pieces of lump crabmeat and pink garlic-dipped shrimp sautéed in butter, mushrooms, and scallions topped the massive mound of fettuccine al dente with parmesan cheese and alfredo sauce. *Abundanza!*

After barely consuming a third of the meal, Patricia declared herself completely stuffed and put the rest in the refrigerator for the next day's meal. She poured herself another cup of tea, devised a strategy for unpacking, and marched into the bedroom with a definite plan.

She recoiled as soon as she looked around. This was going to be a major undertaking. The larger furniture was secured in place, but numerous boxes were littered everywhere.

She looked around, distressed at the many piles and stacks of boxes around her. She grabbed the top box from the nearest pile. It was labeled MUSIC. Needing a calming distraction, she slit the secured tape and removed the packing paper.

Fifty or sixty CD cases were neatly sandwiched between crumpled packing paper. She pulled the plastic cases out until she narrowed it down to a single choice. Happy with her selection, she walked over to the Bose system given to her by her brother and placed the disk into the platter. She closed the drawer and picked up the tiny remote. After pushing a few buttons, the wondrous joyous sounds of Christmas filled the room.

Smiling brightly, she hummed to the holiday tunes of the season as she put the CDs neatly into the holders.

Making her queen-size bed was her first chosen task. Thankfully, it had already been put together by the moving men. But, unfortunately, twelve heavily packed boxes had found homes on top of it. She cleared the boxes, made the bed, and arranged and grouped the accent pillows. Then, she stepped back and admired her crafty handiwork. She smiled. It was beginning to feel like home already.

Next, she placed the drawers into the dresser and sliced open one of three large closet-type boxes that stored her clothes. She fingered through her hung clothing draped neatly on padded hangers, then decided they could wait until another day.

Afterward, she turned to the bathroom, which was piled high with small uniformly stacked boxes. Patiently, she opened each one until the stacked pile shrank to a single box. The marble bathroom countertop now displayed her array of perfumes, makeup, and lotions in multicolored antique glass-etched bottles of all sizes, shapes, and colors. She looked around impressed. The progress she'd made in the last hour and a half was amazing.

Encouraged, she stepped into the living room and looked around the packed apartment trying to decide what to tackle next. Then, the idea of procrastination hit her like a ton of bricks. She needed a break. After all, she had plenty of time. This would be her home for the next year at least.

Patricia took her warm cup of tea, then walked over to the sliding-glass doors and carefully stepped out onto the dark narrow balcony. Pine trees and burning logs perfumed the crisp night, giving the assurance that winter was growing near. She smiled to herself as she held onto the cold iron rail and looked down seven stories to the ground. A heavy wave of acrophobia swept through her and settled in the pit of her stomach. She took a slow cautious step back.

Being eye level with treetops was definitely not for her. Distracting herself, she held tight to the rail and looked up to the magnificent night sky.

Stars flickered like diamond studs against the black velvet of the majestic universe. The North Star shone brightest amid the billions in view. Memories of school-day lectures on the Underground Railroad brought a soaring feeling of pride to her heart. Hundreds of runaway slaves had made their way to freedom by this single point of light in the sky—a most remarkable feat.

The absolute clarity of her new surroundings was a stark contrast to the dismal view from her old apartment. Gone were the condemned buildings, abandoned cars, and dying landscape. Sadness choked in her throat as she realized that changing your address didn't always mean moving away. She would carry the naked sores of her childhood community with her for a lifetime.

A single wooden rocking chair glider, a housewarming gift from Juliet, had been placed on the concrete floor behind her. She sat down with her tea in hand and continued to gaze into the darkness of Virginia, allowing memories within her to heal and rest.

Just as she settled into the comfort of the chair, the bell rang. Cautiously, she walked to the door. "Who is it?" she called out.

"Pierce, Pierce Franklin."

A sly smile as wide as a Texas sunrise greeted her when she opened the door. "Pierce," she exclaimed with breathless surprise, then corrected herself, "I mean, Mr. Franklin." She said it too seductively for her own good.

Pierce peeked into the room behind her, then into her big brown eyes. "You were right the first time." He smiled, and she melted. "I apologize for just barging in on you like this, and if it's too late or you already have company, I understand."

"No, not at all," she said, sounding overanxious.

He held up a white cardboard box tied with a thin string. "I thought you might like some dessert."

"Oh, how thoughtful. Thank you." She paused a heartbeat just to take in the sight of him. He was definitely delicious. "Would you like to come in?" He nodded agreeably. She stepped aside, allowing him to pass.

"I hope I'm not disturbing you." He looked around stealthily for any hint of the man his niece had referred to earlier as Rupert, but it was clear that they were alone.

Patricia closed the door and followed the spicy lusty aroma of masculinity wafting in the air. It had been a long time since the scent of a man had perfumed her apartment.

Boxes of all sizes covered the floor, the furniture, and lined the walls. The only available space was the sofa, so he sat down, leaving enough space for Patricia to sit beside him.

"Where's Kimberly?" Patricia asked nervously as she fiddled with her necklace before sitting on a heavy solid box beside the sofa.

"She's staying with Jasmine tonight. They're going shopping early in the morning. She said they needed to get an early start. Something about Election Day sales."

"Sounds like fun."

"These are for you," he said as he offered the small white box, then openly looked around the apartment and nodded his approval. It was much smaller than he'd imagined, but he liked the layout.

Patricia watched as he looked around. When his eyes wandered to the kitchen, she announced, "That's the kitchen," then motioned for him to follow her. The kitchen was large and roomy, with plenty of cabinet space. There were several opened boxes on the counter and resting on stools. Patricia went over to the stove. "Would you like a cup of tea?"

"Sure."

She went from box to box, frowned, then looked around hopelessly and laughed with embarrassment. "I have no idea where the rest of my teacups are," she admitted freely.

"How about if I ask for a rain check on the tea?"

"You've got it." Through a momentary silence, they smiled awkwardly, then looked away like schoolchildren. "Come on, I'll show you the rest of the apartment."

Pierce nodded and followed dutifully. After touring the rest of the apartment, they went back to the living room. There they talked about anything and everything for the next forty-five minutes.

"I really enjoyed talking with you this evening," Pierce admitted.

"Me, too," Patricia agreed. Their eyes met and held too long. An intense kaleidoscope of emotions filled her. *Pierce Franklin must always be untouchable,* she reminded herself over and over again, hoping the repetition of the words would ice the growing burn inside of her.

Even as she thought the words, her fingers itched to experience the rich mocha of his skin. He was too dangerous, and she had better remember that. Cowardly, Patricia looked away, hoping to break the spell she'd fallen under years ago. But still his dark tormenting eyes watched her, their intensity never wavering.

Her eyes fell upon the white box sitting on the table. "I almost forgot, what did you bring for dessert?"

"Open it."

Her usually nimble fingers nervously untied the string on the dessert box and slowly lifted the lid. Her joyous surprise was evident. She squealed with fervent delight, "Cannoli."

She immediately pulled one from the box and bit into

the lush sweetness. "Umm, this is so good." She licked at the sweet powdered sugar rimming the treat. "I love cannoli." She sighed lovingly. "My mother and I used to make them as holiday presents for the neighbors at Christmastime."

She offered him the box. He took a cannoli, broke it apart, then bit into one half. Powdered sugar sprinkled on his chin and sweater. They laughed as he brushed the sugar away. Then, without warning, he gently took her hand, lifted her cheese-covered fingers to his mouth, and licked away the cream. She watched, hypnotized by the simple seductive act.

As if acting of their own accord, her finger began stroking his smooth face, first wiping the sugar from his chin, then just touching. He closed his eyes, reeling with the feel of her hands on his skin.

The sudden fateful kiss couldn't have been predicted. It was sweeter and softer than the brush of early morning dew and seemed to last an eternity.

When their lips finally parted, they simply stared into each other's eyes until the passion of desire brought them together again.

The savored moments passed as lightning seconds, each building and adding to their mounting unparalleled pleasure. Patricia reveled in the delight of touching, feeling, and embracing the expanse of his chest. She felt the muscles as they rippled beneath the silk fabric of his shirt. He was hard and strong. She was weak and vulnerable.

Without hesitation, she surrendered to the passion of his touch. Each finger caressed a different pulse point with heavenly rapture. She tingled beneath his powerful hands.

When the kiss ended, she held on for dear life and cuddled within his embrace. Protected and adored, she felt the security of his arms wrapped tightly around her body.

"This can't happen," she muttered into his chest, "we can't happen."

"It can, and we can." He tipped her chin upward to meet his eyes. Midnight black, framed in gently brushed lashes, they promised her the world and more. "If we want it to."

She licked her lips, still damp with the taste of his mouth and the feel of his tongue. Yes, she wanted him. But she knew she needed more than one night of passion with this man. She needed a lifetime plus a day.

"You'd better go now," she said, defying the words even as they left her mouth.

"Patricia," Pierce said as he stood reluctantly. Leaving her at this moment was the most difficult thing he'd ever had to do. He nodded, then moved to the door and placed his hand on the brass knob, but refused turn it.

She knew she should have turned away, but she didn't, couldn't. She watched as he walked across the bare wooden floors. When he stopped and turned to her, her heart leaped. Slowly she stood.

Words failed them as their eyes met and sank deeper and deeper into their souls. Patricia rasped and labored for breath. The slam of her heart rocked her to her very core. This man was not for her, she told herself repeatedly. But her heart knew differently. He had seared his mark on her as she had on him. The fight was lost, the battle yielded.

Pierce started walking toward her. After a few steps, he began to move even quicker, gaining certainty of his heart. He knew what he needed in his life; he needed her. Patricia, bolted in place, feebly shook her head no.

When he reached her, he leaned in just enough to press his lips against her cheek. He whispered good night into her ear, turned, and left.

Six

After opening a single eye to the brightness of morning, Patricia instinctively burrowed deeper beneath the warmth of her fleece sheets and down comforter. She laid there, pillow over her head, shutting the world out as long as she could. But then it happened, as it had the day before . . . as it would most likely happen every day from then on.

Patricia growled loudly as the cheerful mourning dove announced his morning ritual from the sill of her bedroom window. She would definitely have to do something about that bird, she decided. For ten minutes she listened in misery to the now familiar coo of the bird singing his solitary tune of woe. It was too early and she was just too tired.

Another sleepless night, she thought. Two days of exhausting moving and unpacking had been followed by two nights of fitful sleep. Again she had tossed and turned all night with amorous dreams of a man she could never have, and she had no one to blame but herself. But it was too late now; she'd tasted the nectar of his mouth and savored the strength of his embrace. She was smitten and pined for a man who wasn't hers and never could be.

Reluctantly she peeled back the comforter, swung her socked feet from the bed, and padded to the bathroom. She stood and looked at herself in the full-length mirror leaning against the wall. The whimsical sight of her reflection brought an instant spark of motivation.

The revealing attire of a sex kitten, satin and lace had never appealed to Patricia. Instead she chose to don an oversize cut-off T-shirt and comfortable cotton boxers. With her hair piled high atop her head in cascading ringlets of flattened curls, she looked more like an oddly dressed rag doll than a thirty-two-year-old woman.

She looked deeper into her troubled eyes. The darkened smudges beneath them gave blatant notice of her recent inner turmoil. If this continued any longer, she'd need a tanker of cover makeup to conceal her angst.

Unknowingly, and with relentless devotion, he haunted her. As she bathed, as she worked, as she slept, he was always there in the near recesses of her thoughts. When the shiver of warm water tingled her skin in the shower, she felt his whispered thoughts. With the gentle satin of lotion on her body, she imagined his stroking hands. He was always there, tempting and just beyond her reach. Never before had she experienced such complete and total distraction.

No, that wasn't quite true. There was once, she remembered, a time when her thoughts had been consumed by the same erratic emotional feelings, when all she wanted to do was melt into the protective arms of the one she loved. The blindness of love had gripped and clouded her to the ugly truth. Then, the sledgehammer of reality had cleared her vision.

But time and heartache had shown her that not everything was as it appeared. As they always say, time heals all wounds, and luckily it didn't erase memories. She'd vowed she'd never make that mistake again.

Wrapped in a white fluffy cotton towel, she returned to the early morning coolness of her bedroom. A flash of vibrant green darted across her dresser with lightning speed, then stopped next to her hairbrush. "What do you want?" she asked aloud.

She gripped the neck and extended her fingers to secure the front of her roommate. She tucked his rear and tail beneath her elbow and brought the scaled creature to her chin. She gently rubbed the dorsal spine of coned spikes against her cheek. He sat patiently within her embrace. "Good morning," she cooed, then gently stroked the underside of the green, scaled, and wrinkled neck with her finger.

"And where have you been, mister?" she scolded. "You were noticeably out of sight last night. You, sir, are supposed to be my protector and keep me from doing something stupid like getting my heart broken and falling in love." After realizing what she'd said, she paused and stared at her likeness in the mirror. A shudder of truth passed through her. "Come on, Rupert, let's get you something to eat."

Patricia filled the aquarium dish with fresh water and added a small dish of specialized iguana food. Rupert turned up his nose at the tender morsels and skittered to the opposite side of the glass container. "I don't have time to hand-feed you this morning, so you're on your own." She went back into the bedroom to dress for school.

The chime of her mantel clock sounded 6:30. Dressed and ready for work, Patricia peeked into the aquarium. Rupert had decided to eat and was well into enjoying his meal. "Very good," she announced to no one in particular, then placed a small dish of halved green grapes near the water.

She reached up and opened the living-room drapes, letting the bright November morning stream in. Her apartment faced east, and dawn was just eclipsing the trees across the open courtyard. She looked to the brightening sky. As soon as she did, her eyes went to the top floor of the building. She knew Pierce lived up there somewhere. Wayward thoughts threatened to push past reason, as he had successfully gripped her heart for a second time that morning.

The ringing doorbell drew her away from her solitary pity party. She looked over at the clock on the mantel above the faux fireplace. It was early, much too early for unannounced visitors.

Patricia, still holding a steaming hot cup of tea, opened the door to a smiling gray-haired intruder. "Good morning, Patricia," the older woman greeted her brightly, as if she'd known her all her life. "I'm sorry I wasn't available when you moved in the other day. I've just been so busy lately. I know I should set aside some time to just sit back and relax. Heaven knows if I don't, I'll be burned out before Christmas day."

Patricia looked at the plump woman with salt-and-pepper hair. She wasn't sure what to think. She wasn't used to having visitors at her apartment in her old neighborhood, so this woman's early morning social call and Cliff's Notes life story was a strange awakening to the reality of suburban life. "Good morning," Patricia finally returned, "how may I help you?"

"I see you're almost ready to get to school, so I won't stay but a minute. Oh, good heavens, where are my manners?" She stuck out her hand to shake. "My name is Helen Hopkins, and my husband is Rudolph, the building manager. We live on the first floor. Apartment Number 101, so if you need anything, give us a call or just knock on the door. I guess you could say I'm the un-official welcoming committee, though I don't know where I find the time."

Patricia grasped her hand and shook with apprehensive concern. "Is there a problem?"

"No, child, heavens, no. I just wanted to welcome you to the building. We're like one big happy family here, so do try to get out and meet the neighbors."

"I'll try my best," she said evasively.

Mrs. Hopkins reached down and picked up a small wicker basket covered with bright yellow cellophane and a big pink bow beautifully tied and draped on top. "These are for you," she announced proudly. Patricia took the basket and peered inside. "They're homemade cookies. I baked them myself. Chocolate chip, macadamia nut, oatmeal, and sugar."

Patricia was speechless. "Thank you," she said, slightly stunned by the generous gift. "This is very sweet of you, thank you."

Helen waved her hand nonchalantly. "You're quite welcome. Kimberly tells me that you usually keep late hours, so we'll do our best to keep an eye on things for you. We're a very close family here at the Regency Towers."

"Thank you, I'd appreciate that."

"It'll be our pleasure." She reached in her pocket, pulled out a folded paper, and handed it to Patricia. "This is an invitation to the after-Thanksgiving social we have here at the Towers every year. It's the unofficial official beginning of our holiday season." Patricia took the paper, opened, and read it. "Just a little gathering of neighbors. Bring a dish or bring Thanksgiving leftovers, we're not picky. Oh, and bring a nonperishable can for the food drive and a Christmas ornament for the tree."

Patricia nodded, making a mental note of her detailed instructions. "Thank you, this sounds wonderful. I'll look forward to attending this year."

Mrs. Hopkins nodded with delight. "Now, finish getting yourself ready for school. We'll have plenty of time for a nice long chat over tea later on." Patricia nodded and smiled. Mrs. Hopkins turned and trotted down the hall to the elevators. She turned. "How's Rupert like his new home?"

Patricia had just pushed the door closed when she

heard the question called from down the hall. "He likes it just fine."

"Glad to hear it. Hurry up now, you wouldn't want to be late for school." The words disappeared around the corner.

Patricia closed the door and leaned against it, shaking her head in amazement. She wasn't quite sure what to make of Mrs. Hopkins. She was certainly a piece of work.

Pierce found himself humming the silly Christmas tune he'd heard playing at Patricia's house the night before. He didn't know all the words, but the tune had stayed with him all night and all morning. With his face half-covered in shaving cream, he stopped, looked at himself in the mirror, and smiled happily while singing loudly and very off-key, "Five golden rings. Four calling birds, three something else, two whatever goes here, and a partridge in a pear tree."

Seven

Time moved even slower than usual as Patricia, secluded in her office, waited. She found herself watching the seconds tick away like a schoolchild eager to end a long day in class. But, unlike a schoolchild, she wasn't looking forward to running home to watch TV or chat on the telephone with friends. She was waiting for the arrival of Pierce.

She opened and reread the E-mail she'd sent to him and received back last week. He'd eagerly accepted her invitation to attend the weekly meeting of the Christmas Ball committee. Patricia frowned. That was before she'd moved into his building, before he'd brought her dessert, and before she'd kissed and nearly attacked him in her living room.

Patricia cupped her hand to her forehead, lowered her head a moment, then looked back up at the clock. The minute hands had barely moved, but she knew that her embarrassment would be complete in less than one hour's time.

Distracted beyond working, she stood and walked over to her office window. Dusk had begun settling over the early evening skies. The weather turned unseasonably warm, giving the sense of winter's delayed arrival. The trees, once lush with summer's blooms, then spattered gold and auburn with leaves sparingly sprinkled about, were now bare.

School had been over for nearly three hours, yet the school's parking lot remained crowded with teachers' cars and with after school activities. Among the several people walking below her window, Patricia watched unwelcome figures as they patrolled the grounds, an increasingly common sight lately. One figure stood out in particular.

He moved with strict military training, back straight, chest out, eyes forward. Never letting his feet stray from their destined path surrounding the main building, he marched in the formation of his own making. Even from a distance, he was a small man. Like his large rough callused hands, his skin, an umber shade of brown, also seemed coarse and rough to the touch.

There was something about him that made her very uneasy. His brow was lowered just enough to give him a constant ominous expression of universal contempt. His full lips were always curled into a menacing grimace, as if he were constantly on the verge of an attack. The feeling he gave everyone in his presence was that of judgmental distrust.

He gave the sense of self-righteous contempt of others, that, together with his paranoia and his delusional sanctimonious attitude, only added to her disquieting convictions. In her professional opinion as a trained psychologist, he was one sick puppy.

Although he'd heeded her request and removed his dark mirrored sunglasses inside the building, he always wore them when he came to consult with his security team. Suddenly he stopped and looked up at her window. His expression betrayed nothing behind his unusual mirrored disguise. He stood and just stared up at the window, as if he'd heard everything she'd just thought about him. Patricia eased away from the tinted windows and shielded blinds, then moved back to her seat. She stood at her desk, letting the eerie naked feel-

ing subside before she sat and opened a file to continue
work.

Finally she concentrated.

Vincent Shields was well aware of his powerful presence.
He knew what those around him thought, and he liked it.
He relished the power his image gave him. He may have
been short in stature, but he was respected and feared by
everyone he met. Those two words would never be expressed about his father. He had become the stronger
man, the better man, the bigger man. People looked up
to him for their very lives. He held their safety in the palm
of his hands. Yes, it was the power, he was the man.

Pecs, abs, triceps, and biceps all rippled, taut. Toned
to perfection, he moved with pride and persuasion. His
exceptional muscular body was perfection. Below the
flimsy offerings of expensive clothing, he was godlike in
his splendor. He was superior both mentally and physically to those desk-clinching weaklings around him,
including his father.

Although his father had the military background and
government connections, it was he and his team who actually did all the work, while his father sat in his office all
day twiddling his thumbs.

He often watched as women ogled his body, wanting
what he had, begging for his attention. But he chose se-
lectively and gave sparingly. Few were worthy of his time.
Then there were those—the blinded ones—who
mocked his presence. They were the ones who truly
wanted him. Like Pat Burke. He knew she wanted him.
It was evident in the way she looked at and spoke to him.
It was in her eyes each time she saw him. She looked
away in shame, but there was nothing of which to be
ashamed. He would help her open herself to him in
order to accept the inevitability of her obvious feelings.

* * *

The sense of a presence first drew her subconscious. Then, the typing on the computer slowed as her conscious processed the shadow standing in the doorway across the room. She jerked up suddenly and gasped. He stood silently.

Breathlessly she asked, "Is there something I can help you with, Mr. Shields?"

He stood a moment without speaking, then he removed his mirrored sunglasses. The snarled smirk pulled tighter across his lips. "You want me," he said rather then asked.

"I beg your pardon?"

"I saw that you were looking at me from your window."

"Actually, I was looking out of the window at nothing in particular. If you were in my line of vision, I hadn't noticed."

A game player, he reasoned and thought to himself. *She can't admit that she was watching me. How could she possibly admit to herself that she wants me?* He nodded with a leer but didn't budge from his position in the doorway.

"Is there something else, Mr. Shields?" she asked, not liking the way he'd begun staring at her lately.

"Yes." He came forward and stood in front of her desk. "I want everything you have compiled from your investigation of the thefts and vandalism."

"I already gave your associates everything of pertinence, Mr. Shields."

He moved around her desk slowly. "You didn't give us the names of the suspects."

"Suspects?" she questioned forcefully. Patricia considered herself a fair judge of character and an extremely even-tempered person, but this muscle-brained Neanderthal was about to pluck her last nerve. "I do not have a list of suspects, Mr. Shields."

He stood directly above her, his legs spread wide and his mighty fists anchored to his narrow hips. "I was told that you interrogated several students about their whereabouts on the evenings of the attacks. Who were those students?"

She stood, holding her ground expertly. "I do not interrogate my students, Mr. Shields. I am a trained and certified child psychologist and counselor. It's my job to speak with students, not interrogate them." Her gaze never wavered from the cold lifelessness of his steel gray eyes.

"My request is nonnegotiable Patty. I want the names, now."

"I don't take orders well, Mr. Shields."

"Perhaps you haven't been ordered by the right man."

"I won't dignify that with an answer."

"Who are you protecting, Patty?" he asked, abruptly changing strategy.

"Mr. Shields, this is a private school. Parents pay good money to send their children here for the excellent education we offer and the nurturing environment we provide. They expect us to treat their children with respect and consideration. I am protecting these students. There are no suspects nor criminals here."

"If that were the case, then you wouldn't need me."

"My point exactly, Mr. Shields. I don't believe we do need you. And, for the record, my name is not Patsy, Pat or Patty. If you find Patricia so difficult to pronounce, you may call me Ms. Burke."

Vincent smiled viciously. "Patricia," he said, letting the syllables tumble from his lips like rocks down a steep hill. "You and I will be working very closely to apprehend the culprits responsible for the school's thefts," he began as he sat his hip on the side of her desk and inched closer to her. "I suggest we get along. Perhaps we could get started by having dinner or even—" He was about to continue when a knock took both of their attention to the office door.

"Am I intruding?"

"Mr. Franklin, Pierce, not at all. Please come in." Patricia smiled brightly, visibly relieved for the distraction.

"It's good to see you, too, Patricia," Pierce said. "Are you finished unpacking yet?"

"Hardly, but it's coming along. It looks a lot better since you last saw it."

"I'll have to check it out. I believe I still have a rain check for tea."

"Yes, you do." Their eyes locked with a knowing smile.

"Excuse me," Patricia said as Vincent walked up and stood beside her, much too close for comfort. "Pierce, this is Vincent Shields. He works with our school's security company. He's here to look into our recent theft problem. Mr. Shields, this is Pierce Franklin."

Pierce immediately glared suspiciously at the slight man before him. Vincent caught and processed the hesitation and made a mental note. Perhaps he should broaden his investigation to include others associated with the school.

Politely, Pierce extended his hand to shake. Vincent looked down at the offered hand, then reluctantly grasped it. They shook with the might and understanding associated with the force of rams butting heads for territorial rights atop a solitary hill. Testosterone seethed through Vincent's veins as his steroid-laden adrenaline kicked in.

Pierce and Patricia continued to converse in niceties, giving Vincent little to add to the conversation. Anger began to bite into his ego. He was systematically being ignored. No one ignored Vincent. At least not for long.

"Why are you here, Mr. Franklin?" Vincent questioned, ending the polite friendly chatter that drifted around him.

Pierce looked down at the mosquitolike menace, then back to Patricia. He answered, "There *is* a Christmas Ball meeting tonight, isn't there?"

"Yes, there is. As a matter of fact, we'd better get started," she said, then turned and leaned across her desk to retrieve her notebook and folder. Both men watched the long stretch of her legs and the sly slit in her skirt promising more as she leaned over. Then, in a knowing instant, Pierce and Vincent stared at each other, both recognizing that a line in the sand had been drawn between them. They nodded to each other, accepting the inevitable rivalry.

"Shall we go?" Patricia asked of Pierce just before she brushed past him and exited the open door.

Pierce and Vincent continued to glare at each other. Vincent nodded. Pierce nodded, then turned and followed Patricia down the hall.

Together they took the same path he had taken to get to her office. Now, very familiar with the basic layout of the building, Pierce paid more attention to the posters lining the walls. "Thanksgiving Dinner Volunteer Program?"

"Some of our students volunteer at a local shelter for extra credit. It helps encourage them to go outside of the security of Wells Academy to help others less fortunate. Kimberly has always been one of our most ardent volunteers. But of course, you already know that and must be very proud of her."

He nodded knowingly. Yes, he was proud of her. No, he had no idea that she volunteered in a shelter.

They passed a poster announcing the Annual Christmas Ball. "I remember attending the Christmas Ball when I was a student here."

"Really?" she answered noncommittally.

"Kimberly mentioned that you attended Wells at the same time Juliet Bridges did." Patricia nodded her head.

"That means you were here when Aidan and I were here."
She nodded again. "It's strange, I don't remember you."

Before she could respond, her name was called. She
turned and paused. "Why don't you go ahead to the conference room?" she said to Pierce. "I'll see you in there."

"Sure," he said as he watched her walk back to the
front door toward an older gentleman with graying temples and bushy eyebrows. Pierce continued to the room
and turned back just before entering. Seeing Patricia in
an animated conversation with another man caused a
knot to twist in his stomach. It must have been hunger,
since his appetite was close to nothing lately.

Pierce turned to face the glass trophy case just outside
of the conference room. He smiled, remembering the
past vividly. Aidan's name was still proudly engraved on
the small brass plate beneath the leaping football player.
Aidan and his team had come in second place that year.
He remembered that particular senior championship
game well. One of their key players had been expelled
and the team had been forced to continue without him.

Pierce noted the year on the trophy's base. It was just
one year before he'd graduated. Aidan had been a senior.
Juliet Bridges had also been a senior that year and, since
she and Patricia met at Wells, that would mean that Patricia had also been a senior. He frowned. Why didn't he
remember her? Slowly, still pondering, he turned from the
trophy case and continued into the conference room.

A conference table large enough to comfortably seat
sixteen dominated the spacious room. Extra chairs lined
the far wall under the three screened windows. A computer monitor and state-of-the-art projection console
system sat in the opposite corner. Pierce moved to the
mat-covered bulletin board and read the many announcements of upcoming events. He scanned the
notices, then turned when his name was called.

"Pierce Franklin?"

"Yes." He immediately held his hand to shake.

"Hi there," a bubbly bright redhead chirped. "I'm Doris Andrews. We met a few times. Your niece and my daughter are best friends," she exaggerated easily. "I also live in the Regency Towers. I've already requested that you be put on my subcommittee. Here's my phone number and E-mail address. You can contact me anytime. I'll be happy to give you a call and bring you up to speed on what the committee and subcommittees have done so far."

"Thank you." He took the offered business card. "That's very generous."

"Oh, it's my pleasure." She was just about to walk away when another woman a third of her size with long stringy brunet hair stepped up. She eyed him like the last dessert in a bakery on Christmas eve.

She petitely held her hand out to Pierce. He shook it cautiously, afraid he'd break bones if he gripped any harder. "Catherine Jones-Holland, welcome, you're on my subcommittee." She stepped in closer and batted her lashes wildly. "I'll be contacting you later this evening to discuss some ideas I've had." With all intentions of continuing the conversation, she was quickly interrupted.

"I specifically requested that Mr. Franklin be put on my subcommittee, Catherine," Doris exclaimed heatedly. A lengthy discussion ensued. Pierce politely eased toward the snack table.

Cold soda, coffee, cookies, and a huge vegetable platter sat on the table surrounded by an assembly of parents, each eagerly expressing ideas and concerns about this year's Christmas Ball. Pierce acclimated himself immediately.

Moments later, Patricia walked into the room. She was immediately besieged and surrounded. Joyful laughter, open smiles, and welcome wishes were handed out generously. She greeted every parent individually, giving each just enough time to express concerns and relay ideas. Pierce stood back and watched her work the room. She smiled openly, shook hands, and disbursed hugs, all with genuine affection. He wondered if there was anyone she couldn't win over.

The meeting began with a few remarks by the principal, Mrs. Simmons, then the recording secretary read the minutes from the last meeting. Afterward, the committee's finance officer read his report, and finally Patricia spoke. She kept her remarks short, indicating that her sole capacity on the committee was as its facilitator and as a bridge to the school's administrative offices.

As soon as Mrs. Simmons left, the meeting heated up when two parents, Doris and Catherine, discussed their opposing ideas for the Christmas Ball theme. Each stated why hers and not the other's would be the perfect motif. Tempers began to flare, and feelings, like falling glass, began to shatter. Patricia interjected instantly.

Pierce sat back and listened as she took complete control of the room. Every ear listened to her soft-spoken words of authority. The solution was simple: The general committee would take a democratic vote. The theme with the most votes would win. She never ceased to amaze him. Her calm easygoing demeanor could tame the wind in a hurricane.

In his world of split-second decisions, timely information, crucial deadlines, and instantly obsolete software, her control was a breath of fresh air.

Pierce's thoughts drifted back to their time together: always slow, placid, and relaxed. Her calming influence wrapped him in a blanket of peace. He could slow down and take the time to relax with her.

A two-hour meeting was all it took to make great strides of progress for the Annual Christmas Ball. It was unanimously decided that this year's theme would be "A Varied Merry Christmas Wish," a theme neither Doris nor Catherine had proposed. Pierce was placed on a sub-committee to research the many ways Christmas has been and is being celebrated around the world. It wasn't exactly his cup of tea, but he decided to do his best to help out.

This year's Christmas Ball was well on its way to being a success as ideas sprang from everyone, including Pierce, who surprised himself by getting right in the thick of the decision-making process. Holding the function in the newly remodeled gymnasium would cut location costs and having the art department sponsor a competition to design tickets, then print everything on the school's computer system, were the highlighted suggestions.

Twenty minutes of additional conversation followed the official meeting's end out to the parking lot. Pierce found himself in conversation with Doris and Catherine, both vying for his sole attention. Yet his eyes continued to drift to Patricia standing just inside the building's glass doors speaking with a lingering committee member.

"I understand your concerns, Patricia, but these are complicated times," Matt stated with deep concern. "There's a real threat out there and we have to be prepared. Some of our students have very influential parents. We can't take these things lightly. We can't take chances anymore."

"I understand that, Matt, but armed security is a bit extreme, don't you think? This is an institute of learning, not a correction facility."

"Shields ProTech is under contract until the end of this year. By then Vincent guarantees to have strengthened our security and apprehended the troublemakers.

He's personally assured me that his company will be out of here in two months."

"Matt."

"He's doing us a favor, Patricia. Two months, just give the man two months."

"All right, Matt, two months, under protest."

"Duly noted." Matt glanced up at the school clock hanging above the double doors in the main foyer. "Look at the time. Marla will have my hide if I'm not home in thirty minutes." He began walking to the front door. "I'll talk to you later."

"Good night, Matt." Patricia watched as Matt hurried across the front lawn, then scurried through the parking lot to his car. He waved at several people still talking beneath the security light, then ducked behind the wheel and drove away.

Patricia spotted Pierce beneath the light immediately. With his perfect angular jaw and exceptional build, he was impossible to overlook. She smiled and was just about to leave the building when she felt a presence behind her. She turned. "Yes?"

Vincent moved in closer and placed his hand on the door, denying her exit. "No need for concern, I'm just securing the doors."

"I wasn't concerned," she said, beginning to push past.

Vincent looked across the parking lot and watched as the two women continued to talk with Pierce. "You're obviously a very intelligent woman, Patricia, so I assume you realize that he's not right for you."

"I beg your pardon?"

He nodded toward the parking lot. "Pierce Franklin, sole owner of PEF Software. I understand he's got a good thing going on over there. I've used his security software myself. I'd hate to see a brother go down because of an indiscretion."

Patricia turned to Vincent. "What are you getting at?"

"I'm merely stating fact. You could do better."

"Good night, Mr. Shields."

Vincent smiled the dangerous grin of an overly confident man. He opened the door and let Patricia pass. "Good night, Patricia."

Eventually the parking lot cleared; except for two solitary figures still standing in the shadows of the main building. They walked to her car.

A brief wave and red taillights left Pierce and Patricia standing at her car alone beneath the overhead light. Pierce looked around, seeing that the other members of the committee were all gone. "Patricia," he said and stepped closer so it was for her ears only. "I'm glad we have this time alone. I wanted to talk to you about the other night," he began.

Patricia lowered her head, embarrassed. "I know what you're going to say: The other night should have never happened. I agree."

"That's not what I was going to say," he interrupted.

"It was a mistake and I apologize," she continued, not paying any attention to what he'd just said.

"Patricia," he interrupted again.

"It was extremely unprofessional of me." She looked up at him, finally hearing his words. "I'm sorry."

He placed his hands on her arms and drew her closer. "That's not what I was going to say," he repeated. He paused a moment to look into her soft brown eyes. Her stomach churned eagerly, but she suppressed the need to reach out and touch him. "There's obviously an attraction here, Patricia, and I think we should explore it"—he took her hand—"find out where it takes us."

Reluctantly, gently, Patricia, pulled her hand away. "Attraction or not, Pierce, nothing can happen between us."

"Why not?"

"Kimberly is a student here, I'm a teacher, it's unethical, and that's just plain wrong."

"What's unethical about the two of us going out and getting to know each other? What, teachers aren't allowed to date nowadays?"

"We date, yes, but not the parents of our students."

"You're not her teacher, Patricia, you're her counselor. There's a difference."

"I'm also acting vice principal, and for the time being, that alone makes it unethical."

Pierce, exasperated by her reasoning, ran his hands roughly over the top of his hair. "Why are you making this so difficult?"

"I'm not trying to be difficult, Pierce. I'm being realistic. As long as Kimberly's at this school and I'm at this school, we can't have an intimate relationship."

He reached over and gently stroked the side of her face lovingly. "Is friendship also out of the question?"

She smiled brightly. "No, of course not." She turned and walked to the door of her car.

"Good. Then, as a friend, I'd like to ask a favor."

She turned to him. "Asking favors already?" He smiled and nodded. She returned his smile. "What's the favor?"

"I have to go check on a house I'm having built. I could use a second opinion, a woman's opinion."

"You're building a house?" She unlocked and opened the door of her car, then slid into the driver's seat.

"Yes. I know you're still busy unpacking, but if you could spare just a few hours, I'd really appreciate it and I'd really like your opinion."

"I'm afraid that's not within the parameters of my capacity as a student counselor."

"How about your capacity as a friend?"

She weighed his request a second, then, without further debate, she decided. "When?" She inserted the key into the ignition. The car instantly roared to life.

"I could set something up with my design firm for Friday evening. Is that too late?"

She closed the door and rolled down the window. "No, Friday evening sounds doable. I'll see you then." She pulled away with a wave and a smile.

Pierce watched the taillights as they faded into the darkness. Slowly, thoughtfully, he got into his car and drove in the opposite direction. He didn't feel like going home just yet. Kimberly was staying with Jasmine, and he didn't want to face the emptiness of the apartment again.

Vincent watched the two shadowed figures interact on the closed-circuit security system he'd stationed in various locations throughout the campus parking lot. A strained vein protruded from his forehead when Pierce touched Patricia. Apparently, she'd decided not to heed his warning.

Vincent pushed buttons on the monitor and adjusted the zoom lens. The new picture captured a close-up head shot of Patricia's smile just before she got into her car. He shook his head in total disbelief. What could she possibly see in Pierce?

Vincent was so keenly watching Pierce and Patricia that he barely noticed the other monitors set up in the small security room located just off the main entrance.

The wall of surveillance monitors showed views of Wells Academy from every possible point. Each of the three stationed security guards were on rounds firmly securing the building. One opened a classroom door, peered inside, then relocked it. Another walked the wooded parameter near the athletic fields while the last shined his flashlight through the doors of the computer labs.

In another grainy black-and-white monitor, Mr. Wilson hummed a familiar television tune as he proceeded down the hall with his pushcart filled with cleaning supplies. The echo of his jingling keys sounded through-out the corridors of the lower level. He usually stayed when there was a late meeting in the building, but this was later than usual. He looked at his watch and won-dered when the security office would close. He had a lot more work to do.

After twenty minutes of driving aimlessly, Pierce found himself sitting in the driveway of his new home. He got out and entered, using the key he'd been given after the outside had been completed. With no electricity, and only the brightness of the full moon through the naked windows to guide him, he walked through the empty chilled rooms of his new home.

The hollowed sound of his footsteps echoed through the vast desolate rooms. Realizing that there wasn't much difference in the emptiness of this home, the apartment, his office, and his life, Pierce paused and stared out of the large living-room bay window. The ex-citement of professional achievement had long ago worn off. Material things had lost luster and friends and companions were nothing more than ego-boosting yes-men or showy, clingy arm candy.

Of course, he had a steady stream of women on call, but none of them had ever stimulated him, not the way Patricia had. There was something special about her that made him want more. Her intellect, her enthusiasm, and her compassion incited something in him he'd assumed had died five years ago: his ability to care.

Guarded, he had been living his life more as an out-side observer, letting it slowly pass him by without much involvement on his part. Perhaps he got that from his mother.

As the wife of a senator, she was constantly in the spot-light, yet she never let anyone get too close. She lived by a simple rule: There was danger in politics as in business. When you're on top, there's always someone out there wanting to knock you off. When you had wealth, there was always someone out there who wanted you down.

With this, she'd kept herself and her family constantly shielded, especially her boys, more particularly Aidan. He was the firstborn and the favorite. Growing up, Pierce and his brother Aidan always had the best of everything, from schools to homes to friends. It wasn't until his family moved back to Florida, after his father retired from office, that he'd realized how much he missed out on as a child sheltered from the real world.

Unlike his brother, Aidan, who had a knack for people, for Pierce, relationships had never been a strong suit. Aidan was popular, personable, and extremely well liked by everyone he met. Pierce, on the other hand, was reserved, quiet, and introverted. He was second string—Aidan's little brother and a pale comparison to the original. In his eyes, he could never measure up to Aidan. He had lived his life trying, and had always failed. Aidan was perfect. He was invincible, that is, he had been until the night of the phone call.

"Mr. Franklin, this is Lieutenant Haskell at the Forty-first Precinct. I'm sorry to tell you that there's been an accident. A car slid on black ice in Rock Creek Park. We need you to come down to the hospital."

Even after five years, the words still rang in his ears as clearly as if they'd been spoken just yesterday. On Christmas day, he'd had to identify the bodies of his brother and sister-in-law, inform his parents of Aidan's death, then bring his eight-year-old niece to her new home and explain why she'd never see her parents again.

Pierce had sat eight-year-old Kimberly down and explained as best he could about the reality of life and death. She'd understood up to a point, like any eight-year-old would. That Christmas morning was her first birthday without her parents. There was no celebration.

Since then, Pierce had abstained from the celebratory rituals of Christmas. There just didn't seem to be any point. Now, strangely enough, the joyous spirit of the Christmas season was buzzing all around him, thanks to Patricia.

Pierce closed and locked the front door, wishing he could do the same to the room in his heart that held his memories. He got in his car and drove to the chilled emptiness of his Regency Towers apartment.

Eight

It was a perfect spring morning in early May, except that it was late November. The weatherman had predicted that the temperature would top out at the middle seventies. Christmas was right around the corner, and winter was nowhere in sight.

A clamorous flock of ducks from the local pond announced their departure to points south as they flew overhead in the familiar V-shaped formation. The crunch of fallen leaves sounded beneath Patricia's feet as she strolled through the school's parking lot, joyfully humming "The Twelve Days of Christmas" while celebrating the beginning of a brand-new day. This was her favorite time of year.

Early arriving students, dressed in the standard gray-and-burgundy trimmed sweaters with the Wells Academy emblem neatly stitched to the knit, waved and called out to her as she passed. It couldn't get any better than this, she assured herself as she passed through the administration area en route to her office. "Good morning," she sounded to the roomful of office workers and teachers.

A pleasant replied greeting followed her as she continued to her office. "Patricia." She turned at hearing her name called. Audrey was walking toward her, carrying her standard walkie-talkie, notebook, and clipboard.

Patricia stopped and waited for her to catch up. Audrey unfolded her half-frame reading glasses, which always hung from a cheap silver beaded chain around her neck, and perched them on her nose. She examined her clipboard closely, then frowned up at Patricia.

"Good morning, Audrey," Patricia chirped brightly. "How are you this morning?"

"Fine," she said with less passion than a moon rock. "I need some time with you this afternoon."

Patricia nodded. "Sure. I'm pretty sure I'm free this afternoon between one and three, but let me check my calendar to make sure." Patricia turned and continued toward her office with Audrey marching close behind. Patricia opened the door to her office and stopped in surprise.

"What is it?" Audrey asked, almost bumping into her from behind. She peered over and around Patricia's shoulder. She immediately saw the sandy dark soil scattered across the floor. "Is that from your plants?" she asked.

Patricia frowned. "From my trees," she corrected. "Yes, it is." She looked around her office. Nothing seemed to have been touched. But the feeling that there was something wrong stayed with her as she moved behind her desk and opened her calendar. "Is 1:30 all right with you?"

"Yes, that will be fine. Don't be late," Audrey said, turned on her heels, and marched on to her next destination.

Patricia shook her head. That woman would never change.

For the next few minutes she sat uneasily looking around her office. Most of her things were of little value to anyone but herself. Her tiny portable CD player sat on the corner of her desk. Her crystal clock, always four minutes fast, sat between the monitor and the telephone. And her favorite fountain pen, sapphire with golden accents, was just were she'd left it the evening before. Everything seemed to be in place. But still, there was something not quite right. She couldn't put her finger on what. She sat at her desk and spread her fingers wide over the closed files. She briefly opened and scanned each one in turn. Nothing seemed to be missing or altered.

She looked over to the bookcase. She noticed that a single book had been moved. She stood, walked over, and replaced it. When she turned, she faced the credenza. That's when she saw it, or rather, didn't see it. The signed baseball that always sat on her credenza was missing.

Smiling at nothing in particular, Pierce hummed a familiar holiday tune as he strolled through the main corridor of PEF Software. His mood could only be described as hopefully encouraged. The fact that Patricia had initially turned down his offer was merely a stepping stone. He could sense her hesitation and was sure he could change her mind.

"Pierce, wait up," Lewis called from behind. Pierce turned to see his friend hurrying to catch up. Breathless, he asked, "what's wrong with this picture?" Pierce was silent as Lewis continued his comedic cleverness. "What massive tragedy, what horrible catastrophe, what unthinkable disaster could put our fearless leader in such a jovial mood?" Pierce merely raised and lowered his brow. "What is up with you, man? I haven't seen you in such a good mood since you decided to go public. What's going on?"

Pierce shook his head and smiled. "Nothing's going on," he assured his friend, then pushed the up button for the elevator.

"Well, then you're going deaf, because I called you three times before you finally turned around."

Pierce shook his head. "I've been distracted lately." The elevator doors opened and they stepped inside.

"I can see that. Did you get that situation at Kimberly's school straightened out?"

"I'm handling it."

"And the counselor?"

"I'm handling that, too," he said evasively, unable to suppress the broad smile that spread across his face. The doors opened at their floor. Both men stepped out and began walking toward the executive suites of PEF Software.

"Wait a minute." A second passed and a huge smile spread wide across Lewis's face also. "I get it, you're *handling* Little Red Riding Hood, aren't you." He mockingly punched Pierce in the arm. "I knew it. Way to bowwow, dawg. You have my undying devotion. You da man."

"I have no idea what you're talking about."

"I bet you don't." Lewis gave a lively chuckled. "Handle your business, dawg." He looked around the empty hallway, then leaned in closer to Pierce. "All right now, give details. What's so special about this one? How was she, any good?"

"You've been married too long, Lewis. You've got sex on the brain. There's nothing going on between me and Patricia Burke."

"Yeah, right. Okay, be like that." Lewis exhaled feverishly, excited. "By the way you described Little Red, umph, I'd be hitting that twenty-four-seven."

"Well, I'm not. Ms. Burke and I are not exactly compatible at the moment."

"That's a tough break." The two men fell into silence as they passed the security desk. Pierce smiled and nodded his greeting; Lewis raised his nose and ignored the uniformed men standing there.

"Patricia Burke, that name sounds so familiar," Lewis spoke up, then thought for a moment. "I know that name from somewhere." He paused a second time, then shook his head, confounded. Pierce shrugged indifferently. "It'll come to me," Lewis eventually promised. "So, since Little Red is out of the picture, I gotta tell you that my sister, Caroline, has been on my back all week for your work schedule. She's got a serious jones, buddy, and I don't think it's entirely because her company designed your new house."

Pierce frowned. This conversation had quickly become tedious. "I told your sister before, I'm only interested in a professional relationship. Anything else is out of the question," Pierce reiterated pointedly.

"Whoa, whoa, don't shoot the messenger." Lewis held his hands up in defensive surrender. "What can I say? You have that effect on the ladies. You always did, you know that. Aidan was the same way. You Franklin men always had them eating out of your hands. But I gotta warn you, man, Caroline can be hardheaded about something she wants. She doesn't take disappointment well."

"She'll get over it," Piece stated dryly.

"Hey, don't get me wrong, my sister is a good woman. That design firm she runs is top-notch. And let's face it, I'd love to have you as a brother-in-law, but"—he leaned in closer again—"but that's between you two. I delivered the message, now I'm out of it. Although, I can tell you one thing, Caroline can be very determined. She's got you in the bull's-eye and she's ready to shoot." His chortle turned to full chuckle.

Pierce ignored the splash of humor. "Not this time. Not with me."

"Hey, as I said before, this is between you and Caroline. I'm out of it."

"Whatever."

"So, you and Patricia Burke, not compatible, what exactly does that mean?" Pierce smiled slyly, giving Lewis all he needed to jump to conclusions. "Aha, I knew it. You're not giving up on Little Red, are you? I knew you hadn't changed. I knew you wouldn't just give up and walk away."

Pierce's smile faded. "It's complicated."

"So just move on." Pierce shook his head. "If I didn't know any better, I'd say you were already hooked."

Pierce smiled. "There's something about her. . . ."

"Man, you can't even commit to a plant. I suggest that you just move on."

"Not just yet," Pierce decided.

"So, what's the problem with her? Doesn't she know who you are?

"That's not the point. There are other concerns at stake."

"Man, you know I have to live my life vicariously through you." They reached the corridor separating their two offices. Pierce kept straight and Lewis turned to the right.

"Grow up, Lewis."

"You've changed, Pierce. Where's the man I lived my life trying to emulate? Where's the take-control man who focuses on nothing else except work? Where's my hero?" Pierce shook his head as Lewis laughed nervously and continued down the hallway to his small office.

By the time Pierce had gotten to his office and closed the door, he was deep in thought. Lewis, although a complete imbecile, was right about one thing. He had changed.

He wasn't the steel-nerved, ice-veined corporate leader he once had been. His hardened edge had vanished. His focus, once solely on PEF Software, had been redirected to thoughts of Patricia. She'd brought a new kind of joy to his life. He liked the feeling.

He pushed the button and the computer instantly came to life. He scanned the numerous communications. There was an E-mail from Wells Academy. He immediately thought of Patricia. He opened the E-mail, but was disappointed to find out that is was from a member of the Christmas Ball committee. They were interested in changing one of the program formats.

To salve his disappointment, he entered the Wells Academy Web site and went directly to *administrative ser-*

vices. Patricia's radiant face smiled back at him. He sat for a few moments and just memorized the planes of her smooth face. There was nothing more beautiful and relaxing than seeing her smiling face everyday.

Vincent was sitting at her desk, scanning an open file when she returned from her meeting with Principal Simmons. Patricia paused just long enough to get his attention. "I understand there was an incident in your office, Patricia," he said without looking up at her.

Patricia walked over and stood in front of the desk. "My baseball is missing."

"Any ideas who might have taken it?" Remaining seated, Vincent looked up at her, expecting a viable answer.

"No." She rudely reached over, closed the file he'd been examining, and glared at him. "Do you mind? These are confidential."

Vincent smiled nicely. "Not at all." He stood and walked around to sit on the edge of the desk, allowing his leg to brush against hers. Patricia reached over her desk and gathered the remaining folders. Vincent ran a short stubby finger down her arm. "You're going to have to be more cooperative than that, Patricia."

She glared at him and moved to her chair. "I said I have no idea who took the ball."

"You must have some suspicions, a notion, a guess, woman's intuition, perhaps."

"Sorry, can't help you." She reached down and pulled a CD from her lower drawer, then slipped it into her portable player on her desk. Soft gentle violins whispered from the small speakers in tune to "Have Yourself a Merry Little Christmas."

"Try harder." She remained silent as she opened and flipped through several files, checking for missing pages. Finding nothing disturbed, she closed them and secured them in her top drawer. "I have to tell you, I keep trying to read your eyes for a sign, any sign."

She looked up at him, and her eyes blazed with a very obvious readable sign. He smirked, having understood well. "You are a remarkable woman, Patricia Burke." He walked over to the credenza and picked up the framed photo of her smiling in the baseball uniform. He absently stroked the image. "A remarkable woman with a remarkable past." He looked over to her. Her expression didn't changed.

"What exactly do you want from me, Mr. Shields?"

He grinned lecherously. "I suppose you could always get your brother to sign another baseball for you." She just stared at him. "Oh, and speaking of your brother, he had an excellent batting season last year. What was he, .360?"

"Something like that," she replied evasively. The rapid scurry of bow on strings ended abruptly with the deliberate clash of cymbals sending the music into a spiraling crescendo.

"You know, I was surprised to see that both you and your brother attended Wells Academy, but oddly enough, only you graduated." Patricia's stomach quivered. Thoughts of those days usually made her physically ill. Vincent grinned, seeing her reaction. "Oh, that's right, I forgot, he was kicked out of school, wasn't he?" He paused for effect. "Something to do with theft and vandalism, I believe." She remained silent.

"He was completely exonerated and his record expunged. It was his decision not to return here," she said, her voice steady and clear, betraying nothing of how her heart raced with anger. Kettle drums beat steadily, keeping the quake of her anger in check.

"Of course it was," Vincent noted sympathetically. "Tell me, how's your mother's hypertension? I hope she's dutifully taking her medication. We wouldn't want her to have another ministroke, would we?"

"She's fine. Thanks for asking."

"Does she still enjoy living in Atlanta with her sister?" Patricia's expression never altered, so he continued. "I'm sure she does. Do you suppose she's still disappointed with you for not moving there with her?"

Patricia wasn't surprised that he knew so much about her and her family. As a security specialist, he had a number of channels at his disposal, she presumed, and had probably already done a complete examination of her background and credentials. "Am I supposed to be shocked or impressed by your snooping into my background?"

"You seem hostile. I'm just performing my job. I routinely investigate the principals involved in an assignment." He finally set the framed photo down and walked back over to the desk. He leaned in closer to whisper, "Understand this: I will find the culprits with or without your assistance. But I'd prefer to have your cooperation. If you feel uncomfortable speaking about this here, perhaps we could meet for drinks or dinner. It might be helpful if you were more comfortable with me. Learn to trust me. Remember, I'm here to protect you." He let his eyes roam over her face and down her body.

She'd been expecting the proposition, and it had finally come. She stood up and leaned across the desk to him. "Let's cut to the chase, shall we? You and I are going to be working together for the better part of the next two months. I suggest we keep our associations as uncomplicated as possible."

Vincent leaned in even closer, a mere few inches from her mauve lips. "Dinner tonight?"

"I'm busy."

"Perhaps another evening."

"Mr. Shields, I don't know how to put this any clearer than I already have. I'm not interested."

Vincent dusted an invisible thread from his expensive

pants to camouflage his annoyance at being rejected. "You realize, of course, that he's not your type." She opened her mouth to speak, but didn't respond. Vincent's mouth watered at her soft-hued lips. "Pierce Franklin," he said simply. "Interestingly enough, I could afford to buy and sell him several times over."

"Congratulations."

"You're playing with fire, Patricia Burke. I'm sure you realize that there are rules against fraternization with guardians of current students." She closed her mouth, afraid she'd say something she'd regret later. "So far, I'm the only one who's seen your little late-night rendezvous under the streetlights." He smiled gleefully. "I could be enticed to look the other way."

"Psychological manipulations or blackmail?" she asked pointedly. The erratic climactic ending of the tune ended with controlled grace in a flutter of gentle keyboard strokes.

"You're a very perceptive woman, Patricia, you figure it out." He stood, smiled again, then walked out. A second later he reappeared in the doorway. "I'd reconsider dinner if I were you."

"Then it's a good thing you're not me, isn't it?"

As soon as Vincent closed the door, Patricia, fuming, picked up the phone to call Juliet, but remembered that she was scheduled to be in rehearsals all day. Angrily, she slammed the phone down, turned her back to her desk, and stared out of the window. She watched the warm breeze tug at the last few leaves on the trees as the hushed chimes of Tchaikovsky's *Nutcracker Suite* whispered gently to her with the familiar trumpets announcing the dance of sugarplums.

It took a good ten minutes for Patricia to calm herself. Letting Vincent's childish antics get to her was totally unlike her. She needed to throw something, break something, or hit something—preferably that something was Vincent Shields. She stood, paced the office with the vigor of a caged cat a few times, then decided to walk.

Out among the students, she returned to herself. Their vigor for life, matched with the excitement and eagerness to learn, was exactly what she needed. She sat in on a history class, then an English literature class. Soon, sparked with the energy of youth, she went back to her office and dove into work until a timid knock drew her thoughts back.

A new student, Jamal Scott, peered around the corner of her open door. "May I speak with you a minute, Ms. Burke?"

"Of course, dear. Come in, close the door, and have a seat."

Being with her students was always the best distraction for her. They were the best, and she would always be there for them. For this particular student, a new arrival, the problem was simple and went back as far as she could remember: the Richies versus the Poories. The student wanted to ask a certain young lady to go to the Christmas Ball, but didn't know how to ask or even if he should.

She refrained from trite platitudes and simply gave him her honest opinion, coupled with enough encouragement to go ahead with his plans at least to ask. The young man left feeling more assured and self-confident.

Patricia was on the mend when she picked up the ringing phone. "Patricia Burke."

"Hi, this is Pierce Franklin."

She recognized his voice instantly. "Yes, I know. Good afternoon, Pierce."

"I was just thinking . . . ," he began.

"Yes," she drawled out, much too sexy for her own good. She spun her chair to look out of the window at the trees' bare branches. "And what were you thinking?" she asked playfully.

The smile in his voice was evident. "That we should

have dinner Friday night before we meet to have a look at the house."

"That's a very sweet invitation."

"So, what's your answer?"

"You know I can't accept. It wouldn't be very ethical."

"Unethical? How? You're not married, I'm not married, I'm not seeing anyone." He paused, then remembered the name Rupert. "Are you seeing anyone?"

"No."

"So I don't see a problem."

"You do like tempting me, don't you?"

"Most definitely."

"Pierce, we talked about this the other night. We can't see each other socially. There are some people who might consider it a conflict of interest."

"Some people?"

"The board of directors, the parents, the principal."

"So, we won't invite them."

She laughed. "Still, I'm afraid I'm going to have to say no, but thank you for the invitation."

"Are you sure?"

"No," she responded truthfully, "but I'm going to decline anyway."

"So, just because you're Kimberly's counselor and assistant principal, you can't have dinner with me."

"Yes, pretty much."

"Then I'll just have to pull her out of Wells Academy."

"You wouldn't do that."

"I might."

"No, you won't."

"So what's my recourse, to celebrate alone?"

"Celebrate, what are you celebrating?"

"Christmas spirit."

"A little early, aren't you? Christmas isn't for another five weeks."

"I haven't had Christmas spirit in almost five years."

"Well, that is cause to celebrate. Congratulations."

"I'd be even more joyous if you'd reconsider my dinner invitation."

"You are persistent, aren't you?" she said wisely.

"It's a simple dinner and a simple yes."

"Nothing in life is that simple."

"You'd be surprised," Pierce assured her.

Nine

The quaint little coffeehouse they chose to stop at was located in a remote area of Reston and seemingly known only to a neighborhood few. The waiter, a young acne-faced teen wearing a clean white apron, immediately appeared as soon as they walked in. He introduced himself in garbled mumbles, then welcomed them to the Café Italiano.

He smiled gleefully through metal braces, proud that he'd remembered the basic greeting and introduction. He turned to the empty room, somewhat confused as to where to seat them. Pierce took the initiative. "How about over there?" he offered, much to the delight of the grateful young man.

They moved toward the center of the room, away from the plate-glass window and kitchen doors. They chose a table near the fireplace. Pierce pulled out Patricia's chair and waited until she was comfortably seated. "Thank you," she said. He nodded as he sat across from her.

The waiter, still hovering, handed each a small handwritten menu, then informed them of the nightly specials. Patricia glanced down the dessert listing and then back to the specialty coffee list. She chose to pass on dessert and just order a cup of herbal tea.

The waiter, whose long blond hair fell each time he lowered his head to write, quickly jotted it down on a small white pad, then turned to Pierce. He closed the menu and handed it back, ordering a cappuccino and slice of mocha cake. The young man nodded as he added Pierce's order to the small pad. He asked if there would be anything else. Both declined. With his task completed, the waiter thanked them and hurriedly disappeared behind the tall counter and then through the swinging kitchen doors.

Alone with Pierce, Patricia uncomfortably looked around the intimate dining area. It resembled an old-world Italian café, complete with wrought-iron chairs, polished brick walls, and marble flooring. She fingered the red-and-white checked tablecloth, then quickly grabbed and placed the matching red napkin across her lap.

She spoke nervously. "This place looks like it's right out of a vintage Italian movie. I like it; it's got real authentic atmosphere, including lovers making out in the corner table."

Pierce looked across the room. A couple sat in a secluded corner, whispering hushed words into each other's ears. Their chairs were close and the man's arm lay wrapped around the woman's shoulder, drawing her even closer. "What makes you think they're lovers?" Pierce asked.

Patricia blushed. "I think that's pretty obvious."

"So," Pierce began as he moved his chair next to hers, "if I were to move my chair like this, and place my arm around you like this"—he leaned into the nape of her neck, letting his warm breath tickle her ear—"and whisper in your ear like this, we might be considered lovers?"

Scalded hot with the flames of desire, Patricia's heart beat rapidly as her hands trembled in her lap. "Point taken. Don't believe everything you see."

"Exactly."

The table fell silent for a few moments as Pierce sat back but kept his chair close. Patricia averted her eyes as the waiter returned with a large circular tray. He placed cream and sugar on the table, then, very carefully, he set each large cup down. He smiled, delighted with his obvious achievement. As soon as the young man disappeared back to the kitchen, Pierce leaned closer. "Speaking of not believing everything you hear and see, I'm still curious . . . who claimed to see Kimberly in the school after hours?"

"Your new home is absolutely beautiful," she answered evasively. Pierce nodded appreciatively, then smiled at her obvious change of subject. "Where did you get the idea for the design? I've never seen anything like it, it's absolutely wonderful."

"Thank you. I wish I could take some of the credit, but I can't. The architect and interior designer I hired are real geniuses." He took a sip of his cappuccino. The sweet rich flavor sent a warm glow down his throat. "They took care of everything. All I had to do was approve their incredible ideas and sign checks. So, my part was pretty easy. I'm glad you like it, that really means a lot."

"Why?"

He sipped his coffee then frowned. "Why what?"

"Why would it mean a lot to you? I mean, why me? You must have dozens of women you could call to see the house."

"True," he said, not making it seem like bragging.

"So, why me?"

He smiled. "Kimberly suggested it."

Feeling somewhat slighted, Patricia steeled her expression with a fixed smile. "I see."

"And," he continued, "because I trust you."

"You don't know me."

"Yes, I do."

She looked at him oddly, then smiled and quickly looked away to the empty fireplace. The appearance of the cold logs neatly stacked on an iron grill in a hearth surrounded by glazed stone drew and held her attention. Suddenly she smiled.

"What?" he questioned.

"Nothing." She waved him off.

"Tell me."

She sighed heavily. "While you were looking around the library, your designer asked me what my personal attachment was with you. She also said that the two of you had been dating for a while. She wanted to know if I considered tonight a date."

"Interesting," he confirmed. She nodded in agreement. He made a mental note to have another talk with Caroline. "Really, what did you tell her, about our personal attachment?"

"The truth, that we were just acquaintances."

"Acquaintances?"

"Friends," she corrected with an uncharacteristic shrug, then repeated with more difficulty, "friends."

"Friends?" he questioned as he reached over and placed his hand on top of hers. "Friends don't get distracted at work and find it impossible to concentrate with the mere thought of you." He looked into her eyes with enough intensity to reverse the axis of the spinning earth. "Friends don't lie in bed at night, sleepless, anticipating the next time they have the opportunity to see you. Friends don't look at each other with wanting eyes the way we do, and they don't devour a kiss the way we do."

The yearning need to kiss him weakened her emotionally as she steeled her resolve. "Pierce," she rasped. Her voice trembled as she pulled her hand away when she spotted the waiter approaching.

"Facts, Patricia," he breathed into her ear, "I'm just stating the facts. You know it and I know it."

The young man appeared again, carrying a tray with Pierce's cake and two glasses of water with lemon. "Will there be anything else?" he questioned, then walked away when Patricia shook her head and Pierce said no aloud.

"You can't just ignore us forever."

She steadied her throbbing pulse. *I have to,* she thought to herself but chose to answer differently. "Tell me more about PEF Software."

Kimberly and Jasmine huddled low behind the desk in the darkened shadows of the administration offices. A soft eerie glow from the computer screen covered their faces as the single sound of the wall clock's ticking second hand lulled them while they feverishly worked.

It was late, much too late for them still to be at school. A small table light and two flashlights lit the computer screen and keys of the keyboard. A pile of books, a stack of files, and two picture frames hid their presence from sight. From the corridor it looked as if someone had simply left a desk light on.

They each had a specified function to perform. Jasmine was to search the manuals for the quickest, safest path and Kimberly was to input the data.

Jasmine sat behind Kimberly with a data manual open across her lap. Using her penlight, she squinted at the tiny typeface, then ran a professionally manicured fingernail across the page to the diagram. She checked and double-checked. Every detail was important, and every command had to be exact. A single mistake in wording or a simple comma or backslash out of place would be disastrous and force them to start from the very beginning, and for them, time was of the essence.

Kimberly's fingers magically roamed the keyboard in perfect precision. Each stroke of a key drew her closer and closer to their goal. She picked up a pencil and wrote a notation in her notebook, then went back to the screen.

To the untrained eye, the computer programming

lingo looked like useless gibberish. But, to Jasmine and Kimberly, it was easily intelligible text. A series of ones and zeros covered the screen, giving the computer detailed instructions through alphanumeric characters.

Following their previously mapped-out sequence, Kimberly backspaced and retyped a command. *Access Denied.* She frowned. "This isn't working. We must have the wrong path."

Jasmine looked up from her manual. "Let me see," she said as she edged over Kimberly's right shoulder. She read the last few lines of type. "You're right, it looks off. Maybe we should have inverted it."

"Nope, I tried that. Nothing happened."

Both girls sat back and stared at the screen. They'd just spent thirty minutes writing a single path. "Try it again." Kimberly leaned up to the keyboard, deleted the last three command lines, inverted, then retyped them. *Access Denied.* Jasmine moved closer. "You're right, that looks worse."

"Maybe if we . . . ," Kimberly began, then let her fingers perform the unstated operation. In a blur of precision and accuracy, they whizzed over the keyboard with lightning speed. When she finished typing, she sat back and stared at the screen. A single finger hovered less than an inch above the Enter key, just long enough for her to turn and look at Jasmine.

Jasmine smiled and shrugged her shoulders. "Let's do it." Kimberly nodded and let her finger drop to the key before Jasmine uttered, "Wait a minute."

Kimberly turned to her, questioning, "What?"

"Did you remember to write this down, just in case?" Kimberly nodded, wrote the path quickly, then pressed the key down.

A second passed. Nothing. Then the hum of the computer buzzed differently. A succession of soft clicking sounds came from the hard drive. The system had accepted the program. The screen ran a series of configurations as listing upon listing of text appeared.

Both girls remained silent as they quickly read the messages detailed on the screen. The system prompted a request, and Kimberly answered. The system referred to an arrangement of data, and Kimberly responded. For each prompt, Kimberly countered with the appropriate response taken from her notebook. Then, without warning, the screen went blank.

The girls looked at each other and smiled as an eruption of giggles surged upward. "Sweet," they sang out in unison. This was it. They were inside the data mainframe.

The computer screen went through a range of applications, then finally rested on a single data screen.

"Oh, snap," Jasmine said as she inserted and loaded another disk into the drive.

Kimberly quickly wrote down the information as it sequenced through. The system prompted a question for printing. She looked at Jasmine, both girls nodded, and Kimberly keyed Print. Within minutes, everything on the screen had copied to the printer across the room. They giggled again.

"That was tight," Kimberly said as the printer began its silent copying process.

The blinking of overhead lights sent both girls diving under the desk. As still as statues, they waited in silence for something, anything to happen. A minute passed with no sight nor sound of another human being. Kimberly began to ease from their secured tomb. Jasmine pulled on her arm. "Where are you going?" She mouthed the words in a half whisper, something she and Kimberly had mastered during class years earlier.

"I have to get out of the system and turn it off," she replied as she continued to move away. Jasmine pulled her back again. Kimberly looked back at her worried expression. "I'll be careful."

Slowly she eased up until her head peered just slightly above the top of the desk. There was no one in sight, so she eased up more. She looked around, then, seeing it was clear, she turned her attention to the computer still displaying the hacked computer site. She followed the prompt, typed in a few commands, and exited the site. Then she began backing out of the system as quickly as she'd entered.

Suddenly, from the corner of her eye, she saw movement. It was Mr. Wilson, and he was coming out of the supply room across the hall with a laptop computer box under his arm. He paused outside of the room, looked around once, then, with his free elbow, hit the light switch, sending the area into complete darkness.

Kimberly slowly eased her way back down next to Jasmine. Her heart was beating so fast she was afraid she was going to have a heart attack.

"That was close," Jasmine said as she cupped her hands over her face and shook her head. "I can't believe that there's somebody here this late. What did you see? Who was it?" she whispered.

"I don't know, I couldn't tell," Kimberly lied. "Come on, we've got to get out of here." She began to stand up until Jasmine pulled her back down.

"We can't leave now. Whoever just left could still be out there. We'll give it, like, fifteen minutes, then go, okay?"

Kimberly nodded agreeably. Rarely did Jasmine come up with good ideas—luckily this was one of those times. "Okay, good idea."

"Besides," Jasmine added, "we still have to turn off the main system before we leave." Kimberly nodded, grateful for the time to calm herself and stop shaking.

Five minutes later, Jasmine and Kimberly were sitting at the keyboard backing out of the computer system. Just as Kimberly was about to exit completely, she stopped and frowned at the monitor. "What's this?"

Jasmine peered over her shoulder and also frowned. Both looked at their watches, then back at the monitor.

"Why would somebody bury a countdown program in the security system?" Jasmine whispered.

"I don't know," Kimberly muttered back absently. She began typing, digging deeper into the school's computerized security program. She frowned when she entered the main program. "Look at this, there's a glitch in here. It's buried as a binary passage. One goes to the monitors and the other goes . . . off. That's strange, why would somebody want the school monitors to turn off in"—she looked at the counter again—"three hours, ten minutes?" she questioned.

"What's strange is that we're digging *into* the system instead of backing *out* of the system. Come on, Kimmy, we have to get out of here."

"But somebody planted some kind of amateur countdown gnome in the security program," she said as she began backing out of the system again. She hit the last key and sent the monitor's screen to black. Together they gathered their notes and backpacks, then crept to the storage room and slipped out of the window.

The girls hurried to their bicycles. As they pedaled down the dark driveway, they talked about the narrow escape. "The only reason anybody would want to turn off the security monitors is to"—they looked at each other—"break in," they said at the same time. They pedaled even faster.

It was the perfect evening and Pierce was the perfect companion. The once-tense conversation had quickly turned to work, politics, and sports. "How do you do it?"

Pierce asked when they stepped off the elevator and he walked her to her apartment door.

"Do what?"

"You asked dozens of questions and got me to talk about myself all night long. I still don't know anything about you."

She smiled. "What do you want to know?"

Gently he leaned in and took her face between his hands. Her eyes sparkled and twinkled with the light like a million diamonds. "Everything." He kissed her lips gently.

She didn't object. "That's a lot."

"I have plenty of time."

"Pierce, you know we can't do this again."

"Shhh." He shook his head and placed a finger over her lips. "The only thing I know, Patricia, is that right now, at this very moment, there's nothing else I'd rather do than be with you, and I know you feel the same way, too. You can't deny it. It's been pushing us together from that first moment we met."

Patricia smiled at his fateful words. "Pierce." She swallowed his name as his mouth descended upon hers in a kiss so sweet and so perfect it could have been designed only in heaven. His arms wrapped firmly around her body in a loving embrace as his hands stroked the line of her neck and down her back. She swayed into his embrace.

When the necessity of air separated them, a lone tear eased down the side of her cheek. He kissed the salty wetness away. She lowered her head. "We can't." She shook her head. "I can't." She quickly turned and disappeared through her apartment door.

Troubled, Pierce walked back to the elevators and rode in solitude to the top floor. His thoughts were frayed with images of him and Patricia together. He slipped the key into the lock and opened the door. The apartment was silent. He immediately went to the library. He picked up a crystal tumbler, added ice, then poured three fingers of twelve-year-old scotch.

He raised the glass of amber liquid and held it to his lips. The stinging smell singed his nostrils. He didn't want alcohol. He set the glass back down on the crystal tray. He knew what he wanted. He wanted Patricia, and he knew that she wanted him. He just needed to convince her that they should be together.

He walked up the stairs to Kimberly's bedroom. He gently tapped on the closed door. There was no answer. The silence coming from her room was odd. He knocked again—still no response. He slowly opened the door while calling out her name. The room was dark except for the glow of the television muted and left on.

Kimberly and Jasmine were fast asleep, one on the bed, and one on the pullout sofa bed across the room. Pierce looked at the green LCD numbers of the clock beside her bed. It was only 11:30, hardly late and hardly bedtime for Kimberly or Jasmine, who oftentimes stayed up on weekends until well past one in the morning.

The unusual sight was curious, but didn't cause alarm. He presumed that they'd been out shopping with Jasmine's mother, then come here and crashed.

Pierce crossed the bedroom to the television and turned it off. He backtracked through the completely dark bedroom, guided only by the hall light. He took a last look at the sleeping girls, then went to his bedroom.

As soon as the door closed, Kimberly and Jasmine sat up and looked at each other. Jasmine got up and went to sit on Kimberly's bed. "So, tell me, who was it, who did you see?"

Kimberly frowned and shook her head. "It was too dark and the person walked in the shadows. I didn't get a good look at their face," she lied.

"Was it a man or a woman?"

"I don't know, it was just too dark," she lied again. Both

girls looked at each other sorrowfully. They had just attained their intended goal when they'd been interrupted and had to abort the mission before completion.

"I'm tired," Kimberly confessed soberly. "Let's get some sleep."

Jasmine nodded, went back to the sofa bed, and climbed in. Moments later, Kimberly sat up and looked over to the sofa. Jasmine was still. The slight burr of her slowed breathing told Kimberly that she was already asleep.

Kimberly turned on the tiny night-light above her bed and opened her computer notebook. She followed down the page until she came to the last few lines. She smiled to herself. They had done it. They had hacked into the Wells Academy archives.

But just as quickly as her smile appeared, it faded. She knew for certain that Mr. Wilson was the thief who was stealing from the academy. She also knew that there was no way she could tell anyone, because she would also have to tell on herself. Neither one of them should have been in the school at ten o'clock on a Friday night.

Kimberly turned the light off and lay back down. Maybe she could leave a note or talk to someone. Her mind whirled at the possibilities. Her uncle Pierce would skin her alive if he found out that she was out at school late at night.

Kimberly looked at the skylight above her bed. Stars twinkled down innocently. She made another wish.

Telling a teacher was out, because he or she would want to know how she knew. What she needed was absolute confidentiality like with a priest, a doctor, or an attorney. The only attorney she knew was Jasmine's father, and he'd have the same reaction as her uncle. She didn't know any priests, and her medical doctor was out of the question . . . but maybe a counselor.

She considered the ramifications and consequences

of telling Ms. Burke. Like a computer, she logically ran scenarios in her mind. She found each one was acceptable, with relatively minimal personal blame.

Patricia crawled to the top of her bed and laid her head against the mound of fluffy satin pillows. She looked around the room, pleased with what she saw. In just a few days, it had been transformed into a picture-perfect bedroom worthy of any magazine layout. Pictures had been hung, shelves had been filled as everything found the perfect place to settle. It looked as if she'd been there for years. Everything was flawless, every *I* dotted and every *T* crossed. Order was her life. She thrived on the precision of balance and harmony.

"I'm so out of control, I feel like I've fallen down a rabbit hole or been sucked up by a twister. This whole thing is moving too fast," she said into the phone.

"I hear that's how it is sometimes," Juliet advised.

"He's like a whirlwind in my mind. Every time I think about him, which is way too often, I giggle and blush like a teenager. I get chills, goosebumps, and, can you believe, hot flashes when he touches me. I can't seem to keep my hands off him when I'm with him."

"Sounds like love to me."

"Love, what is love? A chemical reaction to a given or presented set of circumstances."

"It's more than that, and you know it."

"Please, I don't want to hear any of your lovesick colloquialisms."

"That's the clinical you talking. What you just described to me didn't sound like a chemical reaction. It sounded more like a love attraction."

"He's hands-off, Juliet, but I can't seem to remember that when I hear his voice or see his face. My mind and my heart battle constantly over him. I know what I should do, I know what I have to do, but . . ."

"But what? You know, you were a lot more fun in grade school." Juliet sighed heavily in mock disappointment. "Why can't you just accept what you're feeling and go with it?"

"You know why I can't, no matter how much I want to."

"Patricia, this isn't rocket science. Just sit back and enjoy the ride for however long it lasts."

"But—"

"But nothing, Patricia. Don't you know people have lived an entire lifetime without ever feeling what you feel and want to deny? They'd give their right arm to experience that dizzying whirlwind feeling just once. I can't imagine myself losing hope that I'll never feel that again, and here you are throwing it away because of some possible ethical technicality. Treasure this, Patricia. Make it yours, make it last."

"I don't know." She sighed heavily. "I just don't know."

"Ride the wave, girl, ride the wave."

"You are impossible, but I know this is the right decision for me."

"Suit yourself."

Patricia and Juliet talked, laughed, and mooned over her detailed description of Pierce's new home. They eventually hung up, with Patricia feeling more confident than ever about her decision to stay away from Pierce.

She laid down, fluffed the pillows, and cuddled low beneath the comforter. That's when she first heard the soft rapping. She froze and looked over to the clock on the nightstand. It was well past twelve. She grabbed her robe and rushed to the front door. "Who is it?" she asked in her most steely voice.

"Pierce," he said in an almost whisper.

She opened the door. They looked at each other for a split second before he hesitantly reached out to her. He lightly stroked along her jaw, then threaded his fingers into the hair at the nape of her neck. "I know I shouldn't be here. But I couldn't stay away." She opened her mouth to speak, but he hushed her with a single finger to her lips.

"Let me finish. I've never felt like this before. Ever since the first moment I laid eyes on you, you've been in my thoughts. I can't explain it, all I know is that I just need to touch you." She closed her eyes as his fingers gently massaged her neck, automatically sending her head into its own seductive roll backward.

She opened her eyes to look at him, her heart filled with emotion. What was it about this man that made every fiber of her being yearn? Then she closed her eyes against the sweet sensation of his touch. Her tongue, of its own accord, touched at the corners of her dry mouth, then ran the circle of her lips. His slow sensual torture was excruciating.

A whimper of surprise escaped when he suddenly encircled her waist and scooped her into his arms. She surrendered to a kiss beyond any other imaginable intimacy. Never had her senses been so alive and numb all in an instant, all at one single moment.

He was a master, to be sure. In less than a few moments she found herself backed against the closed and secured front door. All the wagered money in the galaxy couldn't detail how and when she got there. The kiss, as powerful and awesome as a split atom, could have lasted a few seconds, a few moments, or a lifetime. Time had no meaning.

Erotically his lips toyed with the lobe of her ear as he whispered gently, "I want to know everything there is to know about you, Patricia Burke. I know you have concerns about us and I understand. But I need you to know this"—he leaned back, looked at her admiringly, then cradled her face in his hands—"you and I will be together. Nothing can stop that."

She believed him—with all her heart and with all her soul, she believed him. The reality of his truth was simple; she could do nothing other than believe. His eyes displayed such absolute certainty, such complete and utter assuredness, that she was awestruck by his unshakable conviction.

Then, just as suddenly, he stopped, held her away, opened the door, and walked out. Patricia, still stunned and standing at the door, blinked repeatedly. Her mind's eye knew that what had just happened had really happened, but her heart, still reeling from Pierce's embrace, remained uncertain that his presence hadn't been just a figment of her imagination.

Ten

The Christmas season had arrived early and was in full force, as the myriad of holiday displays already embellishing the local shopping center attested. It was only the third week of November, and already the area was filled to the glass-covered rafters with holiday spirit. Jingle bells decked the halls with yuletide cheer on every level while they cleverly adorned Christmas trees, velvet-covered wreaths with sparkling ornamental balls, and glittering gossamer-winged angels hovering above. So as not to be humbugged, Kimberly and Jasmine did their best to garner the holiday spirit while simultaneously lighting the burning fire of spending.

Armed with several credit cards, they arrived at the mall early Saturday morning, prepared to do serious damage. Dressed in stylish jeans, bulky sweaters, and chunky platform boots, they chatted eagerly as they walked the short distance.

Sticking to the usual routine, they grabbed quick café mochas with extra shots of chocolate syrup and sat down at the gourmet espresso bar to plan their shopping strategy.

Jasmine sluggishly raised her head from her crossed arms atop the small café table filled with newly purchased fashion magazines. She lowered her hot pink-tinted sunglasses. "I can't believe we're here so early," she moaned as she sipped her hot coffee. "Look."

She waved her silver polished nails around aimlessly. "There's nobody even here yet. The stores aren't even open. I could have slept another hour. Then Mrs. Hopkins could have made breakfast for us. She makes the best blueberry pancakes in the world. I wonder how she gets all those berries in there without making the pancakes mushy. I hate mushy food. There should be a law that all food must be crisp and crunchy." Suddenly her head popped up. "Umm, do you smell bacon?" She noticed an elderly gentleman walk by carrying a tray of food. "Ohh, he's got one of those big cinnamon rolls. We should get one. I'm starved."

"You're always starved," Kimberly teased, peering over her green sunglasses and checking for chips in her matching nail polish.

"Am not," Jasmine lashed out childishly, then giggled at her blatant lie as she reapplied her glossy lip balm.

Kimberly looked at her watch as she half listened to Jasmine jabber on—about what, she wasn't really sure. She'd been anxious and distracted all morning long. After a sleepless night of tossing and turning in bed, she'd awoken with a major headache. Each time she'd dozed off, the image of Mr. Wilson coming out of the supply closet with the computer box in his arms had awoken her with a nightmarish start.

Sometimes the image had changed to him stopping suddenly and turning in her direction. She would stand, frozen in place as he walked over and began yelling at her. Even now, in the light of day, she shivered. She knew that she needed to tell someone about Mr. Wilson's stealing; she just didn't know whom she could trust.

"Hello. Earth to Kimmy, come in, Kimmy," Jasmine declared when she returned to the table with a huge cinnamon bun. Kimberly looked up at it in surprise.

"When did you get that?" Kimberly asked, seeing the bun and a pile of napkins in her hands.

"Just now. I asked you if you wanted one and you shook your head no, but you can have half of mine if you want. I probably won't eat all of it anyway." She plopped down in the seat across from Kimberly and proceeded to cut the bun in half with a wobbly plastic knife and floppy fork. She picked up one half and pulled the pastry apart, letting the gooey sugared icing drip onto her silver painted nails.

Kimberly smiled and declined the generous offer, knowing, of course, that the entire bun would be inhaled within two minutes' time. Jasmine, never one to decline food, immediately dug into the bun with gusto. Halfway through, she paused and looked down the opposite path. "Oh, my God," Jasmine said, pausing between each word while licking her fingers of creamy icing. "I can't believe it. Check it out, here comes Ms. Burke."

Kimberly turned around to see Patricia walking toward them. Tall, slender, and statuesque, she was dressed in burgundy wool slacks and a matching mohair turtleneck sweater with a black suede hooded jacket. She looked more like a model strutting the runways of New York than a teacher hanging out in the local mall on a Saturday morning.

Jasmine leaned closer to Kimberly's ear. "I can't believe that's Ms. Burke. Look at her, she looks like a model or something. I wonder why she doesn't look and dress like that all the time? She'd be a total hit at school. Gotta give her her props, she's got *it*. I wonder where she shops. We should go wherever she goes. I could so seriously get into the sophisticated look."

Patricia smiled at seeing her two young students. "Good morning, girls," she said brightly as she removed her tinted sunglasses and stopped at their table.

"Hi, Ms. Burke," both answered in unison.

Patricia looked down and frowned at the empty plate of sticky goo and chilled coffee. "Oh, my, I hope that's not supposed to be breakfast."

"Oh, no," Jasmine began until Kimberly interrupted.

Kimberly nudged Jasmine under the table. "Actually, Ms. Burke, it *is* our breakfast. Uncle Pierce isn't much of a cook, so we came here for breakfast." Patricia frowned again. "Do you know how to cook?" Kimberly asked innocently.

"Yes," Patricia smiled with added suspicion, "I can cook."

"Really?" Jasmine began. "You don't look like you can cook. I mean, not that you can't cook, it's just that most people that are cooks are, like, bigger and fatter or something. I think that's because they eat all the food they cook. Like my stepmother's brother-in-law, Nathan. He's a chef at one of those four-star restaurants in New York City, Manhattan, I think. Anyway, he can really cook, but he's as big as a house. But my stepmother's sister is, like, so thin. I think it's because she's, like, bulimic or something. I've seen her throw down. Girlfriend can seriously drop some grub, know what I mean? But look at you, Ms. Burke. You're so thin, you look like a model. You must not eat hardly anything."

When Jasmine finally stopped to take a breath, Patricia quickly spoke up for fear that she'd continue. "Actually, Jasmine, I'm a very good cook and I love to eat."

"Are you cooking for Thanksgiving?" Kimberly asked. "Yes, I am."

"What are you cooking?" Jasmine questioned with added interest.

"The traditional holiday meal with the side dishes."

"Who's coming over, your family?" Jasmine continued.

"No, no one's coming over," she said evasively.

"So, you're, like, cooking, serving, and cleaning up all by yourself?" Jasmine wondered aloud. "That's a shame. Nobody should be alone on Thanksgiving. It's, like, a time for family and friends."

"You know what. You should have Thanksgiving dinner with us," Kimberly invited. "We never cook and Mr. and Mrs. Hopkins always go to their daughter's house for dinner, so Uncle Pierce usually takes me out, but that's getting really kinda old."

"It's very sweet that your uncle takes you out for Thanksgiving dinner."

"I know, but"—she paused for dramatic effect—"I always wanted a real Thanksgiving dinner cooked at home like my mother did when I was younger. You know, turkey and dressing in the oven and tons of pots on the stove cooking."

Patricia's automatic child psychology instinct stepped up. "Kimberly, there are all kinds of celebrations for the Thanksgiving and Christmas holidays. For Pierce to take you out is very special, and you should see it in that light. The traditional Norman Rockwell family setting isn't always what's normal or what's best. Sharing with loved ones, that's the important thing for any occasion."

"So, if you're cooking all that food and no one's coming over and you'll be all alone, where's your family?" Jasmine asked. "Don't they live around here?"

Patricia thought of past holidays spent in Atlanta with her brother's family and her mother and aunt. They were happy times, but also empty. "Most of my family live in Atlanta and no, I'm not going there for the holidays."

"So, what are you going to do? You can't spend Thanksgiving all alone after cooking all that food and stuff."

"I'll have plenty of help." Patricia smiled at Kimberly's concern. "And I don't plan to be alone, Kimberly. For the past few years I've joined my friends at the D.C. Central Kitchen. We volunteer to help feed the homeless."

"You're going to a homeless shelter to eat Thanksgiving dinner?" Jasmine said, her nose crinkled up, appalled by the image of mingling with the homeless.

"No, Jasmine. I'm going to the homeless shelter to volunteer to help serve the meals."

"Oh, I get it," she said in pure enlightenment. "That is *so not* selfish," Jasmine added in openmouthed awe.

"Are you coming to the Towers after-Thanksgiving celebration?"

"Yes, I'm looking forward to meeting more of my new neighbors."

"It's a lot of fun. Everybody gets to bring a covered dish and we all eat leftovers in the community room."

"It sounds like fun."

"Uncle Pierce usually doesn't go. He'll probably have to work," Kimberly added with subdued revelry.

"Well, girls," Patricia said, wondering about Kimberly's overexaggerated sadness, "it's been nice talking with you. You two have a good day. Kimberly, don't forget our meeting this afternoon at the library."

"I won't forget, I'll be there."

"All right, I'll see you at five o'clock. Don't be late." Patricia continued down the mall's path with both girls' eyes trained on her as she disappeared around a corner.

"She is so cool. Can you believe she's going to a homeless shelter for Thanksgiving? That is so cool. I could never see my evil stepmother doing that in a million billion years. She would be too grossed out. To tell you the truth, I don't think I could do it, either. I mean, all those homeless people everywhere. I mean, like, gross. They should, like, go home and eat there or something."

Kimberly looked at Jasmine as she continued to flip through one of the fashion magazines lying open on the table. Kimberly was amazed. As usual, her friend had completely missed the point of the word *homeless*. Kimberly shook her head in wonder. How could anybody be that daft?

"Come on, let's go," Kimberly said as she gathered the dirty plate, napkins, and empty coffee cups. They stood, trashed their cups and plate, and began entering assorted clothing stores.

"What are you meeting Ms. Burke for?" Jasmine asked when they stopped to peer into a shoe-store window.

"I got Ms. Burke to tutor me with English Lit. I have to get through *Pride and Prejudice* with my sanity intact."

"I hear you. I'm getting my sister, Cynthia, to help me. She got an A in English Lit two years ago. She is so smart when it comes to that old English stuff. I absolutely hate Lit class. Mrs. Pain-in-my-butt is always on my case and comparing me to Cynthia, so I decided to give her exactly what she wants. Cynthia and I made a deal: She does all my Lit homework and I do her computer tech stuff. It's perfect. It pays to have an older sister sometimes. Although most of the time she really gets on my nerves."

Jasmine continued ranting for the next fifteen minutes on the merits of having siblings. After ten minutes, she completely forgot her point and just started all over again. By that time, Kimberly had entered a small boutique and begun trying on sunglasses.

Later they stopped to look in the window of a small boutique where they'd often shopped. Several precisely posed mannequins dressed in coordinating outfits looked down at them from their lofty position. Chartreuse bell-bottoms with a tangerine cropped tee and fuchsia fake fur-trimmed jacket caught Jasmine's attention. "Yech!" she said. "Who in their right mind would wear that?" The girls looked at each other and simultaneously responded, "Mrs. Simmons!" Then they laughed heartily.

Moments later they were in the small fashion boutique trying on hats. Kimberly, donning an oversize floppy fedora, primped in the mirror. "Uncle Pierce and Ms. Burke went over to our new house last night."

Jasmine puffed and blew a bright orange ostrich feather sticking out of the pillbox hat. It sat cocked on her crown of tightly curled strawberry blond curls. She tilted it to the back for a more dramatic effect. "Really? How did you find out?"

"He told me," Kimberly said, putting the fedora back and choosing a brown bowler.

"He told you?"

"I asked him this morning if he'd talked to Ms. Burke about my grades, and he told me that he spoke to her last night."

"A date, finally," Jasmine said while tilting a bright red-and-green derby from side to side.

"No, I don't think it was a date, at least not yet. He asked me about the house and I told him to get another opinion. I suggested he ask Ms. Burke because she's got good taste."

"You are so sneaky."

Kimberly eyed herself sideways in the three-way mirror. The velvet top hat was much too large, so she crushed it down onto her head, letting a double puff of tight curls stick out from beneath. She giggled at her reflection. Jasmine came up behind her, wearing a suede Stetson with a turquoise studded band. Together they struck a pose, then giggled riotously.

"Come on," Kimberly said as each put the hats back on the forms. "I am so not feeling this today. Let's roll."

"Hey, check that out," Jasmine said. Kimberly turned. Jasmine pointed over a high stack of cashmere sweaters through the open door of the mall boutique. Kimberly looked in the direction of Jasmine's finger. Her mouth dropped open as Jasmine nudged closer to her ear. She placed the fashionable top hat back on the display post.

"Isn't that Jamal Scott over there? He is so hot. I didn't know he shopped around here. He is so fine. I'm so serious, if I wasn't with Jason I'd seriously check him out. I thought you had decided to hook up with him," she exclaimed loudly. Then she hushed to a whisper, "you really should get with him. I know for a fact that he's been peeping you. Besides, he's so your style anyway. He's an athlete with a serious brain. He's got something like a four-point-one million zillion grade point average. And"—she nudged even closer—"I heard that he's got a good chance at early admission to Banneker, too. So you two are, like, perfect for each other."

"Nah." Kimberly turned away from the hats to flip through the stack of sweaters lying on a display table. "He'd never talk to somebody like me. He rocks and he's got half the female population of Wells Academy after him."

"So?"

"So, look at me. The only thing I have going is that my father was a football player and my uncle owns a software company."

Jasmine covered her ears with her hands. "I'm not even trying to hear this. You know you could have any guy at school you wanted." She dropped her hands and grabbed a sweater from the pile. "Oh," she cooed lovingly, "I love this color. I'm so getting this one. Wait, look at that one."

Kimberly picked up the sweater and held it up in front of her. Jasmine grinned wildly and nodded an exuberant yes. Together they moved to the three-sided mirror to continue their assessment, each grabbing an armful of cashmere. Kimberly watched as Jamal went into a men's store. She smiled. He was definitely a cutie.

Four hours later, Kimberly dropped two large shopping bags on the floor, then plopped onto her bed. She grabbed the remote and turned on the TV, CD, and computer. She picked up the telephone and called Jasmine to discuss their shopping excursion.

"I gotta go," Kimberly said after a long discussion on who was cuter, Jason or Jamal. "I've got to get to the library to meet Ms. Burke."

"That's right," Jasmine remembered. "It's a shame

that Ms. Burke can't just meet you up at your place. If your uncle was there, maybe they could kick it."

Kimberly smiled with devious interest. As usual, Jasmine had come up with a brilliant idea without realizing it. "All right, girl, I'll check you later. Don't forget about the game tonight.

"Bye." Jasmine said before ending the conversation.

Barely a second passed before Kimberly's mind whizzed into action with detailed planning. It wouldn't be too difficult to get Ms. Burke up to the apartment, she reasoned. The hardest part would be to get her uncle Pierce home early. A slow smile of affirmed brilliance graced her young innocent face as she picked up the phone and began dialing.

It was five o'clock and she was right on time. Carrying a heavy backpack, Kimberly hurried up the many marble steps of the Lee Park Public Library. The automated door opened wide, allowing her to breeze right in. As soon as she walked past the central information desk, she spotted Patricia sitting alone at a table with several books piled in front of her.

"Hi, Ms. Burke," Kimberly said, heaving the backpack into the nearest available chair.

"Hello, Kimberly." Patricia smiled at the sweet face. "Take a seat and we'll get started."

Kimberly sat down and pulled several pieces of notebook paper from her backpack. She pulled out a pen and sharpened pencil and began writing the title, *Pride and Prejudice*.

Patricia opened the book and they began. First she outlined Jane Austen's background, her personal challenges, and the basic influences of her life from childhood through to womanhood. She gave a brief synopsis of the story, then reviewed the list of characters, their motivations, and their influences, complete with a character map of their interrelations.

Then, taking on the first five chapters, they discussed the complexities of life in rural England in the early 1800s with particular emphasis on the separation of classes resulting from economic status. The focus shifted dramatically when similarities to Wells Academy were addressed.

"So, in other words, Elizabeth Bennet and Darcy were doomed because of their class difference," Kimberly stated after writing her final notes.

"No, not necessarily. Although economics were the main reason for class differences in that era, there were many other ramifications involved. It's true, marriage outside of one's class wasn't as prevalent in a civilized society. Most stayed and wed within their own class structure. Those who ventured beyond their class were met with alienation and animosity."

"So, in other words, the rich stayed rich and the poor stayed poor."

"There were exceptions, which is what Jane Austen tells us in the story. Both Elizabeth and Mr. Darcy learned to alter their perspective on life, class, and each other. Subsequently, they allowed their feelings for each other, and not their class differences, to dictate their future. In the end love had more to do with their marriage, not class structure. Unfortunately, differences and prejudices will always be prevalent in some form in human nature."

Kimberly nodded her head in understanding. "So, it's sort of like Wells Academy."

"How so?" Patricia asked with interest.

"You know, the Richies versus the Poories. The rich kids don't associate with the poorer kids on scholarship, so everybody stays separate. There really are two different class structures and two different schools." Patricia remained silent. "Was it like that when you went to Wells?"

"Pretty much. But there were exceptions, as there still are today."

"What exceptions?"

"I went to Wells on scholarship, which technically made me a Poorie. My best friend Juliet's family is quite wealthy, so that made her a Richie. We still became very good friends and still are to this day. So, it's up to each individual to see pride and prejudice for what it really is."

"You were a Poorie?" Kimberly asked.

"I went to Wells on scholarship, if that's what you mean."

"My dad and my uncle Pierce were both Richies. Did you know them when you were at Wells?"

"They were more my older brother's contemporaries."

"But you did know them?"

"No, not really. They were both out of my league, so to speak. And, as you stated, Richies and Poories did not associate with each other."

"But all that stuff changes when you get older, right?"

"Sometimes yes, and sometimes no. Most times it changes because you realize that we're all pretty much the same and you let go of the pride and prejudice. Unfortunately, some people never do let go."

"Wow, so, like, things in 1813 didn't change all that much, did they?"

"I'd like to think that they did," Patricia stated then steered the conversation to form comparisons between the two eras. Kimberly wrote fervently as they talked about the similarities and differences. They cited familiar patterns and modern-day examples.

In total, their session lasted an hour and a half, but seemed to fly by in Kimberly's eyes. She was surprised how much she enjoyed their discussions. None of her other teachers were as honest and open as Patricia. "You should be a teacher," Kimberly said as she gathered her notebook and papers together.

"I am a teacher."

"No, I mean you should be a teacher instead of being a counselor. You're good at being a counselor, but you're really great at explaining things just like a real teacher."

"Thank you, Kimberly, maybe one day I'll go back to teaching English Literature again. But for right now, I enjoy my job as a counselor."

"Rumor has it that you're leaving Wells."

"Really, and when does rumor have me doing this?" Patricia asked while putting on her jacket and gathering her briefcase and purse from the empty chair beside her.

"Are you?"

"It's a possibility."

"Why?" Kimberly asked as she heaved her weighted backpack onto her shoulder.

"There are different stages in everyone's life. At one time I was a student, then I was teacher, now I'm a counselor."

"What stage are you in now? What are you gonna be next?"

"A doctor of child psychology."

"So, it's true, you are leaving?"

"Eventually," she answered without commitment.

Kimberly remained silent until they passed through the automatic sliding doors. As soon as they stepped out into the warm November breeze, she continued. "You said you could cook, right?"

"Yes." They walked to Patricia's car. She unlocked the doors and they got inside.

"Can you make spaghetti and meatballs?"

"Yes."

"Can you teach me?"

"Sure."

"Right now?" Kimberly asked with a pleading tone in her voice.

"Right now?" Patricia repeated. Kimberly nodded enthusiastically. "I'll tell you what. I'll drive you home and we'll stop and pick up a sandwich or something on the way home."

Kimberly looked out of the car window as Patricia pulled into traffic. "I hate eating alone," she said sadly.

"We'll get a sandwich for your uncle as well."

"He's not home."

"Well, then we'll save it for later."

"Can't, he's away."

A suit on a Saturday afternoon would seem overly contrived for the average man, but for Pierce, it was the norm. Whenever he intended to step foot in his office, he dressed professionally. And since he came into the office seven days a week, it wasn't unusual to see him behind his desk, staring at the monitor, dressed in a suit and tie.

The telephone rang four times before he was annoyed enough to notice. Tech support staff for the security software were usually the only people in the building on a Saturday afternoon. So, when the office phone rang, it was picked up by the automated answering system and forwarded to tech support. But this time the automated system put the call through to his private line.

Pierce picked up the ringing menace. "Yes," he said grumpily through the receiver.

"Uncle Pierce?"

"Yes, Kimberly."

"I was wondering if you were going to come home early tonight."

"Why, is there something wrong?" He stopped typing and turned his full attention to the telephone call.

"No, not really," she said quietly, "I was just wondering

if you were coming home early, that's all. I know you've been working really hard the last few months, and I just thought you might need to take a break or something."

Pierce sat back in his chair and frowned at the unexpected and peculiar request. He eyed the pile of papers and days' worth of unopened mail lying untouched on his desk. "Sure." He looked at his watch. "I'll wrap things up and be home within the hour."

"Could you make it more like an hour and a half."

"Why an hour and a half? What are you up to Kimberly?"

"Nothing," she said innocently.

Pierce held back the suspicion in his voice as he turned, saved his file, and exited the system. "Okay, I'll see you in ninety minutes. Are you up for Chinese food?"

"Don't bother bringing anything in, I'll have dinner covered. See ya."

Patricia's eyes widened in dazzled delight. PH1, the Franklin penthouse apartment, was absolutely unbelievable. A showplace of perfect splendor, every fabulous inch was flawlessly designed for optimal comfort and beauty. With an eclectic mixture of postmodern and classic styling, with enough authentic African art to display just the right amount of ethnic pride.

Tranquil elegance greeted her at every corner as Kimberly took her through the downstairs and upstairs rooms. The four penthouse apartments were the only ones designed especially with two floors of living space. When they arrived back at the foyer, Kimberly showed Patricia her uncle's favorite room: his library.

"Here it is," she said proudly. "This is where he spends most of his time when he's not at the office."

Patricia felt as if she'd walked onto the set of a movie studio. Everywhere she looked was luscious leather trimmed with silver studded pins and deep rich mahogany. The decidedly masculine room offered no pretense as to its owner's personality. She could see how this would be his favorite room.

"Here are the books I told you about," Kimberly said as she stood by the built-in bookcases. She opened a glass cabinet and gently pulled a book from the lit case. "Uncle Pierce got it at some auction in New York."

Patricia, now standing by Kimberly's side, took the book and gently fingered the crisped perfect pages. She carefully opened the book and turned to the first few pages. A broad smile crept across her face. "You were right, it's a first edition." A giggle of awestruck giddiness bubbled to the surface. "I've never seen this particular novel as a first edition before." She gently closed the book and turned it over, examining the back cover and spine. "It's beautiful," she choked out, handing the book back to Kimberly.

"Uncle Pierce says it's priceless."

"It is," Patricia assured her.

She watched as Kimberly put the book back in its place and closed the cabinet. She looked around the room again. "This is a very nice room. I can see why it's your uncle's favorite."

Kimberly walked over to the sliding glass doors and pointed down. "Did you know that from right here we can see right into your apartment?"

Curious, Patricia moved to stand beside her. Kimberly was right. From this vantage point you could look right down into her apartment. Patricia had left her living-room light on and her briefcase on the sofa. She made a mental note to keep her vertical blinds closed after sunset.

"Let's get started cooking," she finally said, turning away from the view and crossing the library back to the foyer. She picked up two grocery bags and waited for Kimberly to lead the way with her bag. They walked down the foyer passage to the end of the hall. Passing the large dining room, Kimberly pushed through the swinging door to the kitchen.

Nothing surprised Patricia anymore when it came to the luxury of this apartment. The kitchen, of gourmet style, was more than suitably stocked with cooking essentials and necessities. It was spotless and more closely resembled a stylish magazine layout than a daily eating station.

"We never really cook in here," Kimberly said as she began pulling items from the grocery bag. "The only one who actually uses the kitchen is Mrs. Hopkins when she cooks dinner for us. I don't remember ever seeing Uncle Pierce cooking. When Mrs. Hopkins doesn't cook, we eat out or order in. My grandmother tried to cook one time"—Kimberly began laughing—"but she was worse than Uncle Pierce."

"How is your grandmother?" Patricia asked, remembering the woman well. She had a snobbish condescending attitude and rarely spoke except to remark on that with which she found fault. Some would call her demeanor reserved and aloof; Patricia called it plain old rude.

"You know my grandmother from Florida?" Kimberly asked with surprise.

"We met a very long time ago when I was even younger than you. I'm sure she doesn't even remember me. Very few people do."

"But you were at school with Ms. Bridges, Dad and Uncle Pierce, right?"

"For a short time. But I wasn't exactly memorable." Sufficiently ending the conversation, Patricia pointed Kimberly to the sink. Together they tied on aprons and washed their hands. "Let's get started. We'll make the bread first. Yeast, sugar . . ." She began gathering ingredients on the counter. Soon they were totally engrossed in punching dough down and watching it rise.

Eleven

Pierce was early. He'd promised ninety minutes. but couldn't stay away any longer after receiving that cryptic phone call from Kimberly. He opened the front door not sure of what to expect nor what he'd find. The foyer was dark. He placed his briefcase and a small white box down on the side table and removed his coat and suit jacket. He picked up the waiting mail and white box, grabbed his case, and headed to his library.

He had just taken a few steps when something drew his attention. He turned and noticed something lying on one of the hall chairs. He reached down and picked up a black suede hooded jacket. A delicate fragrance of paradise filled his nostrils. The scent was familiar, but he didn't immediately recognize it. He assumed that the jacket belonged to either Mrs. Hopkins or Jasmine, placed it back on the chair, and picked up the white box.

He went into his library and sat down behind the large mahogany desk. As he began opening the mail, his thoughts drifted to his evening with Patricia. Reflexively, he smiled. He always seemed to smile with thoughts of Patricia.

With curiosity, he paused to listen to the quiet of the empty apartment. It wasn't as quiet as it usually was. The distant sound of activity seized him.

It was the clamor of pots and pans, lively Christmas music, and joyous laughter that first drew his attention. He stood and moved back to the foyer. The soft glow that emanated from the kitchen piqued his interest. Mrs. Hopkins never worked on weekends, and Kimberly was as talented as he when it came to anything dealing with the kitchen.

The talking and laughter grew louder as he passed through the dining room. Slowly, he pushed through the swing doors and stood in the entranceway. Shock registered on his face as his slow, steady smile broadened.

The kitchen was a hotbed of excitement. Large pots wafting steam sat on the stove, a host of chopped vegetables paraded across the marble cutting board, and an oversize loaf of crusted Italian bread was half-cut on the counter. Patricia, her back to him, held a long-handled wooden spoon and stirred the larger pot on the stove. Kimberly, busy chopping something green, looked up and grinned with delight.

"Good evening, ladies," Pierce said, smiling while standing in the doorway, loosening the tie around his neck.

"Hi, Uncle Pierce," Kimberly chirped sweetly and hurried to his side.

Patricia turned, then went still, stunned by the sight of Pierce standing in the kitchen doorway. She looked from Pierce to Kimberly. "You told me that your uncle was away, Kimberly."

"He was," Kimberly said sweetly, nervously, "but now he's back, see?" She reached up impulsively and kissed her uncle's cheek. "Welcome home, Uncle Pierce, dinner's almost ready."

Pierce moved to the stove next to Patricia and peered into a large bubbling pot of red sauce.

"What is that heavenly smell?" he asked as he bent low to peer into the oven.

"It's bread," Kimberly chirped too loud and too excitedly. "Ms. Burke taught me how to make real bread in the oven. We used yeast and sugar and everything."

"She did, did she?" Pierce cracked the oven door and

inhaled deeply, smelling the rich sweet aroma of the second loaf of bread. Then he turned his attention to the first loaf cooling on the cutting board beside the stove.

"Yes, and now she's teaching me how to make spaghetti and meatballs. It was so gross at first, but then it got better and now, look," she sparked loudly. "I'm cooking. I'm actually making dinner for us."

Pierce smiled happily, then tore off a ration of bread and dipped it into the bubbling sauce. He quickly popped it into his mouth just before a drip of red splattered his white cotton shirt. "Hmm, this is delicious," he said.

Patricia turned to Kimberly. "I'm very disappointed with you, Kimberly. You lied to me. You told me your uncle was away."

"He was away, sort of." She looked down, somewhat ashamed, then continued, "But not exactly. I told you that I would probably eat dinner alone since Uncle Pierce would be away tonight. I meant that he would be working late, that's all," she said innocently.

"I see," Patricia said, not buying her embellishments, "so now that your uncle is here, I'll be leaving." Patricia shook her head and began untying the sauce-splattered apron from around her waist.

Pierce placed his hand on the small of her back to halt the apron's removal. "Stay, please. It looks like the two of you have made enough to feed a small army. You did all this work, you might as well stay and have dinner with us."

Patricia shook her head steadily. This was too close; he was too close. He reached down and picked up her hand. She looked into his dark eyes. She searched for her answer in the confusion of her heart. She wanted to say yes, but being this close to Pierce, she dared not. Her thoughts whirled in the quandary.

"Please," Pierce said. Still holding her hand, he raised it to his lips and kissed it tenderly. The smile in his eyes spoke to her heart. Patricia looked into the eyes of the man she'd been in love with since fifth grade. She knew this was a mistake, but she had to do it. She needed once and for all to confront her feelings so that hopefully they could finally be put to rest and she could move on.

Then she heard the answer slip from her lips before her mind processed her thoughts. "Yes," she said. Kimberly whooped, then immediately went back to chopping the green vegetables for the salad.

Pierce's smile was unmistakable. He volunteered to set the table in the dining room while Patricia and Kimberly finished the meal. He found a lace tablecloth and six crystal candlesticks in the side buffet table. He spread the cloth over the large table and placed the candlesticks in the center. He pulled out the matching lace napkins with rings and placed them in the three locations at one end of the dining-room table. He would sit at the head of the table with Patricia on his right and Kimberly on his left. Perfect.

After completing the plate and silverware arrangements, he stepped back to observe his handiwork. He was well satisfied with the job he'd done. He went back to his library and grabbed the small white box. Inside were tasty melt-in-your-mouth butter cookies with colorful sprinkles. He smiled as he placed them on a small tray. They were Kimberly's favorites.

By the time the table was set and ready for the meal, the meatballs had been added to the sauce and the pasta tumbled into the colander to drain. Pierce poked his head into the kitchen to announce that the table was set.

The heavenly aroma drew him to Patricia's side at the stove. Patricia had just added the freshly chopped oregano, basil, parsley, and a pinch of sugar to the pot. She discarded the sprigs of bay leaf and thyme, then ladled several spoonfuls into a waiting gravy bowl.

Pierce lowered his head near the brim of the large pot

and inhaled deeply. The smell was nirvana. He grabbed another slice of bread and was just about to dip it into the pot when Patricia blocked him with the ladle. "Wait until dinner," she said pleasantly.

Pierce frowned. "Just one little dip," he implored to her shaking head. She wouldn't relent, so he was forced to pop the bread into his mouth without the sauce.

"Look, Uncle Pierce," Kimberly said as she proudly displayed her multicolored salad. The counter behind her was a shambles of half-cut celery, radishes, and minced, squished tomatoes.

"Umm, that looks wonderful," he said as he walked over to pinch from her bowl.

She moved the salad away from him, blocking his hand as she had seen Patricia do moments earlier. "Wait until dinner," she instructed. Feeling completely outnumbered, Pierce satisfied himself with a radish chip he pilfered from off the countertop.

"All right, I get the picture. I'm going upstairs to change. I'll be down in ten minutes."

"Good idea," Kimberly said while moving the rest of the radish chips away from him.

The sweet smell of home cooking filled the entire apartment. It had been a long time since anyone, except Mrs. Hopkins, had cooked in the kitchen. Upstairs, Pierce quickly changed into a pair of jeans and freshly pressed denim shirt. He took one last look in the full-length mirror in his walk-in closet. He rolled up the sleeves casually and added a brown leather belt and brown loafers.

By the time Pierce came back downstairs, Patricia and Kimberly had completed his table. Kimberly added a small bouquet of freshly cut flowers and Patricia lit a match to the dripless candles.

"Wow," Pierce mouthed after walking into the dining room. The soft glow of candlelight, the smooth jazzy rhythms, and the heavenly aroma nearly lifted and carried him to his seat.

Patricia looked up past the flame at Pierce. A flush of heat gripped her as he swaggered into the room looking dangerously handsome. "Yeah, wow," she muttered. *Get a hold of yourself, girl,* she warned herself silently. He smiled, and she nearly melted.

They worked in unison to carry the food from the kitchen and place it on the dining-room table. Kimberly brought out the salad. Patricia followed close behind with the basket of warmed bread and bowl of red sauce. Pierce came last, carrying the large wide dish of spaghetti and meatballs.

"Shall we, ladies?" Pierce announced as he pulled a chair back for Patricia, then repeated the act for Kimberly. "Everything looks simply wonderful and smells heavenly," he admitted. Both Patricia and Kimberly smiled at the generous compliment.

They sat and ate while enjoying the cheerful chatter of Kimberly relaying the humorous antics of her and Jasmine's shopping adventure that morning.

"Are you going to the Annual Christmas Ball?" Pierce asked Patricia as nonchalantly as possible.

"Yes, I am. As one of the faculty sponsors, I have to be there."

"I see."

"Do you already have your dress?" Kimberly asked.

"No. Not yet. I think I have plenty of time for that."

"Jasmine and I tried on, like, twenty different dresses this morning. I didn't like any of them. Can I have something made?" she asked her uncle.

"We'll see," Pierce answered.

"Did you know Ms. Burke went to Wells Academy at the same time you and Dad did, Uncle Pierce? You probably had some of the same classes."

Patricia cringed. She did not want this conversation.

"No, we didn't. I wasn't exactly in the same grade level, Kimberly." Patricia interrupted her with the correction, hoping to either end or avert the conversation's present direction. The last thing she needed was for Pierce to be reminded of being in school with her, and to remember the pathetic geek she'd been.

The vision of an underweight, lanky-armed nerd wearing glasses and continuously biting her nails in worn-out, out-of-style clothes and unfashionable shoes was the last thing she wanted to be reminded of. In essence, she was a drooling mass of pathetic hormones.

She shook her head sadly. If Pierce had the slightest inkling of her feelings for him years ago, she would have shriveled up and died from embarrassment.

"Well, your brother was in the same grade, right?" Kimberly asked.

Pierce looked over to Patricia with added interest. His smile was too seductive. "Really? Maybe I know him. What year was he there? What's his name?"

The telephone rang just as Patricia was about to answer. Kimberly instantly jumped to her feet, nearly knocking the chair over in the process. "I'll get it," she bellowed and ran to the kitchen to answer the phone, leaving Pierce and Patricia alone.

Pierce looked at her, patiently waiting for an answer to his question.

Patricia seized the opportunity to change the subject. "Kimberly did very well this afternoon. I think she's got a better handle on the novel."

"What is she studying?"

Patricia sighed with relief. *Pride and Prejudice* by Jane Austen."

Pierce shrugged in distraction. "I never could get into all that class structure stuff. I find it hard to believe any of that could have happened."

"I gather there are no class differences at PEF Software, Inc.?"

"Of course not," he stated righteously.

She smiled at the absurdity of the indignant response. "So everyone is the same at PEF Software?"

"Yes. There are obviously pay differences due to educational background and level of expertise." She smiled in silent dismissal. "You don't believe me, do you?"

"I didn't say that."

"Your eyes did."

She opened her mouth to rebut, but instead decided to take a short trip down memory lane. "Kimberly brought up an interesting comparison this afternoon." Pierce placed his fork on the rim of his plate and gave her his undivided attention. "She compared Wells Academy to the class structure of the nineteenth century."

"And?" he prompted.

"And she made a very astute point."

"And the point was?"

"You went to Wells. Surely you remember the Richies and the Poories."

A blank stare shadowed his face. For an instant Patricia was sure he'd forgotten all about the petty ritual of separation. Then a glimmer of familiarity sparked in his eye. He smiled in recognition. "Oh, yeah, I remember that." He almost smirked.

"Class structure," she said, finishing his statement.

"No. It wasn't class structure. It was"—he stopped, paused, and searched for the appropriate word— "a game. It was all in fun."

"Perceived as fun from only one direction can be seen as hurtful and mean from another direction."

"I'm going to see the Wizards tonight." Kimberly sprang from the kitchen with joyous song. "Jasmine's father has ten tickets to the home game tonight and Jasmine asked if I could go. Can I go Uncle Pierce? Please."

"Sure, enjoy," Pierce said, his gaze still focused on Patricia. Her intense response had proved more insightful than she'd intended. There was obviously more to Patricia than what met the eye.

Kimberly sat down and continued eating hurriedly. She immediately noticed the tension swirling around her. "Is everything okay?" she asked.

"Just fine," Patricia said. "Your uncle and I were just discussing class systems."

Kimberly smiled, "Oh, you mean *Pride and Prejudice*. That is such a cool book once you get through all that old English-talking part. It's really kind of romantic how Elizabeth and Mr. Darcy ignored what people said and just did their own thing and fell in love. That was way cool."

Pierce looked at Kimberly in amazement. "All that from just one afternoon?" he questioned. He looked at Patricia. "You must be some kind of miracle worker."

"Ms. Burke is so good. I wish all our teachers explained stuff like that. It was so easy to understand after we compared it to nowadays."

"Do you think there are class differences today, Kimberly?" Pierce asked.

Kimberly took a huge bite of crusty bread. "Definitely."

"Not with your mouth full, Kimberly."

She swallowed, then sipped from her water glass. "Sorry. Definitely. Wells Academy is a great example of that."

"I thought you liked Wells," Pierce commented.

"I do. I don't have to like everything about it though, right?"

Pierce took a bite of bread and opened his mouth to answer. "Not with your mouth full," Patricia leveled at Pierce. Kimberly broke into laughter. Patricia smiled and

Pierce nodded, chuckling to himself as he chewed the bread.

The phone rang once then stopped. "That's Jasmine," Kimberly announced, jumping from her seat again. "One ring means she's just pulling up to the security booth." Kimberly stood and rounded the table to Pierce. "I already have my overnight bag packed." She kissed his cheek, then kissed Patricia's and darted from the room. "Thanks, bye," she called out as she disappeared down the hall and out the front door in a blaze of farewells.

Pierce and Patricia looked at each other, then laughed until an uneasy feeling of closeness hung in the room. All of the sudden, they were very aware that they were together, alone in his apartment. She was the first to break the awkward silence.

She stood. "I'll clean up the kitchen before I go." She began gathering plates. Pierce followed her, gathering the spaghetti and salad bowls. Within half an hour, the dining-room table was cleared and the kitchen had undergone a drastic renovation. The larger pots were clean and placed back on the hanging hooks above the center island. The sink was cleared of all remnants of cooking and the refrigerator was packed with leftover spaghetti, meatballs, and sauce.

"Would you like a glass of wine?" Pierce asked from across the room.

"No, thank you. I have to go now." Patricia turned the dial, selected a setting, then turned on the dishwasher. With a hushed hum of efficiency it began its wash cycle. Patricia stood at the sink, procrastinating her next move. She didn't want to leave, but knew she couldn't stay.

"Do you really have to go?" His voice was closer. She nodded silently, afraid that the tremors in her voice would betray her.

Pierce came up behind her. "Thank you for dinner. It was wonderful."

"You're welcome," she said, turning to meet the stark intensity of his dark eyes. Her words hung in the air like stars suspended in the heavens. She looked away and pulled at the knotted apron around her waist. The knot tightened in her nervousness.

"Let me," Pierce offered, seeing her struggle with the delicate ribbon of fabric.

"I have it," she insisted, backing away from temptation.

"You just can't help it?"

"Help what?" she asked, breathless.

"Being perfect."

She smiled and blushed. "I'm far from perfect."

"Take my word for it: You . . . are . . . perfect." He moved even closer, stilling her hands behind her back. "Let me," he repeated in a whisper with enough earnest pleading to suggest a single meaning. She knew what that meaning was, and allowed his assistance. The scant space between their bodies vanished like a naughty little secret in the light of day. With firm steady hands he untied the ribbon, then let the apron fall to her feet. Slowly he knelt down to retrieve it, letting his hands find refuge as they slid down the sides of her legs.

Patricia quivered as a sudden rush of excitement took hold when she watched him descend before her. A small glimmer of heaven opened up when she touched the top of his head and ran her fingers through the soft waves of delicate curls. It felt good to freely touch the man she'd been yearning for most of her life.

He responded by pressing his face to the flat of her stomach and winding his arms around her waist. The snug sensation of being wrapped in the strength of his desire was intoxicating beyond words. The intensity of the simple action made her reel with a dizziness that was stilled only when she steadied herself against the counter behind her.

Slowly he stood, the unspoken question answered with

a kiss worth her very soul. In a feverish reply, a tangle of arms and hands touching, teasing, caressing sent a shiver of pending pleasure through the center of her being.

The sweet insanity of love had intoxicated her with its promise of enduring passion. As if in accord, their mouths came together repeatedly in an explosion of heated desire. He was the reason she breathed and the reason she existed.

Then, without warning, he stopped and took her face gently in his hands. He stroked the smooth line of her jaw and ran his finger around her large hoop earrings. He didn't speak, he just stood and stared, asking, begging, pleading to please her. He chastely kissed her forehead, then stepped back in strained restraint. He had opened the door, but left it for her to walk through and meet him on the other side.

The moment she saw the earnestness in his eyes, she knew she would surrender everything to him. Abandoning all she believed to be right and just seemed a small price to pay to call Pierce Franklin hers finally, even for this one single moment in time.

The final twinge of logic vanished as she reached out to him. She grasped the collar of his shirt and brought his lips to hers. There she savored the richness of long-awaited desire. The tender kiss answered his plea with a definitive yes.

A flood of hot passion scorched a path down her body like molten lava down the side of an erupting volcano. With each blistering inch she arched closer and closer to the moment for which she'd long waited. Her legs weakened just as he wrapped his arms around her and lifted her close to his body. She cleaved to him for her very existence.

The thunderous sound of her heart beat louder than a dozen cannons as it throbbed against her heaving breasts. He pressed himself against her. Their eyes connected as if across the decades of time.

"You are so beautiful," he said in a half moan through a thick fog of passion.

With all deliberate purpose she reached out to him, and without a second's hesitation, timidly fingered and undid the buttons of his shirt. The shyness she once felt seemed to seep away with each button. He watched with admiration as if it had never been done in the history of the world. Once his shirt lay open before her, she ran her hands across his chest, then buried her faced against him, devouring all of him.

Slowly he eased the silken sweater from her pants and let it fall free about her waist. His hands slipped beneath the softened cashmere fabric and found the mounds of delight covered by the laced barrier of her bra. Patricia's head rolled back with the thrill of his discovery as her deep throaty moan urged him further.

He reached down and took her hands to kiss.

The dizzying feel of movement seeped continuously through her consciousness as the rhythm of their walking from the kitchen was realized. They passed through the darkened hall to the dimly lit foyer. He turned to the staircase but stopped when her hand slipped from his. She didn't follow.

A furrow of disappointment creased his brow when he turned to her. The soft textured sparks of her brown eyes registered nothing. He stepped down to stand in front of her. She looked up at him, then to the gently flickering light coming from the library. "There," she said decisively, then smiled her reassurance.

He smiled seductively, then took her hand again and led her to his library, his domain, his sanctuary. The subdued lighting enhanced the romantic glow of the gas-burning logs in the fireplace, making the room instantly grow warm with heightened awareness.

Together they moved to the center of the room and
stopped. He turned to her and smiled. She reached for
him. The ineptness of her trembling fingers eased his
shirt apart until it fluttered on his broad shoulders then,
as if animated in slow motion, drifted down to the plush
carpet. Exposed and bare, he reached out to her, running his hands over her soft fabric covering. He lifted
the cloud of cashmere, exposing the orbs of perfection.
His hooded eyes darkened further as his mouth dried
with anticipation.

His knowing hands came to the peaked mounds and
he circled the tips with his palms to maddening stimu-
lation. In a spontaneous reflex, Patricia arched her back
with a benevolent offering to ecstasy.

This slow dizzying dance commenced as they walked
to the large chaise longue. He knelt before her as a
knight before his queen. Then, with deliberate gentle-
ness, he removed her belt, unzipped her pants, and
allowed them to drop, puddled at her feet. With a deep
adoring sigh, he looked up at her. Perfection.

There she stood in awesome spender, clothed in the
scantiest of garments against the dim glow of a fantasy
realized. He stared, memorizing every inch, every plane,
every curve of the body he now knelt to worship.

She lowered her eyes to him, feeling the intense
sparks as they connected with his. The swell of anticipation moved him to grasp her waist and ease her down
onto the chaise. Reclining on the comfort of pillow-
plush velvet, she lay waiting as he removed his pants.

With agility he moved into her waiting embrace. She
sighed and moistened her dry lips, eager to complete
the moment of their joining. But it was not to be. A patient lover could only imagine the sweet agony of his
stimulating care. He drove her to writhe in ardent need.
Teasing, tantalizing, and tempting, he played her body
until every inch was fine-tuned and ready for the cli-

mactic symphony. He reached into the pocket of his discarded pants and pulled a small foil packet. He quickly opened it and protected them.

The instant he joined her, she exploded, bright lights of release tensing her body to surrender. Yielding to his mastery, she wrapped her legs around his waist to brace against the multiple climaxes coursing through her body. She trembled as he dove again, deeper and deeper, repeating the core rhythm of creation. Blinding heat erupted inside as the friction intensified, until once again she soared and crested in a wave of passion.

Deeper and deeper he plunged, filling then emptying her with each stroke, until she ascended yet again. Then together they reaching the highest culmination of life, surrendering to the point of ecstasy.

The flurry of united body movements slowly melted into the velvet cushion beneath them. As their heaving breaths mingled and escaped in ragged retreat, they lay in each other's arms, spent by the force of their mutual attraction. The fall was just as sweet as the climb.

Tiny gentle kisses rained down on her face, eyes, temples, cheeks, then lips. She held the solid tightness of muscles as they spanned, strained, and tensed across his back. The power at his fingertips was frightening. At this moment she would have died for him. Patricia closed her eyes, knowing that the rapture of the past moments had only increased her feelings for Pierce.

What words do you say when no words are possible? Nothing could adequately expressed the height of passion she'd just experienced. Patricia lay back in the cradling embrace of Pierce's strong arms. For her, the moment was awkward as they lay bare to the world beneath the starry night. She, in no uncertain terms, knew that she still loved him now more than ever.

Silence resonated throughout the room, throughout the apartment and, as far as she was concerned, throughout the world. Her heart beat a rhythm un-known to her. It was his rhythm. The rhythm of Pierce. Twenty years ago, she'd never dared to imagine she would ever find herself in Pierce's arms like this.

His face shifted down to her and, with one last passionate kiss, he rolled to his side, taking her with him. She tensed against his perfect form. "Are you okay?" he asked. She nodded her answer, for fear her voice could not be controlled. He shifted again, bringing her even closer. She looked out into the darkness of the night. "Are you sure you're okay?" he asked again. She nodded, still looking away. "Come back," he whispered into her ear.

She turned to him, confused by the request. "I'm here."

"You left. Where'd you go?"

She was touched by his intuitiveness. "I'm here now."

She tensed at the sudden chill in the air. Pierce began stroking the length of her arm. "Are you cold?" he asked, as if their lying there naked were the most natural thing in the world.

"A little," she answered, bristling with a sudden host of goosebumps.

He stood, leaving the warmth of her body. A moment later he returned with a heavenly soft blanket of midnight blue. He draped it over her reclining body, then slid beneath to join her. He pulled her body back against his and wrapped his arms around her, tucking his head in the cradle of her neck.

He maneuvered his hand until it was free of the blanket. Using the remote, he dimmed the flame in the fireplace to an ember's smoldering glow. The room immediately darkened, giving way to the clear full moon shining through the sliding-glass doors.

"It's so beautiful," she said as they both looked out at the huge lunar ball suspended in the night sky.

"It's the harvest moon," Pierce said as he gently massaged her neck and shoulders. He traced his finger along her vertebrae, then down and around her shoulder. "It occurs only nearest the autumnal equinox."

"The autumnal equinox was two months ago," she informed him in her teacherly tone. "I believe it was the third week in September."

"Are you sure?" He rose up to look down onto her profile.

"Positive."

"Serves me right for trying to impress a teacher."

She smiled and snickered, releasing a bit of the tension building across her shoulders. "Ah, now that's much better," he said as he continued to gently rub her shoulders. "I want you to know that this wasn't just a quickie for me," he said. She froze, then suddenly sat up, held the blanket up to her chest, and moved away from him as she looked around for her discarded garments. He lay there, reclined, watching her, still reeling from the haze of desire that swirled around them. "What's wrong?" he asked.

"Nothing," she lied with a weak smile. "Where's the . . ." She began looking around for the bathroom. He pointed to a closed panel-covered door at the far end of the room. She nodded, gathered the blanket and her clothes, then disappeared through the door.

She emerged from the bathroom a few minutes later completely dressed except for her sweater. To her surprise, Pierce stood by the sliding-glass door still completely naked. She blushed and lowered her head in shyness. "It's getting late. I have to get home."

He walked over to her, moving with the confidence that the perfection of his physique required. She marveled, unable to tear her eyes from him. "Stay," he urged gently with his hand placed on the small of her back. Then he gently turned her around to face him. She opened her mouth to reply, but nothing came out. "I re-

ally enjoyed tonight," he added. "I really enjoyed being
with you."

She released a heavy sigh. "I enjoy being with you, too.
But"—she sighed again, realizing there was nothing she
could say—"I have to go." She turned and walked down
the hall toward the kitchen.

She found her sweater lying on the spotless marble
countertop. She picked it up and quickly pulled it over
her head and shoulders. She looked around at the im-
maculate surroundings. Everything was exactly as she'd
found it when she and Kimberly had first walked in with
three bags of groceries hours ago.

The dark hall and foyer afforded her a second to
gather her frayed emotions before she had to face Pierce
again. She looked down at the shaft of muted light coming from the library. She knew she had to offer some
excuse for her peculiar behavior. But how does one say,
I love you. I've loved you since I was twelve years old? The coward in her wanted to run and hide.

She peered into the darkened library with her jacket
and purse secured over her arm. The room was empty,
so the coward in her left.

Twelve

Kimberly sat in class half listening to the school's early morning news report. They were talking about the Annual Christmas Ball, as usual. She raised her eyes to the ceiling in a ho-hum attitude. That's all everybody ever talked about anymore. *What are you wearing? Who are you taking?* It was the pinnacle of the Wells holiday season. It was when the Richies got to strut their stuff and the Poories stayed home. Jamal immediately came to mind. She wondered if he would be attending.

After the general announcements, Mrs. Simmons cleared her throat and began her usual speech on respecting others. "With the holiday season fast approaching, it's very important, now more than ever, to remember those less fortunate . . . blah, blah, blah, blah."

Kimberly immediately zoned out as she twirled her gel pen, then began drawing little circles on her morning algebra assignment. Something had happened and nobody was talking. Her uncle was jumpy and restless, and Ms. Burke had completely disappeared from sight.

She'd even stopped by her office before first period, only to find the door closed and the lights off. She'd knocked anyway but had been told that Ms. Burke had an early appointment outside of the school and was running late. *Running late,* Kimberly thought to herself, *that didn't even sound right.* It probably had something to do with her leaving Wells.

Absently he fingered the circular object in his hand as he watched Patricia get out of her car, gather her briefcase, and hurry to the main building. He sat there, in the warmth of his car, staring at her like a hunter with a lowly deer in his line of fire. He had no idea what had come over him recently. He'd been all but stalking her in the past couple of weeks.

He'd watched as she and the desk jockey toured his new home. He'd watched as they ducked into the tiny little café, and he watched as she shopped with his niece in the grocery store.

He turned off the car's engine and got out of his car. He began walking to the building, then realized what he was still holding in his hand. He went back to the car, opened the large trunk, and tossed the autographed baseball inside.

Patricia hurried to her office. She was late. She hated mornings when absolutely everything went wrong. But it served her right for hiding out at Juliet's place all weekend. She was just too much of a coward to face Pierce.

"Good morning," she called out to the general populace as she quickly disappeared into her office. She was expecting a prospective student any minute, and she needed to gather the materials for her presentation and calm her frayed nerves.

Pierce was still on her mind. Every time she paused for a second he appeared, looking as he had when she'd stepped out of the bathroom: bold and beautiful. A slow easy smile would pull at her lips and her mind would immediately slip into the memories of the evening they'd spent in his library.

Stop it, she chided herself as she stared at the blank computer screen. She leaned her elbow on the desk and cupped her head in her hand. After Saturday night, she was never going to get him out of her mind, thanks to Juliet. . . .

"Damn," Juliet uttered slowly in amazement after Patricia relayed the events of her intimate evening with Pierce. "But in the library?" she repeated for the sixth time after another slow sip of champagne.

"Yes, Juliet," Patricia affirmed definitively, "in the library!"

"Damn, in the library, I'm too impressed." A seventh time.

"Would you please stop saying that?"

Juliet chuckled and looked at a nervous, fretful Patricia, then chuckled more. "Well, girl, all I have to say is, it's about time. You've been dancing around this thing since forever."

Patricia sipped her sparkling wine, then rolled her eyes as she eyed her friend. "Oh, you're a lot of help."

"Hey, don't bite the hand that feeds you. Remember I'm letting you hide out here at my place this weekend." Patricia rolled her eyes again as the giggling Juliet openly broke out into roaring hysterics. "I'm sorry," Juliet offered after three full minutes of side-splitting, tear-falling, hiccuping laughter. "But, you have to admit, this is pretty funny."

"I don't see anything funny about it." Patricia sipped again from her glass. "It was a momentary lapse in judgment caused by my overextended work schedule. I admit, it was a severe transgression on my part, but given my extended period of no interpersonal containment, it was bound to happen."

"Oh, please, girl, can't you just let me enjoy this moment without your instant psychoanalysis bullcrap?"

Patricia leveled a fierce expression of annoyance at Juliet. "You're loving this, aren't you?"

Juliet's blurted laughter was her answer. "For close to twenty
years," she'd choked out through fits of laughter, "you've been
pining after this man. Then, when you finally have him, you
run like a scared bunny rabbit with its tail on fire."

"It's not like that." Patricia pouted. "I just couldn't deal with
it, that's all."

"Deal with what?" Juliet asked.

Patricia took a deep sigh, looked down at her hand, and then
back up at her friend. "He told me that he enjoyed being with
me, and that I wasn't just a quick lay."

Juliet's brow rose with interest. "All right, so he's not very
good with pillow talk."

"I felt like a cheap hooker. It was like being in eighth grade all
over again."

"You were a cheap hooker in eighth grade?" Patricia looked
at her with total exasperation. "Sorry, you're right, that was too
easy. My bad." With much effort, Juliet expunged the perpetual
grin from her face. "All right, let's get serious now." She took a
sip of champagne and cleared her throat for emphasis. "You
make mind-blowing love with the man you've been in love with
for at least two decades, and instead of telling him how you feel
or at the very least talking to him, you chose to skip out and
come here. Is that pretty much how it went?"

"No," Patricia said indignantly, "it didn't happen like that.
Pierce and I were together, then I left," she said matter-of-factly.
Her oversimplified description prompted another raised brow
from Juliet.

Juliet downed the last of her drink. "So, in other words, you
ran out on him."

Patricia yielded. "Yes, all right, I ran. Satisfied?" Patricia followed suit and finished her drink as well.

"I still don't get it." Juliet got up and went into the kitchen.
She hollered to Patricia, "Why didn't you just talk to him?"
Patricia thought for a moment. Juliet had continued hollering
from the kitchen, "You're a professionally trained child psychologist with an IQ of 140. Do you realize that most people, even

in Mensa, would kill to have that number? You're the smartest, most even-tempered, intelligent woman I know, yet every time you're around Pierce, you melt into a bowl of"—she pulled the first word from her mind—*"grits." Juliet returned to the living room with another bottle of champagne.*

"Grits?" Patricia asked sarcastically.

Juliet unwrapped the foil paper and wiggled the cork free. "Whatever. Don't pull semantics on me. You know what I mean."

"As usual, you have so adeptly summed up my dilemma," she said sarcastically. Juliet swallowed her laughter as Patricia shook her head. "He's my weakness, always has been and probably always will be."

"Classic rookie mistake." Patricia sighed heavily. A pop sounded and they watched the cork fly across the room. "So, I want details, don't leave anything out." She nudged closer to Patricia as she refilled their glasses, emptying their second bottle. "Did Pierce just rip your bodice off and take you right there in front of Hemingway, Twain, and Grisham?"

"No," Patricia stated emphatically. She blushed, smiled, then blushed again. "The library was my idea."

Juliet sputtered out the champagne she'd just sipped. "I know I must be drunk now." She set her glass down and wiped the liquid from her sweatpants. "Did I just hear you say that last night's romp in the hay was your idea?"

Patricia shrugged noncommittally.

Juliet burst with laugher and high-fived Patricia as both giggled uncontrollably, spilling champagne all over Juliet's polished hardwood floors.

For the next fifteen minutes, Patricia prudently relayed her evening with Pierce. Uncharacteristically, Juliet sat silent, in awestruck wonder. When Patricia's tale was completed, both women sat dreamily in the silence of the moment.

"Tell me something," Juliet finally asked. "Do you want a future with Pierce?"

Patricia looked at Juliet. The question had taken her off

guard and managed to stump her. For years she'd dreamed of being with Pierce Franklin, but never in her wildest dreams had she imagined herself having a future with him. She was still holding onto that "Richies versus Poories" thing. All the psychology and therapy in the world hadn't changed her core belief. A part of her still felt that she just wasn't good enough for him. . . .

Patricia quickly cleared her thoughts and gathered her materials. It was going to be a long day if at nine o'-clock she couldn't stay focused for the mere fifteen minutes she'd been here. She pushed the print command on her keyboard to make additional copies for her next appointment. As she flipped through to sort the printed copies, she stopped and stared in astonishment. "What in the world?" The buzzer rang, alerting Patricia that her appointment had arrived. Deciding to get to the bottom of the printouts later, she opened her door and greeted the eager parents of a prospective student.

The supply closet had been ransacked.

Patricia stood in the doorway, stunned by the senseless vandalism. She looked around in dismay. The window stood open and a shelf of colored copy paper had been blown everywhere, then saturated by the early morning rain. Several obvious empty spaces testified to missing boxes and equipment. It looked as if someone had deliberately destroyed the small room.

Vincent looked up when Patricia came to the door. He watched as she placed her hand over her mouth and shook her head in despair. He stood in the center of the room speaking with Audrey and several members of his security team. He watched Patricia gather her arms around her chest. Without hesitation, he walked over to the open window. He stood for a moment looking outside, then focused his attention on the window frame. Using a clean white handkerchief, he rotated the lock and unhinged the window. It was already unlocked and open. He had found the point of entry.

Vincent nodded to one of the other security men. The guard instantly walked out of the room, then returned a few moments later carrying a small attaché case. He set the case on the cleared table and opened it up. Inside was every type of crime-fighting paraphernalia imaginable.

Vincent picked up a small tin of gray powder and a large soft bristle brush. He dipped the brush in the powder, then, in a twisting circular motion, he dusted the area on and around the window's sill. As if by magic, a number of finely detailed fingerprints appeared. He peeled the sticky backing from a small piece of cardboard. He placed the sticky film over the fingerprint, then sealed it over the cardboard. He performed the same action on each of the prints he'd dusted. Patricia, who'd been watching intently, tuned to leave. She'd seen enough. The damp colorful full-page confetti scattered all over the room was appalling.

Patricia sat in Audrey's office as she briefly apprised her of the morning's occurrences. "When was it discovered?"

"Mr. Wilson noticed the broken latch this morning. Apparently when the thief left, he didn't close the window tightly this time. It was open all weekend. And, with the cooler night and high winds, the room is just a mess." She turned to the window.

"What happens now?"

"Mr. Shields does his job." Audrey continued to stare out of her window. "The police are on the way. Apparently we have to make out a formal police report for insurance purposes. I never thought I'd say this, but"—she turned back to her desk—"I'm glad Mr. Shields is here."

"Thank you, I appreciate the compliment." Both

women turned around to see Vincent standing in the doorway. Audrey smiled with a new sense of appreciation while Patricia just turned her back.

Vincent stepped into the office and stood at the chair nearest Patricia. She stood to leave. "I'm sure you two have more to discuss, so I'll be in my office if you need me, Audrey," she said, directing her conversation specifically.

Before Vincent could open his mouth, she disappeared down the hall.

"Ms. Burke," Kimberly said as Patricia walked into her office.

"Good morning, Kimberly, what can I do for you?" She sat down behind her desk.

"I wanted to thank you again for coming over Saturday evening. I was hoping that maybe we could do it again sometime."

"I'm not sure that's a good idea."

"Why not?"

"Well, first of all, I'm going to be very busy in the next few weeks with the Annual Christmas Ball and second, it wouldn't be fair to the other students. And I certainly don't have the time to cook for everyone." She lowered her head sadly. "Do you understand?" she asked Kimberly.

Kimberly shrugged. "I guess I was just hoping that maybe you could come over and help me make Thanksgiving dinner."

"I'm really sorry, Kimberly, I already have plans on Thanksgiving. I already told you that."

"I know, I was thinking that maybe afterwards, you could come over."

"I probably won't be home until very late."

"So, could you come over then?"

"Kimberly, your uncle might have other plans for Thanksgiving."

"He doesn't," she spouted eagerly. Kimberly's hopeful expression nearly broke Patricia's resolve.

"I'll tell you what. I'll think about it."

"Really?" she said brightly.

"Get to your next class."

"Thanks, Ms. Burke."

As soon as Kimberly opened the door, she bumped into Vincent. Startled, shaken, Kimberly stepped to the side and continued to her next class.

"That was very touching," he said as he walked into the office.

"I'm very busy. How may I help you, Mr. Shields?"

"How about having dinner with me this evening?"

"As I said before, I'm very busy," she repeated. "And I'm sure you are, too." The telephone rang before he could answer. She picked it up. "Patricia Burke." Refusing to be dismissed that easily, Vincent sat down in a seat across from her.

"Pierce Franklin," came the voice from the other end.

She inhaled deeply, then exhaled a ragged nervous breath. "Hello."

"I gather by your coolness either you're angry about something, or that you're not alone."

"Yes, that's correct." She turned her chair slightly, angling it away from Vincent's piercing glare.

"When can we get together?" Pierce added.

She glanced at her calendar. "I'll have to get back to you about that. My schedule is a little tight at the moment."

"I really need to see you," he said quietly. She didn't say anything. "Please." His ardent plea touched her. She closed her eyes and turned the chair completely around, but still remained silent. "Are you still there?"

"Yes, I am. Will this be for any particular reason?"

"You walked out on me the other night, then disappeared from the face of the earth all weekend. I tried calling. I left messages."

"Yes, I know. I got the messages."

"Are we playing childish games now?"

"No, of course not." She sighed heavily.

"I think we need to talk, don't you?"

"I don't think that would be feasible at this time."

"Tonight then."

"That won't be possible."

"When then?"

"I'll need some time to get back to you on that."

"Tonight, Patricia," Pierce said with determined resolve. "I'll see you tonight. Good-bye."

The phone clicked in her ear. She waited a few seconds before hanging up. A sense of nervous euphoria shot through her like a hot torpedo through iced water. It was too soon. There was no way she could see him tonight. She spun her chair back around to face the desk.

"Bad news?" Vincent asked as he watched her slowly place the phone back into the cradle.

"No." She looked at her watch and stood, a professional courtesy cue for Vincent to stand and leave. He didn't move. She walked to the door and pulled it open. "If you don't mind, Mr. Shields, I have a lot of work to do."

Vincent stood and moved to the door. He took Patricia's hand as he passed. She pulled away. "Good-bye, Mr. Shields." He nodded curtly and walked out in a huff.

She couldn't be bothered with Vincent's hurt feelings. She had to figure out a way to get out of meeting with Pierce tonight.

Angrily, Vincent headed back to the security office. A deep scowl furrowed his forehead, adding to the darkening shadow of anger already creased across his face. He'd been handling Patricia with kid gloves, but all that was about to change. It was time for him to get serious.

If she didn't want him, then she wouldn't get Pierce Franklin, either.

He stormed into the small security room and slammed the door so hard he drew the attention of the two police officers and the three members of his school security team.

"Is that all?" the one police officer asked the security guard with suspicion. He looked at the three uniformed men. They all looked at one another and nodded.

"Yes, that's about it," the lead security guard answered, then looked and nodded agreeably at his partners for affirmation. The other guards continued to nod in agreement.

The police officer walked over to the numerous monitors set up against the side wall. He watched as the monitors switched constantly from students walking up and down the halls to the parking lot area to the library, cafeteria, and back to students changing classes. He fingered the video recorders, frowned, then looked over to his partner. "And nothing was picked up on any of these security cameras and nothing was taped from video monitors?"

"No."

"No?" asked the police officer standing by the door. He moved to the wall of monitors next to his partner. "All these monitors, cameras, and recorders and nothing was picked up on film Friday night."

"That's exactly right," the guard acknowledged.

"Why is that?" the officer addressed the two silent guards.

The lead guard spoke up. "All cameras are shut off Friday night, then reset on Saturday morning. It's standard procedure." He looked to the still fuming Vincent for confirmation. Vincent ignored everything and everyone.

The police officer standing by the monitors closed his small notepad, put it in his pocket, then turned and nodded to his partner. He pulled a card from his pocket and handed it to the lead security guard. "If you happen to remember anything else, give us a call at this number."

"Sure thing, officer," the second guard added eagerly.

Kimberly groaned as she inserted her key into the lock. The only good thing about this day was that it was finally over. "Hi, Mrs. Hopkins," she called out absently after closing and locking the door behind herself. "I'm home," she continued yelling. Following her usual routine, she peeled off her monogram sweater, dropped her book bag on the nearest chair, kicked off her shoes, and trudged into the kitchen. "Mrs. Hopkins," she yelled, then, startled, she stopped in midyell. "Mrs. Hopk— Uncle Pierce, what are you doing here?"

Pierce looked up from the laptop computer that was perched on the countertop beside a plate of chocolate chip cookies and a half-glass of cold milk. "I live here."

"No, I mean what are you doing home? It's too early for you to be here. Are you okay?" she asked, with her head now stuck in the refrigerator searching for a small snack before dinner. After a quick scan, she pulled out luncheon slices of ham, turkey, and cheese, three slices of twelve-grain bread, and jars of mustard and mayonnaise.

"I'm fine," he said as she began assembling her light afterschool snack. He watched with humor as she heaped meat, cheese, lettuce, and tomato slices on the bread in alternate intervals. "Why is it so unusual for me to take the afternoon off once in a while?"

"'Cause you never do," she said, quickly piling everything back into the refrigerator.

"Are you going to eat all that?"

"Sure." Then, without a moment's hesitation, she turned to the massive triple-decker sandwich, picked it up with great difficulty, and took an enormous bite.

"Where's Mrs. Hopkins?" she asked after a second, equally immense bite.

"I gave her the afternoon off."

After another huge bite of the massive sandwich, Kimberly dove back into the refrigerator, then paused and turned to look at the spotless stove. "Did she make dinner before she left?" she asked, frowning with real panicked concern.

Pierce, amused, was tempted to ask her how on earth she could possible even consider eating dinner after making the Dagwood of sandwiches. "No, I'm cooking dinner tonight."

Kimberly stopped rummaging through the refrigerator, stood up, peered over the top of the door, and looked at her uncle as if he'd just grown two heads. "You've never come home early and you've never made dinner before. Are you sure you're all right?"

"Well, things change." He took a bite of a half-eaten cookie and turned back to the computer screen to begin typing. "I'm doing a lot of things I've never done before." To his surprise, the statement was true. In the past few weeks he'd been doing a lot of things that were completely out of character for him. "How was school today?" he asked with his eyes still glued to the computer screen.

After a slow, deliberate scan of his serious expression, Kimberly shrugged, then reached in and grabbed the glass pitcher of orange juice and closed the refrigerator with her hip. She took a glass from the cabinet and filled it with juice. Pierce looked up at her, waiting for a verbal reply. "It was all right, I guess," she finally admitted.

"Did you see Patricia?" he asked. Kimberly tilted her head quizzically, then looked at her uncle. "Did you see Ms. Burke?" he asked again, rephrasing his question.

"Yeah, briefly, but she was busy all day."

"Have you seen Rupert lately?" he continued. Kimberly looked at Pierce comically. "Patricia's Rupert?"

"No, not since the day she moved in. But I did ask her to bring him when I invited her to come to Thanksgiving dinner with us." Kimberly picked up her glass and turned to leave the kitchen.

"What did she say? Is she coming?" he asked, then corrected himself before she disappeared down the hall. "Are they coming?"

"I don't know, she said she'd think about it," she yelled, already halfway up the stairs with her sandwich, glass of juice, book bag, and shoes.

Pierce sat on a stool at the center island and stared at the kitchen entryway. Gradually, he let his eyes drift around the large kitchen. Filled with every modern convenience, it was a gourmet cook's dream. Polished chrome and black lacquer appliances, black Italian marble countertops and black-and-gray speckled granite floor tiles set the tone for the sterile area. Pierce looked at his solitary reflection in the sleek glossy chrome of the refrigerator door.

This is where it had all begun. A slow smile spread across his face as the fantasized image of Patricia slowly appeared behind him. Dressed in scant lace garments that seductively revealed the popular store's secret, she beckoned to him. Pierce's smile broadened as the conjured vision walked closer. She reached out and touched him.

Pierce closed his hooded eyes, feeling the gentle weight of her hands roaming across his shoulders. He rolled his neck and opened his eyes to see her hands spread wide across his chest, then slip low to his waist. The vision looked up into the eyes of his reflection, then vanished.

Impulsive was a word that would never be used to describe him, but he hadn't been himself for some time now. Feeling slightly off balance had become the norm, and he didn't like it.

It was impulse that had led him to leave work early today and it was impulse that had led him to make love to Patricia that night.

Pierce lowered his head in frustration. Another day when absolutely nothing would be accomplished. He tossed his pen down, then pushed and held the delete button on the keyboard until everything he'd just written had disappeared. He wished there was a delete button for other mistakes.

Thirteen

For the past twenty minutes, Patricia had been sitting at the tiny neatly cluttered desk in the corner of her bedroom and organizing, shuffling, then rearranging the files she'd brought home. Bringing work home had always been a distraction; unfortunately, it didn't work this time. She closed the top file, removed her reading glasses, and buried her face in the palms of her hands.

A scurry of iridescent green sped across the papers, drawing her attention. "Not now, Rupert." She gently ran her finger along the bristle of his scales. He instantly darted to the floor, then disappeared through the bedroom door.

A mature person learned from her mistakes, but it seemed that she was doomed to repeat hers over and over. Patricia looked up at the clock. It was getting late, and she still hadn't heard from Pierce. Maybe he had changed his mind and decided not to come. A sliver of disappointed relief snaked through her as she stood and walked over to plop down on her bed.

She ran her hand over the soft ridges of the white chenille bedspread her mother had given her years ago. She laid back and looked up at the white pebbled ceiling while wrapped in the memories of her parents' bedroom.

"This bedspread," her mother had said, "belonged to my mother." Patricia, wide-eyed and amazed—as any child would be, having never known her grandmother—

had listened with particular interest. Her mother had neatly folded the spread and gently wrapped it in tissue, then tucked it into a waiting box. "This will be yours in a few years," she'd promised, "and you will cherish and love it as I have all my life." Her mother had reached down and cupped her tiny face. "No matter where I am, when you lay across this bedspread and look up at the ceiling, I will know that you're thinking about me and you will know that you are loved." She'd kissed her daughter's forehead, then sealed the box with purpose.

As soon as the doorbell rang, Patricia's heart slammed against her chest and her stomach dropped to the floor. She was an adolescent again and the most popular boy in school was standing just outside her front door. She dried her moist palms on the legs of her sweatpants, licked at her dry lips, then said a small prayer for much-needed strength.

As she walked from the bedroom to the living room, she quickly scanned the area for neatness—a usually senseless and redundant act, since she never displaced anything. Her eyes fell upon an anomaly that had been growing more common in the recent weeks. An empty teacup sat on the coffee table and her purse and coat were haphazardly tossed on the side chair. She grabbed her coat and quickly hung it in the closet with her purse as the bell rang a second time. She picked up the cup and hurried to the door.

"Coming," she called out with one last look around the room. Then, without losing her nerve, she opened the door.

Pierce stood there, not smiling. After vacillating for nearly two hours, he'd finally propelled himself to her front door.

"Hi," she said as nonchalantly as possible, but instead, the word came out husky and throaty, with seemingly sexual undertones. *God, he looks good,* she thought before uttering another prayer for strength.

He briefly looked down the length of her. The baggy sweatpants, oversize T-shirt, and woolen socks did little to reduce the swell already beginning to pull at his body. If her intention was to reduce his desire for her by nullifying her usual attractive appearance, she'd sorely miscalculated. "I see you've found your teacups," he said, still standing in the doorway.

"Yes," she said in a haze that was purely Pierce. "Come in," she finally added, after remembering her lapsed manners.

The barest smile faded as he strolled past her. She reveled in the manly scent of his cologne as it wafted around her. When she closed the door, she turned to find him standing in the center of her living room, looking back at her. She turned away, averting her eyes to the sofa. "Have a seat," she offered. He sat and waited for her.

"Can I get you anything? Tea, perhaps, or maybe coffee?" She'd learned her lesson from Juliet well.

"No, thank you," he said. She sat down on the ottoman across for him. "Why did you just leave like that, without a single word?" Patricia hadn't expected for him to delve right into the conversation, but he had.

She stood quickly and walked to the kitchen, cup in hand. He followed. "You're still running away, aren't you?" Her silence was his answer. She poured water into the kettle and placed it on the stove to heat. "Patricia, what is it? What's going on?" He pleaded for an explanation.

"I . . . ," she began, but was unable to continue. "I . . . ," she tried again.

He came to her and wrapped his arms around the curves of her yielding body. "There is something or someone, isn't there?" She looked up at him quizzically.

"Yes. No!" she corrected.

"Rupert?" he asked.

"What?"

"Kimberly told me about him."

"What about him?"

"You tell me."

She frowned, not understanding his line of questioning. Why would Rupert be a problem for them?

"What are you talking about, Pierce?" She wiggled from his embrace, went back into the living room, and looked down into the large glass terrarium. Rupert wasn't there. She continued looking around as Pierce walked back into the living room. She looked to the tall wall unit, then to the sparkling ficus tree by the balcony door, Rupert's usual haunts.

"What are you looking for?" he asked.

"Rupert," she said as she walked past him and entered her bedroom. He turned to follow. She looked around at all the places he liked to hide out. Pierce looked around also, his eyes following her path, not knowing for what he was searching. She walked by him, then eased around the corner through the bathroom door. Seconds later she emerged with a miniature version of the mutant lizard Godzilla tucked comfortably under her arm. She smiled at Pierce. "*This* is Rupert."

Pierce returned her smile with much relief. With a heavy sigh, he sat down on her bed as she slowly walked over to him. Rupert jerked several times in her arm as his tail whipped down her leg. Patricia gently caressed the many wrinkles beneath his neck to assure and calm him. "He's usually a little skittish around men."

Pierce, still staring in amazement at the sight of Rupert, raised his brow at her with interest. "What men?" he questioned. He reached out and cautiously touched the top of Rupert's head, then stroked the skin beneath his chin, noting and following exactly what Patricia had done.

"My brother, when he's in town."

"May I?" he asked, his arms open to receive Rupert.

She loosened her secure grip on Rupert and inched him toward Pierce. "Careful," she warned, "he scratches."

Pierce grasped Rupert just as Patricia instructed. Rupert wiggled uncontrollably and pulled at his sweater, leaving tiny pulled threads. Then, in an instant and flash of green, he leaped from Pierce's hold and scurried across the floor and out the door.

The surprise urgent departure caused Pierce to laugh openly. Patricia, used to Rupert's instant comings and goings, smiled, enjoying Pierce's laughter more than Rupert's antics.

"So, that was my rival," Pierce stated as he turned back to Patricia. She smiled to herself but remained silent. "At least I know what I'm up against."

"Rupert's a male. He can be very territorial. I wouldn't take him too lightly," she said jokingly.

"I'm a male." His tone softened. "And I'm very, very territorial." He reached out and pulled Patricia toward him. She tumbled willingly into his embrace, then into his welcomed kiss.

A minute, an hour, a day, a year—time had no meaning when she was in his arms. The decades of time faded as quickly as sand through an hourglass. At that moment, Pierce Franklin was all Patricia could fathom.

Her willful hands crept beneath the yarn of his sweater, exploring the man seated beside her. Her fingers forcibly dug into the flesh of his back. He was solid male, and her hands enjoyed the sensation of touching him.

An ardent whisper of hopeful thrills surged through her as a low gasp of anticipated pleasure rumbled in his throat. Slowly, gently, they melted back into the heaven of each other's arms. The ease of the reclining movement did little to disturb their mounting passion. The promise of recent memories sparked clearly as their bodies intertwined, fitting and refitting into positions as natural and wondrous as time itself.

The oversize T-shirt miraculously disappeared.

The knit sweater, pulled by Rupert's nails, vanished.

Patricia entwined her arms around Pierce's neck, holding on desperately, lest she awaken from this veiled dream. She inched closer to the source of her desire as the gentle pursuit of want awakened and demanded to be sated.

A burst of teasing, tempting, and promising kisses danced across her face. She ached and writhed in tormented need. With urgency she grasped his face, holding him to her wanton lips.

The kiss, wondrous in proportion, unparalleled in comparison, and superior in execution held her beating heart immobile and her life-sustaining breath stilled. Lasting an eternity's end, the kiss finally faded. Pierce looked down onto her fervid face. Inflamed by her voiceless petitions of longing, he favored her with boundless rapture.

He sought and found the cupped peaks beneath her revealing lace bra. She moaned with his renewed delight. The titillating sensation of his skillful hands drove her beyond the edge. Sparked by her urgency, he descended. He graced her neck with kisses, then her shoulders, then finally, he took her into his mouth.

Precious suction, the tantalizing drawing of his mouth and teasing of his tongue, caused her body to arch in offering. He kissed his way from peak to point.

The magnitude of their desire grew to thunderous proportions as desperate hands pulled and tugged awkwardly at inconvenient clothing. The low rumble of beating hearts quickly phased into the high shrill sound of desperation. With her mind awhirl, she didn't hear the call of alarm. The sound, growing louder, more adamant, finally drew her from the heavenly moment. To ascertain the meaning of the sound, she had to leave the comfortable world of Pierce's arms. She refused.

The sound grew louder until they pulled apart, sluggishly, weakly, like running through wet cement. Each fell to one side of the bed, still hazy from the lost moment.

"Kettle," she scarcely rasped out. "Teakettle." She stood, grappled to put her bra back into place, then dashed into the kitchen. Seeing the stream streaking from the small hole in the teakettle's spout, she hurried to silence the untimely noise. She picked up and moved the scalding water to the protected cooktop, then extinguished the flame, much like her own now-silenced burning.

She stood at the stove, savoring the last moments of lost intimacy. Pierce walked in. He stood behind her and tucked his chin into the crook of her neck as his arms encircled her bare waist. She could feel the still-hurried pace of his heartbeat beneath his sweaterless body.

"This is where I say something really clever," he announced, "but unfortunately, I have no idea what to say. So, for the sake of the moment, pretend I said something really profound." She nodded agreeably. He sighed, heaving as if gripped by inner turmoil. A moment of awkward silence passed slowly.

"And," she breathed out in lingered release, "I guess this is where I respond by saying something equally profound." She turned in his embrace. "So pretend I did that." He nodded and produced a smile so charmingly innocent that it made her heart soar. She shook her head in heedless surrender. "What are you doing to me, Pierce Franklin?"

He held her closely. "I was just about to ask the same question." He shook his head, bewildered. "We have an attraction, a very strong attraction. For us to fight it is senseless."

She twisted from his embrace and walked into the living room. "We have to. This can't keep happening. I can't go on like this," she declared.

He followed her. "What do you suggest?"

"I don't know, maybe"—she paused, disturbed by her thoughts—"I don't know?"

"Maybe what?"

She took a moment to gather her thoughts and reason out the turmoil of questions racing through her mind. "Maybe we should just stay away from each other. Physically, I mean."

Pierce took a step back. "Is that what you want?"

She waited for divine intervention. "No," she answered quietly.

"Then let's just enjoy this special time together for however long that might last." He tilted her chin upward to his waiting lips. He kissed her chastely. "There's something very special about you, Patricia. I like the feeling. I'm not ready to let go of that, not yet." Then, as a second thought, he added, "I don't think I'll ever be."

She closed her eyes to the sweetness of his words, letting the splinter of love pierce deeper into her heart.

Fourteen

"Just answer the question. You saw Kimberly Franklin breaking into the school, didn't you?"

Patricia smiled and remained silent. His accusing tone was enough to completely turn Patricia off, and unfortunately, his pitifully comical rendition of an interrogating cop was enough to bring a slight chuckle from her. But instead she kept her head down and continued filling out her report.

"Do you think this is funny?" he asked with more dramatic flair than necessary. She remained silent, for fear she'd break out in hysterics at any moment. "We'll see just how funny it is when your boyfriend and his brat go before the school board on charges of theft and vandalism and you on charges of moral indecency."

The smirk on her face was instantly wiped clean. Her focus narrowed as she looked up to meet her accuser's hard stare.

"I thought that would get your attention." He turned and took a slow walk around her office, stopping from time to time to poke at nothing in particular.

"Don't you have something better to do on the day before Thanksgiving?"

He leaned across her desk. "I *will* get to the bottom of this, that I promise. I have enough proof right now to have your little friend expelled." Patricia raised her brow in interest. "No need to deny it. I have her finger-prints on the closet windowsill."

"How do you know that they are her fingerprints?"

Vincent smirked smugly at his brilliance. "I got her fin-gerprints from a soda can she trashed. I matched them with prints that I lifted from the windowsill. And what do you know? A perfect match."

"Let me get this straight." She looked up at the smil-ing Vincent. "You took prints from a minor without parental consent? Not only is that unethical, which I hope you realize, but it's also illegal and borderline stalk-ing if I'm not mistaken."

Vincent blew. His eyes bulged and a vein in his fore-head strained noticeably. "I've been watching you, Patricia." He turned to her pointedly. "And your lover." Patricia stiffened her chin at his snide remark. "Your lit-tle affair is over. Do you understand me? Over. So, tell Mr. Romeo desk jockey that he's out."

"I beg your pardon." She surprised herself at how calm and collected she sounded.

Vincent tilted his head in confused idiocy. "Apparently, I wasn't clear enough. Get rid of Pierce Franklin, now."

"My personal life is none of your business, nor anyone else's concern. What I do and with whom I do it has nothing to do with my performance at the school."

"It does if you're intentionally harboring a criminal and corrupting the morals of a minor. And your boyfriend is found to be an unfit guardian."

"A criminal? Have you completely lost your mind?"

"Kimberly Franklin is a criminal, and you know it."

"I have no idea what you're talking about."

"I think you do. Might I remind you that your job is at stake?"

"Might I remind you that slander is a very serious charge? And unless you can prove any of this, I'd be very careful about voicing unfounded accusations aloud."

"Oh, I have proof. Proof of your affair and proof of the brat's vandalism."

"What do you do—sit outside my apartment and watch to see who goes in and who goes out?" she asked jokingly, but then was flabbergasted to see his expression change to surprised guilt. "Stalking, harassment, slander—is there no end to your sick games?"

He glared at her murderously.

She looked at him threateningly. "Good-bye, Mr. Shields."

He turned to walk to the door. "This isn't over," he warned, "not by a long shot."

"Oh, I think it is, and close the door on your way out."

Vincent stormed from Patricia's office, nearly shattering the door frame as he soundly shut the door. This was becoming a recurring action for him. He was more than furious. How dare she treat him like he was just some lowly dime-store cop. He was a security specialist and supervisor of this district. He was single-handedly responsible for the apprehension and imprisonment of seventeen felons. No one treated him like trash.

So what if he'd followed her a few times. It was all in the line of duty. It was his job and his responsibility to secure the safety of Wells Academy. That included its moral security as well. How would it look if a teacher were seducing the male parents? It was his duty to weed out the bad seeds, and Patricia Burke was a bad seed. She was just like her brother. She needed to be expelled.

He entered the small security office off of the main corridor. Two uniformed Shields security guards, laughing, talking, and joking, silenced as soon as Vincent entered in his angry burst of fury. They stared at him oddly, then at each other. They shrugged their shoulders and went back to talking.

Still fuming from his dismissal by Patricia, he barked at them, "Don't you have rounds to go on?" They instantly jumped to their feet, grabbed clipboards, keys, and caps, then hurried out of the small room.

Vincent slammed himself down at the desk. He swiveled the chair to stare at the wall of black-and-white monitors. Patricia was out of her office and walking toward the cafeteria with several students around her. There were always students around her, he noticed, particularly boys. He speculated, then reasoned, *There must be something going on with this scenario.* Patricia with all those boys spelled nothing but trouble. He pressed Record on the monitor and waited for the red light to stop blinking. Satisfied, he caught several minutes of her laughing and talking with several of the young male students and a male teacher. He pulled the tape from the video recorder and unlocked the bottom drawer of his desk.

Several tapes were already inside. He pulled them out and read each title: ELWOOD'S GRILL, CAFÉ ITALIANO, FRANKLIN HOME SITE and NIGHT MEETING—OUTSIDE SCHOOL. He carefully marked the date, time, and a brief description, then printed EXHIBIT FIVE on the tape in red marker, then added it to his collection.

A knowing sneer crossed his face. He'd show her; he'd show everybody.

Pierce walked around his office with his telephone attachment hooked around his ear, speaking into the tiny microphone near his mouth. His house was in its final stages, and Caroline had called him three times since nine o'clock that morning.

"Caroline, I had this same discussion with Angela and Evan just last week. They know exactly what I'm looking for."

"But I need to know Pierce, not the hired help. Remember, I'm the lead designer on this project. I own this design firm, not Angela and Evan, no matter what the magazines and newspapers say."

Pierce smiled as she alluded to the slight she'd been given when a few months ago *Architectural Digest* and several other prestigious magazines and newspapers had praised Angela and Evan for their unique design sense while oddly enough forgetting even to mention Caroline's name or that the two worked at her company.

"You may be the lead designer, Caroline, but they do all the work. I prefer talking to the people who actually do the work. That way we're on the same page and there'll be no misunderstanding or miscommunications to hash out later."

"Don't be ridiculous, Pierce. Everything they do goes through me. Nothing happens here that I don't know about."

"Then you should already know the answers to your questions, shouldn't you? Where are Angela and Evan?"

"They're both out of the office for a few days, or weeks, at a conference, with a client and doing a job on the coast. So, why don't you just tell me the specs again? I'll see to it that everything is done to your liking."

Pierce rolled his eyes. He could always tell when Caroline was lying. She must have done something, because she was stuttering and completely evading his questions. "Caroline, I don't have time to go over all this again. The contractor Angela hired knows exactly what I want. Angela and I took care of that already."

"But I need to know," she reiterated sternly.

A knock on the door drew Pierce's attention. He turned to see Lewis poke his head into the office. Pierce waved him in but held up his finger to give the just-one-minute signal. Lewis looped into the office and walked over to the large bay window behind Pierce's desk.

Pierce hung up and moved to Lewis's side.

"I should have a view like this," Lewis said.

Pierce smiled knowing Lewis too well. "Why is that?"

"We basically do the same work."

"No exactly the same work."

"I should be at the very least a partner," Lewis continued dreaming.

Pierce shook his head and chuckled as Lewis continued. "You and Adian always had the luck. With sports, woman, jobs, you name it. You two had it all. You still do."

Pierce looked out over the mass of trees. "I've worked hard to get where I am today. Luck had nothing to do with it."

"Hey," Lewis instantly began to back off when he heard the sharp tone in Pierce's voice, "don't get me wrong. I'm not jealous of you or anything," he lied miserably. "It's just that a larger office and a salary to match would really show that my abilities are appreciated here."

Pierce, tired of Lewis's same whining pleas changed the subject. "What can I do for you Lewis?"

He turned and sat at his oversize desk.

Lewis walked around to the front and sat opposite him. "I E-mailed you a few ideas I had regarding the phase release assembly. Briefly, if we cut the slip in half, we'll shave a month off the deadline and could still keep the quoted cost the same. That's easy money in the pocket."

Pierce silently assessed Lewis's idea then leaned over and pulled up the design from the E-mail download. He shook his head. "I see what you're saying, Lewis, but"— he hit a few keys to modify the design, then brought the original specs forward for comparison—"your design would require cutting the quality in half as well."

Lewis smiled. "That's the beauty of it. We cut the quality and keep the clients coming back for upgrades and reboots. It can't miss. We'll have them by the balls. There's nobody else they can go to for what they need but us." He beamed with pride. Not only would his idea save the company hundreds of thousands of dollars, but it would also guarantee a very affluent company's income coming in indefinitely. "Eventually we can do the same thing with our other clients. We virtually own the market anyway—we might as well take advantage of it."

Pierce shook his head again. "I'm afraid we can't do this, Lewis."

"But why not?"

"First of all"—Pierce leveled a determined gaze at him—"we don't work like that here. It's not ethical and, as a matter of fact, it's downright fraudulent. Second, cutting quality isn't what we're about. And, lastly, we get and keep our customers because of our impeccable reputation for high quality standards. It's the word-of-mouth references that have gotten us the lucrative and extensive clientele we enjoy, and it's the same word-of-mouth references that have gotten us the big accounts. Once we start cheating our clients, our reputation goes down and the business is next."

Lewis nodded with complete understanding. "Of course. I was just trying to save the company a few bucks and a few months' time."

Pierce stood and placed the earpiece back into his ear. He came around to the front of the desk and waited for Lewis to stand. He did. "Thanks for coming in with the suggestion. We need a good idea man around here. Keep them coming. Next time, who knows."

Lewis nodded and smiled through gritted teeth.

Lewis paused before heading toward the door. "How's the new relationship going?" he queried, completely off the cuff.

Pierce grimaced with confusion at the quick shift in conversation, then he smiled, his thoughts automatically going to Patricia as he leaned back against the desk in relaxed comfort. "We're doing great. We're taking it slow and steady."

Lewis smiled with feigned interest. "Glad to hear it. Although, I must say, I was hoping that we'd be in-laws someday, but I can handle being best man instead." He smiled weakly.

Pierce didn't reply to Lewis's presumptuous remark, leaving an awkward silence hovering in the air. Lewis, sensing Pierce's reluctance, ignored the uncomfortable situation and continued. "Caroline tells me that the house is almost done. How's it look?"

"It's looking really good. We'll have to have you out one day soon."

"My sister's an excellent architect and designer. I just wish I could afford her." He laughed openly at his sly joke.

"Actually, I'm working with one of Caroline's associates," Pierce corrected.

"Oh, really. I thought she designed the house."

Pierce shook his head, then walked back behind his desk and picked up several papers.

"Yeah, well, sure, we've got to get together soon to see that big old mansion of yours. Caroline says it's really grand. How does Kimberly like it?"

Pierce didn't look up. "She loves it."

"What about Patricia, has she seen it yet?" Lewis asked, expecting a negative reply.

"Yes, she's seen it. As a matter of fact, we're stopping by there again tomorrow evening after dinner."

"She's already seen the new house?" Lewis questioned with surprise. "Wow, isn't that the equivalent to bringing the girl home to meet your mother? I guess this thing is really getting serious."

Pierce smiled and shrugged noncommittally. If Lewis had any inkling just how deeply his feelings for Patricia ran, he'd bite off and swallow his tongue.

"Great, well, I'm going to get back to work now." Pierce nodded absently as Lewis closed the door behind him.

Frowning, Pierce sat back down at his desk. He looked

at the downloaded E-mail again. The idea was ludicrous.
No one in their right mind would knowingly bite the
hand that fed him by cheating clients for a few extra
bucks. Maybe it hadn't been such a good idea to hire
Lewis. In the ten months since he'd been at PEF Software, he'd insulted a favorite client, gotten sanctioned
for sexually harassing a secretary, and was now up for re-
view for missing funds and fraudulent expense reports.
Not to mention his latest brainstorm.

Pierce pushed a single key and erased Lewis's brilliant
idea. He had to seriously think about Lewis's position
with PEF.

It was Caroline who'd originally asked, or rather
begged that he hire her brother. For old time's sake,
she'd insisted, since he was Aidan's best friend. Pierce
pulled the earpiece from his ear again. Not only did he
have to deal with Lewis, but Caroline was beginning to
get on his nerves again.

The buzzer on his desk rang. "Yes," Pierce asked of his
secretary.

"Pierce, I just got a call from lobby security. There's a
Vincent Shields waiting to see you."

"Who?"

"Vincent Shields, he says you know him."

Pierce racked his brain for a moment. He had no idea
who Vincent Shields was. "Does he have an appointment?"

"Not that I can tell. I don't see him listed anywhere
within the next ninety days."

Pierce sighed heavily. "Send my apologies. Tell him
I'm in a meeting or something. Have him leave a detailed message. I'll get back to him."

Pierce stood and turned to the window behind him.
The parking lot was practically empty. It was a half-day
because it was the day before Thanksgiving. And for the
first time in as far back as he could remember, he had no
intention of working. He had promised Kimberly that

he'd help her prepare a traditional Thanksgiving meal. It was a very ambitious project, but he was willing to give it his best effort. But first, he had to get through the day.

A slow easy smile crept across his face as he thought about his pending evening. He and Patricia had plans to go to his house, then do some Christmas shopping at the mall together. His smile broadened. Lately, she'd become the only bright spot in his day. Just thinking about her raised his spirits, even after a tedious day of discussions with Lewis and his sister. He couldn't imagine not coming home to seeing her face or listening to her voice over the phone.

Regretfully, he returned to work. It was going to be a long day's wait until that evening.

"What? I'll have your job for this," Vincent yelled, incited by the security guard's treatment. "Do you have any idea who you're talking to? I'm Vincent Shields of Shields ProTech Security. I fire idiots like you three, four times a day."

The security guard, bearing a strong resemblance to Evander Holyfield, nodded curtly and handed Vincent a piece of paper and an envelope. "If you'll leave a message, I'll see that Mr. Franklin's secretary receives it." His monotone voice lacked interest or emotion. He didn't smile or show any sign of anger at Vincent's heated words.

Vincent snatched the paper and envelope from the uniformed guard. He glared a moment, rolled his eyes, and angrily began writing his note.

This was getting out of hand. The lack of respect must have been contagious. He finished writing, tossed the sealed envelope across the desk, and watched as the uniformed guard let it fall to the floor at his feet. They both looked down at the envelope.

The guard looked up and smiled for the first time since he'd arrived. "Have a nice day, sir," he said almost jokingly.

Vincent gritted his teeth and huffed out of the building. "They'll pay for this insolence," he vowed, "they'll all pay." He continued to mumble aloud as he pushed through the heavy glass doors. Then the wind caught the door and slammed it back into his face. Vincent stumbled back, stunned by the sudden turn of events. He quickly regained control over the door, then looked around. Thankfully, there was no one in sight. He pushed through the door again. This time it was caught and held. "I'll get that for you, sir," the security guard said as he stepped behind him with a humorous smirk.

"I don't need your help," Vincent stormed as he pulled away from the door.

The uniformed guard, though bald as a cue ball, saluted mockingly by tipping an imaginary cap and bade Vincent a good day.

As Vincent climbed into his car, he looked up at the top floor. A figure stood at the large window staring down. A low, angry growling sound emanated from Vincent's throat. "You'll get yours," he promised to the man standing at the window. "I'll make sure of that."

Fifteen

Patricia smiled happily and piled a second helping of mashed potatoes atop the first one she'd heaped onto the tray. She loaded the whole thing down with a ladle full of rich brown gravy. The older gentleman grinned eagerly through tobacco-stained sparse teeth. He thanked her profusely, then hunched his shoulders low and hobbled off to find a seat down one of several crowded aisles of long covered tables.

Patricia smiled at the next person in line and repeated the action she had done since early that morning. The line never ceased. There was a steady stream of eagerly awaiting recipients of the Thanksgiving feast available from the outreach mission.

It was an annual tradition nearly eighty years old, since the time of the Great Depression when men, women, and children had been lining up for this holiday meal. It was always an eagerly awaited event that brought together volunteers from all walks of life.

During a rare slow moment, Patricia looked down the row of volunteers lined up behind the extra-long cloth-covered tables. Twenty or so helpers waited patiently as more kitchen volunteers replenished the large pans and deep pots from which they served. Patricia stepped back when she saw Juliet walk over to her carrying a huge tray of corn muffins.

She gingerly dumped the tray of bread into the overflowing cornucopia, then winked at Patricia and walked back into the kitchen. A big strapping man wearing a slightly soiled apron and chef's hat heaved out the depleted pan of mashed potatoes and replaced it with a fresh pan.

The steam from the mashed potatoes' double boiling pans was a welcome relief to the chill each time someone opened and closed the outside door. They'd been arriving since seven o'clock that morning, each clothed in their cleanest, neatest, and best attire, as per the mission's prerequisite. There was an area set aside for personal hygiene and a small room packed with clean clothing and personal toiletries.

Juliet returned from the kitchen, emptied another tray of piping hot rolls into a large basket on the far end of the long serving table, then walked over to Patricia. "Looks like you've got yourself another admirer."

Patricia looked up to see the older gentlemen with his double helping of mashed potatoes waving his loaded fork in the air in hopes of getting her attention. "Shut up," Patricia said through clenched teeth, as she politely smiled and returned the generous wave. Her relief arrived, taking over the serving as she and Juliet took a much-deserved late afternoon break.

"Girl, you and your men," Juliet professed with feigned annoyance as she shook her head in mock disgust.

"Look who's talking."

"Don't even try it. I, unlike some women, who will remain nameless"—she glared at a laughing Patricia—"at least date them one man at a time." She turned, just in time to see the same older man looking around for Patricia. "Aw, look at him, he's smitten." The older gentleman filled his mouth with a large scoop of mashed potatoes and gravy, then smiled across the room. Juliet *tsked* loudly. "You're just going to break his heart, aren't you?"

"Don't push it."

"So, how's it going with Pierce?"

Patricia smiled in spite of herself. "Great. I went over to his new house again last night after work. It's almost done and it looks incredible. After that, we went Christmas shopping for Kimberly. I'm glad I went with him. The man has no idea what a teenager wants these days. Can you believe he was actually going to buy Kimberly a doll?"

"I hope, for his sake, that it was an Usher doll. Because that's all that child talked about when you moved into the apartment."

"I remember." Patricia chuckled. "Were we that bad at that age?"

"You were worse."

"Me? Worse? How so?"

"Does the name LL Cool J mean anything to you?"

"Oh, that."

"Yeah, oh, that." Juliet smirked triumphantly.

"Okay, but, if I remember correctly, you were just as bad with that guy." Patricia snapped her finger several times. "What was his name? Oh, yeah, Fresh Prince, aka Will Smith."

"Well, at least I wasn't as bad as you."

"I wasn't that bad," she said hopefully, "was I?"

Juliet just looked at her until they both broke out in laughter. "But no, Pierce was looking to buy Kimberly one of those fashion model-type dolls. You know, the ones with the triple-D-size chest, fifteen-inch waist, and seven-foot bendable legs."

"Oh, that would have gone over big on Christmas morning. Was he at least going to add the Malibu condo and convertible car?"

"Oh, he had it all hooked up, house, car, clothes, girl-friends, everything."

"What about her male counterpart?"

"Somehow I doubt it." Patricia and Juliet laughed hysterically. "I have no idea what he was thinking."

"Simple, he still sees her as a little girl."

"You're right."

"I hope for Kimberly's sake that you changed his mind."

"Of course I did."

"What did he finally wind up getting?"

"Clothes and an incredible leather coat and boots. A new CD player and some new software for her computer system."

"Sounds nice."

"We also found this beautiful white-gold charm bracelet with a single heart on it. It's so lovely. It'll be a keepsake for her to give to her daughter in years to come, so he's having it engraved."

"You are such a romantic."

"I know."

Juliet nodded toward the opening door as another group of homeless shyly walked into the center. "Looks like we need to get back to work." She glanced up at the large clock on the far wall across the hall as she moved to a new position at the serving table. "We've got another three hours before we're done." Patricia nodded in agreement and smiled brightly at the man stepping up to her tray. She stirred, then scooped up a large ladle of vegetable soup and placed a slice of white bread on the side dish.

Evening darkness came early as five hours later Patricia opened the door of her apartment, crawled across the room, and collapsed on the living-room sofa. She was bone-tired, so she kicked off her sneakers and peeled off her socks. She looked to the bedroom in hopes of taking a nice hot shower, but decided just to sit for a while and relax. Moments later, her heavy eyelids drooped to close just as the telephone rang. She sprang forward, startled by the sudden ringing.

"Hi, Ms. Burke," Kimberly exclaimed cheerfully. "Are you ready to have Thanksgiving dinner with us?"

"Kimberly?" she asked, then sighed heavily. "Oh, Kimberly, I'm sorry, but I don't want to see another turkey until hopefully next Thanksgiving."

"That's perfect," Kimberly chirped exuberantly, "'cause I made spaghetti since that's all I know how to make so far."

Patricia laughed joyfully as she readjusted the throw pillow beneath her head. "I'll tell you what—how about if I see you tomorrow at the community center dinner?"

"Oh." The dejection in Kimberly's voice was obvious. "Okay, I guess you're kind of tired, huh?"

"Yes, I am. I've been on my feet at the shelter all day."

"All right, I'll see you tomorrow then, bye."

Patricia let the receiver slide down her cheek, then onto her chest. She knew Kimberly was disappointed, but the last thing she wanted to do after being at the shelter all day was to be around more people. The thought of disappointing Kimberly was upsetting. She pushed the button and silenced the unpleasant hum of the disconnected line. Maybe after a nice hot shower she'd feel more like herself. She stood slowly and moved to the bedroom. There she peeled the rest of her clothing off and padded barefoot to the shower.

In her long, hot, and refreshing shower, Patricia reveled in the rejuvenating power of hot water. She was almost beginning to feel like herself. With her hair soaking wet, she wrapped a thick white towel around her wet body and opened the door to her bedroom.

The shriek escaped her before she realized it.

Pierce sat on Patricia's bed, twirling her keys on his finger while he secured Rupert beneath his arm, attempting to calm and halt his constant squirming. He immediately stopped swinging the keys when he saw the towel drop

and puddle to her bright red painted toenails. His mouth
went dry, his pulse raced, and his body tensed.

Still stunned and shrieking, Patricia quickly grabbed
the towel from the floor and held it up to the front of
her. "Pierce, you scared me. What are you doing here?
How did you get in?" she asked, near hysterics.

Hypnotized by the red toenails and white towel, he
stood and answered slowly, "I rang the bell and knocked,
but I guess you didn't hear me because of the shower." He
held up the door keys. "You left these in the unlocked
door, so I just came in." Pierce didn't notice that Rupert
had stopped squirming when he relaxed his hold.

Still unsettled by her bewildering visitor, Patricia
backed away from him. "What are you doing here? Turn
around," she instructed firmly as she backed into the
bathroom.

"Why?" he asked, taking a step toward her. Pierce absently stroked Rupert's coarse back.

"Because, I'm not dressed. Turn around," she reiterated more firmly.

Pierce smiled seductively and began unbuttoning his
denim shirt. "News flash," he said, smirking, raising his
brow knowingly. She knew exactly what he meant and
what he was about to say. So she held up a finger to stop
his next words.

"That's different," she continued while peering out
from behind the bathroom door. "Now turn around."

"How is it possibly different?"

"Because I, because you . . ." Exasperated, she gave up,
"Oh, just turn around."

Laughing, he obliged, turned, and stood at the window with his back to the room. Patricia eased from the
bathroom and darted to the dresser to begin dressing.

Hurriedly, she put on her underwear and pulled a
sweater and a pair of jeans from her closet. She quickly
towel-dried her hair, brushed it, and twirled it into a

ponytail with an elastic ribbon. "Okay, you can turn around now."

"I like the colorful sweater you chose, but I would have chosen the black bra and panties instead of the white," he said, still turned to face the window.

Patricia opened her mouth, then closed it and threw a pillow across the room. Seeing her reflection in the glass, Pierce turned and caught it before it hit him. He tossed the pillow back on the bed and walked over to her. He wrapped his arms around her waist and held her close.

"Umm, you smell good." He kissed her passionately. "You feel good," he whispered, then kissed her again. "But I still would have chosen the black ensemble." He attempted to kiss her again.

She mockingly pushed him away in protest. "What are you doing here?"

"Kimberly told me that you were too exhausted to have dinner with us. So, I thought I might come down in hopes of changing your mind."

"Spaghetti?"

Pierce grimaced. "Actually, we prepared a scrumptious Thanksgiving meal of roasted turkey, candied sweet potatoes, green beans, and pumpkin pie for dessert."

"How did you wind up with spaghetti?"

"The turkey is still frozen solid, the candied sweet potatoes are baby-food mush, and the green beans burned to charred sticks."

Patricia successfully suppressed her laughter. "And the pumpkin pie?"

"You don't even want to know."

Laughter slipped out as Pierce joined in. She shook her head sympathetically. "Remind me to pick up some cookbooks for you as Christmas presents. What are you going to do after you move?"

"Full-time cook."

Patricia laughed again. "Spaghetti?"

He nodded painfully. "She's been working really hard since this afternoon." He kissed her briefly. "She's very proud of her attempts."

Patricia sighed heavily and brought his face down to return his kiss, deep and passionate. They reeled with desire in each other's arms until the need for air overtook them.

"Come on," she rasped breathlessly. "For some reason my appetite has suddenly returned." She turned to leave the bedroom. But he captured her arm and pulled her back into his embrace. They kissed again.

"So has mine, but not for spaghetti," he said, whispering seductively in her ear. "What are we doing after dinner?"

"Cleaning up the kitchen. Come on, let's go. Kimberly's waiting."

Sixteen

With holiday music playing joyfully in the background, Patricia spent the following morning, afternoon, and early evening sorting through her Christmas decorations. Seven huge boxes lovingly dragged up from her crowded storage bin were now scattered about her living room.

It had officially begun. Dressed in her favorite Christmas sweater and red velvet Santa Claus cap, Patricia was all set to start the most magical time of the year: the Christmas holiday. Taking advantage of a rare day off, she used the minivacation to begin decorating apartment for Christmas.

Eagerly, she dug into one of the boldly labeled boxes and pulled out several beautifully adorned Christmas stockings. She arranged them on the living-room mantel, hung on a tiny adorned weight representing Santa's sleigh pulled by eight reindeer.

Then she gently unwrapped the guarding tissue and slipped her finger through the small green hoop of a very special stocking. She dangled the stocking from her finger, then held it against her cheek. The fine softness of the velvety material made her close her eyes in hushed wonderment. She smiled lovingly and paused to take a short trip down memory lane.

She'd had the stocking for as long as she could remember. It had originally belonged to her grandmother, lovingly made by her great-grandmother. The sock, ruby red and emerald green handstitched paisley, was still the best part of Patricia's Christmas. She gingerly fingered the tiny handsewn silk stitches of the swirling paisley designs. With each stitch perfectly preserved through the decades, she remembered the stories her mother had told about growing up in rural Georgia with little or no money but plenty of love.

She smiled joyfully. A whimsical pointed and curled elf's toe with knotted golden thread fringe surrounded the top, making it still the most beautiful thing she'd ever seen. Careful not to damage a single thread, she rewrapped the stocking with bleached tissue paper, then placed it on her pillow on her bed.

Next, declaring the impossible, since she was certain she'd neatly packed and secured them, she struggled to untangle several knotted cords of twinkling lights. Ardently, she tested and replaced when necessary each and every tiny twinkling bulb on the white strand of twisted wire. When every tiny light shined with the sparkle of holiday cheer, she lovingly placed the cords around the outside frame of her balcony and along the crown molding circling the entire apartment. She nodded approvingly, then plugged them into the socket. The room lit up like a sparkling waterfall down each and every wall of the apartment.

Later she opened the many carefully boxed and wrapped Christmas ornaments, checking for any signs of damage. Satisfied that they had survived her move and yet another year, she placed them to the side in preparation for their pending display on a very special evergreen she'd choose at the perfect time later on.

On the mantel she laid out her mkeka, the colorful mat she'd hand woven years ago. Next, she reached into the box and pulled out the kikombe cha umoja, the wooden unity cup she'd found in a quaint little African American boutique while visiting Atlanta earlier that year. She carefully unwrapped the tissue paper and placed the cup on the mat. She sat back, tilted her head from side to side, smiled and admired her work.

For her mazao and muhundi symbols she placed fruit and corn behind the kikombe cha umoja. Lastly, she assembled the kinara adding red, black and green candles in their respective places. She sat back and smiled, pleased with her Kwanzaa display. She stepped back and nodded her approval. Four boxes down, three to go.

A steaming cup of Earl Grey tea and the soft sultry styling of Nat King Cole singing "The Christmas Song" helped take her through the early afternoon. Then, spurred by more modern classics, she worked diligently until her apartment rivaled any New York City department-store window display.

Lights twinkled brightly, stockings were hung on the mantel, and animatronic Mr. and Mrs. Claus stood by the front door ready to greet all who passed. Bowls and baskets were filled with pinecones, tinsel, foot-long cinnamon sticks, and silver glass balls. Sprigs of evergreen pine branches draped the doorways and were secured to the balcony rail. Foil-covered pots of white poinsettias were loving and strategically placed throughout the apartment. Statuesque nutcrackers, angels, and santas were placed around as newly wicked candles of green and white stood at attention, to add their wondrous glow to the apartment's yuletide ambiance.

Lastly, Patricia arranged the small majestic nativity scene in the center of the coffee table. In the manger lay a swaddled babe surrounded by the mother, earthly father, shepherds, angels, kings, and a host of animals. Made in Kenya from the wood of the native babobab tree, each crafted piece was carved to perfection and enhanced with banana fiber accents. She stood back to admire her handiwork. Perfect. She declared herself momentarily finished as six large boxes sat empty by the front door.

In shifts of three, she dragged the six boxes back down to her storage locker and returned to the apartment in time to hear the answering machine click off. It wasn't until Patricia heard Kimberly's phone message that she realized just how late it had gotten.

They walked into the festive celebration of the Regency Towers after Thanksgiving social in the community room together. This was the first time she'd been in this part of the building. It was a lot larger than she'd imagined but every bit as joyous. Patricia looked around in childlike wonder as they stepped through the red, green, and white balloon arch above the entrance. Helium-filled balloons danced on the end of brightly colored holiday streamers weighed down by gold and silver jingle bells. Santa's elves and helpers had definitely been busy.

Already crowded with Regency residents, the room was a jubilant outpouring of holiday cheer.

Comfortable overstuffed sofas and chairs ringed the large room, leaving a huge open space in the center for the square red and green linen-covered buffet tables. In the center of that space was a beautifully lit Christmas tree towering to just a few feet from the vaulted ceiling. It sparkled with thousands of tiny white lights as its only adornment.

The Temptations sang of the red-nosed reindeer over the intercom speakers as more families entered the holiday festivities. Patricia smiled with delight as a warm family feeling of inclusion engulfed her with a familiar welcoming embrace.

Dressed in Christmas red and green, with small glass ornaments hanging from her earlobes, Mrs. Hopkins, the unofficial hostess, hurried over to the trio as soon as she saw them enter. "Don't you all look wonderful," she gushed, kissing all three of them. "Look at the three of you. You look like a family portrait already.

"And this is definitely a first." She smiled at Pierce proudly. "Whatever it was that finally got some Christmas spirit in you, I thank the heavens for it," she teased. "It took a while, but I'm glad that it finally happened." She winked at Patricia. "Good for you, Patricia, good for you."

Kimberly, dressed in a red-and-white striped mohair sweater with hip-hugger jeans, smiled brightly and held up a large covered Corning bowl. "I made it myself," she announced proudly.

"Oh, my, when on earth did you start puttering in the kitchen?" Mrs. Hopkins asked as she took the decorative dish and opened the lid. "How wonderful, spaghetti. I don't think anyone has thought to bring spaghetti yet. Good for you, Kimmy. Good for you."

"Ms. Burke taught me how to make it."

Mrs. Hopkins looked from Kimberly to Patricia to Pierce, then back to Kimberly. "Come along, Kimberly, let's take this to the buffet table."

Kimberly smiled happily and followed Mrs. Hopkins to the tables in the center of the room. Pierce and Patricia followed, weaving a path of holiday cheer as they greeted and were greeted by old friends and neighbors while meeting new ones.

The buffet table, loaded with every imaginable holiday treat, was a joy to behold. Finding open spaces to place covered dishes, however, was a feat of miraculous accomplishment and astute maneuvering.

Patricia peered past the table at the pièce de résistance. The tree, lit by spotlights, was surrounded by one table covered with presents of every imaginable size and another covered with ornaments of different sizes, shapes, and colors, both handmade and store-bought.

Pierce leaned over and whispered in her ear. "The pres-

ents are for the children in area shelters. Every year we do-
nate a new, wrapped toy to send to a children's shelter. We
vote on several different organizations every year."

Patricia smiled, proud to be associated with such a
worthy tradition. "How perfectly wonderful."

"Patricia Burke? Pierce? Is that you?"

Patricia turned to see Doris Andrews and Catherine
Jones-Holland waving madly at her from across the
room. She smiled regretfully as they hurriedly approached. Pierce's zealous joy at seeing the two was
evident by his loud inward groan.

Doris, dressed in a simple red and green poinsettia
pantsuit with matching shoes and handbag, elbowed
Catherine at the last minute, arriving at Pierce's side first.

"Hello, you two," the best friends greeted them together with a knowing smile that told both Patricia and
Pierce that when it came to their relationship, the cat
was definitely out of the bag.

Patricia smiled cheerfully and hugged each woman
warmly, as she had always done. "Happy holidays, Doris,
Catherine. My, Doris, don't you look festive."

Doris, extremely proud of her handmade and self-
designed creation, took a slow turn around, which gave
Catherine just enough edge to slip into her place beside
Pierce.

"So," Catherine began, slyly enfolding her arm around
Pierce's, "what are you two up to?"

"Enjoying the festive celebration," Pierce said, nudging away from the perfume-dunked Catherine.

Taking his cue, Patricia swayed and kept the fifteen-
minute conversation on the beautiful decorations, festive
atmosphere, and the upcoming Christmas season. They
stood talking and laughing together until Catherine's
husband came over, which immediately ended all her fun,
and Doris spotted a new dish added to the buffet table.

"Let me guess," Pierce began when they were finally alone again, "they're best friends, right?"

"The very best—they're sisters."

Pierce broke out with laughter held in for years. Not just any laughter, the sidesplitting kind that brought tears to your eyes and left you weak with jocularity. Patricia merely smiled and lowered her head. The last thing she expected was for the calm, cool, and collected facade of Pierce Franklin to crack and overflow at a Christmas party.

Several neighbors came over, bringing holiday cheer and adding to the festivities. Pierce kept the joyful mood merry and entertaining. With Patricia at his side, he owned the world.

Pierce watched as Patricia's eyes sparked quickly around the room. Her face and eyes lit up each time she spotted a new holiday delight. He watched intently, reveling in her response. Seeing her reaction and being here with her was like experiencing Christmas for the first time. The newness of the moment exhilarated him. This was what he'd been missing all these years.

She'd brought out so many wondrous new feelings in him. An unfamiliar sense of belonging gripped his heart. Instinctively, possessively, he took her hand, leaned closer, and whispered in her ear, "Let's grab a table over there." He pointed to a number of small circular tables set up by the large burning fireplace. Patricia nodded agreeably as his arm circled her waist and gently guided her across the room.

The small tables, topped with green cotton tablecloths, were decorated with miniature evergreen trees, white poinsettia blooms, or extra large red and green glass balls with huge sleigh bells. Kimberly came over a few moments after they sat to tell her uncle that she'd be with the teens in the game room.

For the next half hour, Patricia and Pierce sat talking about Christmas holidays past. Pierce told her of his brother's death and how Kimberly had come to be under his care. Surprising even himself, he told Patricia more about himself, his hopes, his dreams, and his fears. She listened patiently as he relayed tales of his childhood and of his strained relationship with his parents.

By the time he had finished talking, he felt as if a burdensome weight had been lifted from his chest. He reached over and took her hands in his. "You have this remarkable talent of getting me talking about things that I haven't thought about in years."

"I'm just a very good listener."

"You're more than that to me." He stroked her face with the back of his fingers. "I hope you know that by now." Touched by his words, Patricia smiled with honored acceptance.

Moments later the music paused and those gathered hung their heads in prayer, thankful for the grace of their union, the bountiful blessing of family and friends. After the prayer, Mr. and Mrs. Hopkins began speaking to the gathering of upcoming events for the new year and reminding all of basic building courtesy and holiday safety strategy.

Pierce stood beside Patricia, who stood beside Kimberly, who smiled up at both of them. Pierce winked and smiled back. He looked at Kimberly, than at Patricia. A sense of completion lifted his soul as he realized that this was what he'd been searching for so long. This was the family he'd always wanted. It hit him like a sledgehammer through wet silk—he realized finally that Patricia was the woman he wanted to share this and every other moment with for the rest of his life.

Although startling in its revelation, he eagerly accepted its truth. He was in love with Patricia, and he intended to keep her in his life forever. He didn't leave her side the rest of the evening.

Empty holiday paper plates littered the trash can as the

assembled gathering waited patiently for the guest of honor. Little faces with big bright eyes squealed in delight as the sound of sleigh bells came from the main entrance. As soon as the red-and-white clad Santa Claus appeared, the young children went wild and ran to his side.

Applause and laughter rang out as several mothers hurried to gather their eager young. Colorful candy canes were dispensed to the small children while the teens strategized the hanging of the donated ornaments. By the time Saint Nicholas had paid his welcome respects, the ceiling-high Christmas tree was completely covered with decorative embellishments, all donated by the Regency Tower residents.

Kimberly, who'd found her way to the back room set aside with a large-screen television, music, and several free-standing arcade games, waved as she rejoined her friends while munching on several of Mrs. Hopkins's cookies from the dessert table.

"Pierce Franklin, for goodness sakes, let the woman breathe," Mrs. Hopkins said as she stepped between the couple. "I declare, you haven't left Patricia's side all evening. It's like you're surgically attached or something." She shook her head and chuckled at her attempted humor. "Come with me, dear, there's someone I'd like you to meet."

Mrs. Hopkins took Patricia's arm and led her to a group of women chatting by the beverage table. Pierce followed Patricia with his eyes. He was still watching her when Kimberly appeared at his side. She intertwined her arm with his.

"I really like Ms. Burke."

Pierce smiled automatically. "I really like Ms. Burke, too." His eyes were still glued to her smile.

"Know what I think?" Kimberly began. Pierce looked down at her with interest and raised a brow. "I think you should ask Ms. Burke to marry you on Christmas day."

Pierce smiled and chuckled. "Is that what you think I should do?"

She nodded her head eagerly. "Definitely."

Pierce nodded his head also. "Definitely."

Satisfied with the course of her plans, Kimberly happily returned to the small room in the back, but turned just a moment to watch Pierce walk over to Patricia and lead her to the dance floor. Kimberly smiled openly. "Definitely."

"Are you having a good time?"

"Yes," Patricia responded, smiling brightly. "I'm having an incredible time." He held her closer. "I'm so glad I came. *This* is what the Christmas holiday is really all about," she said as she looked around at the other couples on the dance floor. There were dozens of couples laughing, talking, dancing, and enjoying the moment. "Family and friends gathered together, celebrating love," she said, looking up at him as she spoke the last word.

"Yes, love," he repeated, enchanted by her beauty, charmed by her words, and entranced by touch.

"Christmas." She sighed contentedly. "It's when dreams are realized and wishes come true. This is why I love the Christmas season. It's the most magical time of the year, don't you think?"

"I'm beginning to." He smiled happily.

The first gentle tap on his shoulder barely drew his attention. The second tap finally did. Pierce turned to see Kimberly smiling up at him.

"May I cut in?" she asked Patricia sweetly.

"Of course."

Patricia stepped aside as Pierce and Kimberly danced. She watched with pleasure. That he was a wonderful uncle, she already knew; that he was a wonderful father was evident.

"Good evening."

An icy chill slivered through Patricia as she turned and came eye to eye with Vincent Shields.

"What are you doing here?" she snarled.

"It's a holiday party for residents. I am a resident."

"You live here?" she asked, completely flabbergasted.

"And why wouldn't I?"

The surprise of seeing the last person on earth she'd wanted to see completely befuddled her. She dropped her purse. It opened and several items slipped out. Vincent bent down to pick them up. Then, as he stood, he brushed his lips against her leg, allowing the dampness of his tongue to taste her dark stockings. She immediately stepped away. "Don't ever touch me again," she warned through gritted teeth.

He smiled lustily, knowing without doubt that she liked it. They all liked it. "I warned you about seeing him," he said as he inched closer.

Patricia smiled pleasantly and with the sweetest spark in her eye turned to him. "Drop dead." She pivoted on her heels and walked over to a group of women she'd met earlier.

Pierce turned Kimberly to see the man standing beside Patricia.

"Oh, that's just that stupid security guard at school."

"I don't remember seeing him here before."

"That's because you've never come here before. He comes every year." She turned to see Vincent again. "He's a joke. Everybody just ignores him."

"He lives here?"

Pierce watched as Patricia glared at the man, then turned and walked off. Pierce frowned, confused by the odd behavior. He wasn't sure what he'd witnessed, but he was sure he didn't like it. He especially didn't like how the so-called security guard leered after Patricia as she walked away. Pierce made a mental note to know more about this particular Wells security guard.

"So, did you ask her yet?" Kimberly asked, interrupting his thoughts.

"Ask who what?" Pierce muttered absently.

"Ms. Burke," Kimberly said, trying to get and keep her uncle's attention. "Did you ask her to marry you yet?" she whispered as loud as she dared, then looked around cautiously, using her best undercover expression.

Still watching the security guard as he made a wide circle around the room, his eyes still glued on Patricia, Pierce shook back to Kimberly's question. "Who? What?" Pierce muttered again.

"You're not paying attention," Kimberly muttered with annoyance. "Did you ask Ms. Burke to marry you yet?" she whispered slightly louder.

"No," Pierce said, still pondering images of the man who had been speaking with Patricia. "Christmas. Definitely."

Seventeen

Early December winds ushered in a cold breeze and promised that a fierce winter season was just around the corner. The sudden change in weather sent the entire city scrambling into warmer attire. Within the span of just a single weekend, they'd gone from sweaters and lightweight jackets to heavy coats, boots, and gloves.

"Mrs. Hopkins," Kimberly rasped as she half ran, half walked through the front door. She shed her heavy coat and removed her hat and gloves, all while hopping around trying to kick off her boots. The entire action took less than five seconds. She tossed her book bag on the nearest foyer chair and headed to the kitchen. "I'm home!" she called out.

"I'm in the kitchen," Mrs. Hopkins called out just as Kimberly came bursting through the doors. "Hello, Kimmy," she said in her grandmotherly tone. "How was your day at school?"

"Okay," Kimberly shrugged then mumbled her reply as she headed for the refrigerator. A quick scan showed that there was nothing in particular she wanted, so she grabbed a glass of orange juice and closed the door.

Mrs. Hopkins picked up a pot holder and walked over to the stove. She lifted the lid and peeked into a simmering pot. A blast of hot steam engulfed her, frosting her glasses immediately. "I just made a batch of chocolate chip cookies. They're in the cookie jar."

Kimberly took a seat at the island counter. "No, thank you, Mrs. Hopkins. I'm not hungry." Kimberly sat with her chin firmly planted in the palm of her hand. She stared absently as the soap opera faded to black and was quickly replaced by a commercial.

Mrs. Hopkins replaced the lid on the pot and turned around to Kimberly. "You not wanting a chocolate chip cookie? Are you feeling all right?" She moved to the counter and sat down on the stool across from Kimberly. She clicked the remote to mute, opened a plastic bag filled with green beans, then pulled a small plastic colander next to the bag. She reached in and pulled a long green bean, snipped the ends, then snapped it into thirds and dropped it into the colander.

"I'm okay. I'm just not hungry right now, that's all."

"Kimberly Franklin," Mrs. Hopkins began, "for the past five years you've come into this kitchen after school and dived into any- and everything edible. Now today, all of the sudden, you're not hungry? What's going on?"

"Nothing, I promise, Mrs. Hopkins. I'm fine," she declared, then added moments later, "can I help you with that?"

Mrs. Hopkins stopped cold and looked at Kimberly. She tilted her head to the side and just stared with her mouth wide open.

"What?" Kimberly asked. "What's wrong?"

"I'm not sure. You tell me. I think one of those body-snatching pods just came and grabbed my baby," she said with a slight chuckle.

"What's a body-snatching pod?"

"It's from an old movie way before your time."

"Huh?" Kimberly questioned, not understanding a word the older woman was talking about.

"First you're not hungry, then you don't want a chocolate chip cookie—your personal favorite, by the way—and now you want to help snap green beans. Something's definitely wrong."

A shy smile tugged at the corners of Kimberly's mouth. "Nothing's wrong and nothing's snatched me. I just want to know more about cooking, that's all. Mrs. Burke taught me how to make bread with yeast and spaghetti and meatballs. I liked helping out in the kitchen."

"Glory be." Mrs. Hopkins looked at Kimberly as if she were from another planet. "You're cooking bread now?"

Kimberly smiled proudly. "Yep, I'm cooking everything. I figured when we move to the new house next month, somebody has to cook for Uncle Pierce."

"Well, Miss Kimberly, that's the best news I've heard all day. I'm proud of you." Kimberly blushed. Mrs. Hopkins finished snapping the beans while patiently waiting for Kimberly to tell her what was on her mind. She got up and walked over to the sink. She let cool water run over the colander and beans.

"I made a wish for the perfect gift for Christmas," Kimberly stated as she eased next to Mrs. Hopkins at the sink. She watched as the older woman tossed and rinsed the green beans in the colander.

"Good for you. What did you wish for for Christmas?" Kimberly, looking all of thirteen, began to smile brightly. "I bet it has something to do with that ushering boy singer, doesn't it?"

Kimberly looked completely confused. Then it dawned on her what Mrs. Hopkins meant. "Oh, you mean Usher."

Mrs. Hopkins went back to her bean rinsing, shaking her head at the absurdity. "Why any grown man and woman would name their child such a name is beyond me. For goodness sakes, Usher of all things. My grandmother was the best usher in Faith Baptist Church. She ushered every Sunday of her natural life. Starched white uniform, white sheer stockings, and white nursing shoes.

Now, she was an usher. When she died she left instructions that she be buried in her uniform, and that's exactly what we did."

"Mrs. Hopkins, you're kinda getting off the subject. We're talking about my Christmas wish."

"Oh, I'm sorry, Kimmy. What did you wish for?"

"I didn't exactly wish for anything for myself. I wished for something for somebody else." Kimberly paused to consider. "Well, it's kinda for me, but it's mostly for someone else."

Growing more curious, Mrs. Hopkins turned off the water, dried her hands, and asked, "What did you wish for?"

"I wished I could have the perfect Christmas. I wished that this Christmas I could have a real family like before Mom and Dad died."

Mrs. Hopkins stopped drying her hands, put the dish towel down, and turned to Kimberly. "Sweet child." She opened her arms wide. Kimberly fell into her hug. "Your mother and father are with the angels. Your uncle Pierce is your real family now."

"Oh, I know that, I just mean I wished Uncle Pierce could find someone nice to be with. I hated all those brainless boob jobs that always hung around here."

"I'm sure your uncle will find a nice lady to settle down with eventually."

Kimberly nodded and took a sip of the orange juice. "Mrs. Hopkins," she said as she leaned across the kitchen counter. "Don't you think it would be a good idea for Uncle Pierce to marry Ms. Burke?"

"Kimberly, whom your uncle chooses to marry is his business, not ours." Mrs. Hopkins took the colander of green beans and dumped them into the steaming seasoned water.

Kimberly eased up next to her. "But they're perfect together, don't you think so?"

Mrs. Hopkins smiled slyly. "Yes, as a matter of fact, I do think that they make a lovely couple. But what we think doesn't matter. It's what they think and what they feel that's important. Either way, it's still none of our concern."

"But what if they just needed a little push to help get them started?"

"What kind of little push?" She looked at Kimberly, not quite sure exactly what she was up to.

"I made a wish on a falling star."

"Oh, is that all?" Mrs. Hopkins said with added relief.

"And I kind of helped it along, sort of."

"Oh," Mrs. Hopkins said as the steam from the boiling broth fogged her glasses again.

"Well"—Kimberly moved back to sit at the counter—"I was kinda in a hurry and I sorta needed this thing done fast. So I sorta helped expedite matters."

Mrs. Hopkins placed the lid back onto the pot and moved back to the counter. She sat down and eyed Kimberly suspiciously, knowing her too well. "Speak English, Kimmy. What did you do?"

"When I heard that there was going to be an empty apartment in the building, I kind of went into the Regency Towers computer system and put somebody's name first on the list to get the vacant apartment."

"You put Patricia Burke's name at the top of the Regency Towers waiting list?"

"But I didn't hurt anybody."

"It wasn't fair, Kimberly Franklin, and you know it. It was wrong to break into someone else's computer."

Kimberly lowered her head sorrowfully. "I'm sorry."

Mrs. Hopkins, always one to feel bad after chastising, immediately went to the cookie jar and pulled out a fat cookie, loaded with chocolate chips and pecans, something that always worked with her own children. She handed the cookie to Kimberly on a cloth napkin. "You were wrong and we won't speak of this again. Is that understood?" Kimberly nodded her head in understanding. "And you won't do it again, is that clear?"

Kimberly nodded her head a second time, took the cookie, and began nibbling at the edge as Mrs. Hopkins went back to her pot. "There's more," Kimberly said quietly.

Mrs. Hopkins stirred the beans around in the simmering broth. She placed the lid on top of the pot, then turned to move the cookie jar by her side. She sat back down at the counter across from Kimberly and waited patiently for her to continue.

"I kinda also went into the school's computer system to get some information."

"You did what?"

"I needed to know some more information about somebody. I tried the Department of Motor Vehicles, but they didn't have as much as I thought they would. Then I tried the Social Security office, but they had even less. I had no choice but to go into the school computer."

"Miss Kimberly Franklin, there is no way for you to justify your actions. You were completely and totally wrong, plain and simple. You went snooping into places you knew were off-limits. The DMV and Social Security, for goodness sake. Do you know how much trouble you could be in if you had gotten caught?"

"But I was very careful not to get caught. I made sure to back out exactly as I went in so there wouldn't be any footprints."

"Going into government systems is against the law. Going into any system that doesn't belong to you is against the law, and you know it."

"But I had to make sure that she was right for Uncle Pierce."

"Kimberly."

"Yes, I know." She lowered her head in shame.

After a few moments of disturbed silence, Mrs. Hopkins pulled out another cookie from the jar and gave it to Kimberly, then she slid down from the stool.

"One more thing," Kimberly began again. Mrs. Hopkins hopped back up onto the stool and took the lid off the cookie jar. "While I was in the school's computer the last time—" she began.

"Wait a minute, wait a minute, *the last time*? Exactly how many times have you been in the computer system at school?"

"Just a few times."

"How many is a few times?"

"Six or seven times maybe," she mumbled, barely audible.

"Kimberly Franklin, I am so ashamed of you. You know that was illegal. What if you were caught? Do you have any idea how dangerous that was? What if a teacher or the principal walked in and caught you riffling through the system?"

"Oh, they wouldn't have seen me, 'cause I broke into the school at night when I knew nobody was there. I went into the system, then left as soon as I got what I needed."

Mrs. Hopkins reached into the jar, pulling out a cookie, and took a huge bite. This was sounding more and more like one of her soap operas from television. She could just see Melissa Crane confessing something like this to her comatose great-aunt Jeannie and her paralyzed and headless uncle Luther. Lord knows they did have problems, but nothing like this one.

"What on earth would you need in the school's computer system?" Kimberly opened her mouth to explain, but Mrs. Hopkins halted her by holding up her hand to stop. "Why don't you just start from the beginning," Mrs. Hopkins said.

Kimberly took another bite of her second cookie and started at the beginning. "I made a wish on a falling star and I just wanted to help out a little. I needed to get some information on Ms. Burke."

"Ms. Burke?"

"Yes, she was part of the Christmas wish I made."

"The Christmas wish?"

"For Uncle Pierce. I wanted to give him Ms. Burke."

"Why on earth did you want to give Ms. Burke to your uncle?"

"For a Christmas gift. He has everything else, I just wanted him to have love, too. That's when I chose Ms. Burke for him. But I needed to know that she was right for him. So I went into the school computer system. Then, while I was in the system, I found out that not only did Ms. Burke go to school at Wells, but she was also in some of my dad's classes. So I found his yearbook and looked her up. She wasn't anywhere, not a single photo. So Jasmine and I decided to find out what happened to her."

"What do you mean, what happened to her?"

"Her name wasn't mentioned anywhere in the yearbook."

"Maybe she graduated some other year."

"I checked that. It's on record that she got her diploma the same year as my dad."

"So why wasn't she in the book?" Intrigued, Mrs. Hopkins questioned with as much zeal and excitement as she had when watching her soaps.

"Ms. Burke graduated three years early. She started out in Uncle Pierce's class, then got skipped to Dad's class. She graduated early, then went to college when she was fifteen. Can you believe it? She must have been really smart. Anyway, I thought that maybe she'd be a good match for Uncle Pierce. Then I overheard her say that she was looking to move closer to school, and that she'd applied here at the Regency. That's when I sort of helped out by putting her name at the top of the waiting list."

Mrs. Hopkins shook her head and frowned but leaned in closer to hear the rest.

"It was all my idea. I couldn't find a good Christmas present so I decided to give him Ms. Burke."

"Kimmy, you can't give a person as a gift."

"But she's perfect for Uncle Pierce, you said so yourself."

"Kimberly Franklin, you should not be meddling in your uncle's affairs."

"I know, but they really like each other, they have from the very beginning. You should see them together. Uncle Pierce has never been happier. He's even looking forward to Christmas 'cause he knows he'll be spending it with Ms. Burke. Uncle Pierce hated Christmas, but now look at him. He's walking around humming 'The Twelve Days of Christmas' and shopping for presents."

"Be that as it may, you were wrong and you're going to have to confess and tell your uncle what you've done."

Kimberly held out her hand for another cookie.

Mrs. Hopkins obliged and waited patiently to hear more confessions. "Go on, what else?" she questioned.

"I saw who was stealing stuff at Wells. I saw them do it."

"You what?" Mrs. Hopkins shouted aloud, completely taken off guard.

"I didn't mean to, I just looked up and there he was, going into the supply closet and coming out with a computer box."

"Oh, heavens! Have you told anyone else?"

"No. Jasmine was with me at the time, but she didn't see what I saw."

"Oh, Lordy. We have a mess of trouble."

"I won't tell anyone, I promise."

"You have to tell, Kimmy. Did the thief see you?"

"No."

"Are you sure?"

"Yes. I'm sure."

"Good. Now we've got to get in touch with your principal so that you can confess the whole story."

"But then they'll know that I was there, too. I'll get into trouble and Banneker will take my admission away."

"Hello," Pierce called out from the foyer. "Anybody home?"

Both Mrs. Hopkins and Kimberly jumped, froze, and stared at each other. Mrs. Hopkins turned the cooked green beans off and set the pot aside just as Pierce entered the kitchen.

"Good afternoon, ladies," he spouted happily. Kimberly looked at Mrs. Hopkins and seemed to groan inwardly. She knew what she needed to do.

"Good afternoon, Pierce," Mrs. Hopkins said sternly.

Pierce pecked Mrs. Hopkins on the cheek. "How was our show today? Did Melissa finally find out that her new husband is a louse?"

Mrs. Hopkins, for the first time in a long time, had forgotten all about her soaps. "To tell you the truth, Pierce, I have no idea. I forgot they were even on."

Pierce frowned, sensing immediately that something was wrong. Mrs. Hopkins not watching her soaps was bad enough, but for her not even to remember to look at them was major. "What's going on?" he questioned.

"Kimberly," Mrs. Hopkins said as she gathered her things from the kitchen. Kimberly looked away, dreading the next few minutes. "Dinner's in the oven and there are green beans in the pot on the stove. Just put the whole pot in the refrigerator when you're done. I'll see to it tomorrow." She picked up the cookie jar and handed it to Pierce on her way out of the kitchen. "I'm going home now. You and Kimberly need to talk."

Pierce eyed Kimberly suspiciously. She was pensive and sober. Nothing unusual there. "Kimberly? What's going on?"

It took over half an hour for Pierce to finally get the whole story behind Kimberly's late-night excursions.

Shock, anger, and disbelief. Kimberly grimaced. Pierce was furious. The lecture had changed, at least. Unfortunately, it lasted twice as long.

The knock on her door startled her. Patricia called through, "Who is it?"

"Pierce."

She brightened immediately and hurried to the front door. She swung it open to see a very stoic Pierce standing next to a very miserable Kimberly.

"Hey, you two," she looked from face to face and then back again. It didn't take the sixth sense or psychic ability to see there was a problem. "What's going on?"

Pierce looked down at Kimberly with annoyance. Patricia also looked down at Kimberly, puzzled. "Maybe you'd better come inside and sit down."

Eighteen

"She did what?"

"That's the same thing I said when I first heard."

"That little scamp," Juliet said with a laughing tone in her voice. She chuckled silently.

"What, may I ask, is so amusing?"

"This whole thing. Oh, Patricia, get over it. It was just a little innocent stunt to play cupid. What's the harm? And it worked, didn't it? I say good for her."

"Juliet, do you realize this little stunt of Kimberly's could cost her admittance to Banneker's Computer Summer Program? I don't think Benjamin Banneker School of Computers, Mathematics, and Science will approve of her little stunt."

"You won't let that happen," she said assuredly.

"What am I supposed to do? My hands are tied. She broke into the school, then into the computer system, all to do a background check on me because she wished for the perfect present to give her uncle."

"All right, so she was a little misguided."

"Misguided?"

"Come on, don't tell me you'd let a thirteen-year-old cupid go down hard on this one. She was just trying to put two people together."

"She broke the law, Juliet."

"She took the initiative. You sure as hell weren't going to."

"Don't you dare put this on me."

"Oh, please, you've had a thing for Pierce for twenty years. Every man you've ever been involved with has always come up short of the perfect Pierce Franklin. Then, finally you get your chance at happiness and you deny it. So what if the kid bent the law? She handed you something you've wished for all your life."

"She didn't just bend the law, Juliet, she broke it."

"Did she actually get into the Department of Motor Vehicle computers?"

"No, she couldn't."

"Did she get into the Social Security computer system?"

"No, but . . ."

"So, what's the problem?" Juliet asked.

"The problem is, she broke into the school and hacked into *my* computer. Am I supposed to overlook that?"

"Who's to say that you didn't give her permission to check your computer out? She's a computer major, right? You've said a dozen times that she knows more about your system then you do."

"Don't you dare start putting together her defense. She broke the law. I can't help her."

"Oh, please, since when did you become such a gestapo hard-ass?"

"Don't defend her, Juliet. She's not some kind of cybercupid. She's a kid who went too far."

"Are you listening to yourself?"

Patricia paused a moment. Juliet was right, as usual. There was no way she'd let Kimberly ruin her future over this. The initial shock of being spied on and set up was upsetting, but to punish someone harshly for a lapse in judgment was not right. She knew, just as Juliet knew, that in the end she'd find a way to get Kimberly off the hook.

Patricia opened her mouth to answer, but stopped when she heard the repeated rapping on her door.

Audrey knocked again, turned the knob, then poked her head in through the open office door. Patricia smiled and held a finger up for a moment. "Juliet, let me get back to you later." They rang off as Audrey stepped into the office.

"Hi, Audrey, what can I do for you?"

Audrey frowned and walked around the office silently. "Patricia, we need to talk."

"This sounds serious."

"It is."

Patricia's mind whirled as Audrey sat down slowly across from her. Pierce must have called her this morning and come clean about Kimberly's night visits.

"What's going on, Audrey?"

"That's what I'd like to know." She looked directly at Patricia.

"What do you mean?"

Audrey opened an envelope she'd been holding and pulled out the folded paper inside. She handed the letter to Patricia. "This was delivered in this morning's mail. It's unsigned."

Patricia took the letter and briefly scanned it, then instantly reread it more carefully. "Oh, my God."

"Is this true, Patricia?"

Patricia took a deep breath and looked Audrey directly in the eyes. It was over. She was caught. "Yes, it's true."

"How long?"

"A month, more or less, something like that." She passed the letter back across her desk.

"My hands are tied on this one, Patricia. I have to go before the board. I have no choice. You've made your bed, now you have to lie in it," she said, "so to speak."

Patricia nodded her acceptance of the situation. "I understand. Would you like me to . . ." She choked up with emotion. "I can go out on personal leave right now, immediately."

"No, nothing changes, not until the board meets and reviews the situation." She stood and came over to Patricia, who also stood. "To tell you the truth, I'm not exactly sure what the morals clause says about this. So, since you're scheduled to begin staff exchange development sessions with the county school system, why don't you continue with that?"

"This was all my fault, Audrey. I was wrong. I knew exactly what I was doing. I'm sorry to have to put you and the school through this."

"The board will meet and give you every opportunity to explain yourself and your actions." She turned to go, then, without looking at Patricia, added, "Personally, I feel you should be fired immediately." She spun around quickly. "I am sickened by your irresponsible, thoughtless, reckless behavior. You have not only put yourself in danger, but you have put the entire school and its faculty in danger because of this. Your lack of restraint and good judgment is appalling, although I am not completely surprised by this action of yours. Coming from you and your kind, I expect no less."

Patricia smiled, much to Audrey's surprise. "It took you twenty years to get that off of your chest, didn't it? Ever since I came to this school you've had a problem with me and my kind. It's been twenty years, Audrey. Get over it. Scholarship recipients are here to stay.

"The pure rich history of Ida B. Wells Academy was founded on equality for all children, not just the ones who could afford it.

"It seems you've forgotten the purpose of the school and the vision of our founder. Ida Wells fought all her life for equality for all. Not just for black, white, or rich, but all people. She refused to move from a cable car and denounced discrimination seventy years before Rosa Parks and the civil rights movement. Maybe you should take a page from her book and check yourself. Everybody deserves an opportunity to be here, not just the wealthy. If you don't see that, then maybe you're in the wrong school."

Audrey gasped. "Let's just see what happens, shall we?" Audrey smiled stiffly. "Now, I must get back to work. I still have a school to run. Are you ready to go?"

"My schedule is clear for the next two weeks. I don't expect the sessions to take much longer than that."

Audrey nodded her understanding. "I'll contact you with the time and place of the board meeting. In the meantime, I'll expect you will carry yourself accordingly. I suggest you end this relationship as soon as possible. No need to make matters worse." She pulled the door slightly to as she left.

Patricia was shaking. It had taken twenty years, but she'd finally put Audrey Simmons in her place. Her mind raced to the dozens of times Audrey had belittled, insulted, and mocked her just because she was poor. Yes, she felt good.

"I told you to leave him alone. You should have listened to me."

Patricia looked up at Vincent's triumphant expression as he stood in the doorway. She smiled brightly in return. "Good morning, Mr. Shields."

Vincent frowned and pushed away from the door frame. "You seem awfully chipper this morning, particularly for someone in as much trouble as you're in."

She looked at him quizzically. "What trouble would that be, Mr. Shields?"

Vincent frowned. This wasn't going as he'd anticipated. He assumed that by now she'd be crying hysterically. "I hear that your little romance with Pierce Franklin is common knowledge now."

"And?"

"And a school counselor having an affair with the guardian of a student is unethical, but I'm sure you're aware of that." He smiled smugly and waited for her reply.

Patricia smiled without responding, but instead reached into her top drawer and pulled out a small legal pad and began to write. "Why did you send the letter, Mr. Shields?"

"What letter?"

"Did you not sign because you felt that you weren't worthy?"

"What?"

"Tell me, does this give you a feeling of power?"

"Yes, as a matter of fact, it does."

Patricia nodded and made a brief notation. "How often do you have these feeling of inadequacy?"

"I am not inadequate," he practically yelled.

She made another notation. "Tell me about your father, Henry Shields."

"My father had nothing to do with this."

"I see." She scribbled on the pad again.

"What are you writing?" he raved as he leaned across the desk.

"Nothing for you to be concerned about," she stated calmly. "Let's talk about your childhood, shall we? Tell me your first memory."

"What? I know what you're doing." He pointed an accusing finger at her. "You're trying to psychoanalyze me, aren't you?" She smiled and continued writing. "Stop it, stop it," he hissed. "This is not about me. It's about you and your boyfriend." She smiled again and laid her pen down.

Not getting the satisfaction he expected, Vincent turned to leave, then paused. "One more thing." He smiled smugly again, trying to regain his composure. "My security team has taken care of your vandalism and theft problem."

"How did you do that?"

"We found an empty computer box in the custodian's

closet. Apparently your Mr. Wilson has been helping himself to the school's supplies."

"That can't be right. It doesn't make any sense."

"It doesn't have to. He was caught red-handed trying to dispose of the empty box. End of story." He stormed from the office.

Troubled, Patricia relaxed back into her chair. It didn't make sense. There were too many questions that were still unanswered. Why would Mr. Wilson suddenly begin stealing after working at the school for more than twenty-five years? How could he have possibly gotten into the security system and altered the monitor cameras? There was definitely something else going on, and she was going to find out what it was. But first she had to trace the computer security system back to its source.

"What's this?" Pierce picked up the hand-addressed envelope that his secretary placed on top of his personal mail pile.

"Security left this for you a few days ago. You told me to take care of it, but I don't think it has anything to do with software. But I think you might want to see it. It's a personal matter." She shrugged and picked up the ringing phone.

Grimacing, Pierce took the resealed envelope and pulled out the folded paper. He read the letter, then placed it in his breast pocket and marched into his office. The sour turn of his day had turned into an even more drastic downward spiral. Just as he sat down and pulled the letter out to reread it, Lewis poked his head through the door.

"Hey, Pierce," Lewis began, cheerfully loud.

Pierce continued reading. "Not now, Lewis."

"Hey, no problem, dawg. I just came by to bust your

chops. I did a little checking up on your Little Red Riding Hood."

"You did what?"

Lewis continued, unaware of Pierce's rising ire. "I knew that name sounded familiar, so I asked around to some of the old crew. Nobody remembered at first, but then we started talking and it came to us. Why didn't you tell me you were going out with Ratsy Patsy?"

Pierce looked up at Lewis in complete confusion. "What are you talking about?"

Lewis laughed. "You have to remember Ratsy Patsy. The mousy little brainy girl that told on her brother while we were at Wells. She got him kicked off the football team, then expelled, and almost did the same to all us. It was the first time we'd lost the senior football championship in years."

Pierce was completely lost. "I don't have time for games, Lewis, I'm right in the middle of something." He refolded the letter and put it back into the company envelope.

"Eighth grade—your brother, her brother, me, and a few of us played a little prank at the school. She found out and told on us."

"Who are you talking about?"

"Ratsy Patsy, Patricia Burke. You're dating Ratsy Patsy, a Poorie. You turned down an opportunity to be with my sister for a Poorie. I can't believe it, a Poorie."

"Lewis, get a grip. That was over twenty years ago, man, grow up."

"Me? You're the one sticking a Poorie. Just remember, when you wake up on the wrong side of the tracks, you usually go to sleep there as well, so watch your back."

"Excuse me?"

"Yo, man." Lewis threw his hands up in mock surrender. "I'm just joking with you. If you want to get a piece from some Poorie, that's your thing, whatever."

"Would you get off the Poorie thing?"

"Ah, see, you weren't there. Ratsy Patsy"—Pierce shot him a warning look—"I mean Patricia was this super-brain that, like, breezed through school. She should have graduated with you, but she was so smart she graduated with our class."

"So, she was smart, big deal."

"She wasn't just smart, she skipped through Wells and practically went directly to college."

"Why don't I remember any of this?"

"The Poories and Richies didn't associate."

"You were friends with her brother. I'm sure he didn't have any money."

"Oh, well, he had potential. Dude could shoot hoops from half-court, toss a football thirty yards, whack a ball into the outfield, plus kick a soccer ball in the goal fifty feet away."

"So, even though he didn't have money, he was still accepted," Pierce concluded.

"Well, I didn't say he was completely accepted, I said he was okay. Dude was a winner; we dug winning."

"This is unbelievable. I can't believe my brother actually went along with this crap."

Lewis laughed so hard that tears streamed down his face. "Are you kidding? Your brother, Aidan, came up with the whole Poorie-Richie thing. It was brilliant."

"Aidan did what?"

"He was the brains," Lewis said proudly.

"What?" Pierce repeated, not believing what he was hearing.

"Oh, yeah, he was the man," Lewis stated proudly. "He was brilliant. We kept those scholarship Poories in their place. I really miss that dude."

"What is wrong with you?" Pierce asked rhetorically.

"What do you mean? I'm just keeping it real."

Pierce continued to shake his head while Lewis babbled on, still stuck on stupid. He couldn't believe what he was hearing. How was this possible? He knew Aidan was more like their mother, but until now, he'd had no idea how much. Was Aidan really that much of a fool?

"Yo, Pierce, you do what you want to do. I'm going back to my office." He stood and moved toward the door.

"Correction." With that one word, Pierce halted him in his tracks.

"Yo, Pierce, check yourself, man. I'm only trying to come correct. I want you to know that I got your back on this, man."

"I don't need you to have my back. You're fired."

"Excuse me, you can't fire me for something that happened—what did you say?—almost twenty years ago." He sat down and smiled smugly.

"True, but I can fire you for submitting fraudulent paperwork, not to mention sexual harassment."

"What are you talking about? What fraudulent paperwork? I never turned in any fraudulent paperwork. And pretty miss secretary isn't going to place charges. You saw to that."

Pierce smiled menacingly. "I beg to differ." He reached down, pulled a file from his briefcase, and tossed it across his desk. "You turned these into accounting."

Lewis scanned the paperwork. His eyes grew wide with surprise. "I . . . these . . . you see—" he stuttered.

"Good-bye, Lewis."

"Fine. I don't need this hassle, and I don't need this job." He threw the file and its contents across the desk and onto the floor. "I've got ten companies waiting in line for my services. I don't need you. You know what, man? You're pathetic. That Poorie's got you whipped. I'm glad I sent that letter to the school. She should be fired, not me. You should have stayed with Caroline. At least with her you'd still have your balls." He pulled the identification card from around his neck and threw it. Pierce caught it easily as he picked up the phone. "She's just using you, man, to get back at Aidan. Don't you see that?"

"Get me security." He was instantly connected. "This is Pierce. Lewis Carter is no longer with PEF Software. Please escort him from the building."

"Look, Pierce, man, this is all a mistake, I swear. I can fix this. I need this job, man. Come on, we go back a long way, don't fire me. Come on, listen, I'll call Caroline, you two can go out, do a little this, a little that. Everything will be fine. I swear, man."

The heavy knock drew both men's attention as the door opened and two uniformed security guards stepped inside with wide smiles on their faces. They nodded to Pierce. "Gentlemen, please help Mr. Carter exit the building."

"Fine, man, you be like that. Keep your stinking job. I don't need it. I hope you and your Ratsy Patsy have a wonderful Christmas." With that holiday sentiment, the security guards escorted Lewis to his office, then out of the building and off the grounds.

Pierce sat with his back to the desk for a long time. He stared out at the bright December morning. An hour ago he'd been on top of the world. Funny how quickly things changed.

He pulled the hand-scrawled letter from his pocket and reread it again. There was no mistake. Lewis had just validated its allegation.

Jasmine practically ran to catch up with Kimberly as she walked into the study hall. "Where have you been? I've been looking all over for you," she rasped out breathlessly as she arrived by her friend's side.

"I had computer lab all morning. What's up?"

Jasmine nudged closer to Kimberly and began to

whisper in her ear. "You are never going to believe what I just heard."

Kimberly, in an unusually bad mood, declined to guess and asked Jasmine simply to get to the point.

"I just heard that Ms. Burke got fired."

"What?" Kimberly stopped walking and stared at Jasmine.

"Ms. Burke just got fired."

"Fired?" Kimberly asked, as if the word were foreign.

Jasmine nodded her head. "That's what I just heard," she confirmed.

"Fired for what? How? Says who?"

"I don't know, nobody knows."

The first thing Kimberly thought was that somehow somebody had found out about her late-night visits, and since it was Ms. Burke's computer, had blamed her.

Kimberly rushed to Patricia's office and swung open the door, only to find it empty and dark. "It's true," she said in a saddened whisper, then closed the door behind her and went to study hall.

Pierce's day had been hell, and Kimberly was back to her bitter sulky self. When he got home, he dropped everything and went straight to the library. He searched the bookshelves until he had finally come up with that for which he was looking. He pulled the book down from the shelf and opened the cover.

The familiar crackling of pages long since sealed sounded through the room. Pierce turned page after page for some inkling of understanding. For hours he sat at his desk, flipping through the pages of his brother's yearbook, searching for a clue to Patricia's motives. Could she really hate his family still, after all these years? He came across his brother's young smiling face. The same old anger rose up instantly. Adian had been

driving much too fast. He'd never known what hit him.
He and his wife had died instantly. Perhaps it was time to
let the demons go.

There was never any love lost between the brothers.
They'd always had a strained relationship. Aidan was
more like their mother, and Pierce was more like their
father. The natural clash had only grown wider as they'd
gotten older. Being born number two was not a choice,
but being number two was. So Pierce had always vowed
never to be less or have less than the best.

Angrily he slammed the book shut and threw it across
the room. There had to be something he was missing.
And there was only one place to get the answers. He
stood, picked up the yearbook, and set it on his desk. It
was late, but she'd still be expecting him.

Pierce went directly to Patricia's apartment. He rang
the doorbell and waited for her to answer. The door
opened a small crack, then it widened as Patricia appeared. She smiled, pleased to see him, as usual.

"Hello," she purred seductively, then stepped aside,
pulling the door with her. Seeing Pierce standing on the
other side of the door was the best thing to happen to
her all day. The thrill of love deepened in her heart each
time she saw him, and this time was no different. She
sighed heavily, anticipating their evening together.
"Come on in."

Pierce remained still. His face was emotionless, his
stance was stoic, and his eyes were cold as ice. "You went
to Wells Academy when my brother did."

"Yes." Her smile slowly dissolved from her face.

"And you knew Aidan?"

"Yes."

"And Aidan started the Richie-Poorie thing?"

"Yes."

"He and his friends got your brother expelled?"

"Yes."

"You were the one who saw Kimberly that night at school, weren't you? You and your little security guard came up with something to finally even the score? You used Kimberly to get back at Aidan. You used me."

Patricia looked at him as if he'd gone mad. "Do you actually believe I would use you or Kimberly to get even with Aidan for something that happened more than twenty years ago?"

"Answer my question, Patricia. Are you the one who saw her in the school after hours?"

"Yes, I saw her."

"So, you lied to me, then kept on lying. Then, of course, we slept together. How did that fit into all this?"

"I don't need a lecture on morals from you."

"So, one word from you and she'd lose her admission to Banneker, just like your brother lost his scholarship to Wells. This is what they call payback."

"It's true, I hated Aidan for a long time, and it wasn't just because of the Richie-Poorie thing. He made my life hell. I was the one who they all picked on and made fun of. I was the smart skinny kid with glasses and cheap old clothing. Scholastically, I was years ahead of everybody my age. I was twelve years old, in the eighth grade, surrounded by older kids who hated my guts because I was smart and poor."

"The sins of the father are visited upon the child."

"I would never avenge my pain on a child. You should know that."

"No, I shouldn't."

"You know how to let yourself out," she offered.

Pierce nodded curtly and turned. Patricia remained silent as she watched the front door close behind him.

Pierce pushed the button for the elevator. It opened almost immediately. Without looking, he stepped inside. "Pierce Franklin." He looked up to see a familiar woman standing in front of him.

Not feeling particularly sociable, he simply stated her name. "Juliet Bridges?"

She smiled. "You remembered, how sweet."

"How long has it been?" Pierce held the elevator door open.

"Oh, don't start that good-old-days crap."

Pierce smiled for the first time all day. From what he remembered of Juliet, she had that effect on a lot of people. Her quick tongue was legendary for equally biting wit and brutal lashings. Born with a silver spoon in her mouth, she bit any and every hand that dared keep her down or try to take advantage.

"I gather you're here to see Patricia," she asked.

"No, not anymore." The friendliness in his eyes faded.

Juliet looked surprised. "That doesn't sound good."

"Did you know she was after my family?"

"Who's after your family?"

"Don't play games, Juliet. Your friend has a problem."

She looked at him in warning. "I'd chill on that if I were you."

"She played me." He stepped into the elevator.

"Impossible." Juliet stepped out of the elevator.

"You don't know your girl like you think you do. She comes with an agenda."

Juliet laughed openly. "You are so wrong," she said as she continued down the hall.

Juliet held out a third tissue as tears continued to stream down Patricia's face. Her hiccuped speech was as impossible to understand as Pierce's cryptic pronouncements. "Shh, just slow down and tell me what happened," Juliet said.

Juliet, having never seen Patricia in such a state, held her tight and soothed her as best she could. "Patricia, you're going to have to calm down and tell me what happened." Another round of garbled gibberish flowed from the weeping Patricia.

Eventually, after two cups of steaming hot tea, Patricia was able to talk.

"I'm on academic probation pending a hearing with the board of directors," she confessed tearfully. "I'll probably get fired. My career is over. It's all I ever wanted. How am I supposed to become a child psychologist if I can't keep my hands off my patient's parents? Who's going to want me around their family? My God, what was I thinking? I knew it was wrong, I just could not stop." As soon as she stopped speaking, her tears began to overflow again.

"Patricia, your career's not over. This is just the beginning for you. Remember that shingle you're going to hang out in a few years."

"No shingle, not anymore. That dream's gone, over."

"That's ridiculous. Of course you'll have a shingle. You already have me booked ten years in advance, remember. Who else is going to listen to and put up with all my craziness?" She hugged Patricia closely and gave her another tissue. "Believe me, fifteen years of dancing on toes and getting two dozen roses afterward can make anybody crazy. I need you."

Patricia almost laughed. "It's over. Pierce didn't even give me a chance to explain about Vincent Shields."

"So?"

"What do you mean, so?"

"So what? We all know Pierce is a pigheaded, moody, obstinate, selfish jerk. What else is new? He's a man, what did you expect?" Juliet paused with a knowing smile. "On the other hand, he's also totally irresistible, charming, smart, and the man whom you love. He knows that you're the best thing to ever happen to him."

Patricia shook her head. "Not anymore."

Juliet struggled to piece together everything Patricia

had told her. "Pierce is upset because he thinks that you are in cahoots with a security guard to discredit his niece. That doesn't even make sense."

"I also told him that I hated his brother."

"Oh, I'm sure that was a nifty icebreaker." Another half-smile peeked out as Patricia wiped her damp face.

"It was," she said sarcastically.

"Look. Pierce is a big boy. Everybody knew that Aidan and Pierce didn't get along. He knows his brother was a jerk. And that's not speaking ill of the dead, that's just telling the truth. You opened up an old wound. Sometimes they're the hardest to heal."

"I shouldn't have told him."

"Yes, of course you should have. Being truthful in a relationship is never the wrong thing to do. You told him the truth. The only way to live in the present is to let go of the past."

"I had my fling, the sex was great, it's time to move on," Patricia said sorrowfully.

"It was more than a fling, so don't tell me you're just going to give up?"

Patricia nodded her head. "I have no choice. It's over."

"At least give him a chance to step up to the plate and be a man about it."

"It's over, Juliet."

"But . . ."

For the first time in a long time, Patricia got the last word. The subject was ended.

Juliet stood before PH1. She smiled radiantly as she thought to herself, *As they say in my business, it ain't over till the fat lady sings, and I ain't heard a single note.*

"Twice in one day. To what do I owe the prestigious honor of Juliet Bridges at my front door?"

"Let's not mince words. We both know why I'm here."

"Fine," he said and stepped aside.

She strolled in past him. "Let's do this."

Pierce showed Juliet into the library. She looked at the velvet lounge chair and smiled knowingly as Pierce took his place behind the desk. He offered her a beverage, she declined, and for the next half hour they discussed Patricia.

"So, you just leave her out in the cold to take the rap."

"She's with the security guard."

"Oh, my bad. I thought that you were in love with her."

"My feelings for Patricia have nothing to do with her deception."

"Get over yourself, Pierce, Patricia wasn't in cahoots with this Vincent Shields. It would make no sense."

Pierce opened his briefcase and pulled out an envelope. He handed it across the desk. "Read it," he offered.

Juliet reached out, opened the envelope, and removed the letter. She unfolded the paper and read it. She laughed as she read it a second time, reading some of the more humorous parts aloud: "Dear blah, blah, blah . . . evidence and testimony provided by Patricia Burke . . . capacity as a student counselor . . . incriminating evidence . . . implicating said Kimberly Franklin . . . vandalism . . . your presence is requested . . . details to follow . . . blah, blah, blah." She peeked over the edge of the paper and chuckled again. "He misspelled four words."

Pierce was stoic. "I don't see the humor."

"It's signed by Vincent Shields," she stated, as if to give the letter all the credence it deserved because of the author.

"And?"

"You actually fell for this. Damn." She shook her head regrettably. "And to think I gave you more credit."

A harsh chill of anger swelled inside Pierce. Juliet

looked at his expression and laughed again. "Okay." She began finally to calm. "Let's start at the beginning with the basics, shall we? How well do you know Vincent Shields?"

"What?" Pierce was completely confused by the question.

"It's a simple question, Pierce. How well do you know this man?"

"I don't."

"And you're willing to give your future happiness up for someone who you don't even know? How well do you know Patricia?"

Pierce remained silent. Juliet smiled. "I'll take that as a 'very well.' Does it make any sense, given your knowledge of Patricia, that she would do what is implied here?" She handed the letter back across the desk. "Does it make any sense for her to side with this Keystone Kop, even for twenty years of revenge?" Pierce glared at Juliet. "Patricia loves kids and they adore her. Is she the type to purposely hurt a child?"

Pierce stood and walked to the sliding doors. He looked out into the night.

"Let's talk about your personal relationship for a minute. She put her career, her reputation, everything on the line to be with you." He kept his back turned in silence. Juliet stood and walked up behind him. "Do you intend to have her lose everything because of her love for you?" He didn't answer. "I guess I was wrong. You are just like your brother: selfish and cruel."

Juliet smirked, turned, and picked up her discarded coat and purse. "Look, you do what you have to do. I have a rehearsal first thing in the morning. I suggest you give this a lot of thought before you just throw everything away." She walked to the library doorway, turned, and looked back to see him still staring out into the night. "Nice room," she said approvingly, then walked out.

Nineteen

The crowded lot was packed with customers mingling about, each in search of the perfect Christmas tree. Children dashed between the low-hanging evergreens, squealing in delight, sensing the season upon them. Couples strolled arm in arm through tightly standing trees, trying to decide on a single one.

Pierce wasn't in the best of moods. Juliet had seen to that. He hadn't been since the day he'd spoken to Patricia about her involvement with Shields and the investigation of Kimberly. Although she didn't deny knowing he was investigating his niece, she was vague as to what part she'd played. His mind buzzed with questions, all of which she'd refused to answer.

Kimberly purposely slammed the car door, bringing a level frown from Pierce. "Why do I have to be here?" she groaned grimly.

"Because it's your tree, too."

"I don't want a Christmas tree this year."

"Sure you do. You always want a tree."

"Yeah, but we never have one, do we."

"We're having a tree this year, Kimberly," Pierce said sternly, bringing an abrupt end to the discussion.

Kimberly opened then closed her mouth. She glared at him, then rolled her eyes. "You're just doing this because she wants you to."

"Because who wants me to?"

"Caroline," Kimberly singsonged the name.

"Caroline has nothing to do with us buying a Christmas tree. I've bought trees ever since you were born."

"Yes, she does," Kimberly mumbled under her breath. "She's hanging around you again, just like before."

"Her design company is building our house," he reminded her needlessly.

"It's already done," she snapped instantly, bringing another frown to his face. "Why does she have to keep hanging around when the house is finished?"

"She's an old friend."

"She's a leech," she mumbled, just low enough for Pierce to miss it.

"What about this one?" Pierce asked as he stopped to examine a straight tree with full bushy branches.

"I don't like it," Kimberly said without even looking at it.

Pierce nodded and continued walking. He turned the corner of the first aisle and began slowly walking through the pillars of evergreens in the second aisle. The two had been snapping at each other for the past two weeks. Neither was in the holiday spirit anymore. Pierce had hoped that with the Christmas season barreling down on them, they could at least be civil. He was wrong. He continued walking, knowing that she would eventually catch up.

Kimberly stayed in the first aisle. She refused to move. With her lips pouting, she crossed her arms over the bulk of her winter coat and dragged her feet in protest. It was cold and she didn't want to be here. He was just making her come out to torture her.

"Kimberly?"

She turned to the recognizable voice. "Hi, Ms. Burke," Kimberly said, smiling for the first time in days. She immediately ran to Patricia, threw her arms around her waist, and hugged her tightly.

Patricia, slightly taken back by the overwhelming adulation, hugged her back. "My goodness, what a warm hello! How have you been? How's school?"

"School is good, but we miss seeing you."

"I know, I miss being there. But I'll be back in a few days."

"You're coming back?"

"Yes, Kimberly, of course I'm coming back."

"But what about what everybody's saying about you?"

Patricia looked particularly confused. "What is everybody saying about me?"

Kimberly shyly looked down at her new leather boots and dug her toe into the rough stony gravel. "That you and one of the parents at school were having a thing together and that you got caught and were fired." She shrugged, not wanting to say the words too loud.

Patricia grimaced at hearing about the unforgiving rumor mill and the confusing gossip it insisted on churning out. "Kimberly, you can't always believe everything you hear or see."

Kimberly looked up, smiling again. That's all she needed. As far as she was concerned, Ms. Burke was innocent and her Christmas wish was still on. Then a shadow of doubt crossed her young face. "But why aren't you at school anymore?"

"I'm working on a project for the county public school system." Kimberly continued to look confused. "Think of me like a library book loan."

"So, you still work at Wells Academy?"

"Yes, I still work at Wells Academy."

"Did you hear about Mr. Wilson?" Kimberly said with a sudden change of subject.

"Yes, I heard."

"Everybody was really surprised."

Patricia nodded. "Do you still have that notebook with

all the school codes written down?" Kimberly nodded slyly. "Good, I'd like to borrow it."

"Okay," she whispered. "But don't tell Uncle Pierce. He made me promise to get rid of it."

Patricia nodded. "I'll take care of it for you."

"Kimberly?" Pierce called out as he rounded the corner and came face-to-face with Patricia. An unexpected smile leaped from his eyes, then they clouded with remembered anger.

"Hello, Pierce."

"Patricia," he said painfully, then turned to Kimberly. "Kimberly, we have to get this over with. Let's go."

Kimberly looked at him as if he'd lost his mind. Here was the perfect opportunity to get back together, but instead he wanted to leave. "But we just got here," she whined.

"I don't see anything here for us."

Patricia, stung by the implication of his words, shifted the large wreath in her gloved hands.

"Are you buying that, Ms. Burke?"

"Yes, I am."

"Do you have a tree yet?"

"No, not yet," she replied, watching Pierce turn away from the corner of her eye, "I'm still looking around."

"Uncle Pierce wants us to buy a tree, but I think I'm too old for Christmas trees and all that Santa Claus stuff."

"Oh, Kimberly, you're never too old for Christmas. This is a very special time of year. A time for family and friends to come together in celebration."

"Is your family coming to visit you this Christmas?"

"No."

"Are you going to Atlanta?"

"Yes."

"You are?" she said, surprised. "When are you leaving?"

"After the Christmas Ball, Christmas day."

"Uncle Pierce is going to the ball, aren't you, Uncle Pierce?" Pierce looked at his niece, knowing exactly what she was up to. He nodded slowly and threw her a warning nod. "He's got a tux and everything."

"That's nice."

"Jamal Scott asked me to go with him and Uncle Pierce said I could, but he's going to chaperone since he thinks I'm too young to date."

"I'm sure your uncle knows best. Jamal is a wonderful young man. I'm glad you accepted."

"He's really cute, too," Kimberly leaned in and whispered.

"Yes, he certainly is."

"What are you wearing to the ball?"

"I haven't decided yet," Patricia said.

"Kimberly, I think we should let Ms. Burke get back to her shopping."

"Yes," Patricia agreed, "I still have several gifts to purchase."

"Okay, bye, Ms. Burke," Kimberly said sweetly. Pierce nodded curtly.

"Good-bye Kimberly, Pierce." She smiled brightly and started walking through the aisle of trees.

Kimberly and Pierce turned in the opposite direction and circled back toward the beginning of the second row. Pierce turned the corner and began walking down the aisle, while Kimberly lagged several feet behind. She pulled a few needles off a low-hanging branch, then caught up with her uncle, who had stopped to examine a tree. "Why don't you and Ms. Burke hang out anymore? Is it because of me?"

Pierce stopped walking and looked down into his niece's dark eyes. They glistened with moisture. He wasn't sure if it was the bitter cold or emotion. "No, Kimberly, it's not because of you. We decided that we didn't have as much in common with each other as we thought. It happens all the time with grown-ups."

"I know that, but I hoped, I mean, I thought that you and Ms. Burke would be different."

"Sometimes things don't always work out like we hope they would."

"I guess I just miss talking to her."

"You can talk to her at school, can't you?" Pierce stopped to size up a possible selection.

"No, I can't."

"Why not?"

"She's not there anymore."

Pierce stopped walking. "Why isn't she at school anymore?" He asked with more concern then he intended.

"They have her doing staff development stuff instead of being a counselor. So she's not in the building. But, if you asked me, I think they were trying to get rid of her."

"What are you talking about, getting rid of her?"

"Because of the letter Mrs. Simmons got."

"What letter?"

"The letter that said that Ms. Burke was having an affair with a married parent."

"What?"

"That's what everybody at school is saying."

"An affair with a married man, that's ridiculous."

"That's why they say she got fired."

"Fired?" The word stung in Pierce's mouth like acid.

"I heard that the board is supposed to be meeting and deciding what to do about it. Everybody says she's going to lose if she doesn't explain the letter."

"Who sent the letter?" Pierce frowned, growing more and more irritated by the recent turn of events.

"I don't know, nobody does. All Ms. Burke has to do is deny it, but she won't. She said that her personal life is nobody's business."

Pierce remained silent for a few moments, his thoughts

solely on Patricia. Then he froze as it hit him. Lewis had mentioned something in his mad ravings about writing a letter to make things right. Pierce's frown grew deeper. Juliet had told him that Patricia's future was on the line. But he hadn't taken her words literally. Juliet was right: He was no better than his brother.

Twenty

Patricia stood at her desk and stared down at the pile of paperwork that had accumulated in her absence. The board of directors had called an emergency meeting to handle the newly arising angst surrounding her letter of resignation and the pending accusation against Mr. Wilson.

She sat down and turned on her system. The bright flash of circuits coming to life beamed at her. Then the screen turned a deep rich blue and prompted her to input data. She placed her hands above the keyboard. The answer was in here somewhere, and she was determined to find it. She began typing.

The school's computer system was integrated technology. A single computer inside the building could conceivably access the entire system, which was why Kimberly needed to be in the building and couldn't access the system from home. Patricia typed in her code, pulled out Kimberly's notebook, and went to work.

She reasoned that if Mr. Wilson hadn't stolen the computers, someone else had to have. But who? It wasn't hard to follow Kimberly's notes and access the security system. Using a graphing and probability program, she input the dates of the thefts and correlated them with the arrival of the security team. She smiled at the results.

She quickly passed through the security screening and clearance. It was a lot easier than she'd anticipated. No wonder they were having security breeches from all directions. As she delved deeper into the system, she accessed password and encryption sequences until finally she reached the time sequential mode.

She found it. Buried deep in the system was a binary switch that split the alarm sequence in half. One part performed the routine security program, while the other half accessed a silent self-diagnostic program, which shut the system down for a determined period of time.

"Interesting."

She reviewed the altered alarm code and entered it into the graphing and probability program. It was a match. Each time the security alarm system was scheduled to malfunction or self-diagnostic, there had been a theft—proof positive that it was an inside job, as the police had originally suspected. "Got ya."

She was on a roll. She grabbed the bio that Matt Glover had sent her months earlier and input more data about Shields ProTech Security. A large amount of information appeared on her screen, including prompts for further research.

She cross-referenced the data with Internet resources and came up with an astounding listing of thefts that coincided with Shields Security.

It was beginning to make sense. She pushed Print.

Two days later, Patricia had compiled a very impressive folder containing all of her research into the school thefts, Vincent Shields, and Shields Security. She sat at her desk staring at the folder. Oddly enough, she was incredibly serene and calm considering that her entire career would be decided in the next few minutes. She relaxed and waited until she was summoned.

Since there was other business to attend to, she presumed that she was the last order of business on the agenda. She stood and walked to her window. December had ushered in a strong cold wind that whipped at everything in sight. The barren tree branches bent and sagged each time the cold wind blew.

A spark of black caught her eye a second before it disappeared through the front gates. It looked like a black Jaguar, but it couldn't be. Why would Pierce be here?

The ringing phone spun her thoughts to the present. She picked up on the second ring. "Yes."

"Patricia," Audrey said, "we're ready for you."

"I'm on my way." She picked up her folder and took a last look around the office.

"Patricia," Matt began, "with much debate and with the added inducement of one of the school's more prominent alumni, the board of directors has come to the conclusion regarding—"

"Matt," she interrupted, "before we address the issue of my future here at Wells, I'd like to say a few words about the dismissal of Mr. Wilson."

"That's really not necessary, Patricia. The whole thing has been wrapped up and Shields Security has installed new guards on the premises."

"That's exactly what I'd like to address: the guards."

"All right, proceed."

She pulled several pieces of paper from her folder and placed them in front of each board member.

"I did a background security check on Mr. Wilson." She paused to give them time to go over the information in front of them. "As you can see, Mr. Wilson has a tenth-grade education with no formal training in computer systems. He doesn't own a computer and is quite frankly skeptical of the whole process. He doesn't even use the automated teller machines."

"What does this have to do with his stealing computers? Maybe he stole them to sell or give away, who knows?"

"Possibly, but I don't think so," Patricia added, then continued while placing another sheet before them. "With the help of an outside consultant, I also did a security check on Shields Security. It seems that there have been seventeen vandalism and theft incidents associated with companies just weeks before Mr. Vincent Shields arrives to supervise.

"By coincidence, the installation of the same three-member security team preceded all seventeen occurrences. If you'll also note, the vandalism and thefts began two weeks after Shields installed its new team. Then, apparently, they are transferred after the case is solved, leaving the accused culprit claiming innocence, but still obviously discharged from their duties."

"Excuse me, Patricia, but that's what they do. Shields Security goes in after the problem and cleans it up. They did the same thing at my company," Matt stated emphatically.

"Exactly. But we've never experienced thefts of this magnitude until the three security guards arrived. Have you?" she asked of a now troubled and considering Matt.

"But they are trained—" Audrey began.

"Yes, Audrey," she interrupted, "they are trained in all aspects of security, including surveillance." This time she handed each member of the board a copy of the official police report, including the officer's on-call notes that stated a possible internal manipulation of videotapes.

Audrey frowned as she scanned the report briefly. "This states that each time the thefts occurred, the video recorders were timed to go off from the source?"

"Yes."

"Mr. Wilson doesn't have the capability to access and alter the security system."

"No, he doesn't, thus, it's impossible for him to have

perpetrated the thefts." Patricia smiled smugly. Her case had been made as the eye of suspicion turned elsewhere.

The room went silent as each member considered the consequences of their actions. "Well, Patricia, thank you for bringing this to our attention." Matt nodded around the conference table. "In light of the preceding report, I move that we reinstate Mr. Wilson at his earliest convenience." All agreed instantly.

Matt's movement was seconded. "Now to the matter at hand. Patricia," Matt began, "the board of directors has come to the conclusion that there were no violations intended by you as a member of this staff. We have checked with our code of ethics and morals clauses and found that there were no violations forthcoming. I have your letter of resignation here, but the board feels that we cannot accept it under these circumstances." He pushed the unopened envelope across the desk to her.

"Thank you," she said, smiling graciously, relieved to have this finally over with. She turned to leave, then stopped. "Oh, there's more." She pulled the last paper from her folder. "This a list of other schools and business with the same pattern of compromised security. You might want to inform them of our findings." Matt immediately grabbed the list. He gasped slightly. His company was the first listed. "Oh, and one more thing: The school's security system is scheduled for another binary diagnostic between 3:41 and 4:09 this morning. You might want to make advance preparations with the local police. They might be interested to see who shows up at the rear door."

Twenty-one

"A Varied Merry Christmas Wish" was magnificent.

Who would have guessed that the Ida B. Wells gymnasium was under this converted vision of Christmas magic. As if it were a master of disguise, the simplest of decorations brought forth the most exquisite transformation imaginable.

White artificial Christmas trees sparkling with tiny green lights lined the perimeter of the room, giving it a snow-covered feel. Groupings of white and silver balloons floated like silver-lined clouds, covering the rafters and completely blocking out the familiar gymnasium ceiling. They were held together by curly streaming ribbons that drifted just above arm's length.

The band, set up opposite the entrance, was dressed in formal tuxedo white and played Christmas tunes with rhythm-and-blues, jazz, country, and rock-and-roll grooves. The mix, though uncharacteristic, was classic Christmas.

The back wall was set up buffet-style with the entire length of the large area catered with Christmas specialties from around the globe. The culinary preparations were highlighted by a massive six-foot walk-through gingerbread house decorated with jumbo gumdrops, foot-long licorice, twelve-inch lollipops, and gallons of thick glossy white icing. The splendid sight drew a steady crowd as Doris and Catherine sold pricey raffle tickets for those who wanted to give the gingerbread house a more permanent home.

Patricia arrived early that evening, but entered the Annual Christmas Ball late and alone. Dressed in a sleek black tuxedo gown with white accents, satin heels, and silver diamond-studded accessories, she looked around in awe. For this night, she'd chosen to wear her hair pulled up in a smooth French twist. She was stunning.

Immediately besieged by students and parents, it took half an hour just to greet and briefly speak to each one.

"Ms. Burke."

Patricia stiffened instantly. The last thing she wanted or needed was to lose her fervent joy because of a crab apple Christmas Grinch. She turned, expecting the worst.

"Patricia, I'd like to speak with you a moment, please."

Patricia inhaled, then blew out heavily. "Of course, Audrey." Together they stepped back out into the hall.

Audrey handed Patricia back her resignation. It was torn in half. "I can't accept this," she stated.

Patricia was stunned. "I thought you'd not only accept but throw a party to get rid of me finally."

Audrey frowned, hurt by Patricia's assumption. "Patricia, I wasn't born with a silver spoon in my mouth. In terms of this school and its slang, I would have been considered *less* than a Poorie. I'm sorry if you feel that I have been particularly rough on you. I assure you that my intentions were solely to make you the best person you could be. If I tend to be harder on those less fortunate, it is only because I know well the road that they must travel. Doors, both private and public, will slam in their faces. So, I want my scholarship children to be stronger, tougher, and more determined to succeed. I want them to be like you. I never told you this, but I am very proud of you. You turned out exactly as I'd prayed."

Patricia was stunned silent.

Audrey slipped the torn resignation into Patricia's

hand. "Let's go back and enjoy the celebration, shall we?" Patricia nodded absently as Audrey continued. "By the way, I noticed that you were tardy. As acting vice principal, that is unacceptable."

Patricia laughed, and Audrey smiled. Then they walked back to the Christmas celebration.

Patricia watched Pierce as he walked into the gymnasium with Kimberly and Jamal Scott. Several women's heads immediately turned in his direction. He was gorgeous in his black dinner tux and matching band-collar shirt.

The perfect couple, Kimberly and Jamal held hands. Jamal smiled proudly. With Patricia's tutelage, he'd finally gathered enough courage to ask Kimberly to the ball. Patricia was so happy for them. He looked handsome in the fitted dark suit that she'd helped him choose at the mall.

Kimberly wore a sweet lavender silken gown that seemed to flow with each step she took. It had three spaghetti straps per shoulder and had a shortened jacket made of chiffon. Her hair, glittering, had tendrils of tiny curls gathered at the crown and a sprinkle of crystal beads.

"There's Ms. Burke," Kimberly whispered to her uncle. "May I go over and say hello, please?"

Pierce nodded absently. There was no way he could not have seen her. She took his breath away. She was stunning in her black-and-white halter satin tuxedo gown and wrap.

He watched as Kimberly and Jamal hurried over to join the small gathering around Patricia. They spoke for a moment or two, then Patricia opened her arms wide and Kimberly fell into her loving embrace. Patricia and Kimberly smiled, laughed, and talked animatedly for another few moments, then Kimberly turned and pointed in Pierce's direction. Their eyes met across the room in a sadness made even worse by distance. She nodded her head in greeting; he responded in like.

Jasmine and Jason appeared next to Kimberly and Jamal. The two young men exchanged greetings by shaking hands in the cool way kids did at that age. Jasmine and Kimberly shrieked with stunned excitement and hugged each other several times.

They kept a polite distance for the remainder of the evening, she on her side of the gymnasium and he on his. Kimberly, darting between the two, finally found a comfortable place by her uncle's side when Jamal and the guys gathered to talk sports.

"You look so beautiful tonight," Pierce said in amazement. His sullen teenager had turned into a beautiful butterfly right before his eyes.

"Thank you," she said, smiling proudly. "Ms. Burke said the exact same thing." She hugged his waist lovingly.

Pierce took Kimberly's hand and led her to the dance floor. He looked down into his niece's sparkling eyes. "I wish I could go back and do some things differently, like being a better uncle."

"But you're a great uncle, Uncle Pierce."

He smiled down at her; he couldn't help it. "Look at you, you're all grown up." Just as he was about to continue, he felt a tap on his shoulder. He turned to see an eager young man smiling, enamored with Kimberly.

"Sir, excuse me, sir, may I cut in?" he asked.

Pierce chuckled silently and stepped aside. He walked over to the punch bowl, picked up a paper cup, and filled it.

"Hello, Pierce."

He turned. "Hello, Patricia."

A pregnant silence hung between them as they just looked into each other's eyes. "Well, here we are," she said, looking around anxiously, "back where it all started." Pierce nodded slightly. "I heard what happened at the board meeting. Thank you for coming to my defense with the board. I understand you were extremely persuasive regarding my position here." She paused and looked away. "I asked them to accept the resignation."

"Why?" he asked, distressed.

"It's time for me to move on."

"Thanks for keeping Kimberly's name off the record."

"She was a big help in clearing Mr. Wilson and snagging the real thieves. So, all of her hard work breaking into my computer actually paid off for someone."

"Yes, it did," he said, nodding agreeably. A second pause hung in the air as Pierce reveled in seeing her again. "We should talk," he began until she interrupted.

"What's done is done," she said calmly, then smiled graciously. "I hope you have a good time tonight." She walked away, proud that she didn't break into tears or run screaming from the room.

Twenty-two

Patricia walked into the darkness of her apartment alone. She kicked off her satin evening shoes and tossed her purse and wrap on the coffee table next to the Kwanza kinara. She stood there for a while, in the middle of the room, staring at nothing in particular. She didn't feel like crying, but she did anyway.

Stepping over her packed luggage, she walked over and stood at the balcony doors. Instinctively, she turned on the Christmas lights. The sparkle of the rooms did little to lift her mood. Her eyes drifted to the darkness on the top floor as they always did and probably always would. It was over.

She turned to the magnificent tree displaying all the wonders of Christmas past. Ornaments celebrating her birth hung side by side with remembrances of graduation, her first home, and student gifts. She plopped down on the sofa, just as the phone rang. She picked up on the third ring.

"Are you okay?"

"Sure," she lied.

"Do you want me to come over?"

"No."

"Do you want to come over here? I'm actually going to attend the cast party. You can be my date. I'll even buy you dinner."

Patricia chuckled at Juliet's attempt at levity. "I'm fine,

really. It's not like it's the first time this has happened. You go ahead and enjoy yourself. I'll call you tomorrow."

"Promise."

Patricia smiled at her friend's concern. "I've always called you on Christmas day and always will."

"Okay." Juliet accepted her at her word. Every Christmas since the day they'd met, Patricia had called and wished her a merry Christmas. "By the way, I opened my gift."

"Juliet, how could you?" Patricia admonished jokingly.

"Oh, please, when have I ever waited to open a gift from you?" The tiny crystal etched and engraved ballerina toe shoes hung in the honored center position on her Christmas tree. "Thank you, I love it."

"You're welcome."

"While we're on the phone, why don't you open my gift to you now?"

"Nice try, but I will be opening my gift on Christmas day as customary. So you'll just have to wait."

"Aw," Juliet mockingly moaned, as defeat mixed with laughter led to a meaningful silence. "Are you sure . . ."

Patricia finished her words of concern. ". . . that I'm okay? Yeah, I'm going to be just fine. You go ahead, have a great one for me. I'll call you tomorrow. Bye." Patricia smiled as she hung up the phone. She was truly blessed to have a friend like Juliet.

Feeling better would be far too optimistic, yet her heart lifted enough to propel her from the sofa to the kitchen. She'd chaperoned all night without once grabbing anything to eat. She opened the refrigerator and looked in just as the phone rang again. "I'm fine," she sang out as she picked up the phone in the kitchen.

"Ms. Burke?"

"Kimberly?"

"Ms. Burke, can you come over?"

"Kimberly, is that you?" Static crackled in her ear.

"Yes."

"We have a bad connection. I can barely hear you. What's wrong?"

"Uncle Pierce needs you."

"What?"

"You have to come over, it's Uncle Pierce."

"What's wrong with Pierce?"

"I don't know. There's something wrong with the house lights. They keep going on and off."

"Where's your uncle?"

"Can you come over?"

"Kimberly, where's Pierce?"

"Working on something."

"What's wrong with Pierce? Where are you?"

"We're at the house. I have to go. Can you come over, please?"

"Kimberly, what's going on?" The line went dead. The cold hand of panic gripped her heart. There was something wrong with Pierce. Kimberly was in trouble. It didn't matter. All she could think about was getting to them as quickly as possible. She immediately slipped back on her heels, grabbed her purse and wrap, then rushed out of the door.

She drove like a madwoman. Each turn she took, each yellow light she ran, seemed to make the journey take that much longer.

With high beams glowing, she maneuvered the dark streets. Their hidden patches of black ice were no deterrent, even as her car slid into several slow-motion skids.

Finally she had reached the entrance to the planned community complex. A single floodlight shown brightly on the welcoming sign. With arrows pointing to the various model homes, she followed the path on which Pierce had taken her many times before. It was a lot darker than she remembered or maybe with Pierce she just hadn't noticed.

She turned down the newly paved street. More darkness.

Inching forward, she peered through the windshield, searching for some sign of life. But all she found was darkness. "There it is," she whispered aloud as her headlights pointed the way to the sole house standing proudly at the end of the winding road. She pulled up into the driveway, the only car in sight.

She turned off the engine and looked around the darkness. The only lights shining guided the way along the basket-weave brick walkway to the front porch. She wrapped the shawl around her shoulders and cautiously got out of the car. A gust of arctic wind blew the car door shut before she could manage it.

The gentle click of her heels echoed against the silent hush of the wooded surroundings. She followed the curved path to the front door, grateful for the hooded landscape light that showed the way. She stepped up onto the porch and quickly glanced through the surrounding windows. There was no sign of anyone. She rang the doorbell. There was no answer. She rang again then again, still no answer. She knocked the metal handle against the brass plate, then tried the doorknob. It turned with ease and she went inside.

"Hello," she called out as soon as she entered the foyer. "Kimberly. Pierce." She looked around. The security key panel she'd seen Pierce deactivate was dark. At least she wouldn't be arrested for breaking and entering. "Hello," she called out again.

She moved farther into the house. "Kimberly, Pierce," she repeated until she noticed the glow of light.

The whole house was dark except for a dim shaft of light in the living room. The echo of her heels clicked against the oak hardwood floors. The place was completely empty. She moved to the living room, where she'd seen the glow of light. There, in the middle of the room, stood a twelve-foot Christmas tree with a shaft of light beaming onto a single ornament hanging from a branch. Curious, she moved closer. The ornament, just at her eye level, was a simple red ribbon. Odd.

She plucked it from the tree. The red ribbon was attached to a black velvet box trimmed with gold. She pulled the ribbon's tie and let the small box fall into her waiting hands.

"I've been waiting for you for a long time."

Startled, she jumped and spun around, stunned to see that Pierce had entered the room behind her. Darkness from the foyer still shrouded his face. She stepped back nervously.

He wore a tuxedo, a perfect tuxedo. He'd casually undone his banded collar, leaving the ends open. Handsome could never even begin to describe how he looked standing in the doorway at that moment.

Her heart raced so fast she was afraid that it was about to explode right out of her chest. How was she ever going to stop loving this man? "Kimberly called me," she rasped out finally in breathless panic. "She said there was an emergency, a problem, that I should come quickly." She looked around the empty room, still nervous. "Where is she?"

"She's around," he stated nonchalantly as he stepped farther into the room.

Panic gave way to concern. "Is she all right? She sounded like she was in trouble."

He smiled and nodded his head. "Kimberly's fine," he assured her calmly.

Concern eased to caution. "So, what was the emergency? She said she needed me."

"She does."

His slow steady walk toward her made her even more nervous. Beneath the sophisticated gown, stylish shoes, and fancy hair, she was still an insecure little girl waiting all alone for the popular boy to notice her. And he finally had.

"What's going on, Pierce?" she stated bravely after mustering all the strength she had.

"Kimberly does need you, but so do I." He stood within arm's reach of her. "I need you, Patricia."

"You what?"

"I need you. I love you. You're everything I ever dreamed of, everything I hoped for, and everything I ever wished for. You complete me, you make me want to be a better man, the man I always hoped and thought I could be. How I survived this long without you in my life is a wonder. All I know is that I can't go a single second longer without you in my life forever. I love you, Patricia." The warmth of his love washed over her like fog over a moonless sea.

She gasped in delighted surprise, letting the bright red ribbon fall to the floor. Pierce bent down and picked it up. As he knelt, he took the box from her hands. Tears began to form in her eyes as he opened the small box and presented it to her. The diamond ring, slightly smaller than the size of her missing baseball, sparkled beneath the beam of light. This couldn't be real. This was her only dream, her only Christmas wish for as long as she could remember.

A flood of tears rolled down her cheeks as she watched him remove, then place the diamond ring on her finger. She was speechless. All she could do was stand there crying her eyes out. "Patricia, would you do me the honor of becoming my wife?"

She didn't answer.

Pierce stood and gently wiped the tears from her face. She lowered her head, shaking it steadily as the tears continued to roll.

"You were right when you said that this was the most magical time of year, when dreams are realized and wishes come true. Make my Christmas wish come true," he whispered. "Be my wife, be my love." He tilted her head upward. The sincerity in his eyes caused her knees to weaken. Pierce wrapped his hands around her. "Will you marry me?" he asked.

"Yes."

At that exact instant, the surrounding darkness slowly faded into a glow of thousands of tiny white lights twinkling and sparkling through the branches of the Christmas tree.

Smiling, relieved, Pierce pointed upward. She followed his eyes to the ceiling. Mistletoe. They kissed in an explosion of love that would surely last for many Christmases to come.

Kimberly, holding the two connected ends of the extension cords in her hands, giggled to herself as she peered down the stairs, seeing her uncle and her brand-new aunt standing in front of the twinkling tree.

Her Christmas wish had finally come true. She'd found the perfect gift of love for her uncle and the perfect gift of love for herself. Smiling, she looked up through the foyer window as a shooting star speared through the night sky.

> *Star light, star bright,*
> *First star I see tonight,*
> *I wish I may, I wish I might,*
> *Have the wish I wish tonight.*

She closed her eyes real tight and made the most ardent, fervent, heartfelt wish she could think of. "I'd like a baby cousin next Christmas, please."

I heard the bells on Christmas Day
Their old, familiar carols play,
And wild and sweet
The words repeat
Of peace on earth, good will to men!
—Henry Wadsworth Longfellow

Merry Christmas
and Happy Holidays!

Best Wishes,
Celeste

Dear Readers:

I hope you enjoyed experiencing the joys and triumphs of Patricia and Pierce's story. Finding forgiveness isn't always easy. Finding love is sometimes even harder. But, thanks to a little help from Kimberly, Patricia and Pierce will experience many seasons of everlasting love. Sharing this timeless holiday romance was **A Christmas Wish** come true for me. I hope it has brought joy and happiness to your holiday season.

In April 2003 BET Books will release my third novel, **Since Forever**. It is a classic tale set in the glamorous world of Hollywood featuring reclusive child star, Alexandra Price and superstar action hero Lance Morgan. From the very first page to the last, it's pure excitement. You are thrown into the privileged world of Hollywood's rich and famous. The glitz and glamour of Tinseltown, the seductiveness of the Mediterranean and the sophistication of New York's Fifth Avenue add to the backdrop of this compelling story of romance, intrigue and forgiveness. Shrouded in mystery, intrigue and deceit, **Since Forever** adds new meaning to the old adage, "there's no business like show business."

Lastly, I would like to take this opportunity to thank all who wrote about my debut novel, **Priceless Gift**. I truly enjoyed reading and answering every letter and E-mail you sent. Many of you asked about the future of Mamma Lou and the Gates family. I am pleased to announce that Louise Gates is at it again and her grandson, Dr. Raymond Gates, is her next target in **One Sure Thing**, due to be released October 2003.

For more information on the "Christmas Wish Contest" or to read more about my upcoming titles, including sample chapters, stop by my Web site at http://www.celesteonorfleet.com. Or, if you would like to receive an **A Christmas Wish** bookmark and be placed on my mailing list send a #10 SASE to: Celeste O. Norfleet, P.O. Box 7346, Woodbridge, VA 22195-7346. I love hearing from you so please continue to write and send E-mails.

Best wishes and season's greetings,
Celeste O. Norfleet

ABOUT THE AUTHOR

Celeste O. Norfleet, born and raised in Philadelphia, Pennsylvania, is a graduate of Moore College of Art and Design with a B.F.A. in Fashion Illustration. She has worked as an Art Director for several advertising agencies and now does freelance design for area businesses.

An avid reader and writer, Celeste has sold several more books to BET/Books. She is a member of Washington Romance Writers and Romance Writers of America and lives in Virginia with her husband and children.